MW00940624

ABYSS

SWATI M.H.

Kismet Publishing

Cover: Cover Me Darling

Photographer: Ren Saliba

Editing: Silvia's Reading Corner

ALSO BY SWATI M.H.

Elements of Rapture Series

Adrift

(Forbidden, single dad/nanny, grumpy/sunshine, age gap)

Ascend

(Marriage of Convenience, single-mom, friends to lovers romance)

Ablaze

(Brother's best friend, friends-to-lovers, one bed, firefighter romance)

MomComs Series

Mother Pucker

(Hockey star, single mom, reverse age-gap, doctor/patient romcom)

Feel the Beat Series

My Perfect Remix

(Single-dad, friends-to lovers romance)

My Beautiful Chaos

(Fake-relationship, second chance romance)

My Darling Neighbor

(Enemies to lovers, surprise pregnancy romance)

<u>Fated Love Series</u>

Kismet in the Sky

(Slightly forbidden, second chance, workplace romance)

Surrender to the Stars

(Enemies to lovers, hospital romance)

AUTHOR'S NOTE

Content warning: This book is intended for mature audiences. It deals with themes related to bullying and death that may be triggering for some readers.

To Mom:
Please skip the spicy scenes. But, since there are quite a few, please just skip this book entirely.

"I hate the way you talk to me, and the way you cut your hair. I hate the way you drive my car. I hate it when you stare. I hate your big dumb combat boots, and the way you read my mind. I hate you so much it makes me sick; it even makes me rhyme.

I hate the way you're always right. I hate it when you lie. I hate it when you make me laugh, even worse when you make me cry.

I hate it when you're not around, and the fact that you didn't call.

But mostly I hate the way I don't hate you. Not even close, not even a little bit, not even at all."

— KAT STRATFORD, 10 THINGS I HATE
ABOUT YOU

Chapter One

KAVI

From: Kavi <<u>specialk_jain@gmail.com</u>>
To: Nathan <<u>nathans@gmail.com</u>>
Date: June 2 4:43 PM
Subject: The Waiting Place . . .

First day of work. Wish me luck.

And yes, I know what you're going to say. I
haven't worked in the food industry before.
I haven't worked in *any* industry before.
But I just need something to tide me over
for three months. Then I can do the thing
I've been waiting my whole life to do.

Speaking of, I haven't painted in two
months. I can practically see your eyes
popping out.

You know how I get without the smell of
paint after a while. I just haven't had the

time! Last month was crazy leading up to graduation, and this month I was trying to find a damn job. How many places did I tell you I interviewed at? Fourteen?

And I doubt I'll have the energy after this shift. From what I could tell, they're short-staffed and overworked. I'll be lucky to have the energy to brush my teeth before going to bed.

Anyway, I'll tell you how it all goes. Here's to hoping my tray skills are stronger than my basketball skills.

Or my tennis skills.

Or my dance skills.

Shut up. And stop laughing.

xoxo
-Special K

I've only messed up twice tonight.

Not too shabby, in my humble opinion. Though, I have no one else to weigh in and tell me if that's normal on the first day except my boss, Arlo, since they're all busy running around like chickens with their heads cut off. Arlo doesn't look impressed.

For a high-end restaurant, I would have expected more staff and fewer delays, but hey, what do I know?

Suits me just fine since I'm not much of a talker, anyway.

Besides, it was just two plates delivered to the wrong

table, and an eggs Florentine instead of eggs Benedict sent to the guy at table seven, who still seems to be holding a grudge against me, what with his red-faced glare and exaggerated frown. Apparently, he's very particular about having spinach in his eggs.

As I see it, people who order eggs for dinner are psychopaths, anyway.

"No, Arlo, I'm not serving his table again. The guy's an asshole," Stella whines, her expression a mix of agony and a plea as she glances across the room at a table in the back. She's the server I shadowed last week for an evening, who's been working here for a year.

Arlo keeps his eyes fixed on the computer screen at the waitstand while addressing her. "He's also part owner of the establishment you're employed by, in case you forgot."

"Then have someone else serve him. See if you can maybe free up Kevin. Or, I don't know, *you* can do it, but I won't. No tip is worth dealing with a man who has a pitchfork for a tongue." Her gaze narrows when she finds me placing some extra menus in the designated cubby. "Have Kavi do it."

Gee thanks, Stella! Why wouldn't I want a verbal beatdown on my first day from Mr. Temperamental Dung beetle over there?

Arlo takes an exasperated breath. "Kevin already has too many tables, and Kavi's too new—"

Agreed. Kavi's too new.

"It's not rocket science," Stella interrupts. "He might be nicer if he knows she's new." She wraps her arms around her chest. "Arlo, I stayed back to help you fold the silverware way past my shift yesterday. I even came in on my day off last week when we were short-staffed. The least you can—"

"Fine." Arlo's jaw shifts slightly before he blinks at me without an ounce of the empathy I'm starting to feel for myself, given Stella's high opinion of our boss and overlord. "Kavi, take table sixteen—the booth in the back with the two gentlemen. Make sure to take a bottle of the limited-edition vintage Dom Perignon. It's what he likes."

"Yeah, because apparently, a fourteen-hundred-dollar bottle of champagne is just a bottom-of-the-barrel, budget-friendly choice for the rabid beast to keep his snarl at bay," Stella mumbles with a tightened jaw before replacing it with a mile-wide fake smile when a family of four walks to the stand.

I hesitate for a few seconds before finally walking toward the bar while Stella directs the family to the other side of the room.

While the bartender looks for the bottle, I run my hand down my black skirt. It's on the shorter side, well above my knees, and tighter around my waist and ass than I remember it to be, but it'll do. I'm just happy I found it in the pile of clothes in my closet I was waiting to donate. With less than a hundred dollars in my bank account, it would have killed me if I had to spend any of it on a skirt.

My normal attire consists of bargain-basement and thrift-store finds. Occasionally, I'll rummage through my mom's closet, but since most of her things are about a decade or two out of style, I'm usually stuck with jeans, some sort of graphic T-shirt, and my trusty old pair of Doc Martens. It's a win when neither my jeans nor my T-shirt have holes in them, but a purposeful fashion statement when they do.

If only the popular rich bitches from high school could see me now.

Taking a calming breath, I walk over to the table in the back with the bottle of champagne that costs more than my car, two flutes, and a couple of ice waters on a tray.

One of them, a younger man—likely a few years older than me, and also of Indian descent—stops speaking when I approach, turning to me with a smile. I set the waters and empty flutes in front of each person and regard the other . . .

Oh . . .

The other is . . . He's . . .

Am I having a brain aneurysm? Why am I losing my grasp on my vocabulary when I should be composing sonnets about this guy's jawline, writing dissertations about his ridiculously chiseled face? Seriously, the man looks like he was carved by angels themselves.

And I haven't even moved past his face.

He doesn't grace me with an acknowledgement—not even sparing me a look—so I continue my perusal down to his smooth, pink, and oh so kissable lips. They're surrounded by salt-and-pepper stubble that looks more than a few days old, but not because he hasn't had the time to shave. No, it's intentional.

Everything about this man—from the way his obscenely broad shoulders look both tense and relaxed, to the way he continues to stare ahead, watching me in his periphery, to the way his jaw ticks subtly—is intentional. Purposeful and confident.

He doesn't have the time to be casual or spontaneous.

My eyes continue down, past his unbuttoned collar, settling on the divot at the base of his neck. There should be no reason for a divot to cause my vagina to pulse like she's under duress, but here we are, fluttering and pulsing like she's about to take flight.

His biceps are basically trying to rip out of his suit, his thick forearms—one banded with a watch that probably costs as much as a house—peeking out at the end of his sleeve. His thick fingers, attached to massive hands, are steepled on the table almost as if he's trying to refrain from tapping out a bored rhythm.

I've just dropped my eyes to get a glimpse of his wide thighs—*How much time does this man spend in the gym?*—when a cleared throat has them landing back on that divot. I mean, snapping to his lips. Er, his eyes.

His very sharp, very irritated blue-gray eyes. "You're new."

"Uh . . . um," I stammer, trying to come to. How long was I out? *Five minutes? Five hours?* Jesus Christ, did I fall into a coma? I place the tray against the bottom of the booth and wrap my hand around the champagne bottle. "Yes. Um, I'm Kavi. I'll be your server today—"

"Where's Stella?" His deep voice, along with his two-word interruption, like a veiled threat, causes my stomach to dip. "I don't like dealing with new staff."

"She's, um . . ." I look around, as if perhaps Stella might materialize out of thin air, before wiping my sweaty hand over my skirt. "She's serving other customers. But I can assure you, I'm perfectly capable of—"

"Then tell Arlo I've asked for Kevin."

"It's fine, Hudson." The other man waves his hand, speaking to Mr. Personality. "Stop giving the poor girl grief."

"I'm not here to be a guinea pig for new staff, Dev. I expect prompt and exemplary service," he snaps.

Jesus. Asshole much?

I'm not sure how I do it, given my racing pulse and shaky legs, but I throw my shoulders back, tilting my head up. Mom always says that when faced with fear—or, in this case, a fire-breathing dragon with a stick up his butt—half the battle can be won with good posture.

"I assure you, the service will be everything you expect." His narrowed glare at my response has me withering slightly before I look at the bottle in my hand, having no recollection of how it got there. I lift it to show him the label. "Do you . . . I mean, would you care for champagne?"

He doesn't respond, going back to looking straight ahead, but the other man—Dev, I believe the snarling lunatic referred to him as—gives me the same pitying look I'd be giving myself if I could, sliding his flute forward. "I'd love some."

I take a stilling breath, hoping my apprehension regarding the bottle in my hand doesn't show. I haven't opened a champagne bottle before, but I've seen people do it plenty of times. Honestly, how hard could it be? I'm sure those catastrophic videos online where the cork goes flying through a window or up into a lightbulb are probably just exaggerated scenarios for comic relief.

I look to my right—no windows close by—before I look up, feeling better about the fact that there are no lightbulbs above us, either.

It's going to be fine. I'm just all up in my head about it. It's really not that big a deal.

Pulling the wrapper off the top, I smile with feigned confidence at the two men awaiting their drinks.

Well, I smile at one.

The other can catch the next train to hell, if I have anything to say about it.

Still, my traitorous eyes brush over the way his hands flex, not missing the lack of a wedding ring on his finger. That doesn't mean he's not married, but let's be honest, who the hell would marry his grouchy ass?

The gray at his temples and in his stubble, and the age lines at the corners of his eyes say he's not young—probably in his mid-forties—but there's also a ruggedness around his features, like he's spent time in the sun or working with his hands.

Pressing my thumb to the top of the cork inside the wire cage, I untwist the wire tab, taking that moment to breathe in through my nose and out through my mouth as discreetly as possible.

Shoving the bottom of the bottle inside my abdomen to keep it steady, I take off the wire cage and place both thumbs under the cork. I push with all my might when I hear one of the men murmur hesitantly—something about never taking off the wire cage—before I feel the cork release and go flying with a *pop*!

As if I'm watching it in slow motion, the cork goes soaring, connecting with the gorgeous grump's forehead, eliciting an *oof!* out of him before bouncing off to the side.

My eyes widen in horror as his hand flies to his head, and I quickly put the champagne bottle on the table and lean toward him, trying to form an apology while hoping to . . . hoping to do something. *Anything!*

But in my haste, with my heart hammering like a thunderstorm, I accidentally topple over his ice water, too.

He huffs audibly, trying but failing to move aside inside the booth, as cold liquid sloshes over the table and into his lap. Wet spots decorate his white button-down shirt, and his jaw tightens so hard, I'm afraid he's going to break it.

Time freezes right along with my breath and my heart as his shocked eyes sear my face. A red welt blooms in the middle of his perfectly symmetrical forehead, and given the way his hands are now fisted on the table, I can tell his mild irritation has shifted to barely-controlled rage.

"Oh my God!" My cheeks burn as I stammer out an apology, barely hearing the other man snicker. "I'm so, so sorry!"

I reach for the black napkin around his silverware, sending his fork flying across the table, before bending over and patting the ridiculous amount of water pooled on his lap.

My brain tells me to get a hold of myself—*to stop patting his fucking crotch!*—but it's as if my body is decoupled from its commands. My eyes prick and my face burns at a thousand degrees as blood rushes through my ears.

I'm not going to cry, I'm not going to cry.

A calloused hand wraps around my wrist, halting my movement, and if I wasn't heating up with embarrassment, I'd actually have goosebumps fly across my skin. But as it stands, I feel nothing but mortification.

His gaze softens as he examines my pooled eyes, and for a moment, it seems like the edge of his anger fades, but all too soon his nostrils flare again. "Stop."

"God, I–I'm so sorry." My eyes snap to the red welt on his forehead. "Are you okay? I didn't mean—"

I lift my hand instinctively to touch his head—*Please, God, save me from myself*—when his snarl squeezes past his lips. "I said, *stop*." At my nod, with a stray tear dropping onto his wet hand, he releases my wrist. "Send Arlo here at once."

I rise from his lap, still nodding with my shoulders slumped. So much for good posture and winning battles against dragons or whatnot.

"I'm so sorry," I whisper, wanting to shut myself inside the nearest bathroom and live out the rest of my days there.

His words hit my back as I'm rushing to the waitstand, avoiding the sympathetic gazes of everyone watching. "Oh, and Ms. Kavi? That's about all the incompetence this restaurant can handle for one day. Please turn in your badge and clock out. This will be your last day working here."

From: Kavi <<u>specialk_jain@gmail.com</u>>
To: Nathan <<u>nathans@gmail.com</u>>
Date: June 3 10:22 AM
Subject: Left in the Lurch

Okay, so imagine the worst possible situation on your first day of work, and then multiply it by twenty.

Yup, you're looking at the first server in history to spill ice water on her boss's lap, after sending a champagne bottle cork flying into his forehead.

Needless to say, I'm looking for a job. Again.

I'll spare you the details and give you a chance to catch your breath since I know you're bowled over with laughter, but can you be serious for a second?

What the hell am I going to do now? I needed this job so fucking bad, Nathan!

Before you start with a lecture, let me remind you that you curse plenty, and I only do it when the situation deems it appropriate. I've deemed this situation appropriate for a couple of fucks, a few shits, and at least one damn.

Three months, and then I'll be working at my dream job with a paycheck that'll cover everything we could need, but until then . . . I needed this.

I guess it's time for me to ask for help, huh? God, you know how much I hate that. But if I don't, I'm not sure how we'll even manage to pay rent.

Enough about me, though; I'll figure it out. What have you been up to?

Also, are you seeing this crazy weather? When have we ever gotten this much rain in Northern California? It's been twenty-eight straight days at this point, and I'm sorta over it.

xoxo
-Special K

P ressing the key fob in my hand, I try my luck again, but of course, I should know better. It hasn't worked the past thirty-five times I've tried it, so why would it suddenly work now?

Shoving my key into the lock on my car door, I turn it, barely hearing the *click* above the splattering of rain and tires driving through the puddles on the street behind me. Whatever. It's not like I have anything of value in there, anyway. Just some paint supplies.

Looking both ways before crossing, I trudge through the rain, my coral-colored Doc Martens now the color of mud. Sheets of rain beat down on my covered head, crawling down my nose and lips in a steady stream before falling from my chin, as I try my best to protect my small purse under my raincoat.

They're calling it the wettest spring in the Bay Area in over a decade. I was alive a decade ago, and I don't recall *this* much rain. It's getting to be a real hassle, if you ask me. The incessant storms have turned the streets into watery and hazardous mazes, we haven't seen the sun in weeks— annoying because this is supposed to be sunny California!— and every step feels like I'm playing puddle hopscotch.

I shake off some of the water from my raincoat under the awning of the coffee shop before entering. Swiping the bottoms of my shoes on the sodden rug in the front, I unsuccessfully try to wipe off the mud from them while casting my gaze around the room.

Rain, shine, or catastrophic tornado, Madison Case is never late. At almost five-feet-ten inches, with naturally platinum blonde hair, she's also damn near impossible to miss, so it's no surprise when I see her tucked into a chair in the back, pounding something out on her phone with her rapidly moving fingers.

Pulling off my raincoat and hanging it on the coat tree

nearby, I pad over to my friend, the squishy sounds of my damp steps lost to the hum of the shop.

"Excuse me." I drum my short orange fingernails on the table, making her eyes snap up to meet mine. "I was wondering if you could help me find a Professor Madison Case around here?"

Madison's entire face lights up, her bluish-gray eyes sparkling as she shoves her phone into her purse and leaps up to wrap me in her arms. "God, doesn't it feel like the end of the world out there? It took me an extra fifteen minutes to get here with the pileup on the highway."

I hang my purse on the back of the chair before taking a seat in front of her. "And yet, you're still here before me."

She rolls her eyes. "Habits formed by a dad who could have been an army general." She waves the air between us as if trying to move on to the next subject. "Anyway, tell me how you've been? Congrats on graduation, by the way! What's next? Gosh, it's been too long since we caught up."

Oh, where do I start?

Madison and I met at a volunteering event her dad's company hosted a few years ago during the holidays. We were chosen to be on the same team to pack bags of groceries for the needy and deliver them around San Francisco. It was during that eight-hour event that I found a lifelong friend. And that's saying something since I don't have very many of those to begin with. Perks of being a wallflower and all that.

Plus, you could say I have trust issues.

So, while we don't hang out often, we make it a point to meet up every couple of months to catch up.

Madison is a chemistry professor at the University of California in Berkeley, and one of the most generous and kind-hearted people I've met. There's not a thing the woman wouldn't do to help even a stranger on the street, let alone her friends.

Which is why I feel guilty even coming here with an agenda.

I know she'd help me find a job to tide me over for a few months, but A.) I hate asking for favors, especially from friends, because it always makes me feel like I'm using their friendship, and B.) I hate asking favors from a person who will literally stop at nothing to help me, despite how busy she is.

I wiggle out my credit card from my purse, rising from my chair. "I'll catch you up on everything—I also want to know how the wedding planning is going—but we're going to need coffee first. Tell me what you'll have." When Madison tries to get up with her designer purse in hand, I shake my head. "Nope, you got me last time. This one's on me."

"I didn't realize you were counting," she huffs, placing her purse back on the table, but I appreciate when she doesn't argue.

It's not a secret that Madison's well-off. From what I understand, that wasn't always the case, and her humble, down-to-earth demeanor is a testament to that. But given my current, barely held together getup—a faded black tank top with a large strawberry illustrated in the middle, jeans that definitely weren't ripped when I bought them, and Nathan's weathered red-and-blue flannel tied around my waist—along with the fact that she knows I still drive my dad's old Mazda and have school loans I'll be paying off for the foreseeable future, it's obvious I'm not rolling in dough, but I'm grateful she doesn't make me feel that way.

"Well, I am," I sass at her with a smile, though she knows I'm teasing. "Now, tell me what you want."

Seven minutes later, I'm sauntering back to the table with a medium mocha latte for Madison and a kid-sized black coffee for myself. I'd wanted my favorite crème brûlée macchiato, but by the time I got to the counter and realized a kid's cup of coffee would be eighty percent cheaper, I figured I'd save the extra cash.

I take a sip, trying not to make a face when it burns my tongue. "Are you all set for the big day? It's coming up so soon!"

Madison hums around her first sip, putting the cup down and smiling from ear to ear. She's been dating her girlfriend, Brie, for almost five years, and the two decided to take things to the next level earlier this year. They're supposed to be getting married mid-summer.

At twenty-nine-years old, Madison's about four years older than me, with one hell of a good head on her shoulders. She's accomplished more in one life than most people could in two. From having made huge contributions leading to break-throughs in renewable energy, to publishing influential papers in the field of chemistry, to all the charity work she does, she's a force to be reckoned with. And the person she gives all the credit to is her dad.

Apparently, he was only seventeen when she was born and raised her on his own, while trying to figure out a future for the two of them. And what an incredible future he carved, given his multi-million-dollar Earth Sciences business. From the little I know—given I've never seen or met him—Madison and her dad are more like best friends than a typical father-daughter duo.

"We're ready! Well, for the most part. There's always last-minute things, but nothing I'm stressed about." She chuckles. "Brie, on the other hand, thrives on stress, so no matter how many times I've assured her that everything's going to be fine, she finds reasons to freak out. We got your RSVP a few weeks ago; I'm so glad you'll be there." She wags her brows. "No plus-one?"

I wink at her, hoping to hide behind the veil of jest. "Plus-ones are for people who get bored by themselves. I, for one, have no problems with my own company."

I don't mention the fact that plus-ones are for those who seek them out, or any relationship at all, for that matter.

It's not that I haven't explored relationships in the past, because I have. But things usually fizzle out after a few dates, probably because I'm guarded. It takes time for me to open up to someone. Whatever the reason, no one has ever worked hard enough to look beneath the layers, to stick around long enough. And, truth be told, I've never found someone worth letting in that far.

She takes a sip of her drink, winking at me from above the rim. "Well, if that changes, you can always add one at the last minute. We're keeping things pretty casual."

I smile at her. "I can't wait. And if you need any help at all, let me know."

"Okay, now tell me what's happening in Kavi-land! What's next for you now that you've graduated? Masters in art therapy, right? That's pretty damn exciting!"

"Thanks. Yeah, it is exciting," I agree, turning the cup on the table clockwise and chewing my bottom lip. "I got a full-time position as a therapist at a children's hospital in Portland that starts after the summer—"

Madison's hand clamps over mine, cutting off my words. "Kavi, that's awesome! I'm so happy for you!"

I blush. "Thanks."

I've never been good with compliments . . . or words in general. I'm definitely better with people I care about, but getting to know someone new or making conversation for the sake of doing so has never been my forte. If I have friends, like Madison, it's because they've tried to get to know me. But even so, I don't divulge enough for them to know much.

Maybe it's because I've never found myself interesting enough. Maybe I've just always liked listening and observing more. Or maybe it's because I tend to be the overthinking type, never sure of what to say. By the time I figure it out, the moment's usually long gone.

It's one of the reasons I've always loved art—it doesn't require my words, just my thoughts. It's the only place where my feelings are enough. Where *I* am enough. The place where I'm both completely in control and completely free.

The place where mistakes result in new possibilities, not catastrophic endings.

"What are you doing until then?" Madison asks after taking another sip of her drink.

My face heats at the thought of asking her for help; I've never been good at that, either. "Actually, I'm desperately looking for a short-term gig. Something to be a stopgap until I start my job."

Her brows furrow. "Do you want me to ask around at the university? There's always a need for temporary positions. I can also ask Brie if she needs anyone to help at her law firm —"

"Actually," I clear my throat, "I saw a position at your dad's company, Case Geo, for a temporary admin position.

Her eyes widen as realization sets in. "Oh, that's right! My dad's looking for a person to fill-in while his admin is on maternity leave this summer." She blows out a breath. "But, as much as I love the man, I'd never wish for a friend to work for him."

My brows wrinkle. "Why?"

She huffs out a breath, as if wondering where to start, chuckling at the end. "Girl, my dad's not easy to please. It's why I'd never work for him! We'd kill each other!" She throws her head back, laughing as if she's made the best joke before her eyes turn sympathetic. "I'll recommend you for the position if that's what you want—it would work out in terms of timing for you, too—but . . . I don't want you to hate my dad."

I reel back. "Hate him? Why would I hate him?"

She sighs. "He's the best man I know and the best father a girl could ask for, but . . . he's also a big grump with soaring-high expectations when it comes to his employees. Me and a couple of his close best friends are the only ones who truly know him, but otherwise, he tends to keep people at arms' length."

Maybe her dad and I have something in common already.

I snort. "Well, as long as he's even marginally better than the jackass who came into the restaurant last night, I should be fine."

I try not to visibly cringe as I recall the gorgeous asshole's face as he got torpedoed by a stray bottle cork. God, what a disaster. If I *never* think about that incident again, it'll be too soon.

"What?" Madison leans forward, tucking a blonde strand behind her ear.

"Never mind." I shake my head. "Don't worry about me hating your dad. If he raised someone like you, then he can't be that bad." My shoulders slump as I watch a raindrop trace its way down the window, merging with a larger droplet before meeting Madison's gaze again. "Things are a little tight and . . . I need this."

The overdue notice on the counter for this month's rent curdles my stomach. Between Mom's jobs as a customer service rep and Uber driver, and my paychecks from my TA position, we've been able to cover our living expenses, including rent, utilities, and food until now. But whatever was in our savings has been long depleted from Dad's medical and funeral bills.

Money has been tight ever since I graduated and lost my TA position. And while relocating to a more affordable area around the Bay is an option, it comes with the cost of potentially downgrading school districts and compromising my brother's education. Not to mention the huge adjustment Neil would face at a new high school as he gears up to be a senior next year.

Change isn't easy in high school. I know that better than anyone.

Madison's hand falls gently on my forearm. "Hey, I get it. I know how tough it's been ever since your dad died." I don't clarify that it was tough long before that, too. "Don't worry, I'll get you the job with my dad. In fact, consider it done, okay?"

"Thank you." I lay my hand on top of hers, closing my eyes, and once again appreciating the fact that she's not treating me like a charity case by just offering me money.

She shifts, snorting. "Well, don't thank me yet. This might not be the blessing you're thinking it'll be. My dad is—"

"You won't hear a single complaint from me, I promise. If he agrees, the only thing I'll feel is gratitude."

Madison smirks, a playful glint in her eyes. "Let's see if you're singing the same tune in three months. And don't let this temporary admin position fool you. It'll pay well, but volunteering to juggle live grenades might be easier. But hey, more power to you if you can do it. Just remember, I warned you."

Later, as I insert the key to unlock my car, watching the rain gently patter over the pavement, I can't help but wonder if I've asked for more than I can handle. My gaze lands on a puddle near my tire, trembling with every falling droplet, much like my heart seems to be . . .

As if it can sense the approach of a much bigger storm.

Chapter Three

HUDSON

MADDY

Don't be late, Pops. I don't want to have to play the my-dad-is-a-workaholic-and-doesn't-have-time-for-his-daughter card, but I'm not above it.

The corners of my mouth lift as the text bubble lights up on my phone, but movement in front of my office door catches my eyes.

Belinda taps the doorframe, her brows raised before she's even asked the question. Even at five-foot-one and eight months pregnant, she commands attention. Besides the fact that the woman is meticulous at everything she does, her ability to look me in the eyes and not sugarcoat her words are the reasons I hired her to be my admin. Unlike everyone else, she doesn't tiptoe around me. Hell, there are days I feel like I'm the one tiptoeing around her.

"You're going to be late. And you know how much Madison hates that. If you leave now, you might still make it to dinner without getting an earful from your daughter."

I shut the screen of my laptop. She's right. No amount of work—from the slides I still have to do for the board presentation, to the contract I still need to revise for the new airport site my company's excavating—is worth Maddy's wrath. Nor is it worth missing out on a date with my daughter. Plus, I hate tardiness myself—timeliness being one of the first things I instilled in her as a kid—so I'd deserve her wrath if I was late.

Rising, I grab the suit jacket hanging on the back of my chair. "Why are you still here?"

Belinda locks a hand on her hip, her brown hair dusting over her shoulders. "And where else am I supposed to be? I'm here because my asshole boss refuses to leave until," she turns her wrist to look at her watch, "seven-ten PM, and I feel bad leaving before him."

I put my phone in my pocket and head toward the door, feeling like shit because the woman is literally on her feet and chasing one fire or another all day. Her doctor specifically told her to take it easy this month, given her spikes in blood pressure. I've asked her to work from home, but she refuses, stating she needs to be here or things won't get done right.

And they call me a perfectionist.

"We need to find a replacement for you. Put everything else aside and make it top priority. If we can find someone in the next week or so, hopefully you'll have enough time to train them."

She walks ahead of me, heels tapping on the tile, and I try to avoid the empty office across the hall from mine. Let me rephrase: I can't glance at it without balling my fists so tight, I might draw blood from my palms. Even after two years, the stench of betrayal lingers heavily around it, threatening to seep into the walls.

I've always run a tight ship, demanding exemplary performance and unwavering dedication, but after the way shit went down two years ago . . . let's just say, I've taken any hint of leniency completely off the table. Now, I value loyalty as much as hard work.

Belinda speaks over her shoulder. "It's easy for you to say, but interviews, background checks, HR approvals . . . they all take time. And let's not even mention your stellar track record with admins—"

"Hey, you've stuck around for three years."

She shoots me a wry look. "Count your blessings." At the slight lift of my lips, she continues, "You'd already fired three admins before me, and when I took one month off last year to go on my honeymoon, you fired the temp!"

"He started off our staff meeting by asking everyone to express how they felt that day using emojis."

Belinda presses her lips together like she's trying not to laugh. "In any case, I need to add 'emotional resilience' to the job requirements."

Something in her words triggers an image in my mind—a face I haven't been able to erase from my thoughts for three days.

The way a single tear rolled over the bottom of her lid before falling on my hand, burning my skin like it was acid. The fear and uncertainty in her amber-colored eyes. The glint of a tiny diamond on the right side of her upper lip.

Her anxiety was palpable through her shaky hands and her stuttered words. And the asshole in me—the one who failed to acknowledge the fact that she was probably half my age— couldn't stop myself from homing in on the way her lips trembled, the way they parted when our eyes connected.

And those fucking hands hesitantly trying to mop up the ice water she'd spilled on my lap . . .?

Jesus. There was no reason for the raging boner I had,

given my dick was practically frozen inside my pants, but clearly my brain wasn't in charge of my body.

It wasn't until my friend Dev's snickering reached across the table that I snapped out of whatever trance I was in. I noticed her bent over with her face practically in my crotch, her ass inside that short-as-fuck skirt on full display for the entire restaurant.

And I saw red.

I'd already had a hellish workday, and my mood was at an all-time low. My irritation spiked, overshadowing the impending migraine from a damn cork launched at my head.

What I wanted to do was tell her to go put some fucking clothes on, to stop waving her ass in the air for the table of men behind her, who were more than happy to get an eyeful. But what I ended up saying left a bitter taste in my mouth afterward. Like those words shouldn't have even formed in the first place.

"That's about all the incompetence this restaurant can handle for one day. Please turn in your badge and clock out. This will be your last day working here."

A part of me wanted to take them back, especially as I watched her walk away, shoulders deflated. But I couldn't.

Because who would I be if I couldn't stand by my words? If I didn't follow through? If I let things slide, even once?

Isn't that how I got into my current predicament, by letting things slide? I can't even look at the damn office that's been empty for two years.

Belinda's voice snaps me out of my thoughts. "Hurry up and get out of here before Madison starts blowing up my phone looking for you."

I'm just about to enter the elevator when Belinda rushes over, making me worry she's going to topple. "Oh! I wanted to ask, do you need anything for your meeting in Portland tomorrow? I already have you checked in on your morning flight."

I shake my head. "I'm all set. Now, will you please stop working?"

She huffs, "I will as soon as you find me a replacement." Her brows rise, a hopeful look in her eyes. "Who knows, maybe we'll have the perfect person walking through these elevator doors on Monday."

MADDY CUTS a piece of her salmon before forking it into her mouth and taking the last sip of her Sauvignon Blanc. Both our waters need refilling as well.

My gaze travels around the restaurant, looking for Stella, and I exhale a frustrated breath. She's been rather inattentive with our table today, and I'm inclined to put her on the spot the next time she comes over. This is not the type of service I expect at my restaur—

"Dad," Maddy's voice steals my attention. "It's a busy Thursday night, and I'm not going to die without a refill on my wine. Stop looking around for Stella; she'll come by soon enough." She takes another bite of her salmon before looking at my empty plate. I'd devoured my entire meal ten minutes ago. "Gramps would have loved this place, you know. He would have been proud of everything you and Uncle Jett have accomplished."

She studies my reaction carefully, surely noticing the way I tense at the mention of my younger brother and co-owner of this restaurant. But because the last thing I want to do is rehash my complicated feelings about my brother and his betrayal, I simply nod.

She's right; Dad would have been proud.

Witnessing his dream of opening a restaurant serving

some of his favorite seafood dishes come to fruition would have given us one of his rare smiles. It's what he'd always wanted, and what both Jett and I envisioned after he died.

We'd both grown up working on Dad's fish charter, navigating the waters of South Lake Tahoe. Unlike the life we live now, there was no golden veneer. No struggle for power and prestige; no expensive champagne and handmade watches.

Just the scent of lake water, hard work, and humility.

Sure, Dad managed his business differently than I would have. His decisions—like giving employees too much leniency for tardiness, or not setting standards of exemplary service on fishing trips, or not scrutinizing his finances carefully—used to drive me crazy.

But it was those decisions, and the fact that I practically watched Dad's small business turn to dust due to his oversight, that hardened me in my own ways. Even at a young age, I knew I'd do things differently if I ever ran my own company.

"How's work?" Madison asks, sitting back in her seat. "Did you guys secure that contract with the new airport? What are they called?" She snaps her fingers. "Rose City Skyport, right? Will Case Geo excavate the new site?"

I pinch the bridge of my nose.

Just the thought of the hurdles we've jumped through for this client has my head pounding. If they weren't so strategic for my efforts to establish Case Geo as the premier company specializing in environmentally conscious airport planning, I wouldn't be bending over backward, revising our standard contracts for them. But as it stands, with the ridiculous amount Case Geo stands to gain from this client alone, they've got me by the fucking balls.

"We'll secure them." My jaw tightens, recalling our clients are also shopping around with our rivals—the same ones my brother and my ex-girlfriend left to work for.

"We're the better choice in terms of expertise and experience."

Maddy leans forward, her eyes gleaming in that way I've seen all her life, when she's preparing to ask me something she knows I might object to and brace myself. "Hey, Dad . . ."

At twenty-nine, being an immensely accomplished person herself, there's not a whole lot my daughter asks from me, but I won't deny that I like being the person she can still come to when she does need something.

It's just that her requests are now a bit more . . . worrisome than the ones she used to ask for as a kid, like ice cream for dinner or to borrow my sports car to impress her then girlfriend. For example, her request to go shark cage diving for her birthday because her fiancée refused to. Needless to say, I tried not to pass the fuck out when a tiger shark zoomed toward us. Even with my extensive appreciation of marine geology, I've never been happier to set my feet back on solid ground.

She steeples her fingers together under her chin, as if she already knows she might need to pray for this one. "So, I need a little fav—"

"No," I respond before she can use those wide blue eyes to pierce my resolve. I'm no idiot; the kid's been conning me with that look her whole life, and she'll probably succeed again today.

I won't admit it, but I've always been a willing sucker for it.

I suppose it's the guilt that sometimes comes from being a single parent—the one where you play both the good and bad cop. The worry you've worn the bad cop hat more than the good one lately, wondering if you're not enough to fill in for the missing parent, the one she probably yearns for every single day. And though she tells you that you're enough, that you've always been enough, you still wonder if she's just sparing your feelings.

At only seventeen and living in different states, her mother and I weren't destined to be together. She was visiting her friend in Lake Tahoe over the summer when we ran into each other at a party that led to a one-night thing.

A year later, she dropped Madison off at my doorstep with a note admitting she wasn't meant to be a mom. And though she'd left her phone number scribbled at the bottom of the note, I never called her.

In fact, neither did Maddy—not when I gave her the phone number when she was eight, and then again when she was a teen.

I can only guess what her reasons were for not reaching out to her mom, but mine were simple: I don't chase after quitters, never have and never will. And her mom had done exactly that when she'd flown back to Tahoe with our three-month-old—never having told me she was even pregnant—to drop her off at my door and fly back without a single word spoken to me. She may have left me her phone number to ease her conscience, but in my mind, the doors of communication were closed.

"You haven't even heard what I have to say!" Maddy throws her hands up. "It's not bad, I promise. In fact, it'd be really good for you."

I highly doubt that, but I ask anyway. "Fine. What is it?"

She's about to answer when Stella comes back to our table to pour us both more water and asks us if we want refills on our wine. We both agree, but I notice she doesn't make eye contact with me.

I stop her before she can leave with our empty plates. "Is there something you want to say, Stella? You've been a bit lacking in your service—"

"Dad." Madison tilts her blonde head, reminiscent of her

mother's hair color, giving me a warning look. While I raised her to be disciplined and tough, I'm realizing, now that she's all grown up, sometimes those traits backfire on me.

I take a breath, softening my tone toward Stella, and hating the fact that I even care. She makes a decent paycheck working here and has been one of our best employees, but if hard work is no longer something that interests her, then I have no qualms about telling her to hand in her notice. "It's just that you seem off lately."

There. That's about as nice as I can manage.

Stella swallows, blinking rapidly as her head swings from Madison to me. "It's . . . we're understaffed and overworked. I'm pretty sure you can see that. But you've fired the two servers we've hired over the past three weeks. At this point, it doesn't seem like you even want to give people a chance to learn—"

"Maybe if you would spend more time letting them shadow you, I wouldn't have to interact with servers who are clearly unprepared."

"None of us have the time or the bandwidth to train a new person extensively, and some of this is trial by fire. We need to allow people to make a few mistakes."

"Absolutely not," I grit before catching Maddy's raised brows again. She's . . . disappointed, and that irks me like nothing else. I close my eyes, trying to center myself for a moment. "Fine. I'll go a little easier on the next person, but perhaps wait until they're a bit seasoned before they're in charge of my table."

"Thank you." Stella's shoulders release with a sigh before she walks away to get us more wine.

Maddy's half smile is obvious behind the fingers over her mouth. "I'm proud of you, Dad. Looks like an old dog *can* learn new tricks after all." At my responding glare, she quickly adds, "So, about that woman you're going to hire to replace Belinda for the next three months . . ."

Wait a minute. Did I just miss some vital information I don't recall ever getting?

"What woman? What are you talking about?"

"You're still looking for Belinda's replacement, aren't you?"

"Yes, but—"

Maddy steamrolls right past me. "I have a friend who desperately needs a job for a few months. She just graduated with a masters in art therapy and has a permanent position with a hospital in Portland starting at the end of summer, and—"

"How does that have anything to do with a company that specializes in Earth Sciences?" That pounding headache I referred to earlier is getting worse.

"Dad, she's smart and talented. I'm positive she can learn whatever you need her to. She's just had a rough year and has piled up a few bills. And while she hasn't been an admin before, I've volunteered with her at multiple events. She's very dedicated and a quick learner. She even teaches free art classes to kids suffering from anxiety on the weekends."

When I don't respond, I swear her eyes get rounder and her bottom lip pops out. It doesn't matter how old your kid gets, I can attest to the fact that it's fucking hard to say no.

"Please, Dad."

I groan, running my hand over my face. There aren't many people who can muscle me into doing things, but one of them happens to be my biggest weakness and the woman sitting across the table from me. The other being my best friend, Garrett. "Fine. Have her come in for an interview with Belinda tomorrow. I'll be in Portland but—"

"Yay! Thank you!" Maddy covers her lips with the tips of her fingers and sends me an air kiss. "I owe you big time. And if it's not too much to ask, can you not fire her like the servers Stella was talking about? I know you're a stickler, but just remember, she's my friend, too."

My jaw tightens as I shove away thoughts of the amber-eyed, anxious woman I'd fired a few days ago. "The only thing you owe me is a dance at your wedding."

Maddy lifts the new glass of wine Stella just brought us, and I clink mine with hers. "Oh, come on, you know I'd never forget my pops."

I take a sip. "Now, tell me all about how the wedding planning is going."

Chapter Four

HUDSON

Waiting for my coffee in our building's lobby, I flip through my email on my phone, hoping for an update from Rose City Skyport (RCS) regarding the status of our contract negotiation, knowing I won't find anything.

Last Friday in Portland, my team and I answered our prospective client's questions the best we could, but I have a feeling they'll be having similar discussions with our competitors this week. And I'm pretty sure we won't secure their formal answer until that all unfolds.

My nostrils flare as I stare mindlessly at an email from my finance department, not really registering the words. It's not an unexpected reaction, given this is a familiar response to anything that reminds me of my brother and the woman I had come to care about.

Shaking off my irritation, I grab my coffee from the bar and saunter into the elevator, mentally gearing up for the day. Thankfully, I squeezed in a workout this morning with my best friend, Garrett, a pilot out of the Bay Area. Though it's become rarer since he and his wife Bella had their daughter, we try to meet up at the gym whenever we can manage it.

A smile pulls at my lips when I think about the videos he showed me of her trying to walk, but my good mood takes an immediate nosedive when the doors to my floor open.

My lingering smile drops when my gaze settles on the woman sitting behind Belinda's desk.

Cascading waves of dark silky hair—well past her shoulders—frame her face, brushing against the paperwork in front of her. Her thick lashes flutter before she puts the end of her pen to her bottom lip, engrossed in whatever she's reading. And though she hasn't looked up, with the glint of that piercing over her top lip, there's no mistaking who she is.

And . . . is that a homemade cake in the portable cake box in front of her?

Belinda messaged me late Friday evening to tell me the woman Maddy sent her way turned out to be a great fit and was ready to start on Monday.

But surely, she couldn't have meant the same one . . .

Surely, the universe wouldn't send the *same damn woman* to ruin my mood again.

Hoping there's some sort of explanation for why she's here—*because why the fuck is she here?!*—I clear my throat, making her jump. In her scramble to rise from her seat, she knocks her coffee off her coaster, catching it right before it topples, but not before a drop of it lands on the corner of her paperwork.

"Shit!" A flustered pair of amber eyes find me before recognition sets in and they widen to saucers. "What are you . . ."

"I'd like to ask you the same thing." My gaze rushes down her attire—a faded gray T-shirt with a fucking orange slice illustrated on it that says, 'Peeling Good,' tucked inside worn denims, secured by a sparkly white belt, and an oversized men's blazer folded at the sleeves. "What the fuck are *you* doing here? And what are you wearing?"

She looks down at her ridiculous outfit as if noticing it for the first time. Her head snaps up and a glint of something—annoyance, perhaps—sparks in her eyes before it turns to uncertainty again. She closes her eyes and murmurs something that sounds like, *"You've gotta be kidding me,"* before she straightens her shoulders.

"Are you . . . you're Mr. Case?" She doesn't wait for my response, gleaning the answer, possibly through deductive reasoning or likely from the thunderous look on my face. "Right. Well, I'm your new admin."

"No, you're not." I scoff because this has to be a joke. And not a very good one. "Where's Belinda?"

"She's—"

"I'm right here. Sheesh!" My very pregnant admin waddles in behind me, holding the side of her belly and breathing heavily. "I was just using the little girls' room." She looks from me to the still-bewildered-looking woman behind her desk before swinging her head back in my direction. "What's the problem? Hudson, this is Kavita Jain, the woman Madison—"

No.

Hell no.

"She's not going to work." I stride right past her desk, not sparing another glance at *Ms. Peeling Good* and her frayed jacket.

"But—" Belinda's heels tap furiously on the tile behind me as she tries to keep up. "Hudson."

Behind my desk, I move a few manila folders off my laptop, still grappling with the fact that the woman I fired last week from my restaurant—a woman who's flitted through my thoughts more than I care to admit—is the *same* one my daughter recommended and is now back to working for me.

What are the fucking chances?

The door to my office shuts as an irate-looking Belinda stares at me. "Want to tell me what your problem is? Why are you acting like a child this early in the morning?"

I open my laptop before shrugging off my suit coat and managing an inscrutable expression. Something I'm adept at. "There's no problem. I get a say in the people we hire, especially when they affect my job directly, and I don't want her."

Belinda steps closer, her head tilting. "Is it her attire? I admit, it's a bit on the casual side, but I can—"

"It's not." I take a seat in front of my laptop, keeping my eyes on the screen. "Her attire is only a drop in the bucket of all the reasons she's not a good fit. I just don't want her working here."

"What? *Why?*" I don't have to look at her to know her eyes have practically turned to slits. She's nothing if not skilled at poking and prodding until one of us loses our shit.

I pretend to be intrigued by something on my screen.

"Hudson, you're being unreasonable."

"Fire her. Find someone else."

Belinda's hands land on the edge of my desk, and I make the mistake of meeting her fearsome and tired gaze. "Hudson Case, either you tell me exactly what's gotten up your wealthy ass or prepare to hear an earful."

I snort, letting that be my response. Aren't I *already* getting an earful?

Apparently that wasn't the most prudent thing to do, because Belinda's hands land over the top of her belly as she fumes, "I hired that woman out there; a woman your own daughter vouched for, by the way. When I messaged you on Friday about her, you told me to trust my instincts, which is precisely what I did. She's sharp, attentive, and a quick learner. So, you either give her a chance or end up with no admin in the matter of a few weeks."

I squint at her. "Is that a threat?"

"No." She shakes her head, picking off a non-existent crumb from her belly with eerie calm. "It's a fact."

My eyes flick back to my screen and I keep my mouth shut.

How do I explain that I want that woman out there at a minimum of a ten-mile radius from me with no knowledge of her whereabouts or address?

How do I reveal that, for reasons surpassing the incident at the restaurant, everything about her irks me?

Her breathy gasps, the rise and fall of her chest, and the flush that sweeps over her cheeks whenever she's embarrassed.

Her fucking heart-shaped lips . . .

She's the definition of a walking, talking migraine.

"Alright." Belinda raises and drops her arms to her sides in exasperation. "Fine, I'll tell her to go home because, for whatever reason, my boss doesn't find her to be a good fit. But guess what *you're* going to have to do?" When I chance another glance at her, she flashes me a smug grin that says she knows she's on the verge of victory. "*You're* going to have to tell your daughter why you fired her friend without a fair shot. And rest assured, *that* will not be an easy conversation."

My hand balls into a fist around a pen as my molars grind, and I recall the promise I made to Maddy at the end of our dinner—to give her friend the benefit of doubt and a fair shot.

I rub my temples with the tips of my fingers, watching as Belinda struts back toward the door with her nose in the air.

Goddammit! How do the women in my life always seem to get their way?

"Fine," I grit, keeping my voice low and my eyes trained on my screen, stopping her in her tracks. "Keep her. But I swear to God, Belinda, the second she becomes a bigger headache

than she already looks like, I'll fire her and bring you back with that newborn of yours. So, make sure to train her well."

With her hand on the doorknob, Belinda turns her head to the side, and I don't miss the triumphant smile flickering at the corners of her lips. "Yes, boss. But just so you know, it'd be illegal for you to ask me to come back during my leave. I'm pretty sure I can sue you for the gazillions you wipe your ass with, so unless it's to congratulate me on my new bundle of joy, don't call me." She flips her hair off her shoulder. "Oh, and that's definitely not a threat; it's a promise."

I GLARE at the white plate, covered in see-through plastic wrap, for the tenth time.

A swirl of Nutella decorates the slice of pound cake under the wrap. Even from its place at the corner of my desk, the sweet scents of vanilla, chocolate, and butter seep through the covering, agitating my senses. It's the same scent that lingered inside my nose days after the restaurant incident, and now I feel like my fucking brain is floating in it.

And the small orange Post-It note with the words, *Thanks for chasing away the rain* stuck to it? It's pissing me right the fuck off.

Who the hell bakes a cake for their first day of work?

She came in an hour ago, trying to be confident with each stride toward my desk, though I didn't miss the way she fiddled with the bottom of her blazer. Not that I was looking, since my eyes never left my laptop.

I also never wondered if said blazer was her own or if she borrowed it from her boyfriend because she got dressed at his house this morning.

I never wondered about that, but the thought managed to piss me off, regardless.

"I . . . I'm learning to bake." Her soft voice, the same as I remembered from the restaurant and then from this morning, grated against my ears. *"I got this recipe book called Thirty Easy Bakes to Know by Thirty. I've been trying each recipe, and—"*

"Ms. Jain, as riveting as your culinary endeavors sound, I don't have time for the diatribe." I didn't spare her a glance. *"Please make sure you close the door on your way out."*

A pink tint had settled at the tops of her brown cheeks when she dropped her eyes to her clasped hands and nodded, abruptly turning to leave. But before she made it through the door, I'd glanced up, not knowing exactly why I was holding my next words with all my might at the tip of my tongue.

To stop her?

But why the fuck would I want to stop her?

If this was going to work, then there was no reason to become too familiar. There was no reason to let her think I appreciated gestures of the type. I'd gone down that route in the past and look where it landed me—with my girlfriend in bed with my brother, and a betrayal that rocked the foundation of the company I'd worked so hard to build.

In any case, in three months, she'll be on her way to her art therapy job to do whatever the fuck it is that art therapists do, and I'll still be running a multi-million-dollar company here in California.

So I dropped my eyes back to my computer, but not before letting them trail down to her exquisite ass, full hips, and thick thighs, practically ripping the seams of her denims.

I've never been attracted to thin, fragile-looking women —the types that look like they'd break in the arms of a six-foot-two, two-hundred-plus-pound man. My eyes are magnets for round hips and soft curves, a round and plentiful ass. There's something so hot about being able to grab handfuls of a woman's ass, watching it bounce while being buried deep inside her.

As soon as the door clicked, I shoved those thoughts right out of my mind. As it was, I wouldn't be able to get out of my seat sporting the boner inside my pants for a good time to come.

The woman is my daughter's friend, half my age, and from every encounter till now, somewhat of a hot mess.

Not only that, but acting on or even *thinking about* someone who was now working for me was out of the question. Not that I was even remotely interested in her.

I'd broken that rule in the past—dating someone from our marketing department and thinking I could trust her, only to have her stab me in the back, right alongside my brother. I'd be a fool to go down the same road again.

No matter how sweet and innocent the woman sitting at Belinda's desk looks, I don't know her, nor do I want to. Sure, Maddy's opinion of her holds weight, which is why Kavi even has the job, but it won't be the reason I let someone cross the boundaries I've firmly set.

After typing and deleting the same damn sentence in an email four times, I slam my fingers onto the keyboard before running them through my hair.

Belinda left an hour ago, as stated in the email she sent me. About as big of a fuck you as I expected, given she barely spoke to me all day. I heard her and Kavi murmuring throughout the morning before they eventually went to lunch together.

Evidently, she's still pissed off about my reluctance to hire the art therapist with the work experience of a toddler in her stead. *Well, go right the fuck ahead, Belinda. I'm not losing sleep over it.* Because if I'm going to be strong-armed into keeping this woman around for three months, then she'll have to deal with my retorts and objections while she's around.

If she sticks around.

My eyes drag back to the plate, and I huff before bringing

it toward me. Ripping off the note, I stall on the words written on it again—on every letter curved and contoured, as if painted with a brush. She even drew an umbrella over the words.

Thanks for chasing away the rain.

My gaze inadvertently finds the droplets clinging to the windows in my office, the gloom from the lack of sun over the past few weeks barely noticeable in the evening. The rain hasn't let up all day, and the forecast says it has no inclination for doing so in the foreseeable future.

What the fuck is she talking about?

Chasing away the rain?

Not knowing what to do with the dessert—not wanting to relent by eating it, nor wanting to throw it away—I shove it inside my leather bag.

Thirty minutes later, well past the time most of the staff has left, I pull my suit coat back on. Stowing my laptop inside my bag, and careful not to squish the cake, I head out of my office. As usual, my eyes harden, along with my jaw, at the empty office across mine.

Shoving away memories, and the subsequent crack to my heart, of the day they both came to my office to tell me they were going to work for our rivals—with my girlfriend at the time telling me she'd slept with my brother—I stalk down the hall, heading toward the exit. The last thing I expect is to see movement at Belinda's desk.

It's well past eight and pouring buckets outside. So why the hell is she still here?

My legs still, a frown pulling at the corners of my mouth. "Why are you still here?"

"Hi! Um . . ." She rises awkwardly, making the chair roll back farther than she intended. She swipes a strand of silky hair behind her ear, giving me a glimpse of . . . *Are those plastic orange slices hanging from her ears?* The woman has the strangest taste in fashion. "Belinda said she stayed until you left. So . . ."

Right. Belinda usually comes to my office to tell me to leave before she threatens to sue me for something.

"I don't expect that from you." I scowl—which seems to be my permanent expression around this woman—watching her tangle her hands together nervously. "In fact, I don't expect *anything* from you."

She flinches, as if my words physically assaulted her, and before she can form a response, I turn to walk to the elevator.

She isn't Kenna, and this isn't like me.

Sure, I'm surly and demanding; I've been more so after the way things went down with Jett and Kenna, since they also managed to take a few key staff with them. But have I ever been this callous?

I'd lost faith that day, in the people I thought I could trust, in the way I'd run my business until then. In me.

To think my own fucking brother—the kid I'd practically helped raise, my flesh and blood—would shove a dagger in my back. For what? And why?

I don't give two-flying fucks about Kenna—she lost her place in my life and my heart the minute she told me she'd slept with my brother because I wasn't "around enough"—but I have thought about asking him if it was worth it. Was it worth it to gut the person who always stood by his side? Who helped make him who he is?

I haven't asked though, and I probably never will. Like I said, I don't chase quitters.

I'm inside the elevator, with the doors closing, when I think I hear a sniffle.

Fuck.

I jab a finger on the *Open Door* button right as my hand juts out to try to keep the doors open, but it's too late. The doors force closed, and I'm stuck inside with my stomach in knots.

The weight of my own bitterness presses against the walls of my chest as the elevator descends.

The doors finally open, revealing the lobby downstairs, the doorman scrolling his phone at the front and pellets of rain still streaming down the windows.

I have half a mind to push the button for my floor again and go back up to talk to her . . . to apologize. Shit! I don't know.

But instead, I find my feet moving me toward the exit before I'm settling into my truck inside our parking garage. I toss my laptop bag onto the passenger seat before slamming the bottom of my palm against my steering wheel. "Goddammit!"

I throw my head back against my headrest as the sound of her sniffle echoes inside my ears. I'm a fucking asshole, venomous and cold.

When did I become this way?

Glancing at the seat next to me, I pull out the stupid slice of cake she made, which is only slightly flattened inside my bag.

Peeling back the plastic, I dig in with the fork she'd tucked inside as well. It's spongy and sweet, with just the right amount of chocolate. In a few bites, I've eaten the entire thing.

But it does nothing to sweeten the bitterness inside my conscience.

Chapter Five

KAVI

"**W**hat do you mean, it's dead?" I ask my mom, turning the knob on our laundry machine as if she hadn't tried that herself. I open and close the lid and push the Start button, hoping for a miracle. "It was working fine a couple of days ago."

I don't mean for my tone to sound accusatory, but it comes out that way, anyway. It's just that my mother—*God love her*—can be a bit of a klutz when it comes to household appliances. It's not intentional, and she's so remorseful afterward, but the woman was born cursed with the worst of Murphy's Law when it comes to electronics.

Last month it was our blender—"*I don't know why, it just blew up!*"—and a few weeks before that, it was the vacuum. "*It just started smoking. This is the problem with second-hand stuff.*"

And now this.

"I know it was working a couple of days ago, Kavi," she soothes in her thick Indian accent. "But I used it the same way I have all these years, and boom! Dead!"

I'd laugh at her animated explanation if this wasn't the last thing I needed.

I sigh, pinching the bridge of my nose, my mind zipping a mile a minute as I add a new laundry machine to the list of things I need to pay for.

It's been a horrendous day, starting from the moment I discovered my boss, the man who fired me at the restaurant, was also Madison's dad. Not only that, but if I thought he couldn't dislike me more, I was gravely mistaken. If it was possible, his hatred for me might be even stronger now.

Seriously, what are the freaking chances?

I won't deny I'd thought of him often since our first disastrous meeting, but I'd never in a million years expected him to be the head of Case Geo.

Clearly, he was just as surprised to see me. Though, 'surprised' might be putting it mildly. *Shocked* and *irate* might be more in the ballpark of how he looked. His cruel words, telling me he expected nothing from me, still ring in my ears even now, over two hours later.

And if that wasn't enough, I'm now stuck dealing with yet another reason I desperately need this job.

It's like the list of issues keeps growing—there's still that overdue rent notice, a vacuum that needs to be replaced, an upcoming electricity bill, and now a broken laundry machine.

I'm not even going to acknowledge the screeching noise my car has been making every time I turn.

"Come on." My mom grasps my shoulders, turning me toward our small dining room and away from the new reason for my headache. "Let me grab you a plate of dinner. I made your favorite—*puris* and *chole*. I can't believe you had to stay so late on your first day. What kind of heartless boss makes you do that?"

I groan, thinking of said heartless boss, as I allow my mother to steer me into a seat next to my brother. She bustles into the kitchen, the clattering of dishes providing a momentary distraction in my thoughts.

I rest my eyes on my brother, hovering over what appears to be an SAT prep book, studying for the standardized tests at the end of summer.

Neil wordlessly slides a bowl of strawberries in my direction, and I note the smudge of dirt on the side of his face. Lifting my hand instinctively, I wipe it off with my thumb before he grunts, waving it away and going back to his work.

I chuckle at his gruff demeanor but can't help feel the warmth of his simple gesture.

Like Mom, he's been working two jobs this summer—one at the car wash and the other mowing lawns around the neighborhood—hoping to make enough to help out around the house.

And that thought leaves a heaviness in my chest, just like it always does.

He shouldn't have to carry our family burdens just yet. He should be out enjoying his summer with friends, playing video games and watching movies. Instead, he's home every night after an exhausting day of work, studying in hopes of getting a scholarship like I did.

Mom places a plate in front of me, telling me about her day as she walks over to the living room to fold laundry on the couch, when my phone lights up with a message.

MADISON

Hey! How did your first day go? Hope my dad wasn't the grump he usually is.

I bury the snort about to leave my lips. If today was any indication, I'm not sure calling her dad a grump would be sufficient. A self-absorbed prick or a calloused dickface might be more like it.

A beautiful dickface, but a dickface, nonetheless.

But there's no way I can tell her that after she went out of her way to secure me this job. I practically bypassed the HR formalities because of her, and now have a monthly paycheck that almost had me fainting when Belinda told me what I'd be making. With that kind of money, I could save up enough to cover Mom's rent for a few months, take some of the burden off Neil, and pay a deposit for a new apartment in Portland.

I hate the idea of leaving Mom and Neil here on their own, and I wouldn't have if there were jobs in my field available here, but my priority was taking care of them by any means possible. If that meant having a steady income while living in Portland, then it was what it was. Perhaps after Neil goes to college, Mom could move in with me. That's my hope, anyway.

Picking up my phone, I chew on the inside corner of my lip as images of wintery blue eyes, thick wavy dark hair, and that ever-grinding jaw dance inside my vision. The man is an ass, but there's no denying he's a gorgeous ass.

ME

Not at all. You had me nervous when we spoke. He's been nothing but kind and gracious.

Now that I've sent that message, I'm wondering if I laid it on a little too thick. What if she knows 'nothing but kind and gracious' is code for he's a three-headed monster?

But I also remember the promise I made to her when we met for coffee—that she'd never hear a complaint from me—and I intend to keep it. There's no way I'm telling her that not only did I sit there and cry well after Hudson left tonight, but I truly wondered if I should even come back.

That is, until I got home and was reminded that indeed, I had to go back, even if that meant being treated like the gum on the bottom of his Manolo Blahniks.

MADISON

> Okay, now I know you're lying. No one has called my dad kind and gracious his entire life.

Dammit! I knew I went too far.

Panic rises inside me as I imagine Madison dialing her dad to find out the truth, and I quickly type out another message.

ME

> I swear, he's been great. We actually didn't talk much but I can already tell I'll learn a lot from him.

Hoping my answer softens her doubts, I watch the three dots jump around my screen before her response pops up.

MADISON

> Well, I'm glad to hear it. Just remember, it's okay to put my dad in his place from time to time. Ask Belinda; it's the only way to survive him sometimes. And let me know if he ever goes from gracious to grinch. I'm happy to help.

I react to her message with a heart before turning my phone over and digging into my food.

I'm just falling asleep—my eyes closing as if my lids were magnets—when I decide to make myself another promise. One I'm determined to keep.

That tomorrow will be a better day.

It has to be.

THE GUY SITTING NEXT to me must be hard of hearing.

It's the only explanation for why he would turn up the volume on his headphones to a level no human could endure without permanent damage to their eardrums. And now I'll have *Even Flow* by Pearl Jam stuck on repeat inside my head all day.

I hold in a snort, knowing I'll be telling Nathan about this tonight. Not that I care to give him another reason to assert that Pearl Jam is better than Nirvana—because they're not. We've had this argument for years, and I stand by what I believe: Nirvana changed the shape, sound, and color of music as we know it today.

Trying to avoid the gaze of the disheveled, possibly home-less, woman in front of me, who's been staring at me for the past thirty minutes, I turn my head to look out the window, watching the city speed by.

I had no intention of riding the subway to work today, but when the screeching in my car turned into more of a groan a mile out of my neighborhood, I decided to turn around and call an Uber to the station before hollering at my brother to drop it off at the shop. As it is, it would take me an hour to get into the office by car, and now it'll be at least a half hour more.

An hour and a half later, I'm rushing out through the subway's automatic doors, checking my watch for the fifth time in the past ten minutes.

I'd emailed Belinda from the train, telling her I was running late, but even I have to admit it's not a good look on my second day.

With my umbrella barely doing much to shield me from the onslaught of rain, I skirt past pedestrians and try to dodge as many puddles as possible. But not before mud splat-ters over my boots and the fishnet stockings I'd worn under my emerald-green, mid-length skirt.

Great. Just fucking great.

I was so proud of myself for putting this outfit together today, too, having gotten this skirt delivered, along with a few other pieces from an online consignment store yesterday.

Folding my umbrella at the entrance of the enormous Case Geo building, I enter, debating between cleaning up inside a restroom or showing up to the office looking like I just came out of a mud bath.

Settling on the latter, and hoping no one looks below my waist, I pat down my hair, tucking a few wet, wayward strands behind my ear inside the elevator. Rolling my shoulders back, I assess my reflection on the elevator doors, reassuring myself that it's highly possible that Mr. Case isn't even here yet.

I mean, there's practically a torrential downpour out there. It's perfectly reasonable for people to be late with this kind of inclement weather.

Thanking my lucky stars when I find a quiet and conspicuously empty front entrance to Mr. Case's office—with not even Belinda at her desk—I hang my raincoat on the metal tree behind her desk and place my umbrella inside a bin.

I'm just bent over on her chair, wiping off the mud from my Docs with a tissue, when movement in the large conference room in front of me catches my attention.

Without rising, I look toward the room, full of at least twelve people dressed in suits. I hadn't seen them when I'd entered, but looking closely, I now notice the back of Belinda's head, her brown hair slightly flipped at the ends above her shoulders.

But it's when I continue past her head and catch the ice-cold, stormy-blue eyes staring back at me that sheer panic settles in. A part of me wonders if I can tumble off the chair inconspicuously enough and roll under the desk to spend the rest of my day there, before the other part of me decides to follow his glare . . . looking down at my chest.

My very *uncovered* chest, where the tops of my breasts—

swaying inside my lacy cream bra—are on display beneath my gaping V-neck, gray tank top.

I quickly rise, adjusting my shirt and throwing away the muddy tissue, when Belinda exits the conference room, her humorless expression homing in on me. "Hey, Kavi, Hudson wants you to join the meeting since you'll be taking over a few key presentations with some of our clients once I'm on leave."

"Oh, um, sure!" I gather up a notebook and pen, rising from my seat and following her. "I'm . . . I'm sorry I was late. Did you get my email?"

"Yes, but let's discuss that later." She reaches for the conference door, speaking over her shoulder. "Just so you're aware, we're going around the table with our own executive team on some open items and deal blockers."

I nod before stepping inside, and I swear, I can feel a shift in the temperature, though it has nothing to do with how hot or cold it is in here. My eyes—the double-crossing bitches they are—find those same blue-gray ones across the table before I make my way to the open seat next to Belinda.

"Thank you for joining us, Ms. Jain." Mr. Case's head tilts up as he examines me like one would a diseased carcass. "How wonderful that you had the luxury of sleeping in today while the rest of us got up on time since we have to worry about these pesky things called responsibilities and professionalism."

My cheeks heat—no, they catch fire—feeling the side glances from everyone around me. My eyes drop to my lap, burning with unshed tears. "I'm . . . I apologize for—"

"Spare us the theatrics, Ms. Jain, and let me make it crystal clear, in case you still haven't woken up." His nostrils flare and his eyes flick from my chest to my eyes so quickly, I swear I've imagined it. "There are few things I despise more than tardiness and accountability. If you can't be here on time on a daily basis, then please see yourself out and find a different workplace where the staff rolls in with unprofessional attire and muddy shoes." Then, as if he hadn't just publicly humiliated me, he looks to someone still standing at the front, near the projection screen. "Caleb, please continue."

The tops of my ears burn and my chest constricts as I keep my eyes glued to my lap while shame buries itself inside my cheeks. And despite my trembling bottom lip and the rage crawling up my throat, I repeat the same words in a loop in my head, *I will not cry.*

I will not give him the satisfaction of seeing me cry.

I've been through a lot worse.

I'm only shaken from my silent trance when Belinda's hand grasps mine under the table. She squeezes it before her steely eyes connect with Mr. Case's across from us. He looks from her to me, and for a fleeting moment, that same softness I saw once before—if only for a millisecond then two, when I'd dropped the glass of ice water on his lap—appears in his expression once more.

But this time it's me who disconnects our gaze, turning my head to face the front with barely held disdain. My eyes feel like stones inside their sockets while I focus on the release of each of my breaths.

Because fuck him!

Yes, I messed up at the restaurant. I was a nervous wreck on my first day, having unfairly been assigned to a table even the experienced staff didn't want. Yes, I not only accidentally lobbed a fucking cork at his forehead, I also spilled water on his lap and then made a fool of myself trying to wipe it up. And yes, I came in late today.

None of those things were done intentionally, but are any of them big enough offenses to spew vitriol and treat someone like absolute shit?

He already had me fired from my first job. If he didn't want me working here, then why not fire me on the very first day? Why belittle me in such a way, in front of everyone, that if I was even going to have the slightest amount of compassion for his viewpoint, I no longer do?

Because I fucking no longer do.

He's just another heartless, thoughtless—and probably dickless—rich bastard who thinks he can treat people like shit, like all the other useless ones I've met in my life.

I hope all his whites turn pink in the wash.

Barely hearing most of the presentation over the screaming inside my head, I shuffle out of the room as soon as the meeting ends, heading back to Belinda's desk without so much as another glance at him.

Closing my eyes momentarily before taking in a wobbly breath, I remind myself once again what I've said many times throughout my life: No one can make me feel small and shitty without my consent.

Chapter Six

HUDSON

"Just when I think you have something that might resemble an actual heart left inside you, you go and change my mind."

I'm still turned toward the blank projection screen, my hand in a fist over my laptop, unwilling to make eye contact with Belinda.

The room cleared out a few minutes ago, but I knew she would stay back to hand me my ass.

Her voice drips with contempt unlike I've ever heard. It isn't mere disappointment at my choice of words telling an unsuspecting employee to scroll social media on their own time; it's unadulterated disgust for the way I spoke to Kavi.

"You're an asshole, Hudson Case, and if you have even an ounce of decency left inside you, you'll apologize to her."

"Apologize?" I reel back, turning to her, and immediately regret doing so. Not only is Belinda's flushed and furious face at the center of my vision, but I notice *her* through the glass windows, seated behind Belinda's desk. Her eyes are trained on her computer screen, but I get the feeling she has no idea what she's even looking at.

A frown pulls down the corners of her lips and it pisses me off that I'm the reason for it.

I haven't fucking slept.

I swear, between thinking about whether we're going to close this deal with Rose City Skyport and my new admin, I'm running on an hour of fragmented sleep.

The sound of her sniffle reverberated inside my head like it was an amphitheater all fucking night. I tossed and turned, knowing I'd have to see her again this morning. Her pouty, bee-stung lips, those ridiculous curves, and those doleful, amber-colored eyes—the ones that said so much more than she allowed her words to say.

There's a sadness behind her smiles, an exaggeration she's practiced. Like she thinks she has to pay the price for each one day. Like maybe she's paying for them now.

But what I don't understand is *why* I notice. Why, in the short and disastrous meetings we've had, have I noticed the wariness in her eyes or her practiced smiles?

And furthermore, *why* do I care?

"Yes, Hudson." Belinda's head bobs condescendingly. "You know the thing a person says to another person when they've made a mistake?"

"Mistake?" I hook her with my piercing glare, though I know it does nothing but piss her off more. "I'm not the one who came in over an hour late, dressed like I was going to a Bohemian rock concert. I have standards that I expect every employee to abide by. I've made those abundantly clear, and it's what's made this company successful—"

"Oh, wake the fuck up!" Belinda's voice slices through my words, but it's her next words that scrape at a scab that refuses to heal. "It's also the reason Jett was able to take your staff—why they *willingly* left. Because your standards are unreasonable and make for a stressful and resentful work environment. The only reason most people haven't left is because you pay better than our competitors, but remember, time changes all."

It's not the first time I've heard a disgruntled employee talk about my unreasonable standards, but it's the first time Belinda has been this forthright.

Maybe there is truth to her words. Maybe I have held people to standards that no longer make sense, but it's not something I'm willing to admit just yet.

Belinda rolls her chair back with a resigned sigh, as if she's exasperated with what she already knows I'll do. "It's your company, Hudson. Run it the way you want, what do I care?" She rises, gathering a few papers in her arms. "I just thought you should know that things aren't as black and white as they seem. That girl," she throws a thumb over her shoulder, indicating Kavi, "has been nothing but grateful for this job. In just one day, she's taken on more work than I thought possible for someone who doesn't know our industry or our clients. Did you know she reworked the RCS slide deck over the weekend? I thought she could use it to get up-to-speed on the excavation project for them before her official first day, but she sent it back to me with improvements I hadn't even considered."

She walks to the door before turning over her shoulder, her voice defeated. "She told me how badly she needs this job —she wouldn't commute more than an hour if she didn't. Her car broke down today so she had to take the subway. And in case you don't remember this from the days you weren't all rich and mighty, shitty weather and shitty subways equate to delays."

Her words spark the memory of what Maddy told me a few days ago. *"I have a friend who desperately needs a job . . . she's had a rough year . . ."* And before I'm even sure why I'm asking, I hear the words tumble from my lips. "Why does she need this job so badly?"

Belinda halts her movements, closing the partially opened door, and my eyes trail back to the woman at Belinda's desk who hasn't moved.

Even under the harsh office lights, her skin looks flawless, her button nose delicately sculpted on her face. How could a woman be so captivating in her silence, yet be so fucking loud?

She's somehow louder than the blaring sirens inside my head, warning me not to get involved, reminding me that her problems aren't mine. That I have several of my own I still need to heft my way through.

My eyes track back to Belinda, noting a hint of something new in her expression—an awareness of something I'm clearly not privy to. The corner of her mouth pulls into a slanted smirk before she rests her hand on her belly. "You can ask her yourself . . . *after* you apologize."

WORKING my hands into the pockets of my suit pants, I clear my throat. "Ms. Jain, can I see you in my office?"

Kavi's hands stall over her keyboard, though I'm not sure she was even typing anything—merely pretending as soon as she saw me in her periphery.

Belinda murmurs something about needing to use the restroom and waddles down the hall before Kavi swipes me with a side glance.

Her long dark lashes flutter before her nostrils flare so slightly, I'd miss them if I wasn't looking closely. "Why? So you can humiliate me again?" She turns, pulling a sheet of paper out of the printer. "Well, you can save your breath, Mr. Case, because—"

"I'm sorry."

Jesus, fuck, those words practically burned my tongue on

their way out. It's a good reminder why I don't use them often.

Kavi's hand hovers in the air with the paper hanging from her pinched fingers, her nails polished orange. Her mouth falls slightly agape. "Excuse me?"

I exhale a hard breath. Is she expecting me to repeat myself?

Because I don't do that.

"Ms. Jain, if you're thinking I'm going to clasp my hands in front of you and beg for your forgiveness, you'll be waiting a while. I said I was sorry, and that's about as much as you'll get from me."

She rises from her seat, her hand trembling as she releases the paper on her desk before she tucks a strand of that shiny, wavy hair behind her ear. Today, there are plastic kiwi slices dangling from her ears, matching the kiwi on her shirt and the shiny green skirt that tightens delectably over her hips.

The woman has . . . eclectic taste, that's for sure, and I'm not even counting the orange Doc Martens on her feet. Clearly, she has a thing for the color orange, too.

She wraps her arms around her chest, and the movement causes my gaze to dip to her ample cleavage.

Did I just ogle her cleavage and hips?

Not for the first time in her presence, my cock stirs inside my pants, and I remind myself that she's twenty-five. Younger than my own daughter.

I'd pulled up her HR records, including her age and address, in the conference room before I exited. Apparently, she lives on the other side of the damn Bay. Getting here by car is shitty enough every day, having to take not one, but two subways would drive a person crazy—especially given the hours I expect her to work.

"Then, I guess I'll have to think about your apology, Mr. Case, given I don't really know what you're apologizing for."

It's my turn to open and shut my mouth before I repeat her previous words. "Excuse me?"

Is this the same jittery woman who's been nothing but a ball of nerves during all of our interactions? Because right now, she reminds me of the other two women in my life, with her eyes flashing and her upright stance.

She lifts her chin, her rapid blinking and the rise and fall of her chest the only indication of her apprehension. "Over the past week, I not only lost a job because of you, but I've been publicly shamed in front of my new colleagues—"

"Both of those things were your fault!" I seethe.

"Well, then I suppose you have no reason to apologize, do you?"

I raise my arms, letting them fall to my sides. "And yet, here I am!"

The woman is infuriating. A contradiction of bold and timid, soft and unyielding.

Innocence and sin.

Her face hardens before she turns, running her hands over her hips and giving me an eyeful of that fucking peach ass. She settles in front of her laptop again, speaking to it as if I'm no longer present. "Clearly, you need lessons in expressing contrition, because if that's your form of an apology, then I don't accept."

I swear I hold in the growl ready to expel from my throat with everything I have. My hands fist at my sides as I sear her profile with my glare. "Your choice. It's the best you're going to get."

And with that, I storm down the hall to my office for the second day in a row.

◦∾◦

WELL, now I have yet another fucking thing to apologize for.

I press the tips of my fingers to my forehead, closing my eyes and focusing on my breathing.

Except, every inhale is laced with something sweet. Like vanilla and lemons. Like fucking icing and sugar. It's not just infuriating, it's downright maddening.

Only a week ago, I had no knowledge, no memory of this particular scent, except maybe when I entered a bakery. And though I can't say it's overpowering in the way she wears it, it's all I can think about now.

After locking myself in my office post my failed apology this morning, I finally left for a meeting a couple of hours ago.

Except, I found her in Jett's typically locked, off-limits office.

Without taking the time to understand why she was there —apparently, a building manager was inspecting fire alarms, and she was waiting for him to be finished—I unleashed another harsh tirade, telling her to leave the room or risk being fired.

Yeah, not my finest moment, indeed, especially when her irate and hurt eyes flashed at me before she silently moved past me, letting me piece together the situation.

I run my hand down my face.

Just like yesterday, Belinda sent me an email letting me know she was leaving. And just like yesterday, I've given her— and my new admin—more reasons to be disappointed.

Not only that, but Maddy messaged me an hour ago— How are things going with Kavi?—to which I still haven't formulated an answer. But I know that if I don't reply soon, my bloodhound of a daughter will be knocking down my door in curiosity.

Fuck, this is a disaster.

My phone vibrates with an incoming call, and seeing Jared's name on the screen, I take a hopeful breath. He's our main contact at Rose City Skyport and right now, with how shitty my day seems to have gone yet again, all I'm looking for is some semblance of good news.

"Jared, how's it going?" I turn, leaning back in my chair to look out the wall-to-wall windows behind me.

The sun made a fleeting appearance today, shining brightly for all of ten minutes. But now, under the shroud of darkness, only the hints of twinkling lights from nearby buildings bravely glimmer through the ongoing downpour.

"Good evening, Hudson. I have some good news for you." *Thank God.* "The team is ready to sign the contract with Case Geo—"

"Wonderful!" I cheer, running a hand through my hair and imagining my brother and his fiancée's dejected faces when they find out they didn't win the contract. "That's great news!"

"It is . . ." he trails off for a second before speaking again. "However, Silas wants to meet you and Kavi this week before we officially sign. Can you fly over Thursday night? The three of you can go to dinner, and then, if all goes well, we can finalize details and sign Friday morning."

My brows pinch. Did he just say Kavi? How does he know her already, and why does their CEO want to meet her? "Kavi?"

Jared chuckles on the other side. "Yes. Your new assistant? Belinda sent us an email introducing her, since she'll be dialing down at work starting next week. She also attached the updated version of the slides Kavi worked on, and Silas was pretty impressed. Said he wanted to meet her before we put ink to paper. He's old-school like that and always wants to meet the people he works with in person."

My head dips and I find I've been rubbing circles on my sternum, as if trying to release a constriction inside my chest.

What the fuck?

He wants to meet Kavi? A woman I haven't even vetted

properly. A woman who's been nothing but a headache since the moment I met her. A woman who's been the bane of my existence over the past week.

And as if she can hear my thoughts—*probably can, given I'm pretty sure she's a witch*—a knock sounds on my door before she enters.

With the phone still pressed to my ear, I watch her hips sway in her tight skirt as she takes long strides to my desk, paper in hand. Her bulky Docs thump with each step.

My eyes trail up to her cinched waist before briefly halting on her breasts. The woman looks like a perfect figure-eight in her attire, and fuck if that doesn't piss me off just a little more.

I noticed her as soon as she came in this morning, her poor excuse for a raincoat dripping over my carpeted floor. Through the conference room windows, I watched her visibly relax, seeing no one was around, before she rushed over to Belinda's desk and pulled a few tissues out of a box.

Caleb was showing everyone the financial projections on the screen at the front of the room, but at that moment, I couldn't say what was on them or whether he was speaking in English or French. My eyes were stuck to the magnetic pull that was Kavi Jain, as she leaned over, wiping mud off her precious shoes. Her partially wet hair was pulled to one side as she focused on her task.

And when she shifted, her gray shirt shifted with her, the neck dropping to give me—and anyone who faced in the same direction—an expo of her fucking tits.

Tits I'd noticed, whether I wanted to or not, from the second I laid eyes on her. Tits I'd thought about. Tits I'd fucking jacked off to over the course of the past few days.

A snarl built inside me as I curled my hand in a fist, watching those tits swing.

God, how I wanted to fuck them right in that moment,

imagining my cock sliding in between them while she licked the pre-cum off my tip.

And just like that, I was more furious with that image—and the fact that any asshole looking in her direction was probably imagining the same thing—than the fact that she'd come in late.

A smirk ghosts over her lips as she leaves the paper on my desk before turning around to sashay through the door, leaving me completely dumbstruck.

"Hudson? You still there?"

Jared's voice has me bouncing out of my daze before I clear my throat and pick up the paper she left. "Yeah, I . . . let me see what I can do."

I skim through what looks like . . . *a fucking resignation letter?!*

Dear Mr. Case,

Effective immediately, I've decided to disembark the pleasure cruise that is Case Geo. Thank you for giving me a glimpse of your management style and for this very memorable character-building experience. Unfortunately, I won't be staying on for more of the fun and festivities.

Wishing you all the best in dressing-down your next admin.

Regards,

Kavita Jain

Motherfucker!

"I know it's last minute, but this is a big project for us." Jared's voice jolts me once again into action and I'm rising out of my seat as he continues, "We want to make sure any changes in your staff work for us, too, especially for such a key role since your admin is one of our primary contacts with Case Geo and does so much more than just manage your calendar. I don't expect any issues, given Silas already liked Kavi's work, but it always helps to meet in person."

With my heart hammering in my chest, I hang up with Jared and crumble her resignation in my fist. Then, I do something I'd vowed never to do.

I chase after a quitter.

Chapter Seven

KAVI

I wouldn't describe myself as assertive or fierce, save for one situation in my past.

Even when warranted, I don't generally defend myself or have overt emotional reactions leading to tantrums or meltdowns. I don't rage or throw vases against walls; I never pound my feet or jab my finger in the air to make a point.

Instead, I tend to be mild-mannered and inward. Calm and composed in most situations.

It's not to say I don't feel such emotions as anger and bitterness, because I do, just like anyone else. But generally, I keep them bottled up, hidden behind placatory nods, fidgeting fingers, and rapid breaths.

I suppose it's my way of sticking it to those who want to see a bigger reaction. Those who expect me to burst into tears and beg for mercy after having pushed me to my limits.

But on most days, I'm satisfied knowing the joke is on them.

That they'll never get the reaction they're waiting for. They didn't when I was in high school—when I was mocked and bullied for everything from my clothes to my shapely body to the crumpled-up dollars Mom shoved into my pocket for lunch—and they won't now.

Which is why it shocks me to have witnessed a side of myself today I've worked hard to conceal.

Who was that woman demanding an apology and holding her ground? Where did she come from?

Did I really strut into my dickface boss's office to hand in my resignation, dripping with overt sarcasm and disdain? Was that really me, or did I somehow inhabit someone else's body? Someone far more audacious and fearless than I've ever been.

But God, it felt good.

Not that he'll shed a single tear. The gorgeous bastard's probably smirking, silently pumping his fist in victory, but at least it felt good to me.

I would have handed it to him right after the mortifying conference room experience, but I figured I'd take the day to think about it—weigh it out before making a rash decision.

I waited for him all day to give me some semblance of a genuine apology, especially after he hurled his *'I'm sorry'* at me like a worn-out, two-word script, before storming off like a petulant child. But when he raged at me, looking like an angry tomato, no less, after finding me in the restricted office for a routine maintenance issue, I decided enough was enough.

Yes, my family needed this money—*fucking big time*—but Mom would be appalled if she found out I was trading in my dignity and peace of mind for it.

Hadn't I learned my lesson in high school to not let the bullies win?

Hadn't I already lost so much?

Why put myself through something like that again? Why let my self-worth be determined by someone else's impossible standards? Isn't that exactly what I used to preach to *him* when we were younger?

Sure, I'd have to find another job quickly. And if that meant scouring the job boards and doing something for a fraction of the pay, I'd rather do that than sit here all summer, shredding the little self-confidence I've worked so hard to hold on to.

With my heart knocking against my chest, I walk to the elevator with a sense of urgency and determination, trying to keep my feet from tripping on themselves. Every step shoots tremors through my body; every cell revolting, unsure of who I really am.

This isn't me—this bold, self-assured imposter I'm pretending to be—but fuck, I don't want to let her go just yet.

Taking in shuddered breaths, I step into the open elevator and press the button for the lobby when hurried footsteps come to a stop in front of the doors, and Mr. Case joins me inside.

Eyes widened, I try to find my words. "Wh—"

"I don't accept." With one hand in his pocket, he holds up the paper I'd left on his desk, now crumpled.

My mind goes blank and I blink. "I'm sorry? What do you mean, you don't accept?"

The elevator doors close, and I'm trapped as we start descending the forty-two floors.

His nostrils flare as if it's beneath him to have to repeat himself. The jackass. "I mean, I don't accept. You've only been here two days. You haven't even given this a real chance."

I stare at him in complete bewilderment. Just hours ago, he was concocting situations for me to quit, yelling at me every chance he got, and now he claims I didn't give the job a *real chance*?

"Are you on drugs?" I ask, because the question warrants asking.

He huffs out an exasperated breath. Exasperated! Ha! Like he should have anything to be exasperated about! "Drugs might be a good solution at this point."

"What?" I lean in as if to glean some meaning behind his words.

"Never mind," he says with a resigned shake of his head. "Like I said, I won't accept your resignation."

I squint, first at the floor and then at him. "Why? You can barely stand me. Notwithstanding your threat to fire me just earlier today, you've made it abundantly clear that you don't want me here."

He rakes a hand down his face. "We're one final signature away from getting the RCS deal. Apparently, their CEO saw your updates and was impressed. He wants to meet the person who will be replacing Belinda for the next few months."

My mouth falls open in a soft, "Ah," as understanding settles my whirring thoughts. "Of course, that's what it is . . . You *need* me to save this deal. Because what would your clients think if you *still* didn't have a replacement for your admin after knowing all these months that she'd eventually take maternity leave?" I chuckle mirthlessly. "Well, good luck with that, Mr. Case."

He doesn't deign me with a response, both his hands now in his pockets as he stares up at the digital counter displaying each floor we're passing.

And since he doesn't have the courtesy of providing me with more than his silence, I don't say anything, either. Until he glances down at me standing next to him. "So, will you stay?"

I bark out a laugh again. The balls on this guy!

"Perhaps you're incapable of reading the room, or a

blatantly clear resignation in this case, or maybe you're being purposefully obtuse. Either way, let me state it in no uncertain terms. No, Mr. Case, I will not be staying."

I'm jolted back a second later, my hands flying up as I try to find my balance when a warm hand wraps around my elbow, keeping me steady. I blink rapidly, realizing he's pressed the emergency stop button. "Wha . . . what are you doing?"

Aren't there cameras in here? Won't that button set off an alarm or something?

Don't people get murdered like this?

My anxious eyes crash with his before he takes a step forward, erasing the little space between us, and I take a small step back, making more. My palms find the metal bar on the wall behind me as I try to make myself as small as possible.

He towers above me, his hands back in his pockets, with that cool confidence he always seems to exude. The outline of his muscular biceps molds to his shirtsleeves while his chest puffs out even wider, and the scent of pine and lavender cologne has my nipples puckering inside my shirt.

My tongue peeks out, swiping over my bottom lip as I take in his chiseled jaw and that salt-and-pepper scruff that surrounds his plush, pillowy lips.

Jesus, the man is a sculptor's dream brought to life.

And now those lips are turned upward in a smug smirk.

My eyes snap to his, watching as the crows' feet around his eyes dance with mirth. Whatever he thinks he's seen, he can be sure it isn't that, so he can go right ahead and wipe that cocky grin off his face.

Yes, I find him physically appealing—the evidence of my attraction is a warm pool inside my panties—but that's the extent of it, because I'm not in the habit of pining after gorgeous men with the personalities of cacti.

He leans in. "Why did you want this job?"

I raise my head, hoping to make myself look more confident. "Clearly not because of your sunshiny personality. It was for the money, obviously."

"Why?"

I snort. "Why does anyone need money, Mr. Case? To pay past-due bills, student loans, and my mom's lease . . ." I take in a tattered breath, realizing it's too late to take back the unnecessary information. "Why does it matter to you?"

His lips thin. "It doesn't."

"Great," I retort, keeping myself from adding 'asshole' to the end. I shift, unable to help brushing my chest against his to push the start button. "Then you should have no problems letting me get on with my—"

But before I can finish, Mr. Case's hand wraps around my wrist, sending goosebumps not just scurrying up my arm, but traveling the length of my spine and back. "I'll double your salary for the next three months if you stay."

Cue my jaw dropping to the floor. "What?"

His steely eyes pin me in place, his hand still gently holding my wrist. "I'm not in the habit of begging, Ms. Jain."

I pull my wrist from his hand and wrap my arms around my chest, not missing the way his eyes drag down to catch the movement. "Nor are you in the habit of apologizing."

The barest smile strains my lips witnessing the twitch in his right eye. "Is that what this is about? I already apologized for this morning."

"It wasn't good enough and you know it," I retort, enunciating my words. "Not even two hours later, you exploded at me in your brother's old office."

His shoulders straighten as understanding settles in his eyes.

Maybe he thought I wouldn't find out the history behind the locked office, but after Belinda saw the way he treated me today—not once, but twice—we had a long chat about why he is the way he is.

I could tell she wasn't telling me everything, but I gleaned the fact that while he's always had the charm of a damp kitchen rag, his brother's betrayal really messed him up. That betrayal only heightened his need for order, work-ethic, and loyalty.

He huffs, swiveling his head toward the elevator panel, seemingly contemplating his life's decisions that led him to this point. I swear he's quiet for so long, I look over to see if he's fallen asleep standing up.

"Fine. I apologize for my conduct at both the meeting and in Jett's old office." I don't miss the way he tenses saying his brother's name. "It was . . . uncalled for and demeaning."

My eyebrow arches in surprise. Not too shabby for a reluctant apology, though he did look like he'd just taken a swig of brackish seawater.

Seawater, that I hope causes him a bout of temporary diarrhea.

I push my luck. "*And* for being an asshole to me on my first day. *And* for the way you fired me from my job at your restaurant."

"Fine." He scowls. "I apologize for all of that, too."

"So, let me get this straight. You'll double my exorbitant salary for the next three months if I stay on as your admin."

"I'll also need you to take over managing the excavation project here in the city for the new high-rise. It'll require you to be nearby, in case you need to approve deliveries and last-minute changes. Sometimes our clients want to go to dinner spontaneously—"

"I'm not sure I understand." I shake my head. "What do you mean, I need to be nearby?"

"*Nearby*, Ms. Jain. As in, not on the other fucking side of the Bay."

Is he . . .? Is he expecting me to *move?*

"But I *live* on the other side of the Bay. At the moment, my car is at the shop as well, so my office hours are dependent on the subway schedule."

His head lifts defiantly. "That doesn't work for me. You'll need to move to the city, at least for three months."

I'm just about to argue when a loud buzzing interrupts us and a man's voice comes over the speaker. "Hello? Is everything okay in there? The emergency stop was pushed."

Oh, well, thanks for waking up, Edgar!

Keeping his eyes on me, Mr. Case responds, "We're fine, Edgar. I'll restart the elevator when I'm ready."

Restart the elevator when he's ready? He's so casual in the way he says it, like this is just another Tuesday and the elevator is his personal conference room.

Has he trapped other women in here . . . and done things?

Something bitter rolls around my tongue at the thought before slithering down to my stomach as we both wait until Edgar clicks off with a, "Sounds good, sir."

"I can't move to the city, Mr. Case—"

"Call me Hudson. And yes, with the salary I'll be paying you, you can."

"No, I can't." I scoff. "You might be doubling my pay, but what would be the point of that if I'm just spending it on more rent? Plus, I need to be able to get to my mom and my brother in case they need me."

He pinches the bridge of his nose, silence stretching between us, before his eyes train on me again and something passes through his expression. Something he's reluctantly weighing out as evidenced first by the way he swipes his thumb over his bottom lip before squeezing his eyes shut, as if his next words are about to cause him physical pain. "Fine. Then move into my apartment a block from here. You'll have access to my chauffeured car anytime you need to visit your mom and brother."

My mouth falls open for what feels like the hundredth time throughout this strange ten-minute adventure while dangling in an elevator, somewhere between the tenth and eleventh floors. "You can't be serious."

He shifts, taking a step back before pressing some button on the control panel that makes the elevator restart. "As serious as the extra income about to hit your bank account."

"Hudson, I can't live with you."

"Why not?"

My face contorts as I look at him like he's grown three heads. "Because you don't like me. And I, for one, don't want to live with a man who's about as fun as a root canal and can barely even stand to look at me, let alone talk to me. I also refuse to live with someone who isn't very nice."

"Liking or not liking you is irrelevant to this arrangement. And I *am* being nice. It's why I offered you more money, a place to live, and chauffeur service!"

My shoulders stiffen, and for the first time in my life, I watch my own finger jab the air. "No, you're offering those things to me because *you need me*. Don't turn this around to make it look like I begged for it, Hudson. As you might recall, I turned in my resignation fifteen minutes ago."

Hudson's fingers plunder into his dark hair. "Fine, you're right about that, but it's not like I'm champing at the bit to live with you, either. However, given the situation, it makes sense. It's just a mutually beneficial and temporary living arrangement. Nothing more."

"Oh, wow." I scoff condescendingly, rolling my eyes. "If those heartfelt words don't convince me, I don't know what will."

The elevator comes to a stop on the bottom floor, the doors opening to an empty, brightly lit lobby, and I step out, untying my umbrella to be able to step out into the rain, when Hudson's voice has my feet coming to a halt. "Kavi."

The tiniest of flutters dance around my stomach at the sound of my name on his lips, and I turn around to face him. There's a plea in his eyes. And while I don't know him well, I'd say that's a rare look for him.

His throat bobs with a swallow. "Stay".

The clatter of wheels over metal tracks provides a lulling rhythm as I watch the city float by through droplets of rain on the windows.

It's quiet inside the subway car tonight, with only a handful of tired commuters, giving me a chance to get my thoughts straight.

There's a medley of emotions floating around inside my brain, each one outweighing the next—hesitation, unease, excitement . . .

Desire.

It's that last one that has me the most worried, because it has me fantasizing about things I have absolutely no business doing. Like waking up in the same apartment as Hudson Case, or making breakfast together . . .

And then eating it with him in bed.

The thought is so ridiculous, I find my reflection smiling back at me through the glass before my nose wrinkles.

Like he said, it would just be a mutually beneficial, *temporary* living situation. And of course that's what it would be, *if* I decided to take it.

What the hell were my thoughts doing having gone in that direction, anyway? He might be insane—evident by the fact that he actually came up with the idea—but I'm definitely not.

The elevator doors had pinched shut with his last request, and that damn plea in his eyes, hanging in the air between us. It had kept me rooted to my spot, wondering if I'd imagined the entire exchange well after the elevator ascended with him in it.

Because that had to be the only explanation, right?

Moody, broody bosses, who practically snarled every time they saw you, didn't go around offering pay raises and asking you to move in with them. It simply didn't happen.

But it had . . .

And I wasn't any farther along in my consideration of whether I was going to take it.

I mean, how would it even work? The man couldn't tolerate me, not that I was much of a fan of him, either. But how could we live together? And what about Madison? What would she think if she found out?

But the money . . .

A paycheck like that, even for a little while, was unfathomable to me.

At least for a little bit, it would be life-changing for my family. At least for a little bit, we could feel like we weren't all working a million jobs between us, trying to keep the lights on. At least for a little bit, we could all breathe easy.

But did I need the doubled salary for the same work *if* I was going to live with him? It seems excessive and unnecessary . . .

And what about the promises I'd made to myself—to him—after everything? What about all that talk about not letting someone make me feel shitty ever again?

Was Hudson's offer worth testing my self-preservation all over again?

As if my mother can tell I need a reprieve from my thoughts, my phone rings inside my purse and I see her name flash on the screen. Except, her words, her voice, higher-pitched than usual, are laced with thick static on the other end when I pick up.

"Mom?" I bring the phone up to my face, making sure I haven't lost the call. It wouldn't be surprising since we're going through an underground tunnel. I press a finger to my other ear, hoping to silence the cacophony of the subway. "You there?"

Her words come out fragmented. "Neil . . . we're at the . . . taking him into—"

The call ends abruptly, leaving me with a sense of unease and foreboding. It's not common for Mom to call around this time, but maybe she felt the need to tell me something. But what?

I raise my phone, looking for a signal that's not there before sending a text to my mom, telling her I couldn't hear her. While waiting for a response, I remind myself that I'm likely getting worked up over nothing.

The subway comes back above ground, and I call my mom's phone, not getting an answer, before trying Neil's. She said something about taking him somewhere. But when he doesn't answer, I decide to just wait to talk to them when I get home.

Except, an hour later, instead of the coziness of Mom's living room, I find myself in an uncomfortable chair inside an emergency room waiting area with my arm around my mother's shoulders while she prays for my brother.

∾

How is your brother?

My phone vibrates on the countertop just as I'm putting my second contact lens in its case. I squint, trying to read the name on the screen, but quit trying after a few unsuccessful seconds to secure my hair into a ponytail using the black rubber band around my wrist.

We got home twenty minutes ago—half-past one AM—but thank God we all got home, mostly in one piece.

Apparently, after dinner, Neil started complaining about a sharp pain on the right side of his abdomen that he said had gotten progressively worse, to the point where he felt nauseous and unable to walk. Thankfully, Mom made a quick decision to drive him to the ER, where they rushed him in for surgery after a few tests.

Shuffling toward my bed with my phone in hand, I grab my glasses off my nightstand and wiggle them over my eyes. My brows pinch as I read the text a couple of times while my mind tries to make some connection with the number and the text.

I'd received a text from Belinda while I was in the waiting room, informing me she had an appointment in the morning and would be late tomorrow, and it dawned on me that she likely had no idea I'd submitted my resignation.

So, instead of getting into all that with her—though, I'd started trusting her over just a few days of knowing her and knew she'd understand no matter what I decided—I replied, informing her that I wasn't sure if I was coming in tomorrow since I was still waiting for my brother to be out of his emergency appendectomy and had no idea when I'd be getting home tonight.

She'd immediately called me, asking for details and

ensuring I was okay—something I couldn't express to her at the time, but deeply appreciated.

But looking at the text from the unfamiliar number on my phone now, I can only assume it's one person. The person she likely notified with my life update.

Perching on the edge of my bed, my heart pounds as I type back.

ME

He's resting at home but should be back to normal in a couple of weeks. Thank you for asking.

And though I'm sure he won't reply—and had no real reason to do so, given I was still leaning toward my original decision not to work for him—I stored his number in my contacts.

Why? Because I'd apparently developed a new toxic trait of storing numbers of men who've either fired me or threatened to do so at every encounter.

Currently, there was only one person on that list.

I stare at our exchange for a few seconds in silence, wondering if I was leaning toward the right decision. On one hand was my pride—the promises I'd made to stand up for myself—but on the other was my family and their well-being.

Wasn't one so much more important than the other?

We'd just depleted ninety-nine percent of our savings on Dad's medical bills and funeral costs, and now, I couldn't even begin to fathom the slew of medical bills that would rack up after today. Not to mention, Mom would likely have to take time off to be home with Neil until he was well enough to be on his own.

My gut twists with anxiety as a pang of fear pricks the corners of my eyes. Were we ever going to get a break? Could we ever resurface from the undertow we'd been fighting against for the past couple of years after Dad got sick?

The vibration of my phone pulls me out of my thoughts, and I stare back at the relit screen.

CAPTAIN CRANKYDICK

> Despite what you think, I'm not the biggest asshole to walk the earth.

I bite the inside of my cheek, wondering if I was imagining the hint of vulnerability from my crabby boss.

ME

> As long as you believe that, it shouldn't matter what I think.

A string of three dots immediately jump on the screen as I wait for his message before they disappear altogether.

After staring at the screen for another minute, I put my glasses on my nightstand and turn off my lamp before getting into bed. My thoughts are still jumbled, right along with the pressure inside my chest.

I'm just tossing and turning on my pillow, trying to silence my mind when my phone glows from its place on my nightstand.

CAPTAIN CRANKYDICK:

> There's a package for him sitting on your front porch. No worries if you're already asleep; you can get it in the morning.

Before my feet have even had a chance to register their placement on our old laminate flooring, I'm rushing out of my room to the front door.

Swinging it open, I practically trip over the large cellophane-covered basket, secured with an orange bow. I note the wireless headset, a digital reader, a handheld game system, and the various snacks and candy inside before my gaze scours the dark street in front of my house.

The rain has let up, and while I can't see the clouds against the darkened sky, I have no doubt they're still there.

My gaze falls back on the gift basket.

Did he have his chauffeur deliver this? More than likely, Belinda got it all done—thirty-something-weeks pregnant and all.

I'm just about to retrieve it when my eyes pick up movement across the street. I turn on my porch light, lightly clicking the door shut behind me so as not to wake Mom and Neil, before I step out onto our cold porch, the rough concrete biting into the bottoms of my feet.

But dark skies or not, he's hard to miss.

All six-foot-something of him, outlined against the night, standing next to his truck.

He shifts as I pad closer, unconcerned with the thin material of my old Christmas T-shirt—the words *The Grinch stole my heart and my pants* written in cursive over my chest—my short shorts, or my lack of a bra.

Feet on wet pavement, I come to a stop a few inches from him, my eyes falling to the hands he has secured inside the pockets of those ever-present suit pants. My chest rises and falls as I try to steady my heart rate. "If you think this will convince me to stay—"

"It should." The corners of his lips barely lift, but it's the delicate cupid's bow over his top lip that I can't seem to disconnect my gaze from. It's perfectly defined, framing the lush fullness of his mouth, as if drawn by an artist's hand. "Though it's not why I did it."

His eyes trail down my form, a flicker, a flare. The slightest fever grazes across my exposed skin, tightening my nipples into painful buds and sending goosebumps soaring.

His voice ripples through the breeze, low and throaty.

"What did you mean on the note you left with that slice of cake: *Thanks for chasing away the rain?*"

I shrug. "You'd given me a job and well," I look to the side for a moment, "it gave me a chance to breathe. I was . . ."

Drowning.

Suffocating.

Sinking.

I don't finish my sentence, but he seems to pick up my gist. "Which is why I'm asking you to stay."

I don't wrap my arms around my chest, though it would be prudent, and before I can rethink my words, I hear myself speak again. "It would be a bad idea, Hudson."

His tongue sweeps over his lip, a soft blink that does nothing to take away the heat from his irises. "That's the only thing I'm sure of."

I look down the darkened street to my right before facing him again. "Then maybe we shouldn't."

He shrugs, his frown betraying his detached stance. "It's your decision." He nods toward my house behind me. "I thought it would help . . . with everything—"

I'm about to respond with an irritated reply, letting him know I don't need his help, when he speaks over me. "And it's not out of charity or pity. You'd be working for every cent of it. And let me remind you, it would be temporary."

I bite my lip, mulling over his words as the bills sitting on Mom's countertop, future bills surely gracing our mailbox, and small numbers displayed in my meager bank account cloud my vision. "Even if it's temporary, I need to know you won't be an asshole to me at or outside of work again."

"Or maybe you could just develop thicker skin." His lips twitch seeing the tinder lighting up inside my eyes.

My hands fist at my side. "Or maybe *you* can find someone else to take over Belinda's job." I mentally high-five myself for not adding *jackass* to the end of that. "Figure out what to tell your most strategic client when they ask why they have to work with yet another new person."

I turn back toward my house in a huff—not for the first time noting the changes in my personality the man seems to bring out—before I speak over my shoulder. "Thank you for the gifts for my brother. See you *never*, Mr. Case."

But before I can even take one step forward, a warm hand circles my wrist, pulling me back and turning me to face him in the same movement.

His jaw works in an attempt to hide his smile. "That was a joke, but don't get used to it. I don't make them often."

I wrap my arms around myself. "I won't be humiliated and spoken to the way you did to me multiple times today, Hudson."

"I already apologized for those . . . for all of it," he argues.

"Yes, but I want to make it clear." My voice wavers with my next words. "I've seen too many rich assholes get away with things they shouldn't, but I'm not as forgiving anymore."

Silence stretches out between us as he tries to decipher the meaning behind my words, surely wondering if I'll elaborate. I don't.

"I'll try to be . . . nicer."

Jesus. You'd think he was being held at gunpoint or tortured, with the way those words grit out from between his lips.

Still, I suppose I have to give him some benefit of the doubt for trying. I can't imagine he does much of it for anyone besides his daughter.

I lean back on my heels, noting I'll need to wash my feet when I get back inside, before giving him a short nod. "Fine. I'll be back at work tomorrow, but I don't need the additional pay. I was perfectly fine with what I was making before."

He takes a step closer, and it's all I can do not to lean my head forward and take a whiff of his lavender and pine scent. "That's not up for negotiation."

"Hudson, I don't need your—"

"Like I said, it's not charity. You'll be working for every cent of it."

A beat passes between us while I once again consider what I'm signing up for. The money would be a boon with the way things are right now—a relief for both my mom and my brother—but I don't love the idea of Hudson paying me more than any other admin, probably even more than what Belinda made.

I bite my lip, my mind and heart warring with my impending decision. "I don't know . . ."

Disappointment shines in his eyes. He's not a man who begs, but when the word, "Please," leaves his lips, I'm all but a puddle on the cold asphalt at my feet.

"Okay," I whisper, his presence and sincerity pulling my decision out of me.

His shoulders sink with relief while his brows rise in question, unlike his words, which are a statement. "And you'll move in this weekend."

A flurry of hesitation rises inside me again, lodging in my throat. Aside from my dad and Neil, I've never lived with a man before, and definitely not someone I'm working for.

Definitely not someone I'm clearly attracted to, my mind piles on.

"I . . . I—"

"I'll have movers here Saturday morning," he says, not giving me a chance to finish my mumbled musing.

God, this could be a total disaster. "Okay."

"Great." He turns, swinging his truck door open right as I start to saunter back toward the house. "Oh, and Kavi?"

I face him, unable to understand why looking at him always seems to make my heart jog. "Yeah?"

He walks over, his dark hair ruffling with the breeze, and pulls out a black card from his wallet. "Take this."

My brows tangle. "Why?"

"You'll need it to go shopping tomorrow for a new wardrobe." His eyes crawl over my bare legs, incinerating me on their climb and halting briefly at my shamelessly protruding nipples. "You won't have your first paycheck for a few days, and as much as I enjoy your *eclectic* style, perhaps you could find something more appropriate to meet our clients with me in Portland on Thursday."

Say what now? Portland? Thursday?

I glance at the card in my hand before speaking to his retreating form, knowing now that I've re-accepted the job, I can't argue much in terms of the requirements. "I have my own credit card. And what's wrong with my clothes? Maybe it's your company that needs to loosen up a bit."

"Kavi." He takes a breath that feels like it lasts an entire minute. "Use my damn card."

"Fine," I concede, knowing he's got that adamant glint in his eyes. He's also doing that jaw ticking thing, which really can't be good for his teeth. "But I'm not giving this back. I might even take it with me when I move."

He rolls down the window of his truck after getting inside, pinning me with one of his weighty blue-gray stares. "I have a feeling you'll be taking more than just my money when you move."

And even as I watch him drive off, his words linger in the air, following me until I'm back inside.

Chapter Nine

HUDSON

Garrett eyes the plates of food in front of me. "You sure you're not trying to feed a small country?"

I pull the plate of scrambled eggs toward me, shoving the plate of pancakes and bowl of fruit I just emptied aside, and shrug. "Just trying to keep the breakfast industry from tanking. My contribution to the greater good."

My best friend barks out a laugh before digging into his waffles. "That or contributing to the city's food shortage."

It's another rare day where both my and Garrett's schedules aligned and we met up to workout at the gym. I had half a mind to cancel on him this morning, given how late I got home last night and the little I slept the night before, but I couldn't pass up a chance to hang out with him.

Garrett and I actually met at the gym years ago. I helped him correct his form on a couple of exercises and, surprisingly, he didn't think I was a smug asshole for doing so. Ever since, I've not only become good friends with him, but with his brothers, Dean and Darian, as well.

I grin to myself, taking another bite of my eggs and thinking about the time we all went to Vegas and lost Garrett for a night. Turns out, he'd run into Bella—the woman he'd been in love with for four years—and they'd proceeded to get drunk and married.

Two years later, they're the picture of domestic bliss with their two daughters and innumerable cats.

My grin wavers a little as I think about the fun and close-knit family Garrett is always surrounded with—from his kids and wife, to his two brothers and loving parents.

It's not that I'm jealous—I have Maddy and honestly, have never felt the need for more—but at one point I also had kinship with my brother . . . or I thought I did. He was supposed to be both by my side and on my side, much like Darian and Dean are for Garrett, but I suppose I meant less to him than his greed and desire.

And even if I've come a long way in accepting his betrayal for exactly what it was, I can't say it doesn't still sting. Like an old wound, scabbed over but not quite healed.

"How's Maddy?" Garrett's voice has my head and thoughts lifting. "All ready for the wedding? Saw on the invite that they're doing it at your ranch."

I nod. "Yeah, Maddy's always loved the ranch. Ever since I bought it when she was little, she said she'd get married on it." I smile. "Who was I to say no? And as for the other details, you know how she and Brie are."

Garrett chuckles. "Two peas in a *very organized* pod. They probably had the entire thing planned years ago." He glances at me. "What about you? Ready to give your little girl away?"

I sigh, running a hand down my stomach. "I always knew the day was coming. Her and Brie have been together for a long time, and Brie's great—always been like another daughter to me." I look around, not realizing it until now that I even felt this way. "Although, I won't deny I miss the phase you're in, when they rely on you and seek out your advice."

Garrett's brows waggle. "You know, it's not too late to have another one. Even if you are an old geezer."

I snort. "Yeah, an old geezer who just bench pressed your entire weight."

"Touché." Garrett runs a napkin over his lips. "But seriously, you haven't dated anyone since Kenna, right?" His face sours at my ex-girlfriend's name. "Any prospects you care to talk about?"

I lean back in my chair, running my thumb over my bottom lip as an image of the woman I sometimes wish I'd never met flashes across my vision.

For no fucking reason but to annoy me.

Her peach ass in those sleep shorts, so fucking divine, it should be outlawed. And those smooth, bare legs; those thick thighs I've imagined my face in between way more than I should.

The way her nipples protruded through her shirt . . .

Who the fuck wears Christmas pajamas in the middle of June?

"Oh, fuck!" Garrett leans forward, eyes gleaming like a cat spotting a bowl of cream. "There *is* someone!"

"What!?" My head swings from left to right. "Nah, there's definitely not *someone*. What there is . . . is a complication. A pain in my ass."

Elbows on the table, Garrett's smile stretches across his face. For reasons beyond my comprehension, he and his brothers—and their respective wives—have been relentless about getting me to date again.

And while I'm not opposed to the idea of dating, my track record leaves something to be desired, namely honesty, loyalty, and trust. Oh, and I'd love it if she didn't sleep with my brother because I was out of town and she happened to be lonely.

But clearly, my requirements are hard to meet.

"Sounds like an interesting complication," Garrett states.

"I haven't even told you anything yet."

Garrett turns his hands in my direction, in a *'go on'* movement. "Which is why I'm waiting. I'm good at managing complications."

"As proven by your drunken marriage to the woman you pined after for four years." I scoff. "Only for her to cry when she woke up in bed with you the next morning."

"Hey," Garrett lifts his head, "I convinced her to stay, didn't I? And that's what matters. Anyway, this isn't about me. I guarantee, whatever the cause of this complication, it's your fault. Now, hurry up, I don't have all day. Bella's supposed to be going to lunch with Rani and Mala this afternoon," he refers to Darian and Dean's wives, "and needs me to take care of our girls."

I almost argue with his accusation—it's certainly *not* my fault—but shake my head and move forward. "Maddy referred a friend of hers to temporarily take Belinda's job through the summer."

Garrett's eyes bounce between mine, trying to glean some sort of meaning behind my words. "Okay . . ." He drags out the word. "That's good, right? You've been stalling on hiring someone because you're so damn hard to please."

I sigh. "Well, this *someone* also happened to be a woman I fired at *Carl's Catch*," I clarify, referring to mine and Jett's restaurant, named after our dad. "But I didn't know that until she was already hired, since I was out of town."

Garrett runs a hand over his chin like he's struggling with a tough math problem. "I'm not following. So you don't think she's competent? Then why not just fire her?"

I take a long breath. If only it were that simple.

"Because it's not that she's not competent; she is. She's sharp as a whip. Plus, she's Maddy's friend, and . . ." Fuck, I don't really know what I'm even saying. It all sounds like a bunch of random thoughts.

"Holy shit!" Garrett's eyes widen, as if everything just became crystal-fucking-clear to him. Wish he'd enlighten me, because I feel like I'm trying to see through mud. "You like her!"

"What?" I reel back, speaking louder than I intended. "No, I fucking don't! She's . . . she's irritating and exasperating. Wears fucking fruit paraphernalia and shit. And way too much orange." I lean in. "Like these hideous orange combat boots." I shake my head. "She came in late to work yesterday, wearing—"

I stop myself from elaborating, recalling her swinging breasts and how I imagine painting them with my fucking cum. *Jesus Christ*, I can feel the flush rising over my neck. The woman needs to be put away and locked up for good.

"—a tattered T-shirt and fucking *demanded* I apologize to her for calling her out for it in front of our team!" I gawk at him like he should be seeing exactly what I am, that the woman's unhinged.

"And did you?"

I blink. Clearly, my best friend isn't following my line of reasoning, given how calm he seems while I feel like I'm about to burst a coronary.

"Yes, but that's not the point, G. The point is . . ." My mouth sets in a firm line, but my next words don't sound convincing, even inside my head. "She's *not* my type."

Garrett's smile widens, pissing me off. "Then what's the problem? Why are your fucking knickers in a twist at just the thought of her?"

I exhale, frustrated, my breakfast unsettled in my stomach. I was going to finish the bacon and potatoes I'd ordered, but now they don't even look appetizing. I silently curse the raven-haired vixen. "The problem is, our biggest clients like the work she did on some slides and want to meet her."

"So you can't fire her," Garrett concludes, taking a sip of

his orange juice.

I nod. "Bingo." Then I wipe my hand over my mouth and murmur, hoping to bury enough of the next bit so he doesn't hear, and later I can point out that I did, indeed, tell him. "And I asked her to move in with me."

Garrett splutters, quickly bringing his napkin to his mouth, then coughs. The man really ought to take up theater with all his dramatics. "I'm sorry." He clears his throat. "I could have sworn I heard you say she's *moving in* with you."

I glower at him while his mouth hangs open. "It's not what you think."

"I honestly don't know *what* to think. You just went from telling me how she infuriates you to she's moving in with you. Help me bridge the gap here."

I run my hand through my hair, not quite knowing how I'll bridge the gap myself. "She lives on the other side of the Bay and doesn't have a functioning car, or much of a bank account from what I know. She'd need to take a couple of different subways to get to work. And given how much I demand, and the fact that she might need to be on site at a large project here in the city, sometimes at odd times of the day, it just made sense." I shrug, feeling less nonchalant than I'm going for. "It's just a temporary business arrangement. Plus, it's not like I don't have enough rooms."

Garrett presses his fingers against his mouth, seemingly holding back another smile. "Seems to me that you've got it all figured out."

I squint at him, catching the flicker of sarcasm in his tone. "But . . .?" I prompt.

He shrugs. "No buts. I'm just wondering . . ." He pauses with his smile now in plain view. "For a man who has the means of renting any nearby apartment, or even buying her a new car, it's interesting that you chose to move her in with you. Like it was your only option."

I slide a hand over my scruff, not giving him a response. The bastard's all too perceptive, but right now, as it stands, I don't need his perceptions added to the confusion in my head.

"And you know what else I wonder?" I want to say I don't give a shit what he wonders, but he continues, teeth flashing, "When you'll see it as clearly as I do."

MY FINGERS TAP a steady beat on my desk, the end of my pen pressing into my bottom lip as I eavesdrop on my sales team's morning meeting. My physical presence isn't always conducive or welcome in candid employee discussions, so I liked to stay in my office and listen to various department meetings to gain insight into their hurdles and understand their perspectives.

A knock sounds at my door and though I don't spare her a glance, the faint scent of vanilla and lemon permeates my workspace. Even in my peripheral vision, flashes of red, blue, and orange signal yet another of her strange outfits.

Unable to resist the temptation of the proverbial red flag, I turn to her.

Carrying a tall glass of my morning smoothie and what looks to be some sort of muffin, her honeyed eyes skate over me, like sunshine over cold terrain.

She places the items on the corner of my desk, and I take in the soft waves of her dark hair spilling over her shoulders onto a weathered orange shirt that says "Tropic Fever" on it. Her shirt is tucked into faded jeans, with an ugly red and blue flannel around her waist.

She's just about to turn on her heel when I finally speak, averting my eyes to look at some papers on my desk as the voices coming through my speaker carry on about our quarter earnings. "Please take the smoothie with you, Ms. Jain. I've already had my breakfast."

Her eyes linger on the glow of the red mute button on my speaker before she says, "Oh . . . but Belinda said—"

I lift a brow, pinning her with my glare. "Belinda has the morning off for her appointment, which is why she missed the email I copied you both on, saying I wouldn't be needing my smoothie. What's your excuse?"

Her mouth sets stubbornly, the tiny diamond over her lip stealing my attention momentarily. "I didn't have a signal on the—"

I wave my hand, dismissing her. "That'll be all, Ms. Jain. I don't need to hear your sob story."

Nostrils flaring, she reaches to lift the items off my desk when I notice the large scar running down her forearm in a rugged path.

I hadn't seen it before, but then again, I wasn't looking.

She's about to turn back again when, for reasons only God can explain, I stop her once more, my molars grinding. "How's your brother this morning?"

She glares at me. "Recovering. Thank you."

She's turning once more when I throw the pen in my grasp onto the desk. "And that scar on your arm . . .? What's that from?"

Her mouth pulls into a frown, and if she had her hands free, I guarantee she'd try to cover her arm somehow. "Please. Don't concern yourself with me or my *sob story*, Mr. Case. I wouldn't want to take up your precious time."

She's almost at my door when I speak again. Why? I have no fucking idea. It's like a part of me wants her so far on the other side of the earth, I'll never find her, while the other can't seem to get her close enough. "I said take the smoothie, not the muffin."

Lips pursed, she turns yet again, and I swear, if she could

incinerate me with her glower, she would. Taking long strides, in those ridiculous shoes of hers of course, she places the muffin back on the corner of my desk.

I run my tongue over my teeth, feeling a strange sense of . . . excitement buzzing through my veins. "What kind of muffin is this?"

She tilts her head, amber eyes glowing. "Are you sure you want to eat it? I could have laced it with rat poison."

My lips twitch, my eyes taking a leisurely stroll down her frame, my pants feeling tighter. "I'll take my chances."

"Apple cinnamon," she announces in a somewhat bored tone, but I get the feeling she's pleased I wanted it back.

I bring the plate forward, waving the back of my hand to her in a sendoff. "That'll be all."

She wraps her arms around her, my smoothie in one hand, before tilting her head. "Are you sure? Because you're quite the chatty-Cathy today."

I hear my name on the speaker, but it's not anything I need to worry about, so I address her with my business tone again. "Please book our flights and hotel for tomorrow night—"

"I already did it after I got back inside last night."

Oh. How late was she up?

"And what about your . . ." I trail her attire, "wardrobe? You can leave early to shop, if you need."

"I know you're probably running close to the upper edge of Gen X there, Mr. Case, but we no longer have to shop in-store, browse physical catalogs, or use carrier pigeons for our shopping needs. It can all be done on what's called, the *internet*."

My lips twitch but I don't release the smile trying to work its way out. "Please close my door on your way out, Ms. Jain."

Chapter Ten

HUDSON

"Lavender and pine."

Her answer seems to fascinate him, as if she just told him her favorite scent was unicorn breath or diamond-covered marshmallows. His eyebrows rise with a smile. "Ah, a combination of soft and rugged, indoors and out. I suppose I'll have to find a similar scent to put on the next time we meet."

My eyes harden on Silas's son across the table, my hand white-knuckling my fork, but he doesn't notice, given he's turned almost ninety-degrees in her direction, as if she's the only one in this room.

Corbin runs the financial arm for Rose City Skyport and showed up alongside his dad as a surprise guest for dinner tonight. And though I didn't mind his presence at first, that had changed rather quickly.

Over the course of one hour, the fucker has done nothing but derail our productive dinner meeting, directing question after irrelevant question at Kavi. Her favorite cuisine— Indian. Her favorite season—summer. Her favorite color—

orange. *Yeah, surprise, surprise.* The asshole's made it his mission to flirt to the point of exhaustion. Mine, not his.

And though I have half a mind to pick him up by his collar—deal be damned—and throw him across the room, I can't get a fucking read on if she likes his attention.

He wouldn't be a bad choice for her if she did. He's clearly closer to her age, doing well financially, and I suppose, if I was put at gunpoint to admit it, he doesn't look like a troll. He's also made it his mission in life, or at least during this dinner, to make her laugh.

A laugh I hadn't heard until today. A laugh that transforms her features so her eyes crinkle right along with her button nose, and her mouth stretches into a perfect half-moon across her face. A laugh that would put anyone watching her in a good mood without even having the context of what was funny.

Anyone but me.

Because the more she laughs, the more I want to murder the guy next to her. The more I realize her smile—those luminous honey eyes and white teeth—aren't aimed at me, the more I want to pound on this table and demand she stop.

The more she laughs, the more I want to carry her over my shoulder and leave this damn restaurant.

Her eyes glimmer in my direction, dipping to catch the tightness in my jaw and shoulders.

I drag my eyes from her and once again try to bring the conversation back to business with Silas. "So, are we settled on the date? I know we provided the results of the ecosystem assessment around the potential site, along with our solutions for noise and wildlife management, but if you're at all concerned with anything else—"

"No, I think we're all set. Your team gave us a very comprehensive report, and we're confident Case Geo is the right partner for us." Silas swirls the wine in his glass before addressing Kavi, "Though it would be nice to have consistency on your team. I know we only have you for the next three months, Kavi. What are your plans after that?"

A frown tugs on Corbin's lips as he waits for Kavi to speak. Is he already upset by the prospect of her last day? He only just met her. What a douche.

"I'm actually moving to Portland. I have a full-time position as an art therapist at the children's hospital here."

Silas's brows raise, much like his son's. "Art therapy, huh? You'll have to excuse my ignorance, but what does an art therapist do?"

Kavi smiles in response, her gaze shifting from her hands on her lap to Silas, revealing a hint of the nervous woman from our first meeting. She's still there, under the surface, but so is a bolder, more fearless woman—someone I've seen myself.

"Well, not all art therapists have the same approach, but in general, we help people overcome psychological and emotional challenges through artistic expression. Personally, I like working with children, especially those struggling with low self-esteem because of situations in school or at home." She pauses, running her fingertip down the condensation on her glass. "I help kids who may have been abused or bullied channel their emotions onto a canvas."

"That's fascinating, Kavi," Corbin says, his mouth slightly agape. "God, it makes me feel like what I do, running numbers all day and making sure we hit financial targets, seem so inconsequential." His gaze slices across the table at his dad. "No offense, Dad."

Silas shrugs. "None taken. I tend to agree."

Kavi's eyes linger on mine before she drops her gaze, her cheeks hinting at color. Her hand fidgets, tucking a strand of hair unnecessarily behind her ear, bringing my attention to the red strawberry hanging there.

She's wearing a peach-colored chiffon sleeveless top with spaghetti straps that dips to the start of her cleavage. And with nothing adorned over her neck, besides a hint of some sort of shimmering powder, all I can see—all anyone can fucking see—is miles upon miles of flawless skin.

Maybe I shouldn't have given her my damn card to go shopping.

"So, you'll be moving *here?*" Corbin's excitement is hardly masked. "Do you know where you'll live?"

She shakes her head. "Not yet. I've been searching for places online, though."

Corbin's smile becomes more hopeful. "Well, if you're here after the meeting tomorrow morning, I don't mind showing you around Portland."

"She's not," I blurt before Kavi can respond, turning all heads to me. I don't miss the question in Kavi's eyes, knowing we don't have plans to leave until early evening. "I'll have her tied up with some things to ensure the project starts on time."

I take the final sip of my scotch, waving down the waiter for the check. A mix of frustration and confusion tightens inside my ribs like I'm breathing in noxious gas.

I don't drink often or much. On occasion, I'll have a glass of wine or my favorite champagne, but I needed something stronger to get through this dinner.

And though I'm not proud of it, I've already exceeded my limit, including Silas and Corbin's requested celebratory shot commemorating our professional relationship. Kavi didn't partake in that, I noticed, sticking to the same glass of wine all evening.

I'm just signing the check, ready to head to our hotel, when Corbin's words have my pen halting.

He leans in, centimeters from Kavi's cheek, but my ears

catch every word. "Care for another drink? There's a bar next door, a popular Portland hangout."

My pulse quickens.

Does this guy not see how unprofessional this is?

"Actually," Kavi's tongue glides over her bottom lip, "I'm a bit tired tonight. Perhaps another time?"

"Oh, come on!" Silas interjects, elbowing me, as if to pull me into convincing her. "It's just one more drink. God knows I rarely go out. Let's make the most of it."

Corbin's disappointment with his father inviting the two of us flickers in his eyes, but my attention is centered on Kavi. I can't decipher if she's really tired, or if she's refusing because I wanted to call it a night.

"Kavi?" Her name rolls off my lips, forcing her eyes on me. "Are you okay with one more drink? It's perfectly okay to say no."

Her hesitant gaze assesses us before she nods. "Sure, that's fine." She smiles at Corbin, forcing me to look away as an unexplainable pang rattles my insides.

So, I guess that answers my question. She *is* interested.

Fifteen minutes later, I'm standing next to Silas, feigning interest in our conversation, even though my gaze is fixed on my admin, chatting away at the bar with Corbin.

Country Western music blares from the speakers as chatter fills every nook and cranny of the small rustic tavern. The scent of aged wood and cigars envelop my senses, mixing with the smoky sweet aroma from the whiskey in my hand.

I really shouldn't be drinking any more, but this whiskey is the only thing dousing the molten fire running through my veins.

Corbin takes a sip of his drink, offering it to Kavi, who's holding a glass of Sprite. She shakes her head, and he relents, but not before tugging a stray wisp of her dark hair from her lips and tucking it behind her ear.

My molars threaten to crack.

He has no business fucking touching her.

Regardless of the fact that I can't hear them, every laugh, every word between them rings in my ears like a cacophony. Every muscle in my back strains, the skin over my knuckles stretching dangerously as I do what I can to temper my nerves and my breathing.

What. The. Fuck? What is this feeling, and who is this unwelcome guest inside me, blurring my vision and creating a buzz inside my head?

It's not the alcohol I've consumed all night—I know that for a fact. It's something else entirely.

Excusing myself with a quick nod to Silas, I throw back the rest of my drink and head to the bar to ask for another.

I'M NOT DRUNK. I'm merely *slightly* inebriated.

My eyelids flutter as the wind hits my face, the city passing by in a rush of twinkling lights and discordant sounds. I recall asking our driver to open the window, needing the cool breeze on my warm skin, silently thanking the sky for staying dry.

I turn my head to the left when the flash of ebony hair waves inside the car.

Kavi brushes her hands over her biceps, trying to eliminate the goosebumps that have erupted there, and I take in her attire once more.

"I like what you're wearing," I say, leaning in to examine her peach-colored top and her black skirt.

Black like her hair.

Black like the evening sky.

Black like the jealousy that suffocated me from the outside in tonight. Or is it the inside out?

Maybe it's the upside down. That makes more sense.

She doesn't respond, her eyes shifting back to look out the window.

"It's . . . different," I continue, a hiccup interrupting my thoughts. "Less eclectic and more . . . more chic." When she continues her vow of silence, I wiggle out of my suit jacket. "But you know what, Kav?"

She finally turns to me, a peculiar look in her eyes. Something soft—the kind she doesn't reserve for me—something familiar.

Familiar? Why would it be familiar when I've never seen it? Is it because I called her Kav?

Fuck, I like her name. I really like her name and her face and the way she smells . . .

I really like . . .

I place my jacket over her shoulders without much finesse. I saw that going differently in my head. "What does your name mean?"

My eyes are unsteady, but they're steadily focused on her lips. That fucking gem sparkling over them,

If I kissed her, would I feel it on my tongue?

I wouldn't kiss her, though. I couldn't. It wouldn't be right.

For so many reasons . . .

I lift my fingers, counting each one out loud. "Madison." Index finger is up and I'm waving it around in front of my face. "Employee." Second finger joins the first. "Age gap." Third finger comes up and I chuckle.

Brie reads these dirty romance books and was telling me her favorite was 'age gap'. I never got a chance to ask her to clarify that. I mean, technically, unless you were born on the same day as your love interest, wasn't there always some sort of age gap?

Love interest?

The fuck did that come from?

My pinky lifts, and I waggle all four fingers in front of her. "Roommate."

Her brows pinch in confusion as she shrugs into my jacket, but not before running her nose over the collar.

I flash her my teeth. "Lavender and pine."

A stunned widening of her burnished eyes meets mine, cheeks picking up a blush before she clears her throat and juts out the water bottle in her hand. "You should drink the rest of this."

I run the tip of my finger over her orange fingernails, making her fingers flinch and the bottle crackle, before I take it from her. Chugging the entire thing and wiping a droplet from the corner of my lips with the back of my hand, I slouch against my seat.

My head swings her way. "Well, that was a successful meeting, don't you think?"

Her gaze surveys me, questioning if I'm setting a trap. "It was. It seemed like Silas was pleased."

I chuckle, the barbs of something thorny and bitter pressing against my ribs. "Ah, yes. Silas. His son seemed to be pleased, too. Wouldn't you say?"

Lips pursing, she snaps her head back to look out the window, dismissing my probing.

"I'm just saying . . ." I lean in, my breath brushing the shell of her ear. "If I hadn't secured the deal by dinner, you definitely helped clinch it at the bar."

Her head jerks back toward me, my bitter insinuation landing the way I had expected. But she doesn't expect my closeness, my face, lips, millimeters from hers. "Don't be an asshole, Hudson."

I'm distracted by her.

Her little gasps of breaths. Her smooth lips. Her lemony scent.

She swallows, trying to scoot further into her side unsuccessfully, and I'm distracted by that, too. The soft bob of her throat, her tanned skin that looks satiny and sweet. The way her thighs fill out that skirt . . .

"I'm sorry." I roll my head against the headrest with a frown. "I promise, I tried not to be one for as long as I could."

She ogles me. "Oh, did you? I'm sure that was quite the feat for you. Is that supposed to make me feel better?"

I shake my head, my vision shaking along with it. "No, but it is supposed to make you feel *something*."

She huffs out a deprecating laugh, mumbling, "*Unbelievable,*" under her breath.

Our car stops in front of our hotel, but I don't move, my fingers wrapping around her wrist when she starts to pull open her door. A silence hangs between us momentarily after she turns to meet my gaze.

I open and close my mouth, my attempts to articulate a single thought seeming futile. "I'm sorry I embarrassed you tonight," I finally manage, the words feeling heavy over my lips, my chest.

My hand tightens slightly over her wrist like a plea . . . a need for her to understand.

She sighs, whether in frustration or relief, I can't be sure, but if I had to guess, it would be the former. "You didn't embarrass me, Hudson. You almost cost us the deal. A deal your entire company has worked hard for and deserves to win." She shakes her hand. "How could you threaten Corbin like that?"

"Like what?" I say louder than I'd like, immediately regretting it when she flinches. "I told him he either takes his hands off your waist or we'd walk out, deal or not. He was fucking touching you!"

"Yes, and that was reckless of you," she argues, shifting on the seat. "You can't jeopardize something so huge for your company like that. You wouldn't have said it if you weren't drinking."

I smile, thumb brushing the inside of her wrist as my eyes drop to her lips. "You sure about that?"

Her soft breath tickles my skin, chest rising and falling as her raspy whisper hangs in the space between us. "We should get you inside."

I nod reluctantly, running my hands down my face, as she pulls away.

Fuck, what the hell is wrong with me?

I wish I could say it's just the alcohol or the stress over wanting to win this deal over the past few months, but I know I'd be lying to myself.

With some help from the driver, I amble out of the car, my feet not quite recalling what feet are supposed to do. Seeing me struggle, Kavi presses against my side, curling her arm around my waist, while quite literally holding me upright. And because I like the way she feels, and smells, and looks, I pull her closer, my arm wrapped around her shoulder.

We hobble inside, swaying as we do, before stepping into the elevator. At some point while she's tracking the floors changing on the digital counter, I place my nose in her soft hair, unabashedly taking a whiff. "God, you smell so fucking goo—"

I don't finish that sentence, incomprehensibly stumbling back against the wall behind me and taking her with me. Her soft chuckle hits my ears first, alerting the rest of my senses, and my hand clasps around her hip, pulling her ass over my erection. "Kav."

She turns around in my arms, soft hands cupping my face, thumbs running over my scruff. "Hudson, listen to me. I'm going to take you to your room and get you into bed—"

"Now you're talkin'." My dick twitches inside my pants;

though, I'll be honest, I'm not one hundred percent sure he's going to display his Olympic prowess tonight. You know, being *slightly* inebriated and all.

"We have to be at RCS's office by eight-thirty tomorrow, which means only about five hours of sleep." She locks her arm around my waist as soon as the elevator doors open, pulling me forward.

I stumble behind her, trying to stay quiet in the halls, when she tells me to shush.

Jesus. She tells me to shush like I'm a child and not a forty-six-year-old man. Since when did she get this spine and sass?

And fuck, I'm a forty-six-year-old man.

"Do you like age gap?"

Her nose wrinkles as she stalks toward my room. Coming to a stop in front of it, she waits for me to find my key, taking it from my fumbling fingers when I can't steady it enough to open the door.

When the hell did I get this slightly inebriated?

Pushing the door open, she waits inside before I follow. I immediately shuffle over to the bed, falling on it face first. My eyelids feel like dead weights, dragging me down into the pits of a deep slumber.

Seconds later, she's jostling my shoulder. "Hudson?" She tugs at my feet, removing my shoes, before she's back at my shoulder. "Hudson? Can you drink this water? I had Tylenol in my purse. Take it so you don't have a massive headache in the morning."

I roll over, groaning as I drag myself onto my elbows. Taking a sip of the water she offers me, along with the meds, I fall back on the pillow, but not before grasping her hand as she's pulling away.

She lets me tangle our fingers and I stare at her through

hooded eyes. She's fucking ravishing. "You're too good for him, you know."

God, if I was sober, I'd have slapped myself for even speaking—and I know I'll want to go back in time tomorrow and slap myself when I remember this entire night.

She drags her teeth over her bottom lip, a smile pulling at the corners. "Corbin or you?"

My gaze crawls down the length of her body, still inside my suit jacket, but I don't dare answer her question. "Do you like him?"

Her voice is as soft as the light near my bed. "Would it bother you if I did?"

Nope, not answering that, either. "What does your name mean?"

Likely because I'm giving her whiplash, she tries to untangle our fingers, but I tug her closer so her face hangs inches above mine again, her free hand landing on my chest.

Our eyes dance, our breaths intermingling inside the blaring silence.

"Kav."

Her breath stutters, amber eyes flecked with gold and brown. They're so fucking beautiful, especially in contrast against her brown skin. "A poem," she whispers.

My hand cups the side of her face. "It's perfect," I mumble, lids dropping on their own accord. Words slipping on their own accord, too. "You're perfect."

I'm staring at my boss, not that he knows it. And I've been doing so, off and on, for the better part of an hour.

While I woke up with deep, dark circles around my eyes —to which I applied a chilled bottle of vodka from the mini fridge, hoping to de-puff my skin—he looks like he was in the habit of passing out drunk and waking up glowing like a movie star.

Four hours later, with all contractual documents signed and celebrated with our clients, not a single brown hair has shifted out of place from the top of his head. Nor does he display the slightest evidence of a rough night. In fact, in his signature suit and tie, his salt-and-pepper scruff perfectly trimmed, his eyes seem to look sharper, more intense, like storm clouds gathering in the horizon.

Thank God, Corbin let bygones be bygones with what Hudson said to him last night when he saw him getting handsy. Thankfully, I was able to clear the air with him before Hudson and I left, letting him know I wasn't interested in any sort of relationship or even casual dating. He seemed to understand, telling me to inform him if I change my mind.

I won't be.

The longer I stare, the more my boss's crescent-shaped lips pull downward, the creases around his mouth deepening.

"If you have something to say, just say it, Ms. Jain."

Ah, so we're back to Ms. Jain.

Does he even remember anything from last night?

The way he scowled at Corbin all night, as if imagining his death in vivid detail. The way he pulled me into him in the elevator, his body's reaction too difficult to hide. The way his breath floated over my skin, his lids succumbing to the haze in his head as he said those last words.

"You're perfect."

Does he remember any of it, or would he have acted the same with anyone in my position?

His low voice bounces around the small conference room we've borrowed inside the Rose City Skyport's business building, and I pull my gaze back to my laptop, shaking my head. "No, I have nothing notable to say, Mr. Case."

He takes in a long, disapproving breath, as if my answer has exasperated him before pinning me with one of his glares. "Then what's the problem?"

I tilt my head, lowering the screen of my laptop so I'm not hiding behind it, even though I want to. "I don't have a problem. Do you?"

"No."

"Great." I give him an insincere smile. "Then why don't you continue your *Silence of the Lambs* routine, and I'll keep working."

He blinks. "What?"

I lift my screen and frown at the words I was typing on the slides, which no longer make any sense. "Nothing. Never mind."

Another sigh. "Is this about last night?"

I close my laptop screen, leaning back with my arms wrapped around my chest. The movement stirs the air around us, and I tilt my chin down to look at my exposed cleavage as goosebumps rise over my skin. Hudson follows my gaze, not even attempting to disconnect his heated perusal. "I'm wondering the same thing."

His brow arches. "Care to elaborate?"

"Yeah, I'll elaborate." I nod, determined to either shove that stick up his ass even further or take it out and whack him upside the head with it. "From the time I called you this morning, ensuring you got up on time so we could be here for the early meeting, to now, you've only said a handful of words to me—*four*, in fact, if I'm being technical. *'Get me my coffee,'* when I asked you how you were doing this morning." I recount his words, mimicking the small flick of his hand in my direction. "And you didn't even have the decency to look at me when you said them."

A few beats go by as his eyes stay on me. "I'm looking at you now."

"Yes, but—"

He rises from his seat abruptly, closing his laptop. "Come with me."

My brows crease while he stows his belongings into his bag. "Wh-where are we going?"

Our flight isn't for another four hours, and we had plans to catch up on a few pending items from other projects.

Zipping up his bag, he casts a questioning glance in my direction, like he's wondering why I haven't moved. Clearly losing patience, he turns toward the exit, speaking over his shoulder. "To find you an apartment."

Say what?

I quickly stash my things in my bag and hurry after him,

wobbling in my new orange heels. How do people walk in these?

Finding him waiting for the elevator, I saddle up next to him, a little breathless. "What do you mean, 'to find me an apartment'?"

The elevator doors open and we huddle inside. I'm beginning to realize a lot of our notable conversations happen inside elevators.

Bag in hand, he looks straight ahead. "I'm pretty sure I spoke English."

"Yes, but *why*?" I press. "Why are you concerned with finding me an apartment here?"

He side-eyes me, moving his lips minimally as he speaks. "Didn't seem to bother you when Casanova Corbin suggested it."

I'm momentarily caught off guard, almost forgetting to step off the elevator behind him, but spring into action at the last second. Is he . . . jealous? Is that what all that jaw popping and chest-puffing was about last night?

"Firstly, *Casanova Corbin*? Is that the best you can do? And secondly," I follow him out of the building with him ignoring the fact that I can barely keep up with his long strides in this ridiculous skirt and heels. "I didn't get a chance to respond to him because you did that for me."

Jaw grinding, Hudson throws me a grimace over his shoulder. "And what would you have said?"

"I'm here for work, Hudson." I scoff. "You're the one who pays my salary, so I would have said no."

Apparently, my answer only deepens his frown and my boss gives me another one of his disapproving looks.

What the hell did he want me to say?

Three minutes later, we're sitting in the back seat of another chauffeured car, with me chewing on my fingernails. I look out the window, trying to glean where we're going, but of course, I don't really know because I'm not familiar with the city.

I glance at Hudson sitting next to me, typing away on his phone, his watch gleaming as it picks up the sunlight.

I'm momentarily distracted by his long fingers and clean, rounded nails. Was that an older man thing—strong, manly hands that look both soft and rough? I don't recall any men my age having hands like that. And I definitely don't recall staring at them so brazenly, imagining those fingers doing all sorts of fingerly things.

I mentally shake myself out of my daze, recalling what I was going to say. "I'm not really sure what I can afford just yet. Maybe this is all too soon. I don't even know where the hospital is."

Hudson doesn't offer me a visual acknowledgement, speaking to his phone screen. "I made appointments at two apartment complexes near the hospital. We can walk through a couple of units and you can—"

A gasp falls from my lips, my jaw dropping. "You made appointments? *When?*"

He doesn't answer, leaving me to my assumptions.

He made appointments, did research, and looked up where I'd be working?

Why?

Our car stops in front of a well-maintained and manicured apartment complex with an exterior displaying a symmetrical arrangement of light blue-painted balconies and windows. The driver pulls open my door, and I join Hudson as we enter a welcoming entrance gate.

Inside, Hudson speaks to one of the managers while I look at the rental pricing displayed on the boards, along with the various apartment layouts.

I take quick steps toward Hudson while the manager goes back into her office to pick up her keys. "Hudson," I whisper.

"I . . . I can't afford any of these. I'd be spending most of my salary on rent."

I don't mention that my brother will also need a car next year, and that I plan to give him mine once it's fixed and buy myself another used one. All that to say, I won't be able to afford a place with a 'state-of-the-art fitness center' and 'high-end kitchen appliances'.

He gives me a long look so I snap my mouth shut for a moment. But then I decide I need to get my thoughts out before the manager comes back. "I don't know what you think art therapists make, but it's definitely not the exorbitant salary you're paying me." I continue, despite him looking at his watch like he's bored with my diatribe, "Plus, I'm not a fancy-pants like you. I'm perfectly happy with something more . . . dumpy."

"Fancy-pants." He deadpans.

"Yes." Making my point, I jab at his sparkling watch, his cufflinks, and then his tie clip—all items that cost well over my summer salary. *"Fancy-pants,"* I repeat.

He rolls his eyes before following the manager, volleying, "You're not staying at a dump," at me with another disapproving look.

Heels tapping the tiles quickly, I reluctantly follow them both. Just because I look at a place, doesn't mean I have to sign any agreement today.

Fine, I'll look.

After asking the manager about the distance to the hospital, I walk through the one-bedroom unit. The views are pretty from the windows in the master bedroom, displaying part of the Burnside Bridge spanning the Willamette River.

While I'm admiring the beautifully finished bathroom with its free-standing tub, I hear Hudson ask the manager about the security around the complex and whether the apartment staff stayed on premises in case of emergency.

The corners of my lips lift, listening to the baritone of his voice, the concern in his words, masked with confidence and assuredness.

Does Hudson Case *actually* care for my well-being? Well, paint me purple and call me a grape, maybe that alcohol is still in his system!

An hour and a walk-through of another complex later, we're back inside our car, headed to the airport with Hudson looking at his phone sourly.

After seeing my reaction at the very first apartment, he insisted I pay the deposit and secure the place, but I told him I needed to think about it.

There was no question the apartment was everything I'd be happy in, plus it was a five-minute drive to the hospital, but I really didn't want to stretch myself thin when I still had Mom and Neil to think about. The entire reason I'd taken this job so far away from them was because it paid well enough that I could send some money back home with each paycheck. I couldn't splurge it all on high-vaulted ceilings and panoramic views.

"Mr. Case."

Hudson's eyes focus on me with an unimpressed look that has my lips twitching. "I thought I told you to call me by my first name."

I shift in my seat, pulling my seat belt along with me as I turn to him. "It doesn't seem proper given you keep calling me Ms. Jain."

"And what would you have me call you?" His question lingers in the space between us, and I know just as well as he does that we're both thinking about last night.

"Kav," I answer, my voice more a whisper than I'd intended. "Call me Kav. I-I liked it."

His Adam's apple bobs with a swallow, his thick brown

lashes flutter over his eyes as I watch his hand loosen over his phone. "Okay."

Despite wanting to look away from his heated stare, I keep my eyes on him. "Do you . . ." Now that I've started, I almost want to change the direction of my question, but the nagging feeling inside me, insisting I ask, pulls the words from my lips. "Do you remember much of last night?"

Please say no.

Please say yes.

Hudson's mouth opens, and I swear he starts to say yes. I'd swear it if it wasn't mixed with the clearing of his throat. He shakes his head, briefly looking down at his phone. "Just bits and pieces. I don't drink like that often." He scans my face. "I hope I wasn't unprofessional in any way."

I weigh out his answer, deciding to take him at his word. Maybe he is telling the truth, given he isn't in the habit of drinking. Maybe he really doesn't remember much.

I force the images of our groins touching in the elevator and our breaths tangling over his bed from my mind. I give him a reassuring smile. "No, you were a perfect gentleman."

He nods.

"Thank you for . . ." I clear my throat. "Thank you for spending time looking for apartments for me. It meant a lot to me, Hudson."

"You didn't want to lock any of them down, so it's not like it accomplished anything." He goes back to scrolling on his phone.

"Yes, but it still meant something to me," I contend, watching his long fingers again.

I really need a life.

He's quiet for a moment, the turn signal the driver just clicked the only sound inside the car. "Do you have friends here?"

"No." I shake my head, chuckling. "I barely have friends at home, besides Madison, of course. She's great."

Something shifts in his demeanor, something I can't quite read. "Why?"

Regretting my admission, I laugh, trying to lighten the mood that seems to be setting in like a gloom. "Why is your daughter great? Well, let's see. She's kind, thoughtful, funny, and beautiful, inside and out." I feign a gasp, as if realizing something for the first time. "You know . . . I think she only gets *one* of those qualities from you."

I'm banking on the hope that he won't ask which one, but I love the bored look that settles on his features, pretending like he doesn't care.

Mr. Hudson Case. Dare I say, I might just be figuring you out.

"That's not what I meant, and you know it." He lets a silent beat pass between us. "Why don't you have friends besides Maddy?"

It's my turn to swallow, feeling the heat of an intense spotlight warm my skin. I hitch a shoulder up, aiming for casual. "You could say I have trust issues."

My hands twitch on my lap as the memory of a cold, damp wall brushes my fingertips.

For a moment, I'm back, locked inside the tiny chamber in a muggy basement boiler room, left there for hours until I passed out from screaming.

Lifting my arm, I squeeze the back of my neck. My muscles often knot in that area when the musty undertones and a whiff of metal and lubricants clog my senses.

I adjust myself on my seat, hoping to avoid further conversation when Hudson's voice catches me mid-neck-squeeze, pausing my movements.

"Are the trust issues the result of that scar?"

I release a shaky breath, dropping my arm and covering it with my free hand.

Hudson watches closely as I brush my hand over my arm, trying to hide the long, almost decade-old surgical scar—a reminder of the face of cruelty.

Giving up my effort to cover it, I drop my hand and fiddle with the silver band around my thumb. I had it resized years ago, though I've since lost my own. We'd gotten the same words engraved inside it—*'98 and 3/4th percent guaranteed'*—as a reminder of our first argument and a vow for many, many more.

"No," I murmur, smiling wistfully down at my hands. "This scar is a reminder of my strength."

Chapter Twelve

KAVI

10 years ago

The thunderous roars of two modified Dodge Challengers halt our conversation on the front concrete steps of Everbrook Bay Academy. My stomach sinks, beckoning my legs to move faster than they can.

"Fuck," Nathan groans, squeezing his eyes shut while his face goes ashen.

I reach for his elbow, trying to pull him along, while random students avoid running into us on the stairs. "Let's just get inside. They're not going to do anything with teachers around."

Nathan tugs his arm from my grasp, a defeated expression settled over his features. "It's fine, Kav. The deadline was yesterday. Gotta face the music someday."

I place my fists on my hips. "Then let me talk to them. Let me explain the situation—"

"No!" His expression hardens. "I don't want you getting involved. I got myself into this. If I have to beg and plead to get myself out, I will." He runs a hand over his face. "It's not like telling them my asshole dad is in jail will win me any sympathy points. I told you what they said when I took the loan. *'Overdue debts have—'*"

"'*A darkness clause,*'" I repeat along with him. "What does that mean, though? What kind of darkness clause?"

He shrugs as heavy footsteps sound behind us, making the little hairs on the back of my neck stand on end. "I guess I'll find out."

A large hand lands on Nathan's shoulder, and we both turn to face Vance and his crew of heathens. He flashes his teeth at me, reminding me of the shark from *Jaws,* before addressing Nathan, "There's my boy! How's it going, Nate? I was looking all over for you yesterday. Looks like you snuck out on me a little early after last period, though, huh?" His fingers tighten over Nathan's thin shoulder, making him wince. "No worries, though. I'm here now. Ready to settle up? I take cash or . . ." he smirks at his friends, "cash."

The two girls in the circle, Josephine and Paulina, look me up and down, lingering on the hole in my white polo uniform shirt, before giggling. No doubt they're sending silent signals to each other.

My anger flares and I grasp Vance's forearm. "Why don't you get your hand off him, you worthless scum?"

He makes an exaggerated frown, his midnight hair contrasting with his pale skin. "Aww. That's sweet." He looks at Nathan, squeezing his shoulder tighter. "Isn't it, Nate? She might look like the filth my cat dragged in last night, but at least you have someone who cares about your measly life." He steps closer to me, grasping a strand of my hair and curling it around his index finger. "I'm sure she wouldn't look as hideous after a shower and clothes that didn't come from the literal garbage."

"She could stand to lose the *baby fat* that's stuck around for ten years too long, too," Josephine adds, making everyone but Nathan and I giggle.

I slap Vance's hand off me. "You're an asshole." I glare at the rest of them. "You all are."

They chuckle, fist-bumping each other, before Vance's face goes blank, bringing a chill to the late September air. "It's called business, sweetheart." His eyes drop to my old, battered sneakers. "Something you wouldn't understand. I gave him a loan to bail his junkie father out of the sitch a month ago. He was well-fucking-aware when he came to me that he'd need to pay me back by *yesterday,* with interest, or follow the darkness clause."

My eyes narrow on Vance's black ones—fucking black like the pits of hell. "And what is this so-called darkness clause?"

Vance puts his hands into the pockets of his uniform khakis before lifting his shoulders nonchalantly. "Whatever we decide. Think of it as . . ." he snaps his fingers, looking around as if actually trying to grasp a word from the air, "a dare."

My heart races inside my chest, watching Nathan fidget. How could he put himself in this position? How could he take money from the one guy everyone at our whole fucking school knows not to get involved with?

I get that he felt desperate and had no one else to turn to —no one else who had the means to get his dad out of the thousands of dollars he owed to his fucking coke dealer—but to shake hands with a lowlife like Vance? What was he thinking?

Did he learn nothing from what happened to Chris Padilla last year?

Chris was in a bind and needed money for God knows what. Rumors were rampant; some said it was to settle his mom's hospital bills, others said he was trying to get his mom out of a bad situation with his stepdad. Regardless of the real story, he sought help from the school's richest and most conniving loan shark, Vance.

Two months later, his body was found in one of Sarasota's campgrounds.

What I don't understand in Chris' situation is why he didn't ask his rich girlfriend at the time for the money. In a school where practically everyone is the spawn of a Silicon Valley elite, the exceptions being a handful like Chris, Nathan, and myself—the *lucky* few admitted through some social charity quota—with pockets deeper than Santa's gift sack, why not ask someone else? *Literally anyone else!*

I knew that wasn't an option for Nathan, given that his social standing was possibly worse than mine. Still, I swear I want to slap my best friend right now.

My best fucking friend, who is not only the kindest-hearted kid I've ever known, but my ride-or-die in every situation since the first day of kindergarten when we argued about which of Dr. Seuss' books was the best, only to agree that it was *Oh, The Places You'll Go!* after a healthy ten-minute debate involving tears and some amateur name-calling.

The compassionate, albeit anxious, kid who lent me a hand while everyone else laughed when I fell after getting hit with a tetherball.

The fun-loving kid who'd go trick-or-treating with me, year after year, and who'd bring his sister along to spend Christmases at my house because both his parents were passed out drunk or stoned on their couch.

I want to slap the living daylights out of him at this very moment for being reckless enough to ask Vance for even a dollar.

If he had told me even a week ago, we could have figured something out. Maybe I could have asked Dad for a loan, not that he has much to spare, but I know he would have done whatever he could. Maybe I could have asked Alisha—the only girl in our school who continues to be my friend, despite being in the rich kids' crew. Maybe I could have started a Go

Fund Me or something, I don't know. *Anything* would have been better than this.

But he literally told me last night when I asked him why he snuck out of AP English early. After telling him I wanted to murder him for being so stupid, we both sat with our heads in our hands in my room, trying to figure out what to do next.

My dad was out of town for work, and Alisha never picked up her phone. Even if we'd gotten a hold of them, I knew it wouldn't be as simple as just asking for five grand. The money was nothing to sneeze at, and they'd ask questions—questions that could get everyone into more trouble.

God, I fucking hate Nathan's dad more than I ever have. Even more than when he beat the shit out of Nathan two years ago for coming home a half hour past curfew.

And as much as I'm secretly relieved that he's in jail for being caught dealing a portion of his coke to some other junkie, I hate that he left Nathan saddled with having to pay off his dealer. Fucking cretin.

It's the last thing my best friend needs, between taking care of the rest of his family and dealing with his panic attacks and anxiety.

The bell rings, snapping me out of my thoughts as I watch Nathan's shoulders slump.

He clears his throat, trying to find his voice as a few stranglers eye us as they run up the steps. "Wh-what sort of dare?"

Vance's smile widens, his head turning from his crony Dan to Miles, before addressing Nathan, "Since you're asking, I'm assuming you couldn't come through with my money."

Nathan's face falls. "I . . . I tried. I've been working extra hours at the drive-thru and have about a grand I can give you right now—"

Vance tsks, that evil gleam in his eyes. "A grand is not five grand plus interest, now is it, my friend? You'd think that with the free education my parents' charitable donations provide for your schooling here at this world-renowned establishment," he tilts his head toward the entrance of our school, "you'd at least have paid attention in math class."

Nathan rubs a hand over the back of his neck, likely wiping off sweat. "Could you possibly give me an extension? Another month?"

Vance nods solemnly, and a part of me hopes that might be his answer, before he throws back his head, barking out a laugh into the clear blue sky. Suddenly snapping his mouth shut, he leans closer to Nathan, making him flinch. "No. I've already made a tiny exception for you, given I didn't show up at the disgusting little trailer you call home last night and drag your ass out. Today is the day overdue debts are paid."

I can see the tremble in Nathan's hand, the way his chest rises and falls with each breath. "Alright. Tell me whatever this darkness clause is, then."

Vance, Dan, and Miles exchange glances before Vance rubs his hands together, as if excited about the prospect of doling out the punishment. He probably is, the sick fuck. "Meet us in the parking lot at five, eh?" He slaps an arm around Nathan's shoulder, pulling him into his side. "I think you'll be happy to know your darkness clause might actually be fun."

I shake my head, placing my hand on Nathan's elbow. "Nathan, don't. You know he's lying. You know whatever he wants you to do is going to be fun for everyone but you. Let's talk—"

Vance snaps his fingers in front of my face. "Wake up, chubby cheeks. There isn't much to talk about. The terms were clear for your little friend Nate here: pay up on time or pay the price. The rich don't get richer by making exceptions."

I glower at him, my index in his face, even though I'm

scared shitless. "Says who? I could walk into Principal Larson's office right now and—"

Vance and his friends burst out with hearty laughs before he shakes his head at me. "You're not new here. Take stock of your surroundings. Our great grandparents literally built this school from the ground up. Every fucking dollar, including what goes into that potbellied excuse for a principal's bank account, is funded by our families." He points at himself, leaning in to meet my eyes. "Funded by *me*. I'd be really fucking careful before you go stirring a pot of soup you don't intend to eat, you feel me? You wouldn't want your little brother never coming up for air when he goes over to your neighbor's pool to swim, would you?"

The fuck?

Every hair on my body points skyward. How the hell does he know Neil swims at our neighbor's pool? How the hell does he even know where I live?!

Before I can string a coherent sentence together, the five of them start up the stairs. Paulina shoves my shoulder with hers as she passes me, while Josephine glares "Stay in your lane, *trash bag*. It's in your best interest."

Vance turns around at the top of the stairs, a creepy smirk tipping up his thin lips at Nathan. "Five o'clock, Nate. Don't make me wait."

∾

"You can't go, Nathan!" I whisper-yell from my seat at the back of Ms. DeLaney's pre-calculus class three hours later.

We'd been separated all this time with different schedules, but I haven't been able to think about anything but the fact that my best friend is supposed to meet the school's most feared bully in a few hours.

I wish I could talk to someone. I wish we had friends—any friends at all—who could help. But no one would go against Vance and his clan, not even Alisha.

I could potentially text or call Dad, but he's still in Chicago for work, and Mom would probably say I'm inflating the issue. Or she'd tell me to go talk to Principal Larson, which is basically like talking to no one at all. Or worse.

What if Vance does to Neil what I know in my gut he did to Chris?

Nathan keeps his focus at the front of the class, speaking in minced words. You never know who is listening from Vance's crew, so it's important we keep our voices low. "Dan was in history with me last period. He said, apparently, we'll be going on a drive."

My heart stutters. "What do you mean, a drive? A drive where?! That is exactly how people get abducted!"

He shrugs. "What other choice do I have? He's not going to let me off the hook unless I chalk up his money by today, and I can't do that."

"Go to the police! I'll come with y—"

Nathan's head snaps to me. "Do you even know what that would mean? I have a fucking little sister to think about. Not to mention, my good-for-nothing mother. Who knows what Vance and his asshole friends are capable of?"

I huff. "Then I'm going with you. I'm not letting you go —"

"No, you're not, Kav. This doesn't concern you."

"I don't care. I'm—"

"Ms. Jain, is there something you'd like to share with the rest of the class that is more important than parametric and polar curves?" Ms. DeLaney's voice rings across the sounds of papers shuffling, kids turning around in their seats to face me and Nathan curiously.

I shake my head, wishing I could scream, *"Yes, there is something more fucking important,"* but I can't.

I zone out for the rest of class, staring at Nathan's profile, hoping my sixteen-year-old brain will magically come up with an answer.

I'm doing the same thing during our last period, wondering where the hell Vance is planning to take Nathan. Hoping that, somewhere inside his vampire-looking visage, he has a soul, some humanity.

Right around the middle of last period, I've decided to go along with Nathan to wherever it is Vance is taking him. I don't care if Nathan doesn't want me to. If he's my ride-or-die, then I'm his, too, aren't I?

The thought of going along makes me feel better—maybe I can convince the assholes to take it easy, or maybe I can even sneak a few pictures for evidence of whatever they're doing.

Pulling out my phone conspicuously, making sure Mr. Patterson, our chemistry teacher, is still turned toward the board, I quickly text Mom, letting her know I won't need a ride today and that I'll be going to help our art teacher clean up the classroom and set up fresh supplies for tomorrow. Mom will buy the lie, given I was Ms. Ahmad's favorite art student.

I'm just putting my phone back when a folded note is placed on my desk by the girl sitting in front of me.

My brows knit as I pick it up to read it.

Meet me near the storage rooms in the basement at four-thirty. I think I know how to help your friend. I don't want to see him get hurt. -JA

The only person the initials could belong to, and who would know the context for what's going on, is Josephine Andrews. I blink at the words, rereading them a couple of more times. Why would she want to help Nathan?

I raise my head, looking around the classroom. Is this a trap?

Why would she tell me to meet her in the basement? Perhaps to ensure no one sees us, since kids hardly go down there without teacher instruction. But Josephine's older sister is one of the freshman history teachers, so maybe she swiped her keycard?

Tapping the girl in front of me, I wait for her to turn around before whispering, "Who gave this to you?"

"Aster," she replies before turning back around. It's clear from her body language she doesn't want any more questions.

Aster is one of Josephine's minions, so I suppose my assumption for the initials checks out. Aster isn't someone I loathe quite as much as Josephine and Paulina, but I wouldn't say we're friendly with each other, either.

Hell, there aren't many in this school who *are* friendly with me.

I haven't ever been physically bullied here, thankfully. I haven't had girls gang up on me or my clothes stolen out of the girls' locker room.

But the cuts that inflict the deepest wounds aren't meant for the eyes. They're hidden behind cruel words that echo in the quiet of the night, that grate at the depths of your soul, reminding you of how little you're worth.

"Street trash."

"Ugly heifer. Have you seen how her thighs jiggle when she walks? Gross."

"Heard her dad makes the same amount as our lawn guy."

"Heard her and her little brother have to share a room. Incest much?"

Not overthinking the reasons behind the note, I rush out of class. Placing my books inside my locker, I walk down to the basement floor, standing in front of a door that can only be unlocked with a special keycard.

I wiggle the locked knob, wondering how I'm supposed to get inside, when the door swings open. It's not just Josephine on the other side, but Paulina, too.

I eye them warily, about to speak, when a head-throttling punch has me flying backward. The shockwaves of pain barely register as I succumb to unconsciousness.

God, why do I feel so out of it? What the hell happened?

And Jesus, why does my head feel like it's going to topple over?

Only partial whispered words resound in my ears as I feebly struggle against the cold, unyielding floor. I open my eyes weakly but see nothing. Even as I try to blink, my eyes don't seem to adjust to the dark.

I reach my hand out, feeling a wall in front of me. "Hey!" I scream, shoving the wall before turning around as panic and bile rise within me. I can't see a fucking thing. My fingers tremble over the other side of what feels like a vertical coffin. I run my hand up and down, noticing the change of texture—wood. Is . . . is this a door? Feeling my way down, I find a metal doorknob, but it's completely immovable as I shake it.

"Hey! Let me out!" I scream, slamming my hand over the door as hard as I can. "Hey, assholes! Let me the fuck out!"

How the fuck did I get in here? How did they bring me in here?

God, my head. I wince when my fingers brush over my temple.

I pat my pockets for my phone, but I can't find it. Fuck! The cretins took that, too.

Hearing people outside, I press my ear to the door gingerly.

"Aster heard her and Nathan mumbling in DeLaney's class . . . wanting to tag along." The voice sounds like Josephine's.

"Yeah, well, she isn't going to be tagging along for a while." A male voice, perhaps Dan's, rises somewhat above the sounds of various machines in the boiler room. Is he the one who punched me? "Text Vance. Let him know she won't be a problem."

"What if she rats us out?"

A chuckle leaves his mouth, his voice a little louder, knowing I'm awake, what with all my screaming. "What's she going to say when she hasn't seen jack shit? And as for when they ask who put her in there?" There's a pause and another dark chuckle, wrapped in a promise. "Well, if she loves her brother, she'll keep her trap shut."

Chapter Thirteen

KAVI

"I'll walk you through the apartment. You can have your pick of whichever room you want, besides mine."

Hudson's deep voice rumbles around me in his expansive foyer. He puts his keys in a bowl on an entryway table and hands me another set with a small metal orange hanging off it. I roll the orange between my fingers, noting how different and simple it looks in this lavish foyer.

"They're yours as long as you're here," he says nonchalantly, picking up some unopened mail sitting on a tray, reading over the front. His gaze turns my way, noting my silence before flicking down to the keychain in my hand. "Figured it would be easy to recognize your keys since you're always wearing . . ." he waves in my direction, at the strawberry graphic on my tank top, "fruit."

I stare at him, silently because words seem to have escaped me, before finally mumbling, "That's thoughtful. Thank you."

He stiffens, throwing the mail back into the tray. "It has

nothing to do with being thoughtful; just practical and part of our business arrangement. Don't overthink it."

Well, okay then. Looks like Mr. Personality is back.

But, of course, who would I be if not one to poke the bear?

"And that apartment hunt yesterday?" I ask, brows high, my crossbody purse and my backpack around my shoulders. "What was that? Another *business arrangement?*"

Hudson slides his hands into his suit pants pockets, squaring his shoulders while looking down his nose at me.

Goddamn. I've never met a man who could look both powerful and relaxed at the same time. The touch of nonchalance in his otherwise arrogant and professional demeanor, the scent of his cologne, and the way his blue-grays focus on me has me itching to leap forward and bask in his attention and run in the other direction, all at the same time.

He's your friend's dad and your boss. Get a grip, woman!

"That was my *permanent* admin, Belinda, twisting my arm into making sure I helped you find something. Do you actually think I'd have the time to make those appointments or the interest in spending half my day running around town with you?"

Oh.

Well, that stings.

My chest burns, watching him turn on his heels and walk past the fogged glass wall separating his foyer from the rest of the house. I follow behind him, any positive feelings I'd gathered over the past two days turning to ash with each hesitant step.

Of course, he wouldn't have had the time to do any of that yesterday. From what I can tell, the man barely does anything but work. I was delusional to think he'd actually want to spare his precious time with me, voluntarily, taking me apartment hunting.

Clearly, Belinda made him feel guilty, and he did it out of obligation. It's probably why he was so reserved and quiet on the flight back and the ride he gave me back home.

I thought maybe he was reconsidering me moving in today, but when I asked if that was the case, he simply said, "I don't make decisions I have to take back. The movers will be at your place early tomorrow."

And with that, he'd simply driven off, with me watching after his truck in silence for a few moments.

I barely had time to think more about his words. As soon as I walked into the house, Mom was on my tail, bombarding me with questions. *"How was the trip? Did you fly on his personal jet? Did you like Portland?"*

And, of course, the last one that wasn't much of a question at all. *"I only got a glimpse of your boss. You never told me he was so handsome."*

To which I answered, *"I must have forgotten between all the times I told you what a prick he was."*

I won't say it was easy to explain why I was moving in with Hudson to my mother. She understood that it would significantly reduce my commute to work, but she had her concerns about me living with someone who, up until now, I'd only complained about. She also didn't love the idea of not having me around for what she called "my last summer".

As if I was going to die by the end of it.

In the end, though, Mom's always trusted my decisions, so she went along without giving me more grief. Plus, she had more pressing things to discuss, like the fact that she'd accidentally broken our garbage disposal. *"It's possible a couple of avocado pits dropped in there."*

Yes, because avocado pits just loved jumping into drains and causing technical failures.

I spent the next hour trying to get that thing to work again before finally deciding to call a plumber to fix it.

Hudson waves to the kitchen. "Feel free to use anything here. The fridge is always stocked, but if you need anything, I have a running list attached to the front. You can always add whatever you want on there, and my personal shopper will get it for you."

I nod, taking in the grand kitchen and the beautiful appliances. I'm not planning on using his shopper. The fact that he's already paying me enough to take care of my family for the rest of the year is plenty for me. "Do you cook?"

He shrugs. "Being a single dad, I learned a few recipes over the years."

After showing me around the living and dining rooms, both with beautiful views of the Bay, Hudson takes me to one wing of the apartment with several rooms.

He throws a thumb over his shoulder. "My room is on the other side. Here are a few open rooms. I'll have the movers put your stuff in whichever one you pick."

I look through each one and walk into one with a double-sized bed instead of the king-sized ones like in the others. "I'll take this one."

His brows pinch. "You don't want one of the others? This is the smallest of the three."

I shake my head. "It's double the size of any room I've ever stayed in. It's plenty for me."

The corners of his eyes soften for a moment before he nods. "There's an attached bath right through that door. Again, if you need anything, just let my shopper know."

I settle my purse and backpack on the bed, noting the high thread count sheets and the beautiful headboard. The room is modern and tastefully decorated.

Hudson seems to linger in the doorway for a moment. But, right before he leaves, he clears his throat. "If you need a ride anywhere, just let Aaron know." He refers to his driver.

"His number, along with the shopper's, is on the side of the fridge."

"Thank you," I reply, knowing I won't be utilizing either. I plan to wake up early and walk to work every day, and if I need to go anywhere farther, I'll use the subway or grab a taxi.

The lesser I get roped into Hudson's lifestyle, the better. I won't have it after this summer, anyway.

Speaking of which, I really do need to find an apartment in Portland.

I make a mental note to look for places online after I go out for groceries today.

I'm hoping to make the cheesy jalapeño cornbread from my recipe book tonight and take it with me to class tomorrow. The kids are always excited when I bring in goodies I've baked.

Having freshened up fifteen minutes later, I leave my room, only to find the house empty. Or I think it's empty. I can't really tell since it's so quiet. Despite my curiosity, I don't have the courage to go searching for Hudson on the other side.

Nor do I have a death wish.

With the curt and abrasive way he came off today, I'm inclined to stay as far away as possible.

He's right. This is just a business arrangement. We're not two friends cohabiting an apartment together. Nor are we strangers paying equal amounts for space in the same home.

I'm getting paid for being at his beck and call for work purposes, not staying here for my own pleasure.

Grabbing my keys, I make my way out of his apartment, taking the elevator down to the first floor.

Thankfully, the rain has let up, though the dark clouds continue to linger. Walking out of Hudson's high-rise, I catch a cab to a home goods store to purchase a few inexpensive cooking essentials. Afterward, I find a grocery store and grab ingredients for the cornbread and lunches for the week.

I'm supposed to be getting paid this week, so I don't feel too bad about splurging on a few brand-name ingredients versus my go-to generic ones, but I make sure to stay within my meager budget.

With bags hauled over my shoulders, I exit the grocery store, scanning my receipt. Just as I reach the curb to hail another taxi, my boot gets caught in a broken dip in the concrete pavement. My body launches forward, hands instinctively reaching forward to brace for impact as my bags slip down my arms.

I'm so taken aback by the fall, I don't have time to save the baking dish I just purchased. It lands, along with my palms and one knee, on the unforgiving pavement, and I cringe at the unmistakable sound of shattering glass.

"Oof!" I hiss as I stuff the rolling can of sweet corn back inside my bag and gingerly gather myself back to my feet.

"You okay, lady?"

With my head still buzzing from the fall, I turn toward the voice of a stranger—an older black man with a concerned look on his face.

Giving him a small smile for his kindness, noting how the rest of the world continues right past me, I nod. "Yeah, just lost my footing, I guess."

He points at my open palms, and I look down at the bloody and mangled skin there. "You'll need to clean that up."

I tell him I will as soon as I get home before throwing my aching hand up in the air to hail the next cab.

With my knee and hands throbbing, I make my way back up to the apartment. Thankfully, Hudson is nowhere in sight.

Leaving my things on the kitchen counter, I walk over to my bedroom to rinse my hands when I notice the boxes on the floor. Looks like the movers came.

After gently washing my hands with soap, I search inside the cabinet drawers for bandaids, to no avail.

I'm just making my way out of my room to see if I can find a first aid kit somewhere when I notice something. Or rather, the *lack* of some things.

Where are my painting supplies and canvases? I know I packed them last night. Did the movers forget to bring them? God, I hope not. I'm supposed to be taking some of them to class tomorrow.

Ignoring the pain on my palms for a few seconds, I peek inside the room in front of mine—the one that is now flooded with the afternoon sun, which is a rare sighting over the past few rainy days.

Except, instead of the bed and dresser I saw in there earlier, it's now filled with all my painting supplies—my easel placed directly in front of the large picture window, displaying one of my unfinished pieces.

My jaw drops as my mind races to catch up with the changes in the room over the past two hours. Not only did my enigmatic boss clear out the space, but the movers had tastefully arranged all my supplies and canvases inside.

Was this also an instruction from Belinda?

I don't have an envious bone in my body for her; she's been nothing but kind and supportive, even defending me during the public dressing-down I received from Mr. Hot and Cold. But I can't say I'm not curious about how she persuades him.

Speaking of curiosity, I wonder what her reaction was to my move into his home. While she updated me about her pregnancy, telling me the baby would be here any day now, conversation about my move never came up in our recent messages.

So, either she doesn't know or it was too weird for her. I get it; finding out your boss moved his temporary admin into his home to retain a client is definitely a surprising twist.

I'm also unsure if he's told Madison.

I don't know why the thought has my stomach in knots.

While I know her well enough to know she's both laid back and understanding, I don't know how she would feel about me living in the same house as her dad. Would she find it weird, like some sort of breach of friendship rules? Would she understand the situation from my perspective—that I can't afford to live near work, and that it's all a temporary means for the summer?

Not knowing is making me think the worst, and it's something I have to discuss with Hudson before I see Madison again.

Giving up on finding a first aid kit after looking in the hallway bathroom and a couple of kitchen drawers, I begin to unload the groceries, wincing from the ache in my palms.

The soft glide of Hudson's feet over the wooden floor steals my attention from the bags. My gaze fixates on his bare feet peeking out from under—*and there goes my heart kicking into high gear*—gray sweatpants.

They hug his thighs—the very thighs my eyes can't seem to unclasp from—resting snugly around his waist.

But that's not what I'm currently gawking at.

What I'm currently hyperventilating about internally is the rather plentiful bulge that's visible through the thick material. Is he packing a gun in there? A garden hose, perhaps?

Realizing I've gone completely brain dead, I quickly trail up his form-fitting white shirt, noting his large pecs and massive biceps, before finding his eyes.

He tries to hide a smirk, moving past me to grab something from the fridge. "You went shopping?"

I busy myself with the groceries, taking out the box of ground cornmeal. I frown when I find a few eggs broken inside the carton.

Hoping not to draw any attention to my eventful outing, I answer Hudson's question, "Yeah, just needed a few things."

After taking a sip of the protein shake in his hand, he scans the items on his counter. "You could have asked . . ." He steps forward, eyebrows pinched. "Why is that dish broken?"

I remove the whisk and large metal bowls from the same bag as the broken casserole dish, hastily gathering the fragments in my hands. I should have thrown it out in the trash as soon as I got home.

I was really looking forward to making cornbread tonight. I'm sure Hudson has a casserole dish, but I don't want to ask —nor do I want to take his stuff to class tomorrow. I don't want to borrow someone else's things and be responsible for them. What if I break it or accidentally forget it, or—

"Ouch!" I yelp when a sliver of glass slices my palm and blood pools over my cut.

Jesus. Today is just not my day.

Hudson quickly sets his drink on the counter and rushes toward me, pulling the bag out of my hands and discarding it in the trash can.

His gentle yet callused hand grabs mine, bringing it to him. "What—" He scans it closer while I try to pull it back. "Kavi, why is your entire hand scraped up?"

I try to wiggle my hand free, closing my fist as pain shoots up my forearm. "It's nothing."

"It's not *nothing*." Hudson counters, refusing to let me go as he guides me toward the sink. With me in his determined grip, he turns on the faucet and gently tugs my hand under the cool water.

I let out a soft hiss, thanking the Lord that it's not a deep cut. I really can't afford any more emergency room bills at the moment, given I still have to pay for Neil's appendectomy.

Hudson brings over a towel when my hand seems sufficiently clean and pats it down. In the process, however, his gaze falls to my other hand, currently at my side in a fist. With a puzzled expression on his face, he gently pulls it toward him before meeting my gaze. "Open it."

I shake my head, like a kid intent on not getting caught with candy in her fist. "It's nothing, Hudson. Just a scrape."

His jaw ticks. Oh, here we go with the jaw ticking. "Kavi, *open it.*"

I take in a long breath, unfolding my fingers.

His frown deepens. "Jesus. Did you decide to put your hands inside a blender today?"

Again, I try to drag it away from his grasp, but he doesn't let me budge. "That's a little dramatic, don't you think? Even your sunny personality couldn't make me do that. Though, I won't lie, I have thought about it after meeting you."

His frown softens, the tiniest smile playing at the corners of his lips as he examines both sides of my hands. "Let's get you cleaned up and bandaged."

I successfully unlock my wrists from his hold. "I can do it. Just tell me where the first aid kit is."

"Kavi."

Before he can stop me, I rush—okay, stumble—out of the kitchen, without a clue as to which direction I'm headed.

But his outraged voice behind me has me coming to a quick stop. "Kavi, *what the fuck?*"

I turn to find his eyes locked on my leg.

Following his gaze, I wince at the deep red stain over my tights.

Oh, right. My knee.

With the fresh new cut on my palm, I'd completely

forgotten about my knee. But just the mere sight of it shoots renewed bolts of pain through my thigh.

"It's fine," I declare, about to turn when Hudson's voice stops me again.

"Stop." He ambles over to me, grabbing my elbow. "It's *not* fine. You're limping, for God's sake."

"Hudson—"

Before I can say another word, Hudson swoops me up, so I'm bent over his shoulder, my arms dangling near his ass. I'm so shocked by the movement, I lose my train of thought, and vocabulary, for that matter.

A moment later, I'm seated on his bathroom counter, trying to look at everything but his furious face.

Nice tub. Plush towels.

Ooh, I bet that shower can hold a dozen people. Maybe he has parties in there.

What pretty light fixtures—

"Ahh!" I'm taken out of my purposeful avoidance of conversation when he slides an alcoholic wipe over my cut, and I scream. Yeah, I'm a baby like that. Sue me.

He glares at me. "You have a deep cut, scraped hands, and a knee that's probably throbbing, but *this* is what makes you scream?" He goes back to dabbing the rest of my hand with the wipe, murmuring, "Hold still."

Not wanting to prolong this for either of us, I do what he says while I secretly admire his delicious cupid's bow.

"What happened?" He doesn't look at me, focused on his task.

"The pavement came at me like a madman," I mumble.

He aims a scowl at my face. "I told you to write your grocery list down for my shopper. Or you could have called her if you needed something urgently."

I shrug. "I didn't want to bother her."

"Kavi, it's her job. I pay her to do it."

Right. Like he pays me to stay here because this is a business arrangement.

He notes my silence. "You didn't take the car, either."

He must have noticed that somehow, or maybe he spoke to Aaron.

I watch the way he puts ointment on my cut—gently, carefully. "I like the scent of aged perspiration inside the city's taxis."

I get another one of his unimpressed looks. The one that clearly says he knows I'm trying to be funny, but he doesn't find me humorous. And for reasons beyond my comprehension, there is something enticing about making him laugh.

Maybe I'll make it a summer goal: Get Hudson Case to finally break a smile for real on his ever-scowling face.

I clear my throat after a moment. "Thank you for clearing out the room for my canvases. You really didn't have to do that."

"You're welcome."

That's it. Two words, and he's done with that conversation.

Okay, then. I'll just go back to my daily scheduled programming of staring at his cupid's bow.

While he finishes wrapping my hand with a bandage, I trace his face with my eyes, noting the lines fanning off the corners of his eyes. From there, I scan the gray hair at the edges of his forehead and sideburns before returning to count the handful of freckles over the bridge of his nose.

Belinda told me his job used to require him to be outside a lot. He would work right along with his environmental and earth scientists, like himself, examining the soil and managing excavations. But since his company grew, he does less work outdoors.

So why are his fingers still callused?

God, those fingers. What is it about the man's fingers that have me wiggling where I sit? What is it about his clean, short nails, and his—

"Take off your pants."

A record scratch resounds in my head, all music abruptly coming to an end.

Did I hear him right? Maybe I was hallucinating a sex scene with him in it. God knows—*He's the only one who knows*—I've done it before.

I blink at him. "Generally, you'd take a girl out to dinner before asking her to take off her pants."

Hudson glares at me harder. As usual, he doesn't have any laughs to spare at my joke. "Kavi, I said, take off your pants. I need to clean up your knee."

"Absolutely not!"

I make an attempt to jump off the counter, but he's caged me in with his hands on both sides of my thighs, his face inches from mine and his breath fanning my lips. "Kav . . ."

Oh, no. He must know my nickname on his lips is kryptonite.

With my heart thumping, my eyes drop to his mouth again. This time, I know he notices. I mean, how can he not? Especially when I'm licking my lips. I can't help it, it's like an instinctual reaction to those pink pillows of his.

Something sizzles, crackles, and hisses.

A charge that has my nerve endings standing.

Reluctantly, I drag my eyes up to meet his gaze. "Hudson, I'm perfectly capable of cleaning up my own knee. There's no way I'm taking my pants off in front of my boss, for crying out loud."

His eyes flare.

And for a second, I swear he's inside my head, watching me wriggle out of my tights before I sashay toward him like a practiced seductress.

His voice is low and raspy when he finally speaks. "Then I suggest you get the fuck out of my bathroom before I make you take them off."

And with that, I'm hobbling out of there as fast as the charged air can take me.

Chapter Fourteen

HUDSON

Temporary insanity can be defined as a brief loss of rational thinking at the time a decision was made.

Less than two days of living with the woman sitting at her desk outside this conference room, and I can unequivocally claim temporary insanity at the time I made the decision to move her in. There is no other explanation for it.

Why else would I purposely torture myself this way?

I knew it that drunken night when I told that weasel, Corbin, to keep his hands off my admin.

I knew it when my brain no longer had control of my mouth, and I told her she was perfect before succumbing to sleep in my hotel room.

I knew it when she stood in the foyer of my apartment this weekend, filling it up with her vanilla and lemon scent.

And I knew it when I was inches from her lips, seconds from doing something I'd forever regret, when she sat on my bathroom countertop with that innocent expression, searching my face like she was looking for something to grasp. To claim.

I knew I'd lost my goddamn mind and that I shouldn't have ever moved her in.

Barely listening to updates my executive team is giving me, I watch through the conference room window as Kavi rises from her seat, picking up a colorful notebook and pen. She clasps both under her arm before picking up the large platter of cornbread and walks to the entrance.

Against my advice to let her hands heal and stay off her feet, she proceeded to make the damn cornbread on Saturday night. As if she was on a mission to solve world hunger and end wars. As if without baking it, children everywhere would starve.

The pained look on her face, the blood seeping through her tights where her knee was, and her mangled hands had my pulse racing so fast, I was at risk of overheating. The last time my heart had pounded like that was a couple of years ago, when Maddy was in a car accident. Thank God she was okay, but I swear I thought I was having a heart attack when I first heard the news.

I didn't want to, nor did I have any intention of it, but after seeing Kavi wince while using her hands to bake, I came and stood next to her in the kitchen, following the recipe along with her to make a second batch. She clarified that one was for the art class she was teaching on Sunday, and one was for the office.

"Everyone loved the pound cake and muffins I made. I feel like they've come to expect treats around the office now."

I begrudgingly held back an eye roll. I didn't, however, hold back the grumbled rebuke about the only thing they *should* expect is to work the fucking hours I pay them for, but she didn't seem to care or be listening.

No one fucking needs muffins and cakes around here. What they *need* is to get their jobs done.

I won't deny I was a little curious about this art class she taught. For free, apparently. I recall Maddy telling me about it briefly a while ago, but as Kavi buzzed around, telling me about a couple of the kids in her class while she gathered her supplies and snacks, there was a part of me that wanted to go along with her. There was something about the excitement in her voice, the spark in her golden-brown eyes, that betrayed the timid and quiet woman she showed the rest of the world.

Not me, though, clearly.

Somehow, I didn't intimidate her any more. Somehow, she was all about practicing her sass and quips on me.

And, somehow, I didn't hate it . . .

I had to practically beg her to take my damn chauffeured car yesterday. Me, beg!? It's fucking unheard of.

I don't know why she's been adamant about taxis and walking on her own, but at one point, I threatened her to either take the damn car or risk having me haul her over my shoulder and set her ass in it myself.

Thankfully, that made her comply. Probably because she knew I would, given I'd done precisely that on Saturday when she banged up her knee.

But then, today, she got to work an hour before I did. And I know from talking to Aaron that he didn't bring her. The woman is frustrating to an alarming degree.

I don't get up to open the door for her, relishing the way she lingers outside, hoping to get someone's attention.

Her body-hugging cream shirt is tucked into high-rise pine-green corduroy pants that are folded at the bottom. Save for her signature shoes, the outfit looks new—though I can't be sure, given her interesting taste. I wouldn't be surprised if she bought it from a higher-end thrift store.

She sways, this and that way, her pants only accentuating the curvature of her hips, those thighs rubbing against each other so provocatively, I'm tempted to call a break and take care of myself in my private bathroom.

Right as Gail, our head project manager, rises from her chair to assist Kavi, the elevator doors open behind her, revealing the face of someone I've done everything in my power to avoid over the past couple of years.

What the fuck is he *doing here?*

A few members of my executive team turn to follow my gaze, their faces puzzled and anxious. I must look as murderous as I feel.

Kavi hands the platter to Gail before turning to greet him. A moment later, she waves her hand toward another meeting room, giving me an apprehensive look from the window.

I don't think she's ever met my brother before, but knowing him, he hasn't wasted time introducing himself.

She doesn't reemerge from that room.

Not after five minutes, and not after ten.

My hands ball into fists as I try to keep my composure in front of my staff while they continue to pretend they have not seen my brother.

Losing patience, I excuse myself from the meeting, telling them to continue. I head out of the room, stomping down the hall toward the other conference room. My blood rushes through my veins like an untamed wildfire, making me wonder if my apprehension is just based on having to see my brother again or something else.

Something I'm afraid of; something I can't quite put into words.

My irritation spikes when I hear a burst of Kavi's laughter through the door. What the fuck is so funny? And why . . . why, since the time she'd hurtled into my life like a goddamn storm, haven't I been on the receiving end of that laugh?

My brain tells me there are a few reasons it can name, specifically having to do with me humiliating her in public a couple of times and firing her outright once, but I shove those thoughts away.

I got it. They weren't my best moments, nor my best decisions.

But neither was the little slip of my tongue, telling her she was perfect the night I was drunk. Neither was showing her I was raging with envy at the sight of that asshole, Corbin, touching her. And neither was almost kissing her on Saturday in my bathroom.

Jett's voice carries through the door, humor evident in his words.

Between the two of us, he's always been the life of every party. The kid who'd win over his teachers, our neighbors, and even our dad, getting out of trouble for shit he'd blatantly done because of his blue puppy-dog eyes and the flash of his perfect teeth. The man who came into a room and garnered attention just by being there.

The listener, the sympathizer, the fucking jokester.

I just never thought the joke would be on me.

Given the fact that I practically helped raise him, gave him every opportunity right along with me to climb the ladder, manage a huge portion of my business—despite not having the background in Earth Sciences like I did—and be my daughter's godfather, I didn't expect his betrayal.

And that became my single biggest mistake.

For him to leave with a portion of my staff and go to a competing firm? For him to hurt the man and brother who would have stood by his side until the end of time?

Yeah, I'm not sure our relationship will ever recover.

As for the sleeping-with-my-girlfriend part? I could give two shits about that. Sure, it was like icing on the fucking cake at the time because the knowledge came on the heels of him leaving Case Geo, but thank God for small miracles.

Kenna was always needy and selfish. She'd shown me that

time and time again; I was just too lazy to do much about it. She was good company, and I'd never wanted a real commitment, aside from exclusivity. She seemed to be okay with that, so it worked. But I should have seen there was no future for us.

I still remember the day Maddy was in the car accident. I had joined Kenna in New York at a dog show where her purebred French bulldog was up for a "Best in Show" award. I was already having a crazy week at work with my travel schedule at an all-time high, but because of her constant begging for us to spend more time together, I'd canceled an important meeting to be there to support her.

I still can't believe the words that came out of Kenna's mouth when I got the call from Brie, telling me Maddy was in the hospital.

"Are you sure? Or is this another excuse for you to bail on a weekend with me?" She'd kept her eyes locked on the arena where other dogs were being showcased, not even sparing a glance at my face to see how it had gone pale.

I was having a fucking heart attack because my kid was in the hospital, and she thought I was trying to bail on spending time with her? The lack of concern in her voice should have raised the biggest flag in my head.

"No, Kenna. As much as you think the worst of me, this is not some sick plan to get away from you. In case you hadn't noticed, I flew across the country to be here, and now I have to fucking go back because my daughter needs me."

I was rushing toward the exit when she grabbed my elbow. For a moment, I thought she was going to apologize, but what came out of her mouth sealed the deal for me. "I'm sure she'll be fine. It's not like rushing over there is going to get her out of the hospital any sooner."

I knew I'd be breaking things off as soon as I got a chance to sit down and talk to her again. As fate would have it, I never did get

that chance, since the next time I saw her, she and my brother were
walking into my office to tell me they were resigning.

At least he had the decency to look ashamed, but I still remember
the way her lips pursed and the haughty attitude she displayed when
she told me, "Oh, and by the way, we slept together."

Jett messaged me right after to say he was sorry and that
he and Kenna had only slept together once—apparently, on a
night when he was completely wasted—but I'd blocked his
number that day.

I knew that from then on, if he wanted to get a hold of
me, he'd have to do it through my office number or, like he
has today, by showing up at my place of work.

Without more thought, I burst open the door to the
meeting room, convinced I'd see . . . I don't know what I was
convinced I'd see. Jett cornering her, showering her with his
charm and personality.

Instead, I find Kavi standing with her arms crossed in a
corner while Jett is on a chair, relaxed, with his ankle on his
knee. He's leaner than me, but we both share the same eyes
and nose as our father, but where I have dark brown hair, he
has more blond mixed in.

"Good to see you, big brother. Kavi and I were just
talking about you," he says, his smile sweeping over Kavi
before turning to me. "I was telling her about some of our
past shenanigans, running the charters for Dad. Remember
when I used to throw that rubber barracuda into customer
tackle boxes? They'd open it and nearly have a heart attack
when it tried to snap at them."

He laughs, not getting the same response from me, given
I was always the one apologizing to customers for my brother's childish pranks.

I flick a glance at my admin, noting the laughter in her
eyes, which only heightens my temper. "Kavi, perhaps Belinda
never specified this, or maybe you forgot, what with all the

baking that's been consuming your time, but I loathe impromptu meetings. If they're not on my calendar, please tell any unwelcome surprise guest to find a spot appropriately. Or in this situation, tell them to fuck off."

My accusatory tone makes her wince, guilt splashing over her features as she stammers. "I . . . I thought that because he was your brother—"

"Please leave," I cut her off, turning my icy gaze on the person who's the true target for my wrath. "What do you want?"

Chapter Fifteen

HUDSON

"**N**ow I know why none of your other temps worked out," Jett states after the door shuts behind Kavi. He nods in the direction she took off. "None were as stunning as her."

I hold myself back from pulling him up by his collar and throwing him out the fucking window. Jett's always known how to get under my skin, and that's exactly what he's doing now.

Truth be told, as much of an asshole as he's trying to come across, he's not one. His attempt to rile me up has more to do with his own pain than me. He's hurt that he's even having to come to my office instead of being able to reach me by phone like he used to.

Regardless, I don't take the bait. "I don't have time for your bullshit. Either tell me why you're here or leave. You're well acquainted with the exit for this building, as we both know."

Yeah, that was a low-blow, but he's not the only one still hurt.

A flash of remorse crosses his features. "There were

reasons for me leaving, Hud. Reasons you weren't willing to listen to."

"That's right," I cut in sharply. "I don't give a fuck about your reasons, then or now. If that's all you came here to say —"

"I didn't." He rises from his chair, his hands finding his pockets in a similar stance to mine. "I came here because I want to work together again."

I rock back on my heels. "I'm sorry, what? On which planet did you think that was ever going to be possible again?"

He runs a hand over his clean-shaven jaw. "Congratulations on winning the Rose City deal, by the way. We worked our asses off, but I knew we couldn't compete when it came to the sheer expertise you have on the team."

My brain starts to connect the dots. "Ah, so that's what this is about. Your company wants in."

He shrugs. "It makes sense, Hud. You may have the raw talent—the best in the industry—working for you, but we have the muscle. I saw the timeline you guys proposed to them. You're living a pipe dream if you think you can get that shit built by the end of next year without more manpower."

I don't deign to give him a response. He's right that the timeline is tight, but we based it on adding twenty percent more to the workforce in the future just to complete the project. How we'll add that workforce so quickly? That's still something we're figuring out, since most of our work requires niche specializations.

"Look, this could be mutually beneficial to both of us. I'm not asking for an equal partnership—"

"Good, because you already tossed that in the garbage when you had it," I retort.

He takes a breath. "Let's table that comment for a moment; I'll come back to it. Like I said, we're not looking for a partnership, we're looking for a contractual opportuni-ty." He pauses. "I'm not going to lie to you. We were banking on getting the airport contract. We'd hired for it weeks before we actually made the bid. We wanted to show them we were serious, but in the end, Silas and his team valued deep expertise over manpower, and I respect that. But now—"

"Now you have a bunch of staff sitting around twiddling their thumbs," I surmise.

He doesn't respond; he doesn't need to. We both know I'm right, and the reason he's here is to avoid a massive layoff. And a layoff will make his company's stock look shittier than it has on Wall Street over the past year because of their finan-cial projections.

He licks his lips before his expression turns softer—the way it did when he'd get in serious trouble with our dad for the pranks he pulled and he'd come begging me to bail him out because Dad trusted my judgment. "I'm asking you to think about it. It would be a separate contract between Case Geo and us. We wouldn't take any of the credit for the work; only Case Geo would. But yes, you'd be helping us save some substantial losses."

I bite my bottom lip, thinking. But his proposal isn't all I'm thinking about.

I'm also thinking about the fun times we had. Like the summer after Jett graduated with his MBA, and I took him to Norway before he started working for me. We toured, fished, and camped out to see the Northern Lights. It was one of the best few weeks I'd spent with my brother.

We'd become a team after that. He'd slowly started under-standing the business I was running, and I'd given him the leeway to do the things he was great at, like his creativity and staff development. It's why he was so loved within the company. It's why he was able to take so many people with him.

"And as for the point about the equal partnership," Jett says, bringing me out of my memories. "Bro, when did you ever consider me an equal partner?"

My head jerks back. "What?"

Jett huffs out a mirthless chuckle. "I was always your little brother. The kid you helped raise. The one who always got in more trouble than you, who couldn't get anything right in Dad's eyes. And despite the fact that you claimed otherwise, you didn't trust me."

"What the fuck are you even talking about?" My voice rises, along with the temperature of my skin. "*I* didn't trust you? *Me?*" I shove my finger into my chest. "Jett, I fucking gave you one of my biggest business units to run on your own!"

"Only because I'm your brother! Only because you saw me as some charity case!" he retorts. "You didn't give it to me because you believed in me; you gave it to me because I practically begged you! Let's not forget you still had final approval over ninety-nine percent of my decisions."

"Because you ran it like Dad would! You let people walk all over you. Your team consistently missed deadlines, your financials were trash, and you were hemorrhaging company dollars on extravagant team events. You had the largest budget, for God's sake, and you constantly went overboard!"

He runs a frustrated hand into his hair. "And that is why I left, big brother. Because I was fucking tired of having to run things your way. Your focus has always been authority rather than fostering employee morale, but look around, Hud." He paces the room. "I bet you could count the number of happy employees on one hand, *if that*. I mean, look at the way you just treated your new admin, dismissing her like she was an ant."

My stomach drops as I replay my harsh words to Kavi before she left.

I was so blinded by my brother's sudden appearance and hearing her laughter in response to whatever he was saying that I didn't think about my tone. And then, in a low blow, I used her passion for baking as a way of making her feel bad.

Fuck, fuck, fuck!

"You talk about loyalty and trust," Jett continues, "but it goes both ways, brother. Employees need to feel like they can make mistakes without fear of losing their jobs. They need to be able to trust their management to have their backs, treating them as valuable assets, not cogs."

His words cut through me, my breath catching as I take in his candid admission.

Jett moves past me, a frown replacing his usual boyish smile as he places a hand on the doorknob. "I'm fucking sorry I hurt you, Hud. I regret how it went down. I tried talking to you about more autonomy and a broader role, but you dismissed me every time. I reached a breaking point, so I left. And believe me, it was the hardest thing I've ever had to do."

I see the sincerity in his eyes but stay silent, processing it all.

"I never solicited the other staff that left; they followed me on their own accord." He takes a shaky breath, his face dropping with shame. "And as for Kenna—"

"I don't give a shit about Kenna."

"But *I* give a shit about *you*. And giving a shit about someone means *not* hurting them. I knew you guys were already on the fritz, but that didn't change the part I played. We only hooked up that one time, despite what she might have made it seem like. But, drunk or not, I betrayed your trust, and I'm sorry. She resigned from my company a few months after leaving Case Geo, by the way."

His eyes mist over. "You're a better man than me, Hud. You're loyal to a fault and driven beyond what's humanly possible. You're genuine, caring, and resilient. But more than anything else, you're one hell of a big brother. You've taught me almost everything I know. The one thing you never taught me was betrayal, and now I'm reaping that karma."

My knitted brows must convey my confusion, prompting him to clarify, "Because there's nothing worse than not having the big brother you've always loved in your life."

I REREAD the message I sent her over six hours ago; the one currently still sitting on Read.

ME

> I'm sorry. I was a jackass, and that was completely uncalled for.

It's nearly seven, and I haven't seen her since she left me and Jett in the room. I've even gone out to check her desk at least twelve times in the past hour. I know she's around, given the empty platter I lent her is still on her desk, so either she actually had all those meetings to kick off the RCS work all day, like her calendar showed, or she's become adept at avoiding me.

Either way, I feel like shit.

My ears lock onto the sound of soft rustling outside my office, near her desk, and I decide to shut down my laptop, quickly reaching for my phone and keys. I'm about to exit my office when I hear the distinct ding of the elevator.

Shit.

She's leaving without saying anything. She's definitely still pissed.

I hurry down the hallway, catching sight of her empty desk—no platter on the corner—before noticing the elevator doors closing behind her.

I press the button to call the elevator back up, my chest feeling tighter than a guitar string ready to snap.

Today's been a strange day.

From replaying Jett's words in my head over a thousand times to worrying about the way I dismissed Kavi, I haven't gotten a single productive thing done.

It's clear his apology was sincere. I know my brother well enough to know when he's bullshitting, and he wasn't. He knows he fucked up, and I have genuinely missed him.

But can I trust him again? And even if I decided to forgive him, would our relationship ever be what it was? Would I always be waiting for the other shoe to drop?

I look around the first-floor foyer as soon as I'm out of the elevator, hoping maybe I'll catch her leaving, but there's no sign of anyone besides the doorman.

Making my way to the basement garage, I jump into my truck and zoom out of the lot.

A slight drizzle coats my windshield as I scan the street. She must have taken a cab because she'd be crazy to walk this late in the evening when it's still rain—

Goddammit!

I was wrong. She *is* crazy enough.

In her oversized men's blazer, with her lemon-printed umbrella in hand, she's hard to miss. She crosses the street in front of me, platter in tow.

Where the hell is she going? Why is she walking in the opposite direction of our apartment? Is she . . . is she fucking leaving again?

As soon as the signal changes, I turn my truck in the same direction, slowing to a crawl next to her. She does a double take when she sees me roll down my window, throwing her nose up in the air and increasing her speed the best she can on her still-injured leg.

My teeth grit as I watch her walk. I hate that she wouldn't

listen to me and let me look at it. What if she's more hurt than she's letting me believe? "Where are you going?"

I'm sure to anyone watching, I sound like a creeper, trying to catcall a random girl from my window.

She doesn't respond, keeping her shoulders back and her head forward, moving her umbrella between us to try to block me out.

"Kavi, where the fuck are you going? Our apartment is the other way."

She pulls her umbrella back, glaring at me. "It's not *our* apartment; it's yours. And it's none of your business where I'm going."

"The day you agreed to live with me, it became your apartment, too," I yell back. "And yes, it is my business to know where you're going. Why the hell wouldn't you call Aaron or just ride with me?"

She doesn't answer my question, looking down at the platter in her hand. "Is this about your dish? I'm not stealing it. You can have it back."

Jesus. The woman is certifiable.

"Kavi, get in the truck."

"And be in an enclosed space with you so you can be an asshole up-close-and-personal again? No, thanks."

I run a frustrated hand down my face, watching her walk with gusto. Goddamn, the woman is the most frustrating person I've ever met.

Giving up, I grab the nearest parking spot on the street a block away from her and amble out of my car. She likely thinks I've driven off.

Sounds of tires over the wet streets and the scent of fresh sourdough bread hit my senses as I cover the distance between us, jaunting toward her.

Kavi comes to a stop, eyes wide, when she sees me approaching. "Go home, Hudson!"

A few drops of rain land gently on my face so I bend, getting under her umbrella with her. I take it from her, my hand wrapping around hers before she lets go, so I can lift it to accommodate my height. "It's precisely what I'm trying to do, but you're not letting me."

She glares up at me, the stupid platter between us. Even on this dimly lit sidewalk, her honey-colored eyes sparkle like sunshine. "What do you want?"

God, if only that was a simple question. If only I could tell her exactly what I wanted. I haven't quite admitted it to myself, but I'm getting there.

"Your forgiveness, for one."

She turns her head, frustration wrinkling her features. Even so, she's beautiful.

"We keep coming back to the same place. You say something mean and then ask for forgiveness."

"I'll probably do it again, too." When she huffs, I continue, "But I can tell you one thing. I've never asked for forgiveness this many times in less than two weeks."

She squints at me. "Is that supposed to make me feel better?"

My lips twitch. "Yes."

"Yeah, nice try, Mr. Sunshine. I'm over your mood swings."

She tries to grab her umbrella from my hand, but I'm faster, pulling it back before she can take it from me. "I fucked up, Kav. I saw my brother after almost two years, and then I heard you laughing, and—"

"You heard me *laughing?*" she repeats, enunciating the word and making me feel even more idiotic than I already do at my admission.

"Yes, I heard you laughing and . . ." I huff, pinching the bridge of my nose. "I don't know, I just thought . . . I thought—"

"That what? That I'd run off with him, too? So you came charging in like a bull?"

Her words jolt me and I'm tongue-tied for a moment. "You know?"

"Doesn't everyone who works for you? I mean, you keep his office locked up like it's radioactive, you stiffen at the sight of him, and avoid any mention of him. Yes, Hudson, I know enough." She pauses. "I know that some of the staff went with him, as did . . ." she clears her throat, "as did your girlfriend."

"She's not my girlfriend now." Those words leave my lips faster than I thought possible.

"Okay." Kavi shifts on her feet, her orange boots sprinkled and muddy from her stroll.

I take the platter from her hands because it looks uncomfortable and heavy. "I'm sorry. Again. Forgive me?"

She wraps her arms around her chest, and I try my best not to drop my eyes to the way her breasts lift under her blazer. I try, but fail. "I'll think about it."

I nod. "That's fair. Perhaps there's something I can do to hurry you along?"

Her gaze shifts to her right before she bites the corner of her lip. I can't take my eyes off the movement and that tiny diamond I've become so fucking fascinated with. "Well, I was coming to grab dinner at this bakery. You could join me."

My brows draw up. "Ah, so you weren't running away from your monstrous boss. You were merely getting dinner."

She tilts her head. "Let's not misconstrue; I was most *definitely* running away from my monstrous and *beastly* boss, but I was also hungry. I was going to find a way to forgive him while stuffing my face with their clam chowder and sourdough bread."

"Beastly. Ouch."

She tries not to smile at my feigned hurt expression, but it breaks free, anyway. "Only in the biblical sense, not physically."

"Well, that makes me feel better." I lean in, knowing I'm flirting and knowing that she's flirting back. Knowing how much trouble we could get into if we don't stop right this second. "So, *physically*, what are your thoughts about this boss of yours?"

"My thoughts?" She holds my gaze, clearly thinking about her next words. "My thoughts are definitely not of the *good* variety."

Yeah, mine neither.

Chapter Sixteen

KAVI

"I don't know why, but I can't see you working on a fishing charter."

Hudson dips a piece of his sourdough into his bowl of chowder, popping it into his mouth before lifting a shoulder. "Sometimes it feels like a lifetime ago, and sometimes like it was yesterday."

I watch the way his long fingers hold the top of his spoon, the expensive watch around his wrist picking up the lighting from the restaurant before he scoops a bite into his mouth. He's looking down at his bowl, his thick brown lashes fluttering.

Is it normal for a woman to notice things like thick brows and curled lashes on a man? I have no idea, but it's clear that I do when it comes to *this* particular man.

He confuses me.

Like the power and strength he exudes, as compared to the soft and tender side of him—the side that apologizes and cares.

His dismissal stung. The way he tossed me aside with a rebuke in front of his brother today made me feel more insignificant than I'd ever felt around him, even as compared to the way he'd treated me on my first couple of days.

Maybe it stung more because I thought we'd come to an understanding, a mutual respect over the past few days. But with the way he spoke to me, I wondered if I'd imagined it.

Then there he was, standing under my damn umbrella, demanding—not for the first time—my forgiveness. And though I was reluctant at first, I decided that chasing me down and begging me to listen meant *something*. Sure, he was still a colossal porcupine with hemorrhoids, but at least he had the decency to acknowledge it.

And amidst all that prickliness, I glimpsed a soft heart reflecting through his eyes and embedded in his words.

So, true to form, I caved.

Again.

Because, as I was starting to realize, holding a grudge against Hudson Case has never been easy.

"I guess I just can't see you with windblown hair, wearing a weathered shirt, running around handling fishing gear." I imagine a younger version of Hudson with sun-kissed skin and freckles around his nose. "Not when, only until very recently, I hadn't seen you in anything besides a suit."

I run my spoon through my soup, letting the warmth permeating off the surface fill my senses and drown out the thoughts of Hudson in his gray sweatpants. As hungry as I am, my mouth seems to be watering with that image alone.

His responsive smirk tells me he's caught something on my face—something I wish he hadn't. He leans over the table between us. "Why do I get the feeling you'd like to see me *without* my suit?"

My cheeks heat, but I take a quick bite of my soup, hoping to hide the blush I know is creeping in. "You wish, old man. Maybe not having seen the sun in so long is doing things to your head."

Hudson tilts his head back, his eyes hooded. "There's definitely *someone* doing things to my head."

My blush deepens and I wipe the corner of my mouth with my napkin, changing the direction of the conversation before the temperature between us gets any higher. "So, both you and Jett worked on the charter together, and then he started working with you at Case Geo?"

Hudson nods, taking a deep breath as if to clear his mind of whatever it was he and his brother spoke about today. "He helped me build the company in a lot of ways, but apparently, he wanted more. We also own a restaurant together."

I squint at him. "You mean *Carl's Catch*? The one you fired me from?"

His lips twitch. "I don't know what I was thinking. Maybe I'd lost my senses after being pegged by a flying cork? Or possibly it was the cold water in my lap."

I hide my face behind my palms, cringing at the memory of the day. "Touché. It was one disaster after another when the staff decided the newbie was going to be responsible for the boss's table." I raise a brow. "Much like your staff at Case Geo, they're all a little scared of you, you know that, right?"

Hudson looks out the darkened window next to our table, watching people walk by, lights from the nearby establishments glimmering off their umbrellas. "I'm beginning to think change might be necessary."

"Change to the staff?" God, I hope he's not thinking about firing people.

He shakes his head. "No. I mean me. Jett said something similar today. I know I'm a harsh critic; clearly, not easy to please."

I gasp, feigning shock. "*You?* A *harsh* critic? Why, I would never use such foul language to describe you, Mr. Case! Especially not after the way you red-lined the entire document I sent last week, or when you told me I was 'used to accepting mediocrity' when I didn't want to pay the astronomical rent for the apartments we toured together."

He sighs, leaning back in his chair. "You're right. I'm a jerk. I'm sorry . . . again."

"Well, you're definitely improving your apology game." I smile. "We're good. Madison had already warned me about you, so I knew what I was signing up for. So, are you going to accept Jett's proposal for RCS?"

Hudson had updated me on why Jett had come by, proposing that Case Geo contract out with Jett's company for extra manpower on the project.

"What do you think I should do?"

I nibble my bottom lip. "I don't know how deep your trust issues are with Jett, nor do I know him personally, but given what I do know—through you and Belinda—I get the feeling he's not the villain you may have made him out to be in your head."

Hudson starts to say something, and I lift my hand, letting him know I'm not finished.

"I get that the way he left came as a shock for you, but he tucked his tail between his legs and showed up to see you today, didn't he? He apologized for the way things went down between you two and said he missed you—"

"Yes, but—"

"I think it's unfair of you to ask for forgiveness for your own mistakes but not allot the same to others. Especially a brother you clearly care about; someone who was a huge part of your life, someone you helped raise."

Hudson stares at me for a long moment, eyes soft. "It seems you and I have that in common . . . younger siblings we love."

I chuckle, nodding. "My brother can be a shithead, too, but no one could replace him, either."

"Tell me more about you. Have you always lived in the Bay Area?"

I shift in my seat. "Born and raised. I live in a town called Porcelain Castle, which, let me tell you, is anything but a *porcelain castle*. Most people in that town have probably never touched porcelain. So, humble beginnings and all that compared to the high-rise I live in with my boss now." I wink at him.

"My dad worked for a small utilities company for a good portion of his life, but the pay was meager at best. Mom worked, too, but again, their salaries barely covered the household expenses." I smile, running my hands down my thighs. "But the one thing we never lacked was laughter and love. I grew up with a lot of love, despite not having extravagant meals or my own bedroom for a good portion of my childhood."

Hudson listens, something I've noticed he's rather good at. "I know your dad passed away recently. What happened?"

My chest aches from a wound I know will never truly heal. "Doctors said it was sudden cardiac arrest during the night. He went to bed as normal one night, but never woke up."

Hudson frowns. "I'm sorry, Kavi."

I swirl the last bits of broth in my bowl with my spoon, blinking away the mist from my eyes. "Thank you."

Hudson leans back in his chair. "As hard as it may be for you to believe, I grew up much the same way. My mom passed away when I was young, so Dad raised Jett and me for the most part on his own. And though he had the fishing charter, there were years where we barely scraped by financially."

"Well, would you look at that?" I ask, crossing my arms on the table and smiling at him to lighten the mood. "I guess we do have a few things in common."

The corner of his mouth pulls up, not giving me the satisfaction of a full smile, of course. "I bet we have more in common than you think. It just depends on the layers you want to peel back."

I twist my mouth, thinking. "Okay, so instead of things like favorite color or music, let's go deeper. I want to know more about my cranky old boss."

He nods. "Only if you answer the same questions."

"Deal." I tap my lips, thinking about what I want to ask first. "What's the accomplishment you're most proud of in your life?"

He doesn't hesitate. "Madison. Raising her is, by far, what I'm most proud of. My dad and Jett both helped me the best they could, especially when I was attending college, but for the most part, it was just me and her."

I can't help the smile that stretches on my face, my eyes misting at the pride in his features. It's obvious how hard it must have been to raise a child as a teen, but he did it. "And she turned out perfect, Hudson. She's one of the kindest, most incredible people I've met. Not to mention, she's so smart and hard-working."

"You can tell her that she gets all those qualities from her dad the next time you see her." He winks at me, and my heart skips. "She'll love that."

"Yeah, I'll be sure to do that," I lie.

Reading my sarcasm correctly, he waves a hand at me. "Your turn."

I shrug. "My degrees, I think. As you know, going to college when things are tight at home can be challenging. But thankfully, I had a scholarship and financial aid to make it work, along with parents who encouraged me to do so."

Hudson clears his throat. "Your paintings are . . . incredible."

I smile. "You went through them?"

He looks a little embarrassed. "After the movers came, I had them set it in that room and, well—"

"I'm just giving you a hard time. I don't mind." My smile withers. "Painting saved me. It got me through some of the worst times in my life. It's also the basis of what I plan to give back to the world."

"I remember you telling Silas and," his jaw ticks, "Corbin that you wanted to work with kids who had been abused or bullied." His eyes search mine. "Is there a reason you're so specialized?"

It's my turn to look out the window, though I don't even notice the rain or the streetlamps flickering. "My experiences are entangled with my art. They're one and the same in many ways. Every painting is a diary entry. I want to teach kids that they have other means of speaking their minds, even if it's taking their anger and frustrations out on a blank canvas."

Hudson intertwines his fingers together on the table, his eyes lingering on my arm. "Are you ever going to tell me how you got that scar?"

I drop my arms, hiding my scar beneath the table. Damn, the man is way too astute for anyone's good. "Maybe one day, but not today. Anyway, it's my turn to ask *you* a question."

He smiles, letting the topic go.

"What's something you're afraid of that most people aren't?"

He circles his thumbs around each other. I can tell he has an answer to my question, but he's wondering how to phrase it. Finally looking up, he says, "Finding someone worth changing for, only for her to realize I'm not worth the trouble."

Whoa.

His unexpected vulnerability catches me off guard. Is this the same man who walks around with his heavily armored heart, wielding a razor-sharp tongue and bullet-proof standards? "I'm guessing you're speaking from experience?"

He shakes his head. "No, I haven't experienced it, and that's what scares me." He pauses. "What about you? What's something you're afraid of that others might not be?"

I swallow as familiar tentacles of unease threaten to bind me. It's not often that I open up to people. "The dark."

He has no idea how much I appreciate the fact that he doesn't laugh, that he doesn't even question it. "Is that why you have a trail of nightlights along the hall to your room?"

I huff out a humorless laugh. "I used to sleep with the lights completely on, but I manage with just nightlights now. I know there are probably children all over the world who are afraid of the dark, and most adults grow out of it—or they pretend to, at least. But of the various fears I've learned to overcome in my life, that one has been the hardest. I hate the dark."

A waiter comes to our table to ask if he can take away our empty dishes, distracting us from our thoughts. When he leaves, Hudson says, "Okay, my turn to ask."

"Okay."

"What's with all the fruit paraphernalia?" At my giggle, he continues, and I appreciate the way he's taken our conversation to a lighter place. "The earrings, the shirts, the strawberries on your bedsheets . . ."

I raise my brow again. "First, you're sifting through my artwork, and now you're inspecting my linen? You're like a cranky, modern-day Goldilocks, Mr. Case."

For the first time since our paths crossed, Hudson's cheeks turn pink, and he stumbles with his response. He looks so boyish, I'm tempted to take a picture of him. "I-I wasn't *inspecting*—"

I lift both of my hands. "Hey, you have a right to know if a black-market fruit dealer is living with you."

Hudson chuckles softly, and I almost forget what he asked me.

"A few of my happiest memories involve my childhood best friend," I say, as some of those memories flutter through my mind. "Every year, we'd coerce my parents into dropping us off at the nearby fruit orchards and pick strawberries and oranges . . . even kiwi one year. We'd walk through the orchards for hours, laughing and filling our stomachs with way more fruit than anyone should eat in a day. And if they had a little shop, I'd buy a keepsake, like a pair of earrings or a shirt, from there to remember it."

My eyes collide with Hudson's, catching a mix of something I can't quite pinpoint—tenderness or wonder, perhaps?

"What?"

He shakes his head imperceptibly. "A lifetime would be too short . . ."

My heart races for reasons beyond me. "Too short for what?"

Before Hudson can answer, the waiter reappears with our check and the moment dissipates, and I never end up hearing the rest of his sentence.

Chapter Seventeen

HUDSON

I hit Send on an email to my team with changes I'd like to see on the proposed slide deck. I'll be presenting it to a prospect in New Hampshire next week for their upcoming high-rise excavation.

It's the end of the day on Friday, and I know my team will grumble about having to work through the weekend, but it's why I pay them the big bucks. Besides, it's not my fault they didn't get this into my inbox until this afternoon.

My phone lights up on my desk with a text.

MADDY

> Hey, Pops. I'm bringing the wedding planner over to the ranch on Sunday. She wants to take a look around and get a feel for the venue and setting. Just informing you in case you were planning on staying there this weekend. Don't want you to be surprised.

ME

> I get the feeling you're telling me not to stay there this weekend.

Her response comes through a minute later.

> **MADDY**
>
> By all means, you should! We could use more input on where the peonies should go, and whether we should alternate the color of the tablecloths.

I chuckle, knowing she knows the exact response I'll be sending her.

> **ME**
>
> Yeah, I'll be sick this weekend.

> **MADDY**
>
> Speaking of tables, I have you at the one with Brie's parents, her sister, and Uncle Jett. Are you going to be okay with that? I can move him if you aren't comfortable.

I bite my bottom lip, knowing none of this has been easy on my little girl. Sure, she's not little anymore, but that'll never change in my eyes.

No matter the differences between me and Jett, he's always been a doting uncle and one of my daughter's closest confidants. It hasn't been easy for her to see the two of us on bad terms, feeling like she's been tossed in the middle with all our baggage.

Perhaps if he hadn't come to the office this week to apologize, I might have grumbled about sitting next to him, but given the sincerity of his words, the least I can do is not make a fuss.

As for his business proposal to collaborate on the RCS project? I'm taking my time deliberating on it. I emailed him yesterday to send me a proposal of what his team would be willing to sign up to do and any other stipulations. I consider that as leaving the doors open for further chat.

His words have tumbled around in my head hundreds of times over the week. It's not that I'm not aware of my high standards when it comes to my staff, but perhaps it was that he called me out for it right after he saw the way I treated Kavi, or that I'd heard it several times from people close to me, but since that day, I've made a concerted effort to be more—I shudder even thinking it—*warm* to my employees.

I even managed not to snap at someone who glanced at his phone during one of my staff meetings today. Then, I refrained from telling a group to get back to their desks when I saw them laughing in one of the kitchenettes.

I'm really turning over a new leaf in my book.

ME

> No need. I'm fine sitting beside him. Is he bringing a plus-one?

She already knows I'm not, though she's asked me to reconsider.

Besides my friends and their wives being on my ass to find someone, my daughter does the same thing. I can't count how many times she's asked me if she can set up an online dating profile for me. I've said no—not only because I'm not looking to find anything serious right now, but also because it's fucking weird to have your daughter set it up for you!

She's relentless though, so I'm positive once the wedding is off her mind, she'll be back to being a pain in my ass.

MADDY

> He is, actually. Someone named Alaria.
> They've been dating for the past few months.

Something like sorrow or remorse gnaws inside my chest as I read her text and Jett's words—*because there's nothing worse than not having the big brother you've always loved in your life*—

play back inside my head like a doleful melody. Of course, Maddy would know, given she stayed in touch with him, but if I hadn't decided to cut him off two years ago, without listening to anything he had to say, then perhaps I could have, too.

Another text comes in from her before I can respond.

MADDY

> You probably already know, but Kavi is coming, too. How are things going with her?

I run a hand over my stubble, contemplating her question. How *are* things going with my new admin? It's a question I've been pondering for a while.

We've made progress this week, getting into a decent routine, especially since our little disagreement and the subsequent dinner on Monday. We got into it again when I tried to pay for her dinner, and she told me she didn't need any more of my money than was agreed upon contractually. I told her dinners were part of the contract, as were any other expenses while she was living with me.

She then told me I was a jackass, and I decided I really liked her company. I liked it so much, I wished we could have continued talking for hours, sitting at that same table. Everything, from her upbringing to the reasons why she always had a fruit dangling from her ears, to where and how she grew up intrigued me, kept me wanting more.

It also occurred to me how much trouble I was in, given she was leaving at the end of the summer.

I've gotten used to her humming in my kitchen while she bakes and the way she leaves a trail of socks all the way to her room from the laundry room.

We generally eat together in the dining room with our laptops open, and I pretend not to watch the way she chews, or the way she licks her lips, or even the way she leans back in her chair and rubs her stomach, claiming she's stuffed before finding a way back to the kitchen for a bowl of ice cream, taking it to her art room and humming once again while she works.

I still haven't mentioned our living situation to Maddy. It's not that I can't now, but with both her and Brie under pressure with last-minute details for their wedding, the last thing I want is for Maddy to concern herself with changes to my living situation.

I don't expect her to be upset, but I imagine she'll be curious. And with that curiosity will come boatloads of questions, similar to those asked by Garrett. Questions I don't have the answers to, but questions I'll be forced to consider before I'm ready.

I'm not ready to be under that kind of magnifying glass just yet.

ME

Fine. She's not terrible at her job.

MADDY

Wow, Dad. That's like a raving 5-star review from you. You're welcome for the referral, by the way. Feel free to give me a referral bonus in the form of a lavish wedding gift.

I snort, typing out my response.

ME

Pretty sure using my farmhouse, decorating it with peonies and God-knows-what, suffices as your lavish wedding gift.

She has no idea, of course, that I have already booked a villa and flights to Mykonos for her and Brie for their honeymoon.

MADDY

> Speaking of Kavi, I have her seated on the other side, next to one of Brie's friends from college. His name is Adam, and Brie and I think they might really hit it off. He actually lives a half hour outside of Portland, so we're hoping to set them up.

I shift uncomfortably in my seat, as if I'm sitting on hot coals, my good mood plummeting with each word I read from my daughter's text.

I type a response before deleting and retyping it, trying to sprinkle in a little humor. Though, the last thing I feel is humorous as something green and grotesque unveils itself inside me.

ME

> Oh? Is she aware of your side hustle as a matchmaker?

My fingers drum an unsteady beat on my desk as I await her response, my stomach churning like a stormy sea.

MADDY

> Oh yeah. She's excited to meet him.

Yeah, I don't fucking think so.

I don't bother responding, picking up my office phone to call Kavi in before I even know what I'm doing.

Blood pumps through my veins like a turbulent river while my mind swims with the visions of some faceless asshole holding her, touching her . . .

I rise from my seat, pacing to collect my thoughts, when I hear the thumps of her boots in the hallway outside my door.

She knocks before letting herself in, her golden gaze nervously taking in the green goblin fuming back at her. "W-what's wrong?"

I ignore the way her thighs look under the too-short, light blue skirt she has on today, or the way her fucking sweet scent filters through the air, charging at me.

"Are you taking a plus-one to Maddy's wedding?" I ask through thinned lips.

Her dark brows knit. That was not the response she was expecting. "What?"

"She said you weren't taking a plus-one."

"You asked Maddy if I was bringing anyone?" Kavi steps forward, coming to the middle of the room.

"No. She told me you were excited at the possibility of meeting some douchebag they were trying to set you up with."

Kavi's mouth opens for a moment before she closes it, likely wondering where the hell I'm going with my line of questioning. I'm wondering the same, but clearly, I can't help myself. "Okay . . . And?"

I swallow, realizing I've covered the steps between us without even realizing it. "And that's not part of our arrangement."

She scoffs. "I'm sorry, *what?*"

The muscles in my back bunch together. "It's not part of our business arrangement. Dating, bringing men over to my house to—"

Her nostrils flare, her eyes alight with defiance. "When did my dating life become a part of this arrangement? When did *you* decide you had any say in it?"

I step forward, eliminating the inch of space between us. "Since you said yes to moving in with me."

"A decision I had little sway in," she retorts, her mouth forming a tight line.

"I never held a gun to your head, Kavi. You could have simply said no."

She looks at me like I've lost my mind. "What the hell is

your problem? Why are you acting like a lunatic again?"

I lean down, my eyes locking with hers. "My problem is that I will not allow assholes you decide to sleep with into my home."

Kavi looks murderous for a moment, silently glaring at me before a derisive laugh escapes her. "No problem! No one I choose to sleep with will be over at your house . . ." she turns around, looking over her shoulder, "because I'll be at *theirs*."

Before she can take a step forward, I grasp her wrist and turn her around so her chest crashes into mine. My words are minced, my glare deadly. "No, you won't."

A flash of lightning dances in her irises before her lids droop over them and her fingers curl into the space between the buttons of my shirt, fisting it.

Her chest rises and falls in the same erratic way my heart seems to thrum. "Yeah?" she whispers. "And how do you plan to stop me, Mr. Case?"

With a growl, I drag my fingers through the side of her head before grasping a chunk of her wavy hair in my fist. I pull so her chin lifts, her kiwi-shaped earrings dangling gently over her neck. Her luscious mouth with that gem sparkling over her upper lip opens, as if waiting for me. "No plan, only a promise to."

Her soft breath fans my lips, making my cock stiffen painfully inside my pants. "Sounds to me like you're all talk, old man . . ."

This fucking girl.

Without another thought, I slam my mouth to hers, silencing her and pouring every ounce of my irritation into a punishing kiss.

A growl rattles inside my chest as I taste her for the first time. She tastes exactly the way she smells—sweet and tempting, like all the things I could get addicted to.

Like all the things I *shouldn't* get addicted to.

Her lips are soft and plump, moving in time with mine, as our mouths open and our tongues meet.

Her rogue hands climb up my chest, one grasping the hair at the nape of my neck, the other tightening over my shoulder while orange fingernails dig into my shirt.

Something carnal and free hums inside me as I plunge my tongue deeper into her mouth, coaxing a soft moan from her. Our tongues tangle, our chests heave, and our mouths claim, desperately, hungrily.

With a groan, she pushes up on her toes and I pull her hips against mine, letting her feel the way my dick strains for her.

Kavi's eyes are closed, her head tilted to give me access, and God, she feels good in my arms. So fucking good and intoxicating, I wonder if I'd even been alive before this.

I angle her face as our tongues seek more, and she wiggles and mewls against me while I practically hold myself back from dragging her to my desk and fucking her senseless.

She pulls on my hair, opening her mouth wider, letting me take and give. I coast my hand up her waist, brushing my thumb over her breast, and swallow the whimper that escapes her.

Fuck, she is going to ruin me. Destroy me.

My walls, my guard, my every attempt at self-preservation.

She'll leave a trail of wreckage in her path.

I drag my hand up to her neck, feeling her warm skin against mine. Her pulse races under my fingertips, similar to the way my blood rushes through my body, going south. Jesus, I could drown in her; I could asphyxiate and die right here, and I wouldn't be sorry.

I take her mouth brutally, mercilessly, as my hand settles into her midnight hair. I tilt her head the other way, my mouth working against hers, unsure if I'm even breathing. I had no idea how ravenous I was for her all this time.

Maybe it wasn't such a bad idea to hire her as my temp. Maybe this was the most brilliant thing I've ever done.

Reaching a point where we both need to take a breath, but not wanting to let go, I pull away from her, loving the way her mouth immediately forms a frown. Her lips are pink, bee-stung from my kiss and my scruff running over her soft skin, and fuck, if they don't make me feel feral. Like I've marked her.

She lifts her lids, the air still thick between us, not stepping away from me—I wouldn't let her, even if she wanted to. Her hands are still fisting my shirt when she seems to recall where she is or what just happened, blinking rapidly. I'm only a second away from hoisting her up in my arms and pulling that skirt up over her thighs, keeping her stuck inside the fantasy she thinks she was living.

Her hands unfurl, tapping my chest. "Okay, so perhaps you've made your point clear." Her voice is hoarse and raspy, her breath still mingling with mine, when amber eyes drop down to the place where we're still attached, and she inhales a shuddered breath.

Shamelessly, my dick twitches at the sound.

I take a step back from her, though I'm working against every instinct not to, before rounding my desk and sitting back down. It's the only way I can ensure I don't fuck her within an inch of her life, right here and right now.

Turning back to my laptop and pretending to be interested in a document that could be written in Greek for all I know, I say, "I'll see you at home. Please close the door on your way out."

She stands there a moment, probably wondering what the hell just happened, before she starts to back up.

I don't have to look at her to know her hands are clasped

and fidgeting in front of her and she's nodding, even though she knows I'm not acknowledging it. "Y-yes. Okay. I'll just . . ." Her back hits the side of the open door and she winces. "I'll just head—"

She doesn't finish the sentence, rushing down the hall, while my mouth turns into the biggest smile I've had in a while.

From: Kavi <<u>specialk_jain@gmail.com</u>>
To: Nathan <<u>nathans@gmail.com</u>>
Date: June 12 4:43 PM
Subject: A place where the streets are not
marked . . .

Okay, so you're probably not going to like
what I'm about to tell you, being the
overly protective and annoying best friend
you've always been.

I kissed my boss.

There, I said it. Go ahead, tell me what an
idiot I am. Tell me you think I have no
idea what I'm doing. Tell me, because you'd
be right.

Going to have to cut this short because I'm
almost home, but I will not lie. That was

the single hottest moment of my entire
life, Nathan. Like seriously, epic beyond
words. I know you're scrunching your nose,
but I refuse to take it back. :)

Although, now I'm completely unsure of
anything and everything.

I can pretty much guess what you're going
to say, but as usual, I'll be waiting for
your response.

xoxo
-Special K

My hand trembles as I slide the key into his apartment's doorknob, a fusion of adrenaline, lust, and hysteria intermingling into an uncontrollable rush.

That kiss.

Like lightning striking a barren desert.

Like a symphony culminating into a climax.

I throw my keys into the bowl on the entryway table and find my fingers brushing against my mouth. I can still feel the assault of his lips, the graze of his stubble, and the glide of his breath across my skin.

It felt like one of those powerful, lucid dreams. The ones you wake up from in a cold sweat with your heart clutched in your palm, wondering if some part of it was real. Wondering if you somehow traveled to another dimension and lived out your wildest fantasy.

A half hour later, shockwaves still charge through my

system, as if still reeling from the fact that I'd been set alight, blindfolded, and hurled into a dark abyss—one I'll never find footing in.

How did I go from highlighting changes in project timelines one minute, to ending up with my panties sopping wet and my lips tangled with my boss's the next?

One second I was walking away, feigning confidence and throwing barbs at him, and the next, my fingers were curled in his hair just to keep myself balanced.

The way he kissed, rough and self-assured—so much like himself—has me wondering if I've ever truly been kissed before. If so, they were mere pecks in comparison to the sheer devastation he left on my lips. Like a gentle breeze compared to a tempest.

I rush to the fridge, opening the door to grab a bottle of water. I lay the bottle on my neck, trying to cool off my heated skin. You'd think I'd have gotten my heart rate back in control by now, but you'd be wrong.

I pace the kitchen for a few moments, taking a few sips of the water.

I just kissed my boss. My very moody, and incredibly hot, boss.

Holy shit, I just kissed Madison's dad!

My pacing speeds up as I consider the questions flying into my brain like a swarm of restless bees.

What does this mean? Where does one go from here?

How will I even face him again? Can anything ever go back to the way it was after this?

Setting the bottle on the center island, I lean down, propping my elbows beside it, and scrub my face with my palms. "What did you just do, Kavi?"

I'm living under the same fucking roof as the guy! I work for him, for heaven's sake! What the hell was I thinking?

What the hell was *he* thinking?

I mean, this was just as much him as it was me, wasn't it? Sure, I was goading him, but he's the one who slammed his mouth against mine.

God, I wish I had a girlfriend to talk to right now. Someone who could either tell me how stupid I was for making a move on my boss or squeal in excitement with me like a little girl.

Unfortunately, the only girlfriend I'd ever think of calling is Madison, and I can't imagine that conversation going well.

"Oh, hey Madison! So guess what? I think I felt your dad's boner today. Oh, and he kisses like a wild, hungry beast. Wanna discuss?"

She doesn't even know about my change of address.

I'd brought it up to Hudson this week while we were eating dinner, and he casually said it wasn't something she needed to know at this time. I gathered that meant he hadn't told her, but I was too scared to ask why.

Maybe he knows telling his daughter will cause awkwardness between us. Maybe he thinks it will create unnecessary complications having to explain our unconventional living situation.

Or maybe he's embarrassed by it?

Either way, I didn't want to press the issue. We'd figured out a good routine and were coexisting quite nicely as of late, and given the man was as moody as a premenstrual teenager, I wanted to avoid anything that could cause a sudden outburst and disrupt our newfound harmony.

But now I feel even more guilty about everything. How will I ever face Madison again?

Taking my water with me, I traipse to my room, feeling like I'm watching myself in an unscripted movie, where every step I take feels unpredictable and unrehearsed.

I need to talk to Hudson; we need to discuss what just happened. And the best thing would be for it to not happen again.

I mean, as life-altering as that kiss was—for me, at least— it was completely unprofessional and inappropriate. Not only is this my first real job out of college where he happens to be my boss, but above it all, he's my friend's father.

And though the rules were never stated, they shouldn't have to be. What I did feels traitorous and dishonest, selfish and deceitful.

After begging her to get me this job, I go and kiss her dad!? What would she think of me if she knew? Probably that I'm some depraved and conniving bitch out for his money or something.

God, this was all such a mistake.

So why didn't my body feel like it was when he was ravishing my lips like he'd never been thirstier? Why did I practically weep when he stepped away to go back to his computer like he hadn't just caused a flood inside my underwear?

It doesn't matter why.

The bottom line is, it can't happen again.

I'm leaving at the end of summer. I'm living with him and working for him until then. Crossing lines of professionalism will only lead to trouble, heartache, and a dead end. Not to mention, a potential rift with one of my only friends.

With those thoughts firmly set in my mind, I tread to my bathroom for a shower, determined to speak to Hudson when he gets home so we can get this whole lapse in judgment put to bed.

∾

"Can I paint something else instead of the apple you've asked us to draw?" Jojo asks, staring at her blank canvas with her hands resting on her knees while she sits on her stool. Her short ashy brown hair is tucked behind her ears.

She seems wistful today, so I make a note to talk to her after class.

"Absolutely. That's what the class is about. I just brought in the apple I painted when I was about your age as an inspiration piece, but you can do whatever you'd like. But I do want you to talk to me about what you've painted. I want to delve into your brushstrokes and the use of your colors—both give me an indication of how you're feeling."

The seven kids in my class start picking up their paintbrushes. Most have been regulars since I posted my ad for free art therapy months ago. Most come from less-than-privileged or affluent homes and need an outlet to express their feelings constructively, and this class offers them that opportunity once a week.

Fortunately, I was able to secure a small room at the high school near my mom's house, which generously allows me to host this class each Sunday without charging me, so that's been a huge boon. In fact, the school has even supported me by sending out communication to parents for this summer session.

As the kids begin painting, I look out the window, turning the silver ring on my thumb absentmindedly, wondering if Nathan read the email I sent him.

My thoughts then jump to the fact that I still need to reestablish ground rules with my boss, even if every cell in my body rejects the idea, wanting to see those rules break again and again.

Hudson never came home on Friday night. So, after staying up past eleven waiting for him, I decided to go to bed, hoping to talk to him on Saturday. But he didn't show up Saturday, either.

Nor was he there this morning.

I know he's alive, given his responses to work emails over the past two days, but it's clear he's avoiding me. And since he's flying out for a four-night business trip this afternoon to New Hampshire, it appears our conversation will have to wait.

Maybe he'll text me? Call me? Though, if that was the case, why wouldn't he have already? But I suppose I haven't, either.

I keep telling myself it's because I want to have the conversation with him face-to-face, but a nagging voice in my head says I'm a bold-faced liar and the only reason I haven't texted him is because I'm too chicken.

What would I even start with? *Thanks for playing tonsil tennis with me, but let's maybe not do that again?*

I gather, based on his silence and absence, he's regretting what happened. And though I don't regret the kiss, per se, I understand if he does.

He's always so composed, almost dispassionate about anything besides work. So, for him to lose control in such a way . . . I can't imagine he's not reeling from it, wondering how he lost control.

Or maybe he's not.

Maybe it didn't even affect him enough to matter.

Given the fact that he dated someone from the marketing department a few years ago, from what Belinda told me, maybe this isn't even a big deal to him. Maybe he hooks up with women in the office all the time.

Though, with the way he draws lines and keeps things professional with everyone, I can't imagine that being the case, either.

Whatever his reasons are, I'll make it easy for him. I'll tell him we can file our little moment off as a blip of insanity and move forward. Nothing else needs to change.

And as for my guilty conscience about Madison, it'll be my own cross to bear.

I observe Jojo as she adds a good dollop of black to the

navy on her palette before dabbing her brush into it and streaking the canvas. She's so completely consumed in her thoughts as she paints over the same stroke, creating texture, that she hasn't noticed me behind her. I'm just about to ask her if she'll stay after class for a bit to talk when Elijah raises his hand.

I chuckle. "Elijah, you don't have to raise your hand in this class. As long as you're not speaking over someone else, you can feel free to talk."

He points to my painting at the front of the class. "You always say a lot can be learned about the painter by the colors and textures they use." At my nod, he continues, "So why is your apple damaged and bruised on one side? Why are all the colors so subdued, except for the dark blue bruise on the side?"

My eyes linger on my painting, taking me back to the day so much of my life changed, the almost four hours I cried myself hoarse, hoping someone would come get me out of that dark, dank closet, wondering if I'd die in there before I was rescued.

My logical brain told me I wouldn't, that the maintenance staff would eventually come in and find me, but that's the thing about fear . . . It keeps logic hostage, clouding ratio-nality and intensifying despair.

I always loved art. I was good at it, but until that day, I was just a conformist—creating art that made others happy, coloring within the lines, and sticking to the rules.

I started painting my pain after that day, to hell with anyone else's happiness.

"That apple represents a day that, despite the blue skies outside, washed everything in gray for me. For a long time after that day, I only painted in shades of gray and brown. But this painting also represents the last day I allowed anyone to bully and bruise me. I wanted to memorialize the way I looked, the way I felt in that moment, because that's what rock-bottom looked like for me and I planned to rise from it. It took me a while, but I finally did."

A few students stare at me, wondering if I'll elaborate, but this class isn't about my pain or my past—I've had years of therapy to deal with that—it's about their needs and their trauma.

Elijah speaks again. "When did you decide to bring color back into your paintings?"

I smile, thinking about my first email to Nathan. "When I found my best friend again. It was the day I decided I didn't simply want to survive; I wanted to thrive. I wanted to live and use my experience to help others. The day I made that decision, color finally seeped back into my life."

They listen to me intently.

"Sometimes you need the gray to fully appreciate the color. Sometimes it's okay *not* to chase away the pain, the sadness, and the heaviness. It's okay to let it flow through you and express it in your own way."

I walk over to my canvases and pull out the painting I'd created a year later, showing a woman with wavy dark hair, a red and blue flannel wrapped around her waist, and orange boots on her feet, holding a half-eaten red apple as she walks into a bustling city—the Golden Gate Bridge somewhere in the background. "Because sometimes that's what it takes to find color again."

～

I CHECK my phone for the third time.

It's Thursday afternoon and, in all honesty, it's become somewhat of a routine all week. I don't know what I'm hoping for. If he hasn't messaged me all week, why would he message me now? It's painfully clear he's not interested in speaking, aside from copying me on work emails.

Just as I'm gathering my notebook to head off to yet another RCS project meeting, the elevator doors slide open, and Hudson strides out with his phone to his ear.

My heart somersaults in my chest as I run a shaky hand over my skirt unnecessarily. He's engrossed in a conversation about replacing machinery at a client site, his gaze affixed straight ahead. His free hand runs through his hair as he walks on by without stopping.

No hi, no nod of acknowledgment, not even a millisecond of eye contact.

Well, okay then.

A jagged stone lodges in my throat as I watch him disappear into his office, shutting the door behind him without so much as a single backward glance.

My shoulders slump at the obvious dismissal as I trudge to the elevator to get to my meeting.

Why did his avoidance hurt so much?

Was it because I expected him to acknowledge me in some way after sharing such an intimate moment last Friday? Was it because I thought that—at least until that moment—we were getting closer, finding commonalities, even joking around a little, and that was grounds for getting at least some sort of reaction after days of silence?

Perhaps I'm the one who's wrong here. Perhaps I'm the idiot who shouldn't have expected an insignificant kiss to be anything but that, *insignificant*.

Two hours later I'm back at my desk, about to sit down, when Hudson emerges from his office.

He looks down at his phone when he addresses me, "Can you run my suit to the dry cleaners? It's hanging in my office. And on your way back, get me a cup of coffee and one of those apple strudels from the coffee shop downstairs." He takes a step forward, stopping again. "Oh, and book my trip to Portland next week. I'll be meeting with Silas again."

Before I can even respond, he's headed down the hall into a meeting room with a few of his staff, leaving me standing there feeling like the dirt on his shoes.

An hour later, I'm back from running his errands with his coffee and pastry in hand. I head over to his office, knowing he doesn't have any more meetings on his calendar.

I knock on his door before seeing myself in, noticing him standing near the wall of windows behind his desk, hands in his suit pockets as he looks across the city. His broad shoulders, his tapered waist, and his strong thighs have me taking a moment to admire him silently before I take a calming breath and close the door behind me, locking it.

He doesn't acknowledge my presence so, accessing that part deep inside me that holds all my courage, I pace over to his desk and place his coffee and pastry on the corner before clearing my throat. "Are we just never going to talk about what happened on Friday?"

He doesn't respond, doesn't even move.

I huff out a mirthless laugh. "Right. Well, I don't know what I expected from you, but I came in here to tell you not to worry about it, in case you were. It'll never happen again. It *can't* happen again. I'm sorry about my part in crossing those lines—"

"I'm not."

His voice stuns me silent before he turns to face me, taking me in from head to toe, like he's cataloging the various parts of me.

"W-what?" I stammer, completely confused.

Eyes blazing like sapphires in a fire, he strolls over to me, covering the distance between us in a few steps. All my senses catapult and collide at once.

"I'm *not* sorry about it," he repeats.

"But—"

"All I've done for the past six goddamn days is *not* be sorry about it, despite wanting to be. All I've fucking done for the past six days is think of ways to not be sorry about it, again and again."

My mouth drops open as if my jaw has decided to take a mini vacation without informing the rest of my face. "I don't . . . I don't understand."

Hudson curls his hand around the back of my neck, those blue eyes glaring down at me. "Then let me clarify."

Giving me only a second to catch up, his mouth descends on mine, molding and melting. His lips drag over mine in another brutal kiss that's both hunger and longing wrapped into one. His warm tongue glides over the seam of my mouth, demanding access, while his left hand shifts downward, grazing my collarbone before brushing over the side of my breast.

And despite the lectures I'd given myself all week—despite the guilt and the mortification—my mouth responds, opening up like the hungry whore it is when it comes to this confounding man.

Holy crap, is this really happening again?

My eyes close on their own accord, and I lift on my toes to deepen the kiss. My fingers plunge into Hudson's silken hair as I arch into him, partly because my knees are wobbling and partly because I need him closer.

Feeling the hard muscles of his chest under his shirt, I whimper as my nipples harden to stiff peaks behind my bra while a flurry of goosebumps rise all over my body.

Good lord, the way this man kisses—rough and posses-sive, as if he's on a mission to conquer some new land or find buried treasure—leaves me gasping for breath.

And while there should be accolades given to such prowess, I don't want to think about the type of practice he's had to get to this level.

He sucks on my bottom lip, his hand fisting my hair before his tongue starts a duel with mine. I swallow his low groan, feeling the hardened bulge through his pants. Letting my hair go, his hand snakes down my back as if memorizing every inch of me before settling on my ass. He takes a handful of it before pulling our groins flush together.

Another rattled groan escapes him, demolishing all the sense inside me. I no longer know where, who, or why I am— nor do I care. In fact, if someone asked me to count to ten, I'd get lost somewhere around four.

My breath hitches, mind buzzing, as my skin heats up. Every atom inside me feels charged and ready to explode as Hudson kisses me ruthlessly, sending all my logic and reasoning straight into the wastebasket on the side of his desk.

I'm so dazed under the heat of his hands and the taste of his mouth, I don't even realize he's walking us backward to his chair. Bringing me down with him, he pulls me into his lap so I'm straddling him. It's a little uncomfortable, given how tight my skirt is, but that becomes a non-issue when he unzips the side, keeping his eyes closed, and bunches up the material higher on my thighs.

Our kiss continues, burning me from within with each lap of his talented and torturous tongue. My fingers dig into his scalp as I return his kiss with just as much fervor. Hudson's erection presses against my sex, and my body moves over it in time with the small gasps that release from my lips.

God, this is so not good . . . or maybe it's really good, as evident by the heat swirling in the space between my legs. With the wetness seeping out of me, I would be surprised if he couldn't smell my scent. I'm so turned on, I'm practically shaking.

Jesus, so much for all that self-talk and reaffirmations to set boundaries and be professional. One word, one touch, one kiss from this man and I'm a puddle in his lap. Almost literally.

Hudson releases my lips, still tingling and spent, before he drops his mouth to my jaw, kissing and sucking. His hand travels to my breast as his mouth drops to the column of my neck. I slant my head back to give him more access, and he nips my skin, eliciting a soft mewl from me.

"Fuck, Kav," he pants. "Tell me you're sorry about this. Say you don't want it."

I press my hands to his chest and he loosens his hold on me. A rare vulnerability dances in his otherwise wintry eyes.

"I haven't stopped thinking—" I take a quick breath, cutting myself off. I feel flustered, both wanting and not wanting him to know how I feel. "But this would be such a bad idea . . ."

He nods in agreement. "Catastrophic."

I lick my lips, nodding as well, though I'm still in a very compromising position, straddling him. In fact, I'm positive that when I get up, there will be a large wet spot on his crotch as a parting gift from me. Perhaps the thought should embarrass me, but with the various other emotions competing for first place inside, embarrassment is taking a spot near the end.

"I'm your admin, your daughter's friend, and your room-mate," I remind him, running my fingers through the hair at the back of his neck, my body clearly not in line with the words I'm trying to have him heed. "Everything would become so . . . complicated."

His stubbled jaw shifts slightly.

Good God, that salt-and-pepper stubble. How I want it between my thighs, scraping against my most delicate skin.

How is it possible this man looks this hot at forty-something, and only getting more attractive by the day?

"It could be a total mistake," he agrees.

My fingers find the gap between the buttons of his shirt, as if my brain no longer controls them, and I pull him closer. His hands round to the back of my ass as he drags me over his erection again.

My forehead lands against his and a whimper trickles out of me. I bite my bottom lip, seconds from doing something that will forever cross every boundary and obliterate all the rules. "So . . . what do you propose we do, Mr. Case? You know, since you're the boss."

Pulling out my shirt from my waistband, his hand travels under it, skating over my heated skin. He pulls down one of my bra cups before brushing a thumb over my puckered nipple. "That we make the most catastrophic mistake of our lives."

The roll of thunder outside can't drown the roar of blood rushing through my ears as I pull her shirt off and throw it to the side, clasping her nipple in my mouth.

Kavi's thighs shake around mine, a tremor strumming through her body as her hands move from my hair to my shoulders to my chest before plunging back into my hair, as if they're just as needy as her. Her head tips back, a mewl escaping her lips, as I bare down on her puckered skin. "Oh, God. Hudson . . ."

She grinds over me, her hot center pressing down against my painfully swollen cock. Adrenaline and desperation pump through me, replacing the blood in my veins. I'm pure carnal desire.

Still focused on my task, I pull down the fabric over her other breast, pinching and rolling her nipple in between my index finger and thumb. My nose brushes against her skin—soft and warm, with hints of her unique lemon and vanilla scent.

Sliding my mouth over to the nipple I'd been playing with,

I suck it while kneading her other breast. With her hips undulating over me, so needy for that friction, Kavi releases an unsteady breath, giving me an indication of the frenzy building inside her.

I wish I could say I had no intention of being in this situation, this exact scenario, with her. I wish I could say I rolled around the consequences in my head and decided that self-preservation was key to my survival.

I didn't.

Like an unexpected ray of sunshine in the middle of a storm, when the dusky clouds separate and the sun peeks through, that kiss became the only thing I thought about for six fucking days. One taste of her plush lips, and I was dying to bathe in that warmth again.

How many times did I stare at her number on my phone, my thumb hovering over the call button? How many times did I draft a text, asking if I could hear her voice, wondering if she was thinking about what I couldn't rid my mind of no matter how hard I tried?

And every time the temptation became too strong, I talked myself out of it for all the reasons she mentioned herself. She was working for me, my daughter's friend, and living under the same roof. Not to mention, she was leaving at the end of summer.

Any steps in the same direction led to the same result. Disaster.

Yet I couldn't give a damn about any of those things when I walked back into the office today.

Sure, I tried my fucking best not to meet her questioning eyes, or acknowledge her beyond what was absolutely necessary, hoping it would curb my need to touch her, hold her, kiss her again. But I couldn't have been more wrong. If anything, not being able to touch her while she was mere feet from me made my craving worse.

One whiff of her sweet scent and I was done for. I craved her like a famished wolf craves its prey.

I hadn't stopped thinking about her mouth, her hands in my hair, pulling me to her while pushing me away, like she couldn't decide what she wanted more. I hadn't stopped thinking about the sounds she made—the ones I coveted and swallowed—when our tongues tangled and danced.

I'm sure she wondered where I'd snuck off to after our first kiss last Friday, especially after telling her I'd see her at home. She was probably confused, hurt, and pissed I hadn't reached out, and I wouldn't blame her for it.

But I needed time to think, to process what had happened. I wouldn't have been able to if I'd followed her home. Because had I followed her home, I would have likely followed her to her bed, too, and that would have fucked with my mind even more than the kiss itself. So, I slept at the ranch for the weekend, then left for New Hampshire on Sunday.

Kavi arches her body into me, her hips continuing to rock over my erection, and I know we're too far gone to find the lines we'd never drawn.

But I have to make sure we're on the same page.

That this can't happen again.

Letting her nipple go, I tighten my hand around the back of her neck and bring her luscious mouth to mine again. I nip her top lip, the blunt edges of my teeth catching on her skin before sucking it between my lips. Moving to her bottom one to do the same, I groan against her. "So fucking sweet. So perfect."

Kavi trembles as I claim her in a wild and desperate kiss, ravishing her mouth. Her warm tongue wraps around mine, her overpowering sweetness making me feel like I'm being dipped in sugar.

Pulling back and disconnecting our lips, I grasp her waist

in a possessive hold. My jaw sets like hardened concrete. "This can only be a one-time thing, Kav."

Her chest rises and falls as my words sink in. Disappointment flickers across her face before she schools it, replacing her expression with a muted smile. "You mean, to get it out of our systems."

She doesn't pose it as a question, so I just nod. "We go back to the way things were after this. Are you okay with that?"

Her head bobs, despite the downturn of her mouth. "I'm okay with it if you're okay with it."

Something about her response makes me want to argue, even though it's exactly what I'd wanted from her. Perhaps it's the way she accepted it, even as the gold in her eyes lost its tinsel and varnish. Perhaps it's that I wanted her to disagree and plead, even though I was the one who proposed it.

Shoving the thoughts aside, I pick her up and sit her on my desk. Grasping the waistband of her skirt, I wiggle it over her thick thighs, tossing it in a heap with her shirt. Then I do the same with her orange boots.

Jesus Christ, she looks so fucking hot—sitting in her lacy white underwear, with her perky tits hanging out of her bra cups—that my dick wrestles against the inside of my pants, begging to be let free. He wants inside her like he's never wanted anything else before.

Running my hands over the soft span of her thighs, I nod toward her center. "Put your feet on the edge of the desk and open those legs. Let me see how drenched that pussy is for me."

Another gasp hits my ears, her eyes widening, before she does what I ask, hooking her feet on the edge and parting her legs. I'm desperate to touch her. Smell her. Taste her.

I slide the tips of my thumbs over the crease where her legs meet her center, watching her reaction through an unfiltered curiosity. Kavi pulls her bottom lip into her mouth, eyes hooded, letting out a soft whimper that begs for more. A whole lot more.

Sliding the fabric between her legs to the side with my free hand, I take in her glistening pussy. Kavi's chest heaves, her palms pressing against the table behind her as her head falls back. "Please."

Even the slightest touch has her soaking for more. *Soaking for me.*

I glide the tips of my fingers through her wet middle, parting her folds. I can practically taste her on my tongue just from her scent and the way she drips for me. "This has to be the prettiest pussy I've ever seen."

Her response is a moan accompanied by the jerky rise of her center, chasing my touch.

"Do you have any fucking idea how frustrating you've been since the moment you fell into my lap?" I ask in a harsh whisper, continuing my slow, exploratory perusal between her folds.

I recall our first meeting at the restaurant, when she dropped a glass of water in my lap before dabbing it with a napkin. As infuriated as I was, I was still fucking aroused, taking in the ass she swayed freely in the air.

"It seems all your efforts to get rid of me have failed at every turn," she retorts, groaning.

I circle my fingers around her clit, flicking it until I have her jumping under me. "You've been a pain in my ass. The literal reason my dick is constantly rock-hard."

"Mmm," she hums, eyes closed, mouth hanging open as I dip a finger into her, watching the way her pussy swallows it. "I'm going to require visual confirmation of that."

Dipping that same finger deeper, I gradually slip it all the way inside so my palm rests over her sex.

Kavi moans, a flush working up her chest.

Withdrawing my finger, I find her clit again, rubbing it before dipping down to massage her entrance while Kavi chants my name, squirming and moaning against me.

My eyes can't seem to move away from her face, mesmerized by every little flick of emotion that skates across it as I add another digit inside her. Using my thumb, I rub little circles around her nub, making her gasp.

The wet noises from my languid movements have heat crawling over my skin. I can feel the fever rising over me. "Fuck."

I pull my fingers out, bringing her juices to my lips and sucking them clean. Her head tips forward to watch me, lust swirling in her honeyed gaze. There's something so alluring, so beautiful about the contrast of her dark skin and her gold-flecked eyes. She's as hypnotizing as she is delicious.

Dipping my fingers back inside her entrance, I twist and turn them. She's dripping down my palm, widening her legs to give me room to play with her.

Bringing her wetness to my lips again, I suck off my fingers one by one. "You taste just like you smell."

Her hand fists against the table, knuckles whitening, voice pleading. "What do I taste like?"

"Like my filthiest thoughts. Like the kind of sin I'll never find redemption for."

Licking my lips, I press my fingers back inside her, watching her chest rise with every breathy gasp. I work her, turning my fingers slowly while rubbing her clit with my thumb.

She seems to like that, moaning as she grasps her breast. "That feels so good, Hudson. Please don't stop."

Pushing my fingers as far as they can go, I lean down to add my tongue to her clit. She must not have expected that—given her eyes were closed—because she jumps at the contact, moaning outright. Her hand falls to my head as she wiggles under me, her stomach contracting, her thighs trembling around my head.

My tongue swirls around her clit, sucking and licking, while my fingers fuck her, in and out, rhythmically.

Opening her legs wider, she rocks against my flattened tongue, guiding my head with her hand as I work her with my fingers, slow and deep. "Please, Hudson. Please make me come."

I want to laugh at her almost-sob, but I settle for a smile against her perfect pussy, licking and flicking it with vigorous strokes, eating her out like she's my last meal.

The sounds of her gasps, her soaking sex, and my satisfied hums fill the room. She's so fucking delicious, I could devour her for hours. I move my mouth to her folds, sucking each one and making her mewl, before going back to her little nub. I suck it until I know she's close.

Her walls tighten around my fingers the way her hand tightens inside my hair. Her thighs squeeze my head as her hips arch up and, with a groan I'll remember for as long as I live, she comes over my awaiting tongue.

I lap at her for as long as she lets me, while her labored breaths settle and her body slowly unravels under her, melting into a heap on my desk.

Her legs fall over the edge when I rise to my feet. She watches me lazily, her brown skin glistening like warm caramel under the midday sun. She isn't just beautiful; no, that would be akin to calling a perfect pearl that washed up at sea a mere pebble. She's a rarity that defies comparison.

Unbuckling my belt and unbuttoning my pants, I quickly take out a condom from my wallet before letting my pants fall to my feet. "Still wanting that visual confirmation?"

"Yes, please," she pants. "Very much so."

The head of my erection peeks out of the waistband of my boxers, rock-hard and ready to be sheathed inside her.

Dropping my boxers, I pump my cock before I lean over her, my hand next to her head.

Kavi's eyes widen and her mouth parts as she sucks in a hurried breath.

Continuing to pump my cock with one hand, I reach out and brush one of her exposed nipples with the back of my knuckle, loving the way it pebbles under my touch. I dip down to capture her mouth, tugging her bottom lip between mine before kissing her deeper. "I want to fuck you, Kav."

Her hands travel up my shoulder before one tightens at the hair at the back of my neck. "I *need* you to fuck me, Hudson."

Running my dick through her wet seam and gathering her juices around my tip, I make her hiss. Or maybe that was me. It's hard to tell, given I can't hear anything past the pounding of my heart.

I rip the foil with my teeth, gliding the condom over my length before giving her only a second's warning and thrusting into her in one go.

Kavi cries out, her back bowing, her tits hitting my chest, as her eyes roll back into her head. I lean down to bite her nipple, groaning at the feel of her around me.

She's so fucking tight, so wet, I have to give myself a second to breathe. Because if I don't, I'll fucking shoot my load right this second.

With a shiver running down my spine, I wrap my palms around the backs of her thighs and push her legs toward her chest. I watch my cock, pulling it out almost all the way before plowing forward. It's so hot—this vision of our bodies coming together—I'm at risk of catching on fire from the sight alone.

Kavi grits out my name and satisfaction rolls through me. Wanting to hear her beg for me again, I seat myself inside her before pulling out once more and doing it again.

With my eyes locked onto where we're attached, I squeeze the backs of her thighs, loving how exposed she is to me. My pelvis slaps against her thighs with each thrust as her tits bounce, making me feel feral.

"Good God, baby girl, you take my cock like your pussy was tailor-made for me." I pummel her over and over, her juices making the sweetest sounds as my cock slides in.

She lets out a breathy laugh, moaning and arching. "Well, if it wasn't before, it is now with the way you're stretching me out."

I fuck her harder, increasing my speed, making the desk slide forward as my thighs kiss hers. "And these goddamn thighs . . . I can't tell you how often I've thought about my head being buried between them."

She whines, lip in between her teeth, breathing hard through her nose.

"A. Goddamn. Vixen," I grit each word as I pump into her. "Tell me, Kav. These new skirts you've been wearing, the ones that stretch so tight over your ass and your thighs . . . Were they all to tempt me? To make me ravenous?"

She lifts, her hands finding purchase on my shoulders, her breath fanning my lips. "Looks like my plan worked. I told you I'd put your card to good use."

"You know what I'd like to put to good use?" I rasp, grabbing her mouth again in a searing kiss. "This sassy, back-talking mouth. So many times I've wanted to shut you up by shoving my cock inside it."

She clasps my bottom lip in between her teeth before letting go. "We can make that happen."

I kiss her jaw, whispering, "Not today, baby girl."

And since she knows this is a one-time agreement, not ever.

I drive into her, knowing I'm hitting that perfect spot inside her when her moans get louder. Her eyes roll backward, and I know she's getting close. I feel a trickle of sweat roll down my back under my shirt as I hammer into her with a pace I won't be able to maintain for long.

Kavi rolls her hips, creating a sensation that lodges at the base of my spine—a tingling frenzy that seems almost too much to contain. I feel her tightening around me again, so I let one of her thighs go and circle her clit with my thumb.

"Hudson!" Her orange fingernails bite into my shoulders as her walls squeeze my cock. "Oh, my God! Don't stop. Please, please, please."

I'd never stop if that was a possibility. I'd freeze this moment—her getting ready to shatter around me—filing it away as the single most erotic moment I've ever spent with a woman.

This can't be easy on her, given I'm pretty fucking big and stretching her out as far as she can go, but she's taking me like a champ, swallowing my cock whole with each thrust.

Her body starts to tremble as my thumb rubs her clit faster, my name escaping through her lips, her hair dangling down her back. She's so fucking beautiful. The stretch of her neck, her velvet skin, her breathy moans . . . all made to unravel me.

"You're doing so good, baby girl. So fucking good. Keep saying my name, keep swallowing my cock," I urge her, trying to hold my release at bay. "It's all I've dreamt of. Taking you on this desk. Kissing you, eating you out, fucking you."

Kavi gets up, throwing her hands around my neck and locking her legs at my lower back. The angle allows me to get deeper inside her.

We look into each other's eyes while I thrust into her with hard, deliberate strokes, hoping she'll feel me inside her days, months, fucking years after I'm out. Her hands cradle my jaw as she reaches up, pressing her lips to mine. We kiss and breathe each other in, our movements so tender, so raw, they feel lodged inside my chest.

I want to pull away, tell her this wasn't part of the agreement. It definitely doesn't feel the way a one-time hookup would, but I'm too far gone in the moment to do anything but let her take whatever she needs.

I kiss her as I fuck her, when I know I shouldn't do either.

My tongue explores her mouth again, her fingers brushing over my scruff, and for several long moments, we're lost in each other.

Lost, when that's the last thing we should be.

Everything collides inside me, leaving a wreckage I'll be cleaning up long after she's gone. My senses, my mind, and my will are all overpowered by a woman who seems hellbent on taking all my power.

The interruption to my daily scheduled life.

My fucking headache.

I detach my lips from hers, keeping them a breath away as we watch each other. Kavi's hands never release my jaw, her thumbs rubbing my cheek, creating havoc inside me. It's too personal, too intimate, too fucking intense, and not at all what this was supposed to be.

Her walls tense around me and I grip her hips in a brutal hold, my fingers digging possessively into her ass. I can't tear my eyes from her no matter how hard I try, knowing everything is getting blurred—my vision, my feelings. The fucking lines.

When I slowly pull out and plunge in deeper—once, then twice—Kavi clamps down on me, releasing a long moan while her mouth forms an 'O'. "Hudson, I'm . . . Oh, God . . ."

Her eyes squeeze shut as her orgasm rolls through her, spurring my release. I jerk my hips forward a few more times without finesse. My body quakes, crumbling around her, as my lengthy groan fills the room and my dick fills my condom for what feels like hours.

"*Fuck*, Kav." My forehead lands on her shoulder as I heave in lungfuls of breaths, letting the shock waves pass through my body. Her fingernails drag down my back gently before I place a kiss on her shoulder blade. "Fuck me, that was . . ."

I don't have the words. No words would do it justice, anyway.

Lifting my head a few silent moments later, I let my eyes trail over her beautiful face, lingering on the stud on her lip. Her lazy smile punches me hard in the gut, and I steel myself from pulling her into another kiss.

Because doing so might mark the beginning of my end.

A few days later, my phone buzzes on my nightstand and I reach for it, tossing aside the *EarthPulse* magazine I was reading on my bed. It's not like I was retaining any of it anyway, since my mind was elsewhere.

> **BELINDA**
>
> <Photo of baby Evelyn Sky>

> **BELINDA**
>
> Guess who's here! Eight-and-a-half pounds of sweetness.

A smile stretches across my face as I take in the cherub cheeks and golden curls of a very sleepy baby in the arms of her mom, Belinda's soft gaze smiling down at her in awe.

> **ME**
>
> She is really sweet. You sure she's yours?

> **BELINDA**
>
> I've often wondered the same about Madison.

I quickly type out a congratulatory response to her, getting out of bed, not bothering to put my sweatpants on over my boxers.

It's past eleven—Kavi is likely already asleep—but I can't help wanting to give her the news, in case Belinda hasn't texted her already. I could tell her in the morning, of course, but given that I've barely gotten a few minutes alone with her since our rendezvous in my office last Friday, I'm antsy to see her.

I hadn't spoken more than a few words to her this morning when she walked into the kitchen as I was drinking my first cup of coffee. I thought about going back to my room for a T-shirt to wear over my sweatpants, but then she practically tripped over herself and ran into the countertop while she gawked at my chest. That's when I decided I liked her reaction too much to cover up.

Perhaps I'd just walk around the house bare-chested from now on.

Avoiding my eyes, she asked me how my trip was while buzzing around the kitchen, packing cheese scones for the office. I leaned against one of the counters watching her. I'd just gotten back last night after a three-day business trip, and we hadn't spoken much aside from work-related topics. Though I won't deny I was keeping tabs on her.

Per my instruction, Aaron had urged her to let him drive her to work every morning, and my shopper, Tina, had asked for Kavi's shopping list—given nothing was noted on the list I kept in the kitchen. Unsurprisingly, the stubborn mule I was living with refused, saying she was more than capable of taking care of herself.

I'd also sent her a message a couple of days ago to check in.

ME

Are we okay?

Now, I'm not generally one to read in-between the lines, but I got this strange sense she was trying to wave over any personal conversations.

KAV

Yes. Why wouldn't we be? Also, Aaron's mom is in the hospital. I've sent flowers on your behalf.

And when I asked her to drive back home with me today after work, she told me she needed to go to the grocery store. I countered, letting her know I was happy to drive her there, but she refused. I can't help thinking it was her way of avoiding being in a confined space with me. And that thought annoyed me as much as it relieved me.

I open my bedroom door just as my mind warns me to let things lie. *Maybe her creating distance is for the best.* Except, when it comes to the woman sleeping down the hall from me, it seems my mind has little control over my actions.

Throughout my time away from her, I found myself looking off into space more times than I care to count. *Me.* A man so consumed with work, I barely had time to breathe, found myself consumed with something—*someone*—else entirely.

Ever since she left my office that night, giving me the best sex of my life, I've felt depleted somehow—altered and redesigned in a way. As if a toxin had settled into my bloodstream, slowly siphoning out who I used to be, leaving traces of itself in every molecule.

And while the sex was phenomenal, that wasn't the only reason she was on my mind day and night since.

It was that fucking last kiss.

The one where she cradled my face and looked into my eyes as if she was trying to find her way into my damn soul. The way her fingers brushed my skin and her lips touched mine.

I run a frustrated hand down my face, filling my cheeks with air and letting it out. I get laid all the ways to Sunday, and what's the thing that has me spinning out into space? A damn kiss.

Am I becoming a complete sap in my old age? Who the hell else thinks about a kiss when the scent, the feel of a woman, is lingering in their system?

Keeping my feet quiet, I trek down the hall toward the other side of the condo, where an array of nightlights illuminates the area every few feet. There's a little glow dissipating from the bottom of her door as well, and it definitely seems like she's asleep.

Deciding not to wake her, I've just turned to head back to my room when I hear the unmistakable sounds of sobbing.

My body stiffens like a soldier at attention, my ears attuned to the sound, as I listen for another few moments.

She's crying. But beyond that, she sounds like she's in pain, wincing and whining.

Is she still awake? What's she crying about? My stomach rolls at the thought of it being because of me.

But then I hear her mumble some incoherent words that have me thinking she's dreaming.

Not giving myself a chance to change my mind, I shuffle back to her room, gently swinging the door open and stepping inside.

Like fireflies twinkling under a summer sky, her room is bathed in a multitude of soft glowing colors, ranging from orange to yellow to blue from her nightlights, casting comforting shadows over the walls.

Curled into a fetal position on her bed, Kavi's arms are

wrapped around her knees and tucked into her stomach. Her restless movements have pulled her blanket off her body, leaving her vulnerable and uncovered. Even in this dim lighting, the furrow on her forehead, the way her eyes squeeze shut, gives a sense for the demons she's fighting.

"Let me out!" she pleads, kicking off more of her blanket violently. "Please. Someone let me out!"

Without hesitation, I rush to her side. My instinct to comfort her outweighs any warning bells inside my head, telling me to leave her be. Perching on the edge of her bed, I run a gentle palm over her exposed arm, sweeping her tear-soaked hair off her face.

Even in the throes of her nightmare, with her skin cool and damp and her hair disheveled, she's the most beautiful woman I've ever seen.

A knot forms inside my throat as I gently shake her. "Kav," I murmur. "Baby, wake up."

Her furrowed brows deepen as she shakes her head, hands fisting beneath her chin. "You can't do this!" She kicks the mattress, her knee knocking my hip. "Please . . . don't hurt him. I won't tell anyone. I won't . . . I won't . . ."

My chest constricts as I lower my lips to her temple, kissing it gently. Memories flood back as I recall doing the same when Maddy had nightmares as a kid. It broke me to see her be so scared, as if she felt truly alone in whatever she was facing. I loathed that feeling for her, the same as I despise it for Kavi.

"Kav, please, sweetheart." I squeeze her hip, gently jostling her. "Wake up. It's just a dream."

Her body coils under me, eyelids fluttering before blinking awake. At first she still appears to be trapped in the clutches of her nightmare—confused and withdrawn—but a gasp escapes through her lips as her eyes drag up to mine.

"Hudson?" she rasps, almost like she's wondering if she's really awake.

I shift, preparing to get up and give her more room now that I've successfully awakened her, when Kavi throws her arms around me. Before I know it, she's sliding onto my lap, burying her nose into the crook of my neck.

I'm frozen for a moment, my hands halted in the air unsurely. But slowly, as if by instinct or this innate need to protect her, I wrap my arms around her trembling form. I cradle the back of her head, brushing my lips over her temple.

Kavi's chest heaves with sobs, her fingernails biting into my bare back. "Hudson."

This time, my chest catches on fire at the desperate, yet relieved sound of my name on her lips. Wrapping her thighs around my torso, I climb to my feet, and nestle my nose into her hair. "You're okay, baby. You're safe."

She nods, keeping her tight hold on me, not objecting as I guide us out of her room.

"You're sleeping in my bed tonight," I declare to my own surprise, leading us toward her bathroom sink and unplugging the two nightlights there to take with me.

I trail a few kisses on the side of her neck as I carry her down the hall to my bedroom, holding her against my chest as if my heart is beating outside of it.

Fucking hell, what am I saying?

What am I even doing?

I don't know, but right now isn't the time to analyze it.

Flipping the comforter on my bed, I gently lay her on her back. She only loosens her arms around my neck enough for me to lift up but not detach completely. With her arms still crossed behind my neck, I gaze into those beautiful golden pools of honey.

Lifting my fingers to her face, I dab the corner of her eyes with my thumb, wiping away her lingering tears. If there is something I never wanted to witness again, it's her fucking tears. They're like spears stabbing an empty cavity inside my chest, threatening to lodge themselves there.

"I'm going to plug in your nightlights and come right back," I whisper, closer to her lips than I should be.

A moment's hesitation passes before she nods, dropping her arms to her sides.

I slide into bed a minute later, switching off the lamp on my nightstand. I only linger on the thought of what to do next for a second before my hands reach for her. Before I can stop myself, I'm pulling her to me—her chest to mine, her head tucked under my neck, and her arms crossed behind my back—combing my fingers down the strands of her silky hair. I listen to her soft breaths against the dark silence of my room.

Kavi makes circles over my skin with the tip of her finger, her smooth legs slipping between my calves. "I'm sorry for waking you."

Her lips send tremors down my spine.

"You didn't wake me."

A beat of silence passes, and I wonder if she's moved on to another thought, but then she lifts her head, seeking out my eyes. "Then . . . how did you know I was—" Her gaze shifts, not wanting to admit how I found her, in the grips of her nightmare, just minutes ago. "How did you find me there?"

"I. . ." Damn it. I try to make something up, not wanting to admit I left my room to see her, but doing exactly that. "I came to see if you were awake."

Her eyes scan my face. "You came to check on me?"

"Go to sleep." I tuck her face back into my neck, making her giggle.

She finds her way back up to stare at me again. "Were you

—" She licks her lips, her heart thumping against my chest. "Did you miss me, Mr. Case?"

"About as much as I miss my dentist," I respond, hoping my attempt at humor masks whatever this is lingering between us. "I came to tell you about Belinda."

Kavi gasps. "Oh, my God! She said she was feeling something called Braxton Hicks a couple of days ago. Did she have the baby?"

I grin down at her. "A baby girl." I reach behind me for my phone to show her the picture of baby Evelyn.

Kavi coos, holding my phone toward her. "She's perfect. I can't wait to see her. Maybe I'll visit her in the next few days."

I put my phone back, wanting to ask her if she wants kids in the future, but I stop myself. I have no business asking her that.

But for some reason, I'm curious.

She'd make a great mother—sweet, nurturing, and attentive—though there's no question the kid would be dressed in a line of interesting outfits. And for reasons I can't explain, the thought heats the inside my chest like an oven. Igniting, burning, and charring.

The thought of Kavi mothering someone else's baby makes me feel like I'm being boiled from the inside.

Kavi traces the tattoo on my shoulder with her finger, distracting me from my unwanted thoughts. "I hadn't seen your tattoo until earlier today. Is it armor?"

"Something I had done a long time ago."

"It's so intricate, reaching all the way over your heart, like it's guarding it."

I don't answer.

Little does she know, it's taking a lot more than skin-deep ink to guard what's under the surface.

"Do you have any more?"

"One of the Earth on my back."

She nods solemnly. "That makes sense."

"Are you implying the armor doesn't?"

She thinks about it, her tone wistful. "No, it makes sense, too."

The faint scent of warm vanilla fills my nostrils, and I instinctively squeeze her closer, taking a deep breath and shutting my eyes. It's truly inconvenient that she feels so good in my arms.

I reopen my eyes to scan the silent darkness. "What was your nightmare?"

She stiffens. "Just something . . . irrelevant."

I tuck a finger under her chin, lifting it. As much as I know I shouldn't urge, shouldn't get involved, or further sucked in to whatever this is between us, I can't help being curious. "You can tell me."

She sighs, relenting. "It's a nightmare I often have, unfortunately. Being locked inside a dark room, screaming for someone to let me out."

My lips curve downward, my arms tightening over her protectively. "Has something like that happened to you?"

Her forehead meets my chest again with an imperceptible but definite nod, and my hackles rise.

Why was she locked inside a room like that?

I want to ask her, probe further, but her yawn has me keeping my words fastened behind my lips. It's probably not the right time to ask anyway, seeing as she had just awakened from the same nightmare.

She takes an unabashed whiff of my chest, trailing her nose over my collarbone and making my already hard cock strain against my boxers. Everything about her is warm and soft, from the way she feels in my arms to the way she feels inside my chest.

"Do you know how much I love the way you smell?"

I chuckle softly. "I'm starting to get the idea. Plus, you told Corbin it was your favorite scent."

She stills. "You remember that?"

I run a hand through her silky hair, letting it slip through my fingers. "I remember everything." I want to end that sentence with, "when it comes to you," but I hold myself from admitting that out loud.

"Do you—" She clears her throat. "Do you remember the way that night ended?"

"Yes." I'm quiet for a few seconds.

"Did you mean what you said?"

I don't need to ask her to clarify. She means the part when I told her she was perfect. Yeah, I remember that, too.

My lips twitch. "Are you fishing for compliments, Ms. Jain?"

"What? No!" She shakes her head all too defensively. "I was just—"

"I meant every word."

I feel her smile against my skin and fuck, there's that damn warmth again.

I'm sure she can feel my erection between us—I've been stiff since I picked her up in her bedroom—but we're clearly pretending it's not there since we agreed nothing can be done about it, anyway.

It was a one-time thing, I remind myself while wondering why the hell I decided on such a cruel form of torture.

"Can I ask you something?" Her swallow is audible.

"You haven't asked for permission until now."

"After we kissed for the first time in your office . . ." She shifts, and I gather she's digging deeper for courage. "You just disappeared. Where did you go?"

"I have a ranch a few miles outside of the city. I decided I'd sleep at the farmhouse for a couple of days."

She gasps. "The location of Madison and Brie's wedding?"

I nod. "Maddy and I lived in that farmhouse for a few years when she was younger, so she has a lot of memories of it."

"Do you go there often?"

I shrug. "When I can or when I need a breather. I have someone who comes and takes care of it when I'm not there."

"You needed a breather from me."

Clearly, she focused on only a specific part of my response. She didn't state it as a question, but I gather there's one there.

"Only to realize that I liked the scent of lemons and vanilla too much to stay away from it." I bury my nose in her hair. "I guess we have that in common, too."

From: Kavi <<u>specialk_jain@gmail.com</u>>
To: Nathan <<u>nathans@gmail.com</u>>
Date: July 2 7:29 AM
Subject: Simple it's not, I'm afraid,
you'll find . . .

I have more news you're probably not going
to like, so I'm going to keep this short
because the image of your disappointed face
is just not going to help things. I'm sort
of disappointed in myself, too, so don't
worry, I've already given myself the verbal
smackdown on your behalf.

Here it goes . . .

I slept with my boss. Yes, the same guy I
told you I kissed last time.

It kind of came out of nowhere. Or maybe it

was always around us—the electricity, the
tension, and need. Maybe it's been there
since day one, but we finally acted on it.

I'll spare you the gritty details, but
things haven't been the same since. Yeah, I
know what you're thinking: Surprise,
surprise. You slept with your boss and now
he wants nothing to do with you because
he's a misogynist who probably does that to
every woman who works for him. But I fully
believe you'd be wrong to think that of
him, despite his current actions of
avoiding me.

How do I know? Well, you've always told me
I had a good sense for people.

I get the feeling he's been hurt by some of
the shit he went through with his brother
and his ex—a story for another time—and
it's made him guarded. Or maybe he knows
there's no future for us.

Either way, things are a little weird
between us, and while that saddens me, I
have no one to blame but myself. I knew
exactly what he was asking and said yes,
anyway.

Wish me luck in being able to survive
another seven weeks of this.

xoxo

Special K

L ooking at the clear skies, no one would know we'd just had weeks of relentless rain. It's refreshing to finally see birds against the canvas of blue and sunlight blanketing everything in sight after so long.

It's also a perfect afternoon to be sitting outside, holding the sweetest little bundle, swaddled like a human burrito in a pink blanket.

"She's perfect, Belinda," I say, admiring Evelyn's little nose and soft eyebrows. It's as if they were brushed on. "She looks just like you."

Belinda sits back in her patio chair with her cup of tea in hand, dressed in leggings and an oversized button-down. "Except for that hair. That's all from her dad."

"She's beautiful," Madison pipes in, peeking over my shoulder at the baby in my arms, before wandering back to sit next to Brie on the outdoor loveseat. "And so quiet."

Belinda snorts. "Yeah, that's because she's finally sleeping. The booger woke up five times last night, and let me tell you, she was not *quiet* then. She has a set of lungs that can rattle walls."

Madison, Brie, and I giggle. We'd coordinated meeting the baby so Belinda wouldn't be overwhelmed with multiple visits from us now that she had Evelyn's schedule to consider.

The three of us get into an easy conversation with Belinda, telling us about how much her life has changed over the past two weeks, groaning with a laugh when she says she can't remember the last time she properly showered.

"But I wouldn't have it any other way. Life has been turned on its head in the most satisfying way possible." Her eyes soften, watching her baby sleep, before flickering over to me. "Enough about me, though. How are things going at the office? Tell me you're still working there."

I giggle. "Still employed since the last time you checked on me a couple of days ago. Things are . . . good."

I don't mean to hesitate, but telling them that things are tense and charged every time Hudson and I are in a room together wouldn't be the most prudent answer with Madison sitting right next to me.

Not to mention, my stomach has been in knots all morning with the anticipation of seeing her. It's the first time we've hung out since I moved into Hudson's condo, and not telling her feels like a breach of our friendship.

The last time I mentioned it to Hudson, he'd said our living situation wasn't something Madison needed to know about. And now, with the fact that he made it clear we were a one-time thing, I can't imagine he'd be okay with me telling her. And I don't think it would be right to tell her without giving him a heads up.

Ever since the time in his office when he completely ravaged my body and left me deliciously bruised for days after, it's been hard to find a new normal with him. I wish I could say I was the type of woman who could walk away unaffected after he'd told me in no uncertain terms that it was a one-time only deal, but I'm not.

I'm confused, sad, and I don't know . . . hurt, in a way. I have no right to be, but I am. I'm hurt that he just wanted something for one night, as if that's all it would take to get me out of his system. I'm hurt that we can't seem to hold a conversation for more than a few minutes when we're alone. And I'm hurt that he insisted on giving me that one and only time.

I know I'm not being fair, nor am I being rational because I agreed to it when he asked me if that would be okay, but damn it, I am.

It was nice that he was out of town for the week after

because, honestly, I didn't know how to be around him anymore.

I can play the part of his admin during work, return email responses with utter professionalism and nod at the right times during staff meetings.

But what I can't do is go back to the way it was before.

What I can't do is pretend I don't remember the way his eyes brushed featherlight over my face, contradicting the way he sheathed himself inside me. What I can't do is convince my heart and mind that I don't want more.

So the morning I saw him after he came back, half-naked and deliciously sculpted—tattoos and all—I almost fell on my ass and gave myself a concussion. I tried to avoid his gaze, as if I wasn't the least bit affected by his presence, when all I could feel was him around me. His scent, the weight of his gaze, his god-like physique; he was everywhere.

I thought I had it all under control until that night, when he found me in my room in the throes of a particularly terrible nightmare.

The way he held me, calmed me, and carried me to his bed . . . The way his arms never unwrapped from my body through the night . . .

In a way, it made me feel even more disoriented than the dream itself. On one hand, I longed for his touch, happy to have any scraps of his attention. On the other, it threatened to put a crack in the heart I was trying so hard to protect.

Perhaps it's easy for him to separate what happened in his office with the protective and gentle way he held me in his bed, but it isn't for me.

Perhaps returning to an all-business tone comes naturally to him, but it doesn't to me.

Perhaps forgetting is as easy as switching off a light switch for him, but it isn't for me.

I'll never forget.

After having slept better than I had in weeks, I'd woken up in his bed that morning to find him gone, and we haven't spoken about it since.

Belinda's voice brings me out of my thoughts. "Well, I'm glad, and I hope you don't let Hudson push you around. He can be a demanding dick, but he means well." She eyes Madison over her cup. "No offense, Madison."

Madison chuckles. "None taken. I told Kavi before I referred her that my dad's no walk in the park to work for. But it looks like she's handling him just fine."

Little does she know exactly how I've handled him . . .

Hoping to hide the pink rising to my cheeks and bury my guilt, I try to take the conversation in a different direction. Though it's still about Hudson, since it seems all I want to do ever since I met the man is gather information about him like some desperate hoarder. "Has he always been this intense and single-focused on work? Like everything else is just an afterthought?"

Madison sighs. "The only times he loosens up is when he's at the ranch, riding his favorite horse—"

"He has horses?" I interrupt. When Hudson said he had a ranch, I wasn't envisioning a functional one with horses and pigs, but I guess it sort of explains his somewhat rough hands. Maybe even the few freckles on his nose.

Brie laughs, her chocolatey brown hair getting picked up by a breeze. "Oh, yeah. And no one else can handle her. Hudson's had her forever."

"She's like another daughter to him, I swear," Madison chimes in with a soft laugh. "One with more attitude than me. Dad does relax, but it's not often. It's why I've been on him to start dating again, to get himself out there."

An acrid taste fills my mouth, and I look down at the baby in my arms to avoid their gazes, hoping they don't see the way my smile withers.

Of course his daughter would want Hudson to find someone. My mom has only recently been widowed, but I worry about her in the same way. But the image of Hudson with someone—probably leggy, well-dressed, and with an IQ of one-sixty—has that bitterness curdling my stomach.

"Well, given how needy Kenna was," Belinda starts, getting a groan from Madison. "You'll have to find him someone more independent and less clingy."

Madison snorts. "And hopefully someone who won't sleep with my uncle because my dad isn't around enough. It's why Dad hasn't wanted a long-term relationship." She frowns. "He doesn't think he has enough time to offer anyone."

Is that why Hudson insisted on something for one night? Because he doesn't have time for long-term attachments?

Brie shrugs, pulling Madison into her side. "Either that or he hasn't found the right person worth offering his time to. I'd like to believe the latter."

I hold back the bitter noise itching to crawl out of my throat. Clearly, I'm not the 'right person' she's referring to.

And because I can't help it, hunting for every tiny morsel I can get, I ask, "Did he and Kenna live together?"

"No." Madison puffs out a laugh. "Let's just say, I'm lucky Dad could handle living with me for as long as he did, and I'm his daughter!" She shakes her head. "No, they didn't, and that's something that worries me for his future. Other than me, he's never lived with a woman before; I'm not even sure he remembers how to."

Jesus. My face feels like it's on fire.

"Plus, he's so private," Belinda adds. "In all the time I've worked for him, I haven't once seen his place—not even to drop off his dry cleaning."

"Well, don't let that offend you," Brie piles on. "In the five years Madison and I have been together, I only got an invitation for dinner at his house for the first time last year."

Belinda raises both her brows. "Yeah, it would take a very unique woman to break down Hudson's walls enough for him to allow her into his home and his heart. And I just don't know if someone like that exists."

As the conversation changes to updates about Brie and Madison's wedding, my thoughts stay on the previous topic.

Hudson has certainly given me keys to his home. His heart, however? I wonder if he remembers where the keys to that are.

~

"Hello?" I squint at my phone to see the name on the screen again, my voice sleep-laden and groggy. "Jojo? Are you okay?"

I'm already climbing to my feet, trying to find my bearings, when she answers. Her voice is blanketed behind the echoes of rain and thunder. "Hey Kavi," I'm positive I hear her sniffle, "I didn't mean to wake you. I'm sorry, I just . . . I just didn't know who to—"

"Jojo, I'm right here. You never have to apologize for calling me. Where are you?"

She's quiet for a moment, and all I can hear is the rain again. "In my dad's shed. He's not home. Only she is, along with her friends, and I . . . I came here to think. To get away."

Rubbing my eye with my fist, I blink at the time on my old Dr. Seuss clock—three-twenty-two AM—before turning on the lights in my room. I shuffle over to my closet to grab my raincoat, cursing myself for not talking to her after the last class like I'd intended.

One of the other students and I started chatting about something he was going through, and before I knew it, time was up. I'd convinced myself that Jojo had seemed happier since the last time we spoke, when she told me she was having trouble with her stepsister. I figured they'd worked out their differences.

"What are you thinking about?"

"I don't know." She sobs into the phone. "I just don't think it'll ever get better."

The bleakness in her voice sends chills up my arms. "Okay, okay. Can I come see you? Can you send me your address?"

"I don't want you to come here for me. It's raining and—"

"Jojo, listen to me. This is what I'm here for, okay? I gave you guys my number so you could call me, day or night. You did the right thing by calling me. Now, can you please send me your location?"

She's quiet for another beat, sniffling. "She'll see your car . . . Can you park farther away? I'll text you my address. I'm in the backyard, inside the shed."

I hang up with Jojo, knowing she wouldn't have called me unless she had no other option. Rushing down the hall bathed with the glow from my nightlights, on hushed steps, I pull on my Doc Martens in the foyer. Grabbing my keys, I pull out my phone and open the Uber app to order myself a cab. I'm interrupted mid-typing when the sound of feet shuffling on the tile has me looking up.

Hudson's hair sticks up in every direction like he's run his hands through it incessantly, and he's scowling at me like he's just caught me sneaking out. Well, he has, but his glare makes it look like I'm betraying him somehow.

It irritates me, knowing he has no right to act betrayed when I don't owe him anything but what's required for this job.

"Where are you going this late?" His voice is thick and raspy.

I swallow, looking down at my app and continuing to type in Jojo's address, knowing I don't have time to debate.

Hudson and I have been cordial ever since the night we cuddled in his bed after my nightmare, but the fact that he hasn't been around much and we still haven't talked about any of it, I still feel . . . confused. "One of my students is in trouble. She called me, and I need to get to her."

He only hesitates a moment to process what I'm saying before turning toward his room, speaking to me over his shoulder. "I'll take you."

"But . . ." I follow him on hurried steps. "Hudson, don't worry about it. I'm just going to get an Uber and—"

"Kavi." He turns around when I follow him to his closet, giving me one of his hefty, unimpressed looks. "It's not negotiable." He pulls on a T-shirt that conforms to his body, and I try not to watch the way his sinewy biceps flex while he does it. "I'm taking you wherever you need to go. It's not up for debate."

I roll my eyes but, five minutes later, I'm in Hudson's behemoth truck—one of his many vehicles, though I notice he uses this one the most—headed to find Jojo.

I chew my fingernails, looking out the rain-soaked passenger window, before turning the band on my thumb over and over. I repeat the movement a few more times when Hudson's warm hand lands over mine, his touch grounding and reassuring. He entangles our fingers, bringing my hand to rest on his thigh, and I let him.

It seems, at least for the time being, we've both silently decided to put our own issues aside for a more pressing matter.

His thumb caresses my skin. "She's going to be okay, Kav. You'll see, okay? She's going to be fine."

I nod, hoping he's right. "I just wish I'd reached out to her after class last week."

"But she reached out to you on her own. Doesn't that say

something?" He flicks a glance at me. "She trusts you. She knows you'll be here if she needs you."

I nod again, though guilt still pricks my chest.

We park one house down from Jojo's, and Hudson follows me as I make my way over to her backyard. I turn toward him. "You don't have to come with me. I'll just talk to her for a bit."

Under his umbrella, he gives me that blank stare that says he's not going to be changing his mind before nudging ahead of me to open the back gate, motioning for me to enter.

I make my way toward the dark shed, noticing none of the lights are on in the house. In fact, it seems like the entire neighborhood has lost power.

No fucking lights. Just what I needed right now.

My feet have me right in front of the shed, and I take a shuddered breath. My stomach drops and my heart races as I place my hand over the handle when the gentlest of hands squeezes my shoulder.

"I'm right here, Kav. I'll be right out here."

Tears prick the corners of my eyes, and I wonder if I'm feeling choked up because of my fear or because the man who took me out of his system in just one night is the one here with me now, seemingly understanding my fear without me having vocalized it.

Taking another breath to calm my racing pulse and remembering that I can't tell my students to face their fears when I can't face my own, I step into the dark shed.

Thankfully, my phone's flashlight is enough to illuminate the space around me and quell my churning stomach a touch.

I breathe through the feeling of being locked in a small compartment. It's so much like . . .

No. No, I'm not going there.

Forcing my intrusive thoughts away, I focus on finding

Jojo. I spot her in a corner, her head leaning back against the wall.

"Hey," I say, taking a seat next to her on the damp ground. "What's going on?" And then, noticing that her shirt and pants are covered with something wet and thick, I wave my flashlight over her with a gasp. It looks like acrylic paint. "Who did this?"

Her bottom lip trembles. "Max and her friends."

I grab her hand. "What happened?"

She wipes off her cheek before taking a deep breath. "They came into my room and broke the picture frame of me and my mom before ripping the picture inside it. Then, they mixed up a bunch of my paints and flung it all over my room. When I came in to see what was going on, they laughed and one of them threw paint on me."

"Oh, God—" My heart aches for this sweet kid. "Does this kind of thing happen often?"

Jojo shrugs. "It depends on Max's mood. Last week, she destroyed the school project I'd spent hours working on." She chuckles mirthlessly, the sound so forlorn, it lodges something rough inside my throat. "How far back do you want me to go, because this hasn't stopped since Max and I moved in together with her mom and my dad."

She continues to tell me that this seems to happen most when both the parents are away at work. And because her dad was so distraught after losing his late wife—Jojo's mom—and has finally found some happiness again with her stepmom, Jojo hasn't confided in him about the things going on in her life. Namely, her stepsister's bullying.

I squeeze her hand, remembering exactly what it was like to feel helpless. "Would it help if I were there when you talked to him? Just the three of us?"

"What if Max finds out and it gets worse? What if this puts stress on Dad and Jackie's marriage?"

"Do you like Jackie?" I ask, referring to her stepmom. "Does she treat you well?"

She nods, wiping a stray tear. "She may have given birth to a demon, but she herself is sweet. She just doesn't see what an asshole Max is. She doesn't see that I can barely get up in the morning, that I avoid being in the same room as her daughter. My dad doesn't, either." She takes another heaving breath. "I'm just scared to say anything and ruin things for my dad. He's lost so much."

"You have to, Jojo," I say solemnly, referring to her stepmother. God, my heart breaks for her. Even through her own pain, she puts her dad's happiness first. "Listen, your dad loves you, and I have no doubt he'd want to help you if you told him what was going on. And as for being scared, do you want to know something?"

She turns to me in response.

"I'm really scared of the dark. It's so impressive to me when someone can sit inside a small dark room and not let it bother them. I came in here, and that was the first thing I noticed; you were sad, sure, but you were brave. You walked out of your house and came to this shed, despite the power being out, and you called me."

I smile at her, hoping she can see how brave I think she is. "I think it takes courage to work past your fears and call someone, and I am so glad you did. Just as I know it will take a little more courage from you to bring your dad, and maybe even your stepmom, into the fold; to let them know what you're going through. We can work on next steps, but only you can make that decision."

After a few minutes of silent contemplating, with me sitting near her for support, Jojo nods, agreeing to take a chance and talk to her dad and stepmom as long as I'm there.

I pull her into a hug. "I'm so proud of you."

She manages a soft chuckle before she winces, looking down at my raincoat. "Oh no, I got paint all over your coat."

I follow her gaze. "Ah, well, you know what? I think it's going to look even better than it did before."

A half hour later, with Jojo safely back inside her house, I'm back in Hudson's truck, feeling like a mountain has been lifted off my shoulders.

I still can't believe he stood outside the shed under his umbrella the entire time I was inside, like my personal bodyguard and savior.

The fact that he didn't even hesitate to bring me here in the middle of the night, without a clue as to how long he'd have to wait for me . . .

How do I equate that to the man who's barely spoken to me over the past couple of weeks? How do I fuse that with the man who told me all he wanted was one night with me? How do I even believe he's the same irritable and demanding boss I started working for—the one who frowns way more than he smiles?

"You okay?" Hudson watches me turn the ring on my finger, one of those familiar frowns painting his features.

I give him a small smile. "Bet you didn't think you'd be taking all this on as part of our business arrangement."

His eyes stay on the road just as I slip my hand inside his. He squeezes it in that reassuring way of his, one corner of his mouth hitching up. "No. I definitely got more than I bargained for."

"Are you ready to rip up that contract and send me on my way?"

He shakes his head, almost imperceptibly, before he lifts my hand to his lips. "There's a reason it's paperless, Kav."

Chapter Twenty-Two

HUDSON

"Ready to look like the hot father-of-the-bride, big daddy?"

I lift my brow, giving her the glare she's accustomed to. "What have I told you about calling me that?"

Piper giggles, leading me to her area of the salon. "That I should say it with a moan."

I hold back my eye-roll. The woman is a shameless flirt, and if I didn't know without a shadow of a doubt that it was all harmless, luxury men's salon or not, I wouldn't drive an hour to see her almost every three weeks. This time just happens to be right before Maddy's wedding weekend.

In the five years I've been coming here, Piper and I have become friends. She's around Maddy's age and just as smart and good-natured. And while two of her best friends work alongside her as stylists, she's the only one I allow to cut my hair. But that's not a shocker, given routine and consistency could be my middle names.

Piper waves me over to the chair in front of the shampoo bowl, and after taking my seat, I take off my shoes to place my feet into the massager in front of it.

"You know the drill, big guy: head and shoulder massage, shampoo and rinse, then we cut and style your thick, beautiful hair." I hear her shuffle behind me as I get comfortable in my chair. "Want me to turn on a game or anything on T.V.?"

I shake my head. "Too bad I have to wait a few more months before hockey is back on. Did you congratulate your brother on the Stanley Cup win for me?"

Piper turns my chair so my back is to her before her fingers dig into my shoulders, working into each knot. Her brother is Rowan 'Slick' Parker, defenseman for the Boston Bolts and one hell of a hockey player. His life's been plastered all over the news lately after he proposed to his girlfriend at the last winning game where the Bolts took home the Stanley. Apparently, she used to be his physical therapist, but I don't keep up with gossip mills; I'd rather be watching the game instead.

"I did. Can't believe he won his first Stanley and gave me a future sister-in-law, all in one night!" She rolls her knuckles into a particularly tense spot on my neck, making me exhale harshly. "Your shoulders are wound up like coils, big daddy. Worse than the last time I saw you. You stressed about Maddy's wedding?"

I close my eyes, trying to loosen my shoulders the best I can, but as soon as I do, the face of my stress pops into my head.

I take another deep breath, hoping to guide my thoughts elsewhere, but it's no use.

The woman is under my skin, seeping into my bones and places I haven't ever considered letting anyone into. Places that have been vacant for far too long. Places I never wanted to fill in the first place.

But fuck if she's not anything but determined.

The way her eyes glistened when she looked up from her

phone a few nights ago when one of her students was in trouble. She was holding back tears, and it made my chest constrict like I was being wound up from the inside. I hated that look on her face. It didn't matter that I had to fly out first thing in the morning; all I knew was I'd cancel anything —stop fucking time if I had to—to get that look off her face.

Then the way she took those shallow breaths, conjuring up all her courage before walking into the shed . . .

Given the multitude of nightlights in my condo, there are clearly reasons she's scared of the dark—reasons she hasn't felt comfortable telling me—and I hate that she can't tell me. That she won't tell me.

Watching the way her hand trembled and her shoulders tightened before she opened the shed door made me want to pull her to me, lay my lips on her forehead, and convince her that I'd never let anything happen to her. Never.

But I also knew I couldn't say words I couldn't follow through on, because the fact was, she was going to be away from me after this summer and there was no point in hoping I'd be able to protect her from everything.

But fuck, I wanted to.

"You still with me, big guy?"

Piper's voice streams into my consciousness, and I open my eyes just as she turns my chair so I can lay my head back into the shampoo bowl.

"Yeah, I'm still here."

"Want to talk about what's on your mind? You know I don't charge extra for therapy." She giggles, turning on the water and adjusting the temperature.

I make some sort of non-committal response but don't answer.

What would I tell her, anyway? And where would I even start?

Aside from the fact that I haven't quite reconciled what's on my mind with how I'm feeling, I also don't know if I'm ready to bring it all to light through words.

Piper massages the shampoo into my hair, clearly not deterred by my silence. "So, are you all in your head today because of Maddy's wedding or . . .?"

I lay my hands over my stomach and close my eyes. "Or."

"Ah," she responds with a chuckle, as if my one-word response solved a mystery she'd been trying to solve. "You know, I've been waiting a long time for you to tell me about an 'or'."

"You'll be waiting a lot longer then." The spray of warm water around my head, along with the scent of the shampoo she's using, has a few of those coiled muscles relaxing around my neck.

"Oh, come on, big daddy. Don't leave me hanging. Tell me about her."

"No."

"If she's got you this wound up, she's gotta be worth it. I mean, those knots in your neck can only be loosened with a good f—"

"Piper."

"What?" She laughs. "I was going to say 'with a good frolic in the park'."

I give her a deadpan look from my position under her on the bowl. We both know damn well that wasn't what she was going to say.

Piper flashes her teeth at me, her long sandy-brown hair laying on both sides of her shoulders. "You're right. I was going to say 'a good fucking.'"

I shake my head, biting back my smile.

"What's she like?" she asks, toweling my hair after the rinse.

I'm debating on telling her that I'm not having this conversation with her when the word, "perfect," slips out of my mouth, as if it was awaiting the right opportunity to do so. Both Piper and I freeze, both of us afraid to speak for a long moment.

She unwraps the towel from my head and comes to stand in front of me with both hands on her hips. "Hudson 'Big Daddy' Case, are you in love with someone?"

My brows furrow so hard, I'm pretty sure they touch in the middle. "Most definitely not. What the hell is wrong with you?"

Piper's smile spans her lower face, her eyes glittering like a spangled sky. "Oh my hotdogs! The one and only Mr. Frown-salot is in love!"

I get off the chair and walk over to the one in front of the mirror where she'll be clipping my hair and prattling off for the next twenty fucking minutes, wondering why I even came here. "Finish cutting my hair for the last time. I'll be finding a new stylist."

"No, you won't." She snickers. Why? Because, for what-ever reason, none of the women in my life take me seriously. The fucking world might think twice about approaching me, but not the women in my life.

Including the one who I'm definitely *not* in love with.

"Now," she starts back up again once she's got the black nylon cape around my neck, "is she going to be at the wedding this weekend?" When I give her no indication of a response, she continues with her assumption. "Ah, so she is. Are you taking her as your date?"

"No," I snap, feeling a sharp searing sensation in my chest recalling the text I got from my daughter about Kavi being excited to meet Brie's friend.

The thought of Kavi meeting someone unlocked a rabid beast within me. That, and all the sass she gave me after that, led to a kiss—a world-shifting moment—I couldn't stop thinking about for days.

I turn my head, avoiding Piper's eyes in the mirror. Piper turns it back, telling me to look ahead and to hold still, pulling some hair in between her fingers and clipping it.

"Got it," she says as if she's figured it all out with my one-word response. "So, you're not taking her as your date. And I can only assume that's because either she has no idea you're into her or you're not ready for everyone else to know."

My jaw ticks. "Can you just do your fucking job?"

Piper presses the smile she's trying hard not to release between her lips. Her eyes bounce around my face in the mirror, searching. "Oh my God. Does she know?"

"No," I huff. "There's nothing to know. We just had . . ." Fuck, I feel like a prisoner under this cape.

Piper's mouth drops open, her hands freezing over me like she's already piecing it together.

I don't know why I feel the need to tell her anything more, but clearly, I have no restraint today. "We just slept together once, and it'll stay that way."

She drops the hand with scissors to her side. "But why? It's clear you like her."

My stomach sours. "She's moving at the end of the summer."

"So? That's not a reason not to see where things go."

I cup my knees under the cape and massage them with barely restrained frustration. "Can you just cut my hair already?"

Piper ignores me. "Is she bringing a date to the wedding?"

"No, but Maddy and Brie have someone for her to meet—one of Brie's friends." My molars grind, and right when I look at myself in the mirror, I see my nostrils flare. And so does Piper.

"Wait a minute . . ." She blinks rapidly, like a flickering

television. "One of Brie's friends? Maddy and Brie know her?" She pauses, and I feel the weight of her conclusions like boulders over me. So much for that shoulder massage. "How old is this chick?"

I swallow, but don't respond.

Piper squeals out a laugh, putting together whatever it is she thinks she's figured out. "Oh my goodness! If this isn't the most riveting story I've heard all day." She wipes the corner of her eye with the heel of her hand before finally getting to my hair again. "God, what I'd do to be a fly on the wall at this wedding."

"LOOKING SHARP, BUDDY!"

My friend Dev's voice has my gaze disconnecting from my admin. She's in a blush pink dress, sitting in the third row, while guests gather around her taking their seats. It's as if she doesn't realize where she is, because for the past fifteen minutes that I've been watching her from my spot at the backdoor of our farmhouse while waiting for Maddy, Kavi's done nothing but look at her hands in her lap. And I bet, though I can't see it from here, she's playing with that silver ring of hers like she always seems to do when she's thinking.

I turn to shake Dev's hand. "Good to see you, Dev."

"Killer tux and a new haircut. You sure it's your daughter who's getting married today and not you?"

Dev's an executive at his father's multi-billion-dollar tech company, positioned to be taking over as CEO in the next year or so. He's one of the most hardworking and astute people I know, and unlike many of the Silicon Valley assholes I've met over the course of my time in the Bay, he's also a solid guy—humble and possibly one of the most generous people I've ever met.

I wouldn't say he and I are as close as I am with Garrett, but Dev has always been someone I can rely on in a pinch, especially when it comes to getting objective business advice. We've always held each other in high regard and mutual admiration, which is why I make it a point to meet with him every couple of months to talk business and investments.

Incidentally, the last time we met up also happened to be the day I met Kavi, when I left my own restaurant drenched with iced water, trying to conceal both an enormous boner and a headache.

I eye Dev's perfectly-combed hair, but decide to rib him back because that's just how our friendship has been since we met at a business event years ago. "By the looks of your shaggy-ass mane, you might need to go see my hair stylist."

He barks out a laugh. "I mean, if she can work the kind of magic to make your ugly mug look halfway camera-ready, then yeah, I might need to."

"Fuck you," I say without an ounce of malice before leaning around him, realizing he's alone. "Where's Natalia?"

It's unlike Dev to come to an event like this without his long-time girlfriend. And though he's always had tongues wagging around him—what with him being one of the richest and influential men on the planet—he's been off the market for quite some time.

"Uh . . ." His shoulders sag, his lips flattening to a straight line on his face. "Natalia and I decided to part ways, unfortunately. This all happened recently, and I didn't have a chance to catch you up. I felt terrible telling Madison about the last-minute cancellation, but . . ." He clears his throat. "Both Natalia and I thought it would be best if I just attended alone."

I'm sure my widened eyes convey my surprise, but seeing my friend's chagrin, I don't press him for details. He'll tell me more when, and if, he feels the need to. "I'm sorry to hear that, man. Maddy and Brie will appreciate you being here, though."

Before anything more can be said, both Dev and I turn at the clicking of heels on the tiled floor behind us to see Maddy rushing over in her wedding dress.

Dev congratulates her, placing a kiss on her cheek, before squeezing my shoulder and making his way toward the other guests outside. My eyes, however, are affixed on my daughter.

She looks . . .

I'm at a loss for words to describe the emotion bubbling inside my chest. I've looked forward to this day for so long—to watch my little girl walk down the aisle in her wedding dress and take a leap of faith with her future life partner—but in some ways it isn't a day I was prepared for, either. I wasn't prepared for this entanglement of pride and protectiveness. This feeling of knowing I raised her to be fierce and independent, but having this instinctual concern for her wellbeing and happiness, too.

Is this what those people meant when they told me it's always a bittersweet moment for the bride's father?

I blink through the sentiment, making my eyes glassy as I take in my daughter. She's always been beautiful, whether she was in messy pigtails or muddy shorts and farm boots, but today she's shining bright enough to make a sea of stars disappear into the background.

"Oh, come on, Dad." Maddy grasps my hand, much like she used to as a little girl. Her eyes glisten, too, despite her attempt to seem unaffected. "You can't become a sap on me now. I compare you to war generals and dictators. Don't disappoint me, Pops."

"You're a little shit, you know that?" I lob back at her, my words getting caught somewhere in my throat. "But—" My own inhale of breath catches me off-guard. "You look beautiful, Maddy. Brie is a lucky girl, and let me say it once more—"

"I know, Dad." Maddy loops her arm with mine, carrying her wildflower bouquet in the other hand. "You'll find a way to lock her up behind a high-security prison for white-collar crimes if she ever breaks my heart."

"Damn right, I will. Tell her not to forget it. I love her almost as much as you, but I'd burn the world for you."

"I'll be sure to remind her." Maddy squeezes my elbow, giving me a watery but hopeful smile. "Dad, do you realize how much I want this for you, too?"

I side-eye her but don't respond, silently letting her know this isn't the conversation I want to have right now.

She squeezes the same spot on my elbow again. "I'm serious, Dad. I don't want you to be alone." At my mouth opening to defend myself, she continues, "And before you say you're not alone and you have everything you need, including your precious horse-daughter, Kansas, I want you to really consider my words. I want someone beautiful and special to know how beautiful and special my dad is. How he has the most incredible heart in the world. I want you to find someone deserving of you."

I swallow past the lump in my throat. And though I want to lighten the moment by ribbing her about being the sap she claims I am, I don't, not wanting to overlook her sincerity.

Instead, I settle for something that takes the focus off me. "Today is about you. Don't you dare think about your old pops right now."

Maddy wipes the corner of her eye with the back of her hand. "I know it's about me, but you've always made everything about me. You've done everything for me, Dad; given me the love of both . . ." She sniffles, trailing off, though we both know what she was going to say. "I just want to be on the other side one day, giving my dad away, too."

I tap her hand on my elbow, not wanting to prolong this conversation. Thankfully, the music starts right then, and

Brie's nieces walk down the aisle, throwing flowers in each direction.

My gaze lands first on Brie, standing in front of a flowery wedding arbor, wearing a white, one-shoulder suit. Her face lights up as her eyes connect with her bride, her chest swelling with pride and affection.

As I walk my daughter down the aisle in what feels like a surreal moment in my life, my gaze once again searches for the woman it often searches for, especially as of late. I see her turned to the aisle, watching us before her golden-brown eyes collide with mine. Mine takes a detour down to her plump lips before they drag lower, to her exposed neck and shoulders, where miles of flawless tanned skin glows under the setting sun.

She's wearing a strapless pink dress, and if I've ever thought she was the most beautiful woman I've ever met, I'm changing my stance on that now.

She's the *only* woman I've ever met.

Because anyone before her has literally turned to dust in my memories.

After giving Maddy a kiss on her cheek, I place her hand in Brie's, and turn toward the front row to find my seat.

But right as I do, my gaze halts and my brows pinch as a man of perhaps thirty, with highlighted blonde tips in his otherwise dark hair, reaches for Kavi's face. He gently tugs a small stray wildflower out of a ringlet of her hair in a move that's so intimate and easy, it makes violence simmer in my blood. His hand lingers near her cheek, as if he's contemplating caressing her jaw with his thumb before he thinks better of it, and hands the flower to her with a smile.

And here's the kicker. *She fucking smiles back*—soft, shy, and appreciative—as if they'd just shared a familiar gesture.

Disconnecting from the man next to her, Kavi's eyes climb back up to find me. Her smile vanishes when she follows my line of sight, apprehension and guilt thundering over her expression.

If she wasn't able to read my thoughts before, I'm sure she can see them written all over my goddamn face now.

The asshole just wrote his own death sentence, and I'll be happy to deliver.

Chapter Twenty-Three

KAVI

This has to be a picture out of a magazine.

It's the only way to describe the setting—a large wooden barn, adorned with draped linens and glimmering fairy lights behind a wedding arbor woven with delicate wildflowers where Brie stands, waiting for her bride in a white, two-piece satin and lace jumpsuit with a luxurious detachable skirt. Even from my vantage point, seated near the front on one of the wooden benches, I can tell she's barely holding herself together.

The air is sweetly scented with blooming flowers intertwined with subtle notes of hay and damp earth. I silently thank the heavens above, for both Brie's and Madison's sakes, for sparing us from rain today. They had plans to move the wedding into the barn just in case, but thankfully, that doesn't seem likely at the moment.

Shifting my gaze to my hands, I turn the silver band around my thumb. It sounds cliche, but weddings always choke me up. Maybe it has to do with all the love floating in the air, seeping into my lungs with each breath, or maybe it's the fact that the idea of forever feels unobtainable and elusive to me. Not by choice, I've grown accustomed to walking alone, being alone. Sure, I've dated here and there, but nothing has ever lasted, nothing has ever felt permanent, like it was mine. Perhaps it's time to accept that this could be my future at every wedding—always the guest and never the bride.

There's a rustle in the seats next to me as a handsome man, a little older than me, slides between the benches and guests, asking for permission to sit next to me.

I scoot over, wondering why he had to make such a spectacle for this one seat when there are seats left at other benches. Without a seating chart, the guests were asked to sit anywhere besides the front row.

"Hey, Kavi?" he asks, leaning in.

"Yeah," I say hesitantly. "Do I know you?"

"Not yet." He juts out his hand, and I place mine against his warm palm. "But I hope you decide to. I'm Adam, Brie's friend. Maddy and Brie have told me a lot about you."

"Oh!" I say, surprised. "It's great to meet you. They said I'd be seeing you today."

Even at Belinda's house the other day, Brie had mentioned how excited she was for me to meet her friend, going on about how he was a great catch for anyone, but that because he lived in Portland, it would be nice for me to know someone before I moved there.

"I hope you don't mind me being so, uh . . . forward. I don't usually trample wedding guests to come sit by a woman, but then I saw how beautiful you were and, well, I decided I didn't care if I squashed a few to get to you."

The blush creeping into Adam's cheek has me smiling back at him. He's cute, though I'm not quite sure what to think about the blonde tips in his otherwise dark hair. But who am I to judge personal style? Most of my clothes, if not a decade old, come from thrift stores, including the beautiful chiffon pink dress I'm wearing.

Clearly, I'm not one to obsess over what I wear or the way I look. I don't follow trends or go on shopping sprees often, but even I can admit, this dress makes me feel like a million dollars.

And while Adam's compliment has my confidence boosted, it wasn't his eyes I was hoping to please.

No, the ones I was hoping for aren't clear azure skies like Adam's, they're stormy seas swelling under a wild tempest.

It's been . . . complicated between me and Hudson ever since the night in his office. And though we've found ways to skirt around talking about that night, it's been on constant replay in my head.

But aside from his gestures of friendship, like driving me to see Jojo that night and holding me after my awful nightmare, or even ensuring that I got to the wedding in a chauffeured car, he's been nothing but cordial.

But that's just it . . . It's been cordial, friendly, and professional.

But not the same.

So when Brie and Maddy encouraged me to meet Adam, I reluctantly said yes.

He lives in Portland and, from all their accounts, seems like a great guy. And though I'm not particularly looking to fill some deep void or find someone because I'm lonely, I also didn't want to come across as overly resistant. What reason would I have to be that way?

Hudson made it clear we were destined for only that one night, and I'd be foolish to expect anything more. So even though I've hoped he'd take back his words, prayed he'd see that we could be more, I've now decided I can't keep waiting any longer.

I give Adam a genuine smile and don't stop myself from

flirting back a bit. "Well, I won't deny I'm impressed by your grand entrance. I find trampling quite charming."

He flashes his teeth at me, his blue eyes gleaming. Except they don't have the gray in them I'm so enraptured with. "Now I know why Maddy and Brie like you so much." His eyes dip down to my lips before pulling back up to my eyes. "You're cute and funny. It's a hell of a trap."

I blush, unable to come up with a response quite as bold and unabashed as Adam's, feeling slightly uncomfortable under his probing gaze.

Thankfully, Shania Twain's melodic voice fills the air with "From This Moment" playing on the speakers, making guests shift in their seats and stealing Adam's attention off me toward the aisle where the little flower girls scatter petals over the short grass.

Shania's throaty voice echoes down my spine and my eyes search behind the little girls, not only for Madison, but for the man I can't stop thinking about, no matter how hard I try.

I haven't seen him in a few days, but the prospect of it has my heart racing.

Finally, a soft murmur floats through the seated guests as Madison comes into view, holding a wildflower bouquet with her wrist gently tucked inside Hudson's elbow and her gaze set on her bride.

My nose tingles at the sight of her in the stunning white gown with floral embroidery decorating the bodice. Her platinum blonde hair is pinned half up, waving gently in the breeze.

God, have I ever seen a more beautiful bride?

And as they close the distance to the front, Hudson's gaze finds mine. *Kindling, simmering, burning.* His eyes travel over my face, flaring as they dip below my lips to my exposed neck and shoulders, as if cataloging each inch. The heat inside them has my skin pebbling like it would right before a fever.

But while his eyes tell me they like what they see, his words haven't. So as much as I want to hold on to that promise in his eyes, I'd be foolish to think he'll ever tell me what I want to hear.

That perhaps we could be more.

That maybe I'm a shot worth taking.

A soft breeze has tiny flowers and pollen from nearby trees floating to the ground, permeating the air with even more of the sweet scent. I can't believe Hudson raised Madison here, in this picturesque landscape with its country barn and the fenced off area for horses. What must it have been like to have lived here with him?

"Looks like even the flowers want to get closer to you."

I turn toward Adam's awaiting smile as he lifts his hand to pull something out of my hair. His eyes find mine instead of focusing on his task as he presses a tiny flower into my hand.

I smile, disconnecting my eyes from his. "Thank you."

"You're welcome," he murmurs near my ear. "But I was hoping to get you a bigger bouquet at some point."

I chuckle softly, still feeling uneasy with his blatant verbal advances, and lift my eyes to the altar where Brie and Maddy are about to take their vows. But before my eyes can even find them, they collide with a pair of rather enraged ones—reminiscent of glacial icebergs—scowling back at me.

Actually, they're not really looking at me; they're glaring at the man next to me with the severity of thunderous clouds, ready to dole out bolts of lightning as punishment.

Looks like rain is, in fact, in the forecast for today.

∾

INSIDE THE BEAUTIFULLY DECORATED BARN, I'm still finishing up dinner with Belinda and her husband Greg on one side of me, and Adam on the other, but no matter where

I look, all I see is Hudson's impassive face—eyes that seem to be fixed on me no matter who he's speaking with.

Currently, he's talking to two men, who look rather similar, with blonde hair near the bar. One of them has his hair in a well-groomed half-bun at the top of his head.

"Those are Hudson's best friends, Garrett and Dean. They're twin brothers." Belinda leans in to tell me, clearly noticing where my gaze has been lingering. She's so fucking sharp, I have to be careful not to make my growing infatuation with the man obvious. "Dean is the one with the man-bun, and that other man with the darker hair on Hudson's other side is their other brother, Darian. They've all been friends for ages."

I nod, watching them laugh and chat when, all of a sudden, one of them—the one I assume is Garrett—looks directly back at me, following Hudson's line of sight. He smiles and, for reasons beyond my understanding, familiarity and recognition dance inside them, though I'm positive I've never seen him before.

Before I can think much of it, Hudson's brother ambles over with their drinks to join the crowd, and I watch Hudson and him clink their glasses together.

"Oh, and you recognize Jett? You said he came to the office a few weeks ago, right?"

I nod. "Yeah, he came to propose a collaboration with his company and Case Geo for the RCS project."

Belinda elbows me before taking a bite of her fish. Brie and Madison had all the food catered from Hudson and Jett's restaurant. "Between you and me, I don't think Jett was pursuing Case Geo because his company was in need of the money."

My brows furrow as I turn to her, my fork still pinched between my fingers. "What do you mean?"

"I mean, sure, their stock has dropped, but the profits

they stand to make from RCS would be a drop in the bucket for them." She shakes her head before wiping the corner of her mouth with her napkin. "This was Jett reaching out to mend the rift between him and his brother. He fucked up, and he knows it. I know he's tried to reach out to Hudson before, but Hudson has this rule—"

"What rule?"

Belinda chuckles. "Oh, you know our boss by now. He has a million rules, but this one is something about never chasing quitters. In Hudson's eyes, Jett quit on him, quit on their relationship, and fucked up while doing it. Which is why it's taken Jett two years to reach Hudson. Honestly, I'm surprised our stubborn boss actually agreed to work with him and his company." She winks at me. "But I was told it had something to do with what you said to him."

My eyes widen. "Me?"

"Yes. Hudson told me you convinced him to loosen up a bit when it comes to his ridiculous expectations of his employees, and that you lectured him about having a double standard on forgiveness, which is why he agreed to work with his brother again." She searches my face with a smile I can't quite decipher. "He didn't go into much detail because, come on, it's Hudson. The man speaks a total of fifty words a day, if that, but I'm glad you guys are getting along."

I nod, looking back at the risotto on my plate.

Are we getting along? I'm not sure what you'd call the constant electricity and the palpable weight in the air around me and Hudson when we're both in the same room. Would that be called getting along, or would that be more accurately described as skirting around an elephant neither one of us wants to acknowledge?

Still, Belinda doesn't need to know those details, so I settle for, "We are."

"He might be one stubborn mule, but he's a decent man.

One of the best I've met, to be honest, but don't you dare tell him that and inflate his ego any more than it already is. I'm just glad he's warmed up to you because hell, if you had quit, I honestly don't know how I would have trained another admin with a baby attached to my boob."

I chuckle but keep my thoughts to myself. There's no need for her to know that I actually did quit and how Hudson gave me an offer I found hard to resist, so I came back.

Nor does she need to know that, while that offer was at first about the money, I haven't given the money much thought since that day. Yes, while every extra dime is already earmarked for overdue bills, my brother's future, and my apartment deposit in Portland, it's not the reason I've continued to stay. It's never really been the reason at all.

Nor does she need to know that I'm living with him.

My gaze finds Brie and Madison across the room, eating their dinner and whispering to each other, and my stomach sinks at the thought that Madison still has no idea that I'm living with her dad.

I want to tell her. I should tell her. But would it be right of me to tell her without Hudson's consent? I wouldn't want to blindside him like that.

"So, have you found a place in Portland yet?" Adam asks, pulling me from my musings. "I could show you around if you haven't."

"I just signed a lease, actually, right outside of Portland, in Wood Village," I tell him, still feeling this strange mixture of relief and anxiety at the prospect of having found a place to live.

I knew it would only be a matter of time before I did, but any comfort I thought I'd feel after signing a lease a couple of days ago never came. I still feel like I'm in knots inside.

Adam's eyes light with excitement, disbelief. "Seriously? I

live in Troutdale, literally five minutes away from Wood Village!"

"Oh, wow! I've been meaning to ask, what do you do?"

"I actually manage a distillery in Troutdale. You'll have to come visit while I'm working; I'll show you around. All your drinks will be on the house, of course." He winks, as if hoping to entice me further with the prospect of said drinks.

I giggle. "Well, how can I say no to an offer like that?"

He puts down his fork and turns to me, his lips lifting as his eyes trace the curve of mine. "You shouldn't. But can I sweeten the pot a little more?"

I bite my bottom lip, feeling a weird flutter in my stomach. Strangely, the flutter has less to do with our exchange or the almost two glasses of wine I've consumed, and more to do with the fact that I know my boss's eyes are still on me, watching my every move.

But . . . fuck it. I take another sip of my wine, feeling emboldened.

I should feel guilty for using Adam to lure the prowling and hungry lion that is my boss, but I'm blaming the alcohol swimming inside my system for my skewed moral compass at the moment.

"Sweeten away," I say through falsely lowered lashes. "I need more sweet and less cranky-dick in my life."

Adam's brows furrow slightly, clearly not understanding my reference. "How about I take you out to dinner after my shift one day and show you around town?"

I squint at him. "So, let me get this straight. You want to liquor me up, then fill my tummy—"

"And then liquor you up some more," he adds.

"And liquor me up some more, and then take me around town?"

His smile broadens before he scrapes his teeth over his bottom lip. Even in my slightly inebriated state, I can see our faces are closer than necessary. "And maybe, possibly, hopefully after that, I could take you to my apartment to show you where I live."

I pull my glass to my lips again, taking another healthy sip, hoping to put some space between us. "Maybe . . . possibly."

I purposely don't add the 'hopefully'.

When I put my glass down, Adam reaches out to touch me for the second time this evening. His thumb finds the corner of my lip, brushing off a drop of the wine. His eyes soften as he brings his thumb to his mouth, and I'm caught off-guard at how brazen the man is, given I just met him.

Is this normal? I haven't been in the dating scene for a while, but have the rules changed? Are men this obvious about what they want?

My phone buzzes on the table, lighting up with a message, and Adam reads the name out loud.

"Who's Captain CrankyDick?"

Belinda snorts next to me. "Oh, I'm totally going to change his name to that on my phone, too." She pulls out her phone, likely doing just that. "That is fucking gold."

I pick up my phone, telling Adam it's a message from my boss.

CAPTAIN CRANKYDICK

I need to see you in the house. Upstairs, the master room at the end of the hallway. Now.

I look up and find the demanding jackass staring at me while he pretends to be in conversation with his friends.

ME:

I'm not on the clock at the moment, Mr. Case. Please revert your requests to your weekend admin. Oh wait . . . you don't have one. Guess you're SOL.

I watch as he takes his phone out of his pocket and reads my message, his nostrils flaring as he types back his response.

CAPTAIN CRANKYDICK

> Tell me, is it because of the riveting conversation you're having with the twerp who looks like a failed backup dancer for a shitty boy band?

My fingers storm over my phone as my audacity and the need to taunt heightens. If he's going to demand answers, then he'd better be ready to hear what I have to say.

ME

> I fail to see how that's your problem. In any case, yes, I've had quite the lovely conversation with him. He even asked me to dinner and then to go home with him. And since I have nothing tying me down . . .

I hit Send with more than just alcohol thrumming through my veins. I can feel each heartbeat inside them.

When I look up, I find that Hudson's gaze has darkened, but he's not focused on me. Like it was at the wedding, it's on poor Adam. Adam, who's happily slicing the meat on his plate without a care in the world. I'm starting to feel bad for the guy, unaware of his part in the crossfire, when my eyes catch movement striding toward us.

Looks like the lion's decided to come out of the shadows and pounce on his prey.

Chapter Twenty-Four

HUDSON

KAVI

I fail to see how that's your problem. In any case, yes, I've had quite the lovely conversation with him. He even asked me to dinner and then to go home with him. And since I have nothing tying me down . . .

M y hand tightens over my phone, threatening to crack it as my head lifts to find her smiling back at me. It's a smile unlike any I've ever seen from her—reckless and full of innuendo. And while my brain tells me I should reign in the rising tide inside me, my dick is hardening inside my tux.

She knows exactly what she's doing. She knows she's pushing my buttons, but what she doesn't know is those buttons are wired to set off an explosion she's not ready for.

Leaving my empty glass on the bar and my friends and brother chatting, I will my feet not to stomp as I march over to where the asshole, who looks like a Ken doll, takes a bite of his food, eyeing Kavi like she painted the fucking sky.

I've watched him all evening—sitting a little too close,

speaking a little too softly, *breathing* a little too much—and I've decided I've held back enough.

It's been an emotional day, having to officially give away my daughter, and I'm glad to have held my tongue, but I can only hold it in so much.

Sliding my hands into my pockets to hide my fists, I greet Belinda and Greg before asking them about the baby. They've left her home with Greg's mother, and Belinda thanks me for the gifts I had delivered.

I then turn my gaze to Kavi, ignoring the idiot sitting next to her. I won't look at him because doing so could lead to me lifting him by his collar and throwing him out. My desires aside, my daughter and her new bride don't need the drama.

Kavi brings her wineglass to her lips, hiding her goading smile behind it. Glad someone thinks this is funny, but it's certainly not me.

"I need to speak with you, privately."

She bats her long lashes in response to my demand. "Is it work-related because, like I said, I'm off the clock right now, Mr. Case. Plus, I don't want to miss Madison and Brie's cake cutting."

"That's my girl. You tell him, Kavi." Belinda high-fives Kavi before wincing when she sees my unamused face. "Sorry, boss."

My molars grind. "It's . . . *everything*-related, and we should be back before the cake cutting. I wouldn't want to miss it, either."

Kavi throws her napkin onto her plate, making a show of how inconvenienced she feels, and I want to slap her delectable ass right the fuck here. She is on my last nerve, but fuck, what I'd do to get her on my dick, too.

She excuses herself, walking in front of me, when I hear

Ken doll behind me, speaking to Belinda. "Wait, is Madison's dad also Captain CrankyDick from Kavi's phone?"

Belinda chortles. "Yep, that's him."

My eyes stay fixed ahead, resting on the woman who's walking fairly straight, given she practically chugged two healthy glasses of wine over the course of thirty minutes. She entered me as Captain CrankyDick on her phone? I suppose that's not too far off, given my dick has been cranky since the night it was inside her and couldn't be again.

Kavi weaves through the bustling waitstaff, traipsing toward the backdoor of my ranch house. She affords me the small mercy of following my directions in the text, climbing the stairs to my bedroom, and I trail a few feet behind her.

Perhaps I should be worried about sneaking into my bedroom with my admin. Maybe I'd be smarter to conceal the green-eyed monster rising inside me. But at this very moment, when I'm feeling both reckless and alive, I can't seem to give a shit.

Yes, Maddy could find out and ask. Yes, Belinda is probably wondering what I needed to speak to Kavi about so urgently. But I'll cross both bridges when I need to.

Right now, my priority is to figure out why I even asked Kavi to meet me here in the first place. All I knew was I had to get her away from that blonde-tipped asshole before he made the mistake of touching her again. He's lucky it's my daughter's wedding day and I couldn't make a spectacle when he had the audacity to touch her lips.

Lips that belong to me.

A smile that belongs to me and only me.

Jealousy courses through my blood and throbs in my temples. I've never been a jealous man. I've always worked hard for what I've wanted and gotten the fruits of my labor. But Kavi? Kavi's the forbidden fruit I never should have laid eyes on. Or better yet, never should have tasted.

Hands folded over her chest, she struts into my master bedroom. I follow her, locking the door behind me. Thankfully, the noise downstairs will keep our conversation private.

She whips around, her wide eyes assessing me. "What's this about, Hudson? What could be so important that you needed to speak to me right now?"

My heart beats erratically in my chest. "I won't make a habit of watching men flirt with you."

She tilts her head, perplexed. "What? What do you—"

"First Corbin, and now this asshole. You might allow them to flirt with you, but I won't."

Kavi's mouth drops open and, honestly, I stare in astonishment at my own words. I can't decide if I'm more surprised because they're finally out or because I've never felt this strange possessiveness before.

She takes a step forward, incredulity and tension evident in her posture. "What do you mean, you won't allow it? Last I checked, you didn't dictate who flirted with me. Last I checked, you couldn't control who I flirted back with." She stands toe-to-toe with me, placing a finger on the middle of my chest. "You know why, Mr. Case?"

My breath falters as she rises on her toes, bringing her face inches from mine. She's pure seduction and all the reasons I'm spiraling out of control.

Her eyes blaze with intensity and irritation, a deep gaze as endless as an abyss. "Because you made the decision not to."

My nostrils flare. "I made the decision I *had* to. The *only* decision that fucking made sense."

Her finger digs deeper into my chest. "Then what's the problem? Why are we even having this discussion?"

That's the million-dollar question, isn't it? What *is* the damn problem?

I wrap my hand around her wrist. "The problem is, I can't fucking stand it."

"What can't you stand?" she asks breathlessly. "I don't crack codes and speak in riddles for a living, Hudson. I need you to be clear. What can't you stand? That a couple of men flirted with me and you've had to watch, or that I flirted back because I'm free to do so?"

"Yes," I rasp, dipping my head to connect our eyes.

She pauses at my admission, the sharpness in her gaze giving way slightly, but her eyes are still shuttered. "This is what you wanted."

"I know," I retort.

"You haven't spoken a single word to me about that night since—"

"I know." I grip her wrist tighter, pulling her closer. My pulse races as the scent of lemons and vanilla penetrates my senses.

"You said it would be one night, one time—"

"I lied."

She blinks in shock. "What?"

"I fucking lied, Kav. I lied to you and to myself." I grasp her stubborn chin, my eyes dipping to that stud over her lip that I love so fucking much.

Her pupils dilate. "About what?"

"About not wanting you day in and out. About thinking I would only need one night, one time—" I take in a stuttered breath, cupping her cheeks. "I won't watch random assholes speak to you like they stand a chance with you, like they deserve your time."

"Do you deserve my time?" she asks with a haughty tilt of her head.

"No," I answer sincerely. "But I want it, anyway."

Her eyes search mine. "So this is about you being jealous? Is that it?"

"Yes. Yes, I'm fucking jealous," I declare, feeling lighter having let my words free.

"No." She shakes her head, her fingers wrapping around my forearms to pull my hands from her face. "I'm sorry, Hudson, but that's not good enough for me."

She steps away and my body leans forward, immediately chasing her warmth.

"I need more than your macho declarations, claiming me only when you feel threatened. I need something real." A rueful smile tips the side of her mouth. "I don't want someone who thinks he can erase me from his system after one night—"

"I couldn't erase you if I tried," I cut in, leaning against the wall behind me and dropping my hands against my thighs. "Don't you see that? Don't you fucking see that even when I am trying my best to stay away, I can't?"

I stare at her, waiting for her to grasp my admission before coming clean with another. "I didn't need you on the RCS account, Kav. Personnel changes weren't part of the contract; they happen all the time, and I could have pulled in any temp to cover the admin position for a few weeks."

She blinks, a jigsaw coming into place. "You made up a salary I couldn't say no to, a reason why I had to move in with you . . ."

"I'm not ashamed of it, and I'd do it again."

"Why? Why would you do that?"

I lift both my hands and then drop them again, along with all my restraint. It's rare for me to let myself be vulnerable, but with Kavi, no other choice exists. The gates have to be wide open or reinforced with titanium.

"Your orange boots? Your fruit-shaped earrings? Your humming while you bake?" I take a breath, though my heart feels like it's going to rocket out of my chest. "Your paintings, your nightlights, or that diamond over your lip?"

I give us both a moment to absorb my words. A moment where Kavi stares at me, dumbfounded and stunned.

I shrug. "The way hum while you bake. Your orange fingernails, your button nose, or the Dr. Seuss clock on your nightstand."

I give her a tentative smile; tentative and uncertain, when I've never felt either. But it's what this woman does to me.

"I couldn't pick just one," I finish.

After what feels like an eon—like she's just awakened from the stupor she was in—Kavi steps toward me. Her eyes are soft and searching, like she can finally see inside and wants to follow me.

I hold her gaze. "I can't shake you, Kav. I've fucking tried, but I can't."

Her hands cup my face and mine drop to her hips as she makes her way between my splayed legs. "Then don't."

My entire body warms as she lifts on her toes once again, but instead of placing her lips on mine, she sticks her tongue out and runs it over my scruffed jaw. My hands fist momentarily before I palm her ass and pull her against my hardened cock.

I look down at her pillowy breasts, practically spilling from the top of her pink strapless dress, and a low growl shatters in my chest. *I bet her nipples are pebbled underneath.* Kavi's lips drag down to my neck, where she sucks and nips at my skin, soft but sure.

I press forward, giving her a full indication of my need while my large palms knead her ass encouragingly.

She unbuttons my jacket, shoving it off my shoulders, as she trails her lips to my earlobe. Her warm tongue laves it gently before she pulls it between her teeth.

Goading, urging, provoking.

Knowing full well she's drawing out an untamed beast she'll never be able to get back into his cage.

"You gave me all those truths," she whispers, stoking

embers inside me, making me so rock-hard, I'm threatening to detonate. "Now it's time you hear a few of mine."

Her heart thunders, rattling my ribcage.

"Your plush, unsmiling lips, your storm-colored eyes . . ." she dusts her thumb over my stubble as she whispers, "and this scruff that drives me insane."

Her breaths come out in spurts as she lays a hand over my heart. "The heart you guard. The way you kiss. The way you touch. The way you smell." Her eyes bounce against mine. "I can't shake you, either, Hudson, nor do I want to."

Our mouths collide like crashing waves.

Turbulent and explosive, intense and urgent.

Kavi's fingers work fast, unfastening my bowtie and unbuttoning my shirt, as I walk her backward to my bed. Our tongues entangle and thrust as our moans crash between us. There's a ferocity in our kiss and our movements, a need to own and possess. It's not gentle or slow, not sweet and soft. It's untamed and vicious, just like the primal desire inside us. One that's finally been set free.

I'm fevered and delirious as my hands make their way to her breasts. I can't get a good handful with her dress's stiff bodice in the way. She notices, quickly unzipping the side and pulling her dress down. It pools on the floor at her ankles, exposing miles of her skin with nothing but a triangle of pink fabric between her thighs.

"Fuck," I rasp, grabbing handfuls of her perky tits and rolling her nipples between my fingers.

She moans in my mouth, her short fingernails scraping down my chest.

I don't let our lips untangle, my appetite for her intensifying with each drag of my tongue against hers. She tastes just like the first time we kissed, with an added note of wine—delicious and addictive.

"Are you on the pill?" I ask huskily against her mouth.

"Yes."

"Good. Then get your ass on the bed for me," I order, tilting my head to the bed behind her. "First, I need your pussy on my tongue, then I need it to swallow my cock."

Even as she shakes her head, as if resisting my demand, she scoots down the bed, flicking her eyes to the clock on my nightstand. "We don't have time, Hudson. They'll be cutting the cake in less than fifteen minutes."

I lick my lips. "Then you better come fast and hard, because we're not leaving until my tongue is covered with you." I look down at her heaving chest, loving the way her skin glistens, even though I've barely touched her. Trailing my fingertips down her stomach, watching her clench and whimper, I brush them over the elastic of her panties. "Open your knees. I can fucking smell you from here. Fuck, I can even taste you from here."

She drops her knees on the bed, laying back on the pillow behind her, and I pull her to the edge of the bed. Kneeling in front of her, I run the tip of my finger over the flimsy damp fabric against her center. Pulling it to one side, I use my other hand to run another finger through her slit, gathering her juices.

Kavi whimpers, seizing her bottom lip between her teeth just as she grasps the linen on my bed between her fists.

"You like that, baby girl?" I croak.

She makes me feel barbaric, uncivilized and inhuman. I've never felt a hunger like this before, a yearning so fucking deep, it threatens to brand my soul. Yes, I want to own her, possess her in a way I've never done before, but more than that, I want to surrender and lose myself to her, too.

Hell yes, I want to call her mine, but that desire wanes in comparison to the need to be hers. Only hers.

"Mm-hmm," she hums, gasping

I tug on the flimsy fabric, pulling it taut until it's practically tearing before letting it go like a rubber band against her needy center. Kavi hisses, her hips jumping up at the contact, eyes alight with lust and anger, when I do it again. The fabric snaps roughly against her slit, but this time, she mewls.

I don't have to touch her pussy to know it's dripping for me.

"Hudson," she pants.

Chuckling and knowing I don't have much time to play with her the way I want to, I tug the fabric hard, ripping it in the center. Placing my hands on her thick thighs, I lay kisses over her center. My fingertips press into her skin as I alternate kissing and blowing over her dripping center.

Kavi thrashes under me, reaching for the back of my head, a throaty plea escaping through her gritted teeth. "Please, Hudson. I need you."

Her fingers find purchase in my hair and I release another throaty chuckle at how demanding and needy she is for me. She pulls me to her, urging, begging, practically screaming.

And while I'm aware we're limited on time, I have no intention of hurrying through this part.

I run the tip of my tongue up her slit, tasting her once more the way I did on my desk. My cock thickens at the memory of fucking her that day, the way I'm about to today. The woman is nothing I could have predicted, nor seen coming. She's beautiful, no doubt, but where her beauty hooked me from day one, it's her heart, her mind, and her sass that have me ensnared. And I don't want to be let loose.

Kavi squirms under me, her hip chasing my mouth. "Yes. Yes, please," she breathes. "Ooh."

Pressing her legs down on the bed, I open her up like a flower, running my flattened tongue up her center again. Collecting her juices on my tongue, I taste every drop she gives me. She's delicious, her scent heady and so uniquely her that I want to bathe in it.

Focusing on her clit, I pull and suck it into my mouth, slurping at her like a parched traveler at an oasis. I flick and roll it with my tongue, releasing a few grunts over her wet mound. I ravage her with my tongue before sinking the tip inside her entrance.

Kavi's fingernails bite my scalp and her moan echoes inside the room. Her thighs shudder under my hands, begging to be released, and when I finally let them go, they seize my face. My entire head is clasped in her grasp, and even though I can barely breathe, I've never been this turned on. I'd die a happy man right here if I could, doing the thing I love the most—eating out my girl.

My hands clasps her outer thighs as I increase my speed, working her with my tongue to the sounds of her gasps and squeals. When I add my fingers inside her, pumping her with two digits as I continue to suckle her center, she's lost, ready to surrender to her body's bidding.

She lifts her hips, grinding her pussy against my fingers and tongue, using me to chase her pleasure, and I happily oblige.

Lick, moan. Suck, whimper. Lap, squeal. Thrust, gasp.

We repeat the process until her thighs are quivering around me; her screams an octave louder as she comes hard on my tongue. Fisting my hair between her fingers, she unravels and uncoils, sending waves of pride and satisfaction rolling through me.

And before she's even done taking her next breath, I've unbuckled my belt and dropped my pants and boxers.

Her hooded eyes roam over my tattooed chest peeking out from my unbuttoned shirt. "God, are you carved from stone, Hudson Case? You're the most gorgeous man I've ever met."

I've never vied for compliments, but it takes my ego to unparalleled heights that she likes what she sees. I drop to hover above her, one hand next to her head and the other stroking my cock. I slide my tip through her slit, making her squirm. "You know what saying things like that will make me do to you, don't you?"

She shakes her head, reaching up to meet my lips, tugging my bottom lip in between her teeth. "Tell me."

"No, I'll show you."

Lining myself up at her entrance, I thrust inside her in one go. Our groans collide between us, our eyes rolling to the back as I feel her stretch around me as she takes me fully into her body. The feeling is almost too much and not enough at the same time.

I find her mouth again, kissing her as I pull out and push back in, going so deep, I'm not sure I'll find my way back out. She widens her knees and I drive into her again, my biceps quivering from holding my weight. My jaw tightens as I piston into her, and I take as much as I give, fucking her with abandon.

Kavi moans against my mouth, feeling my balls slap the bottom of her pussy. "So fucking good."

Her hands roam over my chest, lingering on the tattoos she loves, before finding my bare back under my shirt. Her fingernails drag down my spine, and I increase my pace instinctively. She's creating a wild frenzy inside me, brewing a storm in the depths of my soul.

"Fuck, yes." I lean on one elbow and gently wrap my hand around her throat, feeling perfectly certifiable with my need for her. "God, I love this pussy so much," I pant, looking down between us where my cock bucks against her. "It's my pussy to fuck and eat. You got that?"

"Yes," Kavi hisses, fisting the pillow behind her, shoving her head back and giving me more of her neck.

"Tell me it's mine, baby girl. Tell me you're mine."

"Head to toe, Hudson," she answers without hesitation. "I'm yours."

We're fucking on my bed, only feet away from my daughter's wedding, but all I can think about is ruining this woman under me for any other man. I want to drench her with me so every inch of her remembers the way I felt. I want to course through her bloodstream and possess her soul.

I hadn't expected today to play out this way.

Yes, I've wanted her since the moment I saw her, sitting at my admin's desk in my office all those weeks ago. Hell, if I'm honest, I wanted her before that. But that today would end up with me confessing shit I hadn't even processed myself? I definitely hadn't seen that coming.

I tried so hard to stay away from her, convincing myself we had no future. But it was just a foolish attempt to outrun time, thinking I could avoid her and keep things friendly until she left. I still have no idea where this leads.

Long-term, short-term, my terms, her terms . . . who the fuck knows?

I should feel sick to my stomach, terrified of not knowing. I'm a man who thrives on control, and not having it feels like trying to maintain balance over shifting sand. I should walk away from this, rescind all the ties and accept the reality that comes at the end of this summer. I should put back all that armor and re-erect all my walls, because in the end, I know she'll shatter what's behind them in a way I'll never be able to put back together.

But I can't seem to.

As if by an undetectable thread I can't seem to cut, I feel bound to her, tangled in a way I've never been before.

And at this moment, that feels okay.

At this moment, being entangled is the only thing that feels freeing.

Tightening my hold on her neck, I drive into her with

punishing strokes, feeling my cock swell and the electricity buzz at the base of my spine. "You ready to come for me, sweet girl?"

"Yes." Kavi wraps her arms around my neck, and I drag my hand down to her clit, working it while I jackhammer into her. My mouth drops to her neck and I drag my tongue over her soft, fevered skin, nipping and sucking it.

A few more long thrusts, with the taste of her sweet skin on my lips and our hearts slamming against the other, and I feel her fracture. Her walls quiver around my cock as she sucks me in deeper before a guttural moan erupts through her lips.

My release begins soon after, and I groan into her neck, coating her insides with my cum.

We're both a tangle of shuddering breaths and sweaty limbs for several long moments until we've both caught our breaths. Her hand is buried in my hair and mine cups her breast. With my face still pressed against her neck, I flick her nipple with my thumb and make her giggle.

"Well, that was quite something." I can hear the smile in her voice.

Releasing her breast, I pull back to look at her, not feeling an ounce of guilt for my part in her disheveled state. "What do you say we do that again tonight?"

She runs the back of her fingernails against my stubble. She wasn't lying when she said she loved it. "I'd say that sounds like the best plan you've ever had. But first . . ."

"Cake," we say at the same time, chuckling.

"Hey! I was wondering when you'd be coming back." Adam stops me at the barn's entrance right as I'm rushing back. He must see the flush over my face and neck. "Are you alright? You look out of breath."

Yeah, I just got railed in every direction by my boss and the father of the bride, Adam. Suffice it to say, I'm a little out of breath.

"Fine!" I answer a little high-pitched. "Just wanted to get back before they cut the cake."

"Well, I'll walk you back to our table." Adam waves toward our table, as if I might get lost walking the twenty feet over there. "Any chance you'd save a dance for me later?"

Approaching our table, I'm about to answer him when Belinda turns around, eyeing me from head to toe and saving me from having to answer Adam. "Did you take a detour through the ranch on your way here?" she quips as I sit beside her.

Adam takes the seat on my other side.

Though I tried salvaging my hair the best I could without a brush, it doesn't look quite as put together as it did when I arrived. I'm sure my cheeks are stained red and—

"Wait." She lifts my hair off my shoulder and inspects my neck. *Shit!* "Is that a—"

With panic coursing through me, I quickly readjust my hair to cover the bite mark on my neck and shoot her a look that tells her not to complete the sentence. I flick a glance at Adam, glad he wasn't listening.

As we all rise to applaud Brie and Madison on their cake cutting, Belinda grins so wide, I'm worried she's going to hurt herself. I should have known there was no way any of my attempts at putting myself back together were going to get past her sharp gaze.

She leans over to me under the cover of the noisy room. "We have some things to discuss, don't we?"

My eyes connect with Hudson's across the room and from his slight squint, I know he can see my anxiety written all over my face.

But I've never been a good liar and, given Belinda is like an FBI agent who could make a stone spill its secrets, I'm not sure it will do me any good to try. Plus, I trust her. She may not approve of what I'm about to tell her, but she's always been sweet to me, and my champion since day one. Hopefully, she won't judge me too harshly—although I wouldn't blame her if she did. Anyway, I just can't keep it bottled in anymore. I don't know her much past our professional relationship, but having a girlfriend to talk to right now would be a relief.

Especially one who isn't related to my boss.

"It's . . . complicated," I answer, ensuring I'm keeping my voice low while watching the two brides feed each other pieces of cake to more applause and cheers. "You're the only one who knows at this point."

"Hell, yeah, it's complicated! He's your boss and your friend's dad!" She hisses her words near my ear to ensure no one is listening. "I mean, are you even going to tell Madison?"

I wince, looking at Madison across the room, smiling as

she wipes the corner of Brie's mouth with her finger before lifting it to her mouth. God, what will she think if she ever finds out? My stomach topples, and though I'd lost my buzz a while ago, I'm completely sober now, as the thought of Madison telling me I betrayed her trust sinks in. What if she never speaks to me again after she finds out? What if I lose the only real female friend I've ever really had?

"I don't think either of us has thought that far," I answer diplomatically, but the words don't feel right, even on their way out.

We haven't thought far at all because we have no idea what *far* even is. Is it to the end of summer or is it past that?

And as much as I want that answer, I also want to take things one step at a time. What if by the end of summer—only five weeks from now—whatever this is between us fizzles away?

The thought of anything fizzling away seems almost impossible, given the chemistry between us. The way he ravaged me not only a half hour ago; the way his hands seared my skin and his mouth wrapped around every needy part of me . . .

The way I can still feel him inside me . . .

My cheeks heat again, knowing I'm no longer wearing any underwear, since my last pair is now sitting inside the trash bin in his bathroom.

Could I ever see this fizzling away? This desire, this need, this combustible energy.

But what if it does for him?

"I can't shake you, Kav."

His sweet admission, along with the downward tilt of his lips as if he was preparing to have me throw his heart back in his face after he handed it to me, swims through my head.

Yeah, we have chemistry, but do we have more? It

certainly seems like it. The question is, how far were we both willing to go for it?

I know my answer . . . but is it the same as his?

"It all makes sense now." Belinda shakes her head, as if shocked it took her so long to figure out. "The way he acted around you, the fact that he never had anything solidly bad to say about you, besides that he just didn't want you working for Case Geo. The way he constantly tried to make you quit because he couldn't fire you. And the fact that he's been glaring at you all night while you talked to—" She motions with her head toward Adam. "It all makes sense now. Old CrankyDick has had it bad for you since day one. I just can't believe I didn't see it earlier!"

We get seated as Brie and Madison take to their first dance as a married couple. I smile as Brie whispers something in Madison's ear, making her throw back her head, laughing. The love between them couldn't be bigger, and it's obvious everyone in the room can feel it, too.

I lean over to Belinda, about to tell her another piece of news that'll probably have her eyes falling out of their sockets —that I'm living with Hudson—when I stop myself. Even though Belinda figured out there was something going on between me and Hudson on her own, something about telling her this bit of information before telling Madison just feels like an even bigger betrayal.

Instead, I opt for something less sensational. "Hey, I wanted to thank you for making those appointments with the apartment complexes in Portland for me to tour."

Belinda looks at me like I've grown another head. "I didn't make any appointments in Portland for you."

Surprise and disbelief tussle inside me as my eyes float back to the man whose layers I can't seem to peel back, no matter how hard I try.

After both brides dance with their fathers, and my eyes

well watching Hudson spin Madison around before kissing her on the cheek, cake is served and the newly wedded couple make their way to all the tables to greet the guests.

It's only a few minutes before they make it to our table, and I've got Madison in a warm embrace, congratulating her.

"Thank you so much for being here. You look absolutely ravishing in pink, Kavi." Madison says, holding my hand. Her platinum blonde hair is done up in a beautiful chignon. She tilts her head conspicuously at Adam, who is engaged in a conversation with Brie. "And what do you think about Brie's friend?"

"He's . . . nice." I was hoping to come up with a better adjective, but it's the best I can do, given my gaze is now connected with the man who left more than just delicious bruises all over my body not long ago. My mind feels like mush as his eyes skim down the length of me, laden with promises I'm ready to let him make.

How is it that he can make my skin heat and my heart race with nothing more than a look from all the way across a room?

"Just nice? Well, if that isn't the most compelling review." Madison giggles.

I squeeze her hand. "No, he's great. It's just . . . I'm not sure he's my type."

She leans into me. "I get it, but if nothing else, you'll have an acquaintance in Portland when you move."

I try to cover my frown with a forced smile, even if the weight on my chest suddenly feels heavier at the thought of moving. "Yeah, that's true."

As Madison and Brie move away from our table, Belinda turns to me, making sure her voice stays low. "Just a word of unsolicited advice. If whatever this is between you and Hudson continues, make sure you tell her yourself." Her eyes bounce around my face. "Madison wants nothing more than for her dad to be happy, but *this* is not something she'll expect. And though she's incredibly reasonable and cares about both of you, I'd assume she'd be hurt if she found out any other way."

Guilt pools in my stomach like it's corrosive. What will Madison think? Will she be disgusted, disappointed in me? What if she thinks I've betrayed her trust in some way.

Taking a sip of my water, I make a silent vow to tell her as soon as she's back from her honeymoon. They'll be gone for almost four weeks. If things are still progressing with Hudson, I'll have no reason not to tell her. In fact, maybe Hudson and I can tell her together.

I'm just about to take a forkful of the cake that's magically appeared in front of me when Belinda swivels her head to look at me aghast, as if realizing something for the first time. "Oh my God! I just thought of something."

My brows furrow. "What?"

Her mouth turns downwards. "You guys haven't . . ." her brows rise to meet her hairline and somehow, she still keeps her voice to a whisper, "in the office, have you?"

I pull my lips into my mouth, holding back any sort of response, to which Belinda says, "Oh, God. I'm going to have to ask maintenance to sanitize everything before I get back!"

I can't help but giggle. Despite how crazy this situation must be to her, I, thankfully, don't find any judgment from her, and that's an unexpected boon in itself.

Nudging her shoulder with mine before taking a bite of my cake, I decide to tease her, now that the cat's out of the bag. "You'll need to tell them to pay specific attention to his desk."

Her mouth practically falls to the floor while I'm practically in stitches. "Oh, you have got to be kidding me!"

"I LOVED YOUR RANCH. There was something so serene and magical about it." I brush my hand over his bare chest, outlining his armor tattoo with my index finger. I love how just that small touch has goosebumps forming over his skin. "And all those wildflowers."

"You're a fan of wildflowers," he murmurs, coasting his fingers over my arm.

We're back in his condo, our bodies still slick from our lovemaking as we lay on his bed. We ripped each other's clothes off as soon as we got home. Thirty seconds after that, he was buried inside me again, taking me from behind with my hair wrapped around his fist.

I wouldn't say I was very experienced sexually until now, but after a summer with him, I'm pretty sure I'll be able to write a thesis or the revised version of the Kama Sutra.

"They're the most honest, unpretentious, and soft-spoken flowers," I muse, delighting in how they were spread all over the grassy patches at his ranch—yellow poppies and baby blue irises.

He tilts his head, looking down at me, his blue-gray eyes less stormy than usual. "They're like you. They're the most beautiful."

Feeling a flush work up my neck, I bury my face in his chest, kissing his pec, and Hudson wraps his arms around me, kissing my forehead.

While I've worked through many of the cruel remarks hurled at me in my teen years—*Have you seen how her thighs jiggle when she walks?*—I can admit they've resurfaced at times I haven't felt my best. It's not that I dislike the way I look. I'm quite comfortable in my own skin, in fact. But with the way Hudson looks at me—lust and admiration in perfect balance—I can't help but feel . . . perfect. Desired.

"What did you say to the Justin Timberlake wannabe to

get him off your back?" Hudson's body stiffens under me and I suppress my giggle.

"Oh, you know. I just told him I'm more inclined toward the grumpy, stick-up-their-ass kind of men, preferably ones who're twenty years older than me. He was a little put off, but took the hint. He was sweet, though."

"I don't give a fuck if he was doused in syrup. He needed to get his eyes and hands off you."

I raise my head and run my lips over his delicious scruff. "I'm going to admit, jealousy looks damn good on you, old man."

He groans. "Good, because I don't share what's mine. Get used to it."

Butterflies swoop through my stomach at his words—*what's mine.*

Sure, it was nice to have the attention that Adam showed me, especially when I had no idea where Hudson and I stood —whether we stood at all. But even as the day progressed, I knew Adam wasn't who I wanted. He was sweet and good-natured, but I guess I'd recently decided sweet and good-natured weren't on my list of attributes to look for in a man.

Settling back over his chest, I inhale his scent I'm so intoxicated with. "I heard you have a favorite horse and that you might love her more than you love Madison."

His chest rumbles with a soft laugh. "Maddy told you about Kansas."

"She did, and I'm not going to lie, she seemed a little jealous of her."

Hudson chuckles again. "I'll admit one thing. I certainly loved Kansas more when Maddy was a teenager. She was the reason I went gray early."

I raise my head to look at him. "I like your gray." When his eyes just glimmer back at me, I continue, "She turned out to be an incredible woman, and that's one hundred percent because of the dad you are. Now, about this Kansas horse of yours—"

"You can't call her a horse when you meet her."

My mouth stays open as I try to process the two things he's said—the when I meet her and the I can't call her a horse. "What do you mean, I can't call her a horse?"

He gets a serious and oh-so-sexy look on his face. "She doesn't like people referring to her as a horse."

I blink at him like he's lost his marbles. "She understands English?"

"Hell, yeah, she does. And she gets offended easily. I've had her for twenty years, and the only reason she lets me ride her is because I call her my little girl. I treat her the same, too."

I grin because the man surprises me in so many ways—hiding away all that sweetness behind his gruff demeanor—I'm having trouble keeping count. "You think she'll let me ride her?"

"Not if you insult her by calling her a *horse*."

I give him a solemn look. "I promise to refer to her as a human."

He kisses my forehead. "Then I'll take you to see her next weekend."

My heart flutters inside its cage at the prospect of spending more time with him. "Why did you name her Kansas?"

"Because she didn't like being called Georgia."

I chortle, my shoulders shaking as I wonder if he even knew how funny he was.

"Madison and Brie must be on their flight to Greece by now," I muse a few quiet moments later, thinking about the entire day, the beautiful wedding, and the two brides.

I loved dancing with them until I couldn't feel my toes, taking a celebratory shot with them at the end of the night, and hugging Madison again before she left in a limo with Brie to head to the airport.

It was a perfect day, but maybe I'm feeling a little extra happy because it worked out in another unexpected way.

With him.

"Have you ever been to Mykonos before?" The timbre of his voice right near my ear has ripples of electricity traveling to my toes.

Is that normal? To be turned on by someone's voice alone?

I shake my head, sliding my bare leg over his thigh—my thick and smooth to his strong and rough. "The only place I've been outside of California is Portland . . . when I traveled with you."

Hudson pulls me back so he can look at me. "You'd never been on an airplane before that?"

"Growing up, my parents were sometimes working multiple jobs to make ends meet. Don't get me wrong, I never wanted for anything, but . . ." I shrug, "flight tickets weren't ever in the budget for us. Plus, I watched this movie where the lights on the flight were all off, and you know, the idea of sitting in a small and dark enclosed space while dangling in the middle of the sky just wasn't something I really wanted to do."

Hudson swallows, clearly considering his words. "Would you travel with me again?"

I want to tease him about making future plans with me, but I have a feeling that will clamp him up and I'm not ready to have conversations where the ending isn't clear.

One day at a time, Kavi. One day and one moment at a time.

"You're the only reason I went the first time, anyway."

He tucks a strand of my hair behind my ear, his thumb dusting my cheek before he pulls me into a kiss. Our lips explore one another, gentler and less hurried than any time before.

I cradle his face in my hands, my hair pooled on each side as I deepen our kiss and he lets me take control. There's something so satisfying, so freeing about being able to kiss the man you're falling for the way you please, without restraint, without thought.

Because you can.

Because he's yours.

I disconnect my lips from his, staring down at his beautiful eyes, well past the point he's ever let me see.

He must see the question in my gaze because he lifts to place a kiss on my lips. "What's on your mind, beautiful girl?"

His husky voice has me pulling my lip between my teeth. "I've never . . ." I drop my forehead on his chest, suddenly feeling stupid for even saying anything. My cheeks heat. "Never mind."

Hudson places his index finger under my chin and lifts my head. "You've never what? Tell me."

I look at him through my lashes. "I've never given anyone a blow job, and . . ."

His eyes darken like a moonless night, the bulge under my thigh pulsating with our intermingled breaths. "And . . ?"

"And . . ." I lick my lips, my nipples pebbling as bolts of arousal slide down my spine, pooling at my core. "I want to . . . with you."

I drag my hand down his taut abs and wrap my fingers around his shaft, tugging and stroking, making him draw in a shuddering breath.

"I want to put you in my mouth," I say, slithering down his body under the light blanket over us. "I want you to teach me what you like as you fuck my mouth."

"Jesus." I hear him say above me as I hover over his erection, loving the sight of pre-cum beading over his tip.

Sticking my tongue out, I go with what my mind tells me

to do, licking the beaded cum off the little slit on the head of his cock.

Hudson jerks under me, and I'm about to ask if I did something wrong when his hand wraps around the back of my neck. "Fuck, baby," he rasps. "That feels so good."

I do it again, rolling my tongue around his tip a few more times when he says, "Now wrap your lips over the head of my cock and suck."

I do as requested, covering the tip of his thick cock with my mouth, laving it with my tongue, and sucking. Wrapping my palm over the part of his hardened shaft not in my mouth, I stroke it up and down.

Hudson's fingers dig into my scalp, an indication that he likes what I'm doing, as I greedily lick and suck his mushroom head.

"Fuck, yes, baby girl," he hisses, widening his legs under me. "Just like that. Now, drag your tongue down the length of my cock." He rewards me with another groan when I do exactly that. "That's it. Now put me back in your mouth, all the way until I hit the back of your throat."

My center pulses with need as my juices seep out, coating my folds and thighs. Hoping to quell my own need, I drop one hand to play with my clit.

Apparently, he can tell exactly what I'm doing, even with me under the covers.

"Don't you dare touch yourself," Hudson commands, tangling my hair in his fist and pulling so I practically pop off his dick. "You don't come until it's my fingers, my mouth, or my cock in that pussy."

I groan as he shoves his dick back into my mouth, telling me exactly what I need to be focused on.

"Now suck my cock like it's the only thing you were born to do."

His words make my core throb and my mouth water. I do

exactly as he asks, working my mouth back up his veiny shaft and teasing his tip. He seemed to like that earlier. I take him all the way in until his tip hits the back of my throat and tears sting my eyes as my gag reflex kicks in.

I've never done this before, never even wanted to for anyone else, but with how sexy, sweet, and beautiful this man is, it's all I've thought about lately. My head bobs over his velvety skin, the slurping sounds from my mouth mixing with the sounds of our breaths as I continue to suck.

Hudson moans, urging me to continue, his abs and thighs flexing under me. "That's it, baby girl. So fucking good. Now, pick up the pace and play with my balls."

I roll his balls in my fingers and continue to pump him into my mouth, tasting every drop of pre-cum he rewards me.

A moan builds inside my chest as I take my lips off him and lick him from root to tip like he's a goddamn popsicle melting in the summer sun. I kiss and suck his head once more before dropping my mouth over his entire length, picking up the pace and cooing at the feel of him on my tongue.

Groaning, Hudson throws the blanket off us, tugging my hair until I'm forced to pull my lips off him. I'm just about to object when, in one fast move, he has me under him, my back on the bed.

With one hand around the front of my neck, he straddles my torso, pumping himself with hard strokes over my chest. The chords in his forearm bunch, his abs contract, and his chest tightens as he glares down at me, his eyes like polished obsidian.

I can't take my eyes off him, as if the mere thought of looking away will make him disappear.

"I'm going to fucking cover you in my cum."

My chest heaves with anticipation and lust as I watch the most beautiful man's control snap. All because of me. His face contorts with pleasure before his mouth hangs open and he succumbs to his orgasm with a low growl. "Fuck."

Streams of cum spill over my chest, the warm liquid running down the middle of my breasts as Hudson rises over me, throwing his head back and gasping as if he just ran a marathon.

When he gazes back down at me, I run my fingers through his release, circling and coating my nipples with it before bringing my fingers to my mouth and licking them clean.

"Jesus Christ," he says. "My fucking fantasies couldn't have done this justice."

"So, I did alright for my first time?"

"You did better than alright," he says with a breathless laugh. "I think you earned yourself a reward."

I tuck my lip between my teeth, feeling my center throb at the prospect. "Yeah? What kind of reward?"

Hudson's mouth turns up at the corners. "The kind that has that sweet little pussy of yours singing on my tongue."

And with that, he drops his lips over my center, taking me into another dimension.

Chapter Twenty-Six

KAVI

I throw a small couch cushion on my brother's face, trying to distract him from his phone. "You know you don't have to work two jobs anymore. We have enough in the account so you can enjoy your summer like most kids your age."

He shrugs, going back to his phone, ignoring my attempt to annoy him. "I don't mind. I don't like dipping into the account."

"Oh, there is more to the story than that," Mom chirps, striding into the family room with cups of chai for the two of us—she knows Neil won't have any. She sits down on the chair across from us, opening the box of garlic knots I baked for them. "Tell her, Neil!"

The glimmer in Mom's eyes tells me everything I need to know, and I swing my grin toward my brother, who slumps further into our couch with a groan. He's well aware of how excited the two women in his life get about any mention of his love life.

"Tell me!" I urge, placing my entangled fingers under my chin and blinking rapidly. "Is this about a girl? Is there someone who watches you from her window while you mow her parents' lawn?"

He glares at me unamused, which just makes me giggle more. It also warms my insides to know he's going through normal teenage things. Especially since my own teenage years were spent hiding inside my room, trying to come to terms with everything that had happened, things I should have never experienced.

I throw another pillow at him. "Tell me!"

"There's a girl by the name of Lilac—" Mom starts.

"Lyla," Neil corrects her, going back to scrolling his phone. His hair lays like an overgrown mop over his forehead.

Mom waves her hand in the air like potato-potahto, taking a sip of her tea. "Yes, yes. That's what I said. She's become quite fond of our Neil—"

Neil looks up. "Mom, she's never even said a word to me. She literally doesn't even know I exist."

"Yes, yes," Mom huffs, as if this is all extraneous information that really doesn't embellish her story in the least. "But that's just because she's pretending not to. You know, playing coy so you will approach her. It's what we women do, don't we, Kavi?" She looks at me for agreement. "It's just the way we flirt."

I'm not entirely sure I agree, but I nod anyway to placate her while my brother rolls his eyes. "She has a boyfriend, Mom."

I wince, but my mom keeps going. "Well, relationships at this age rarely last, so keep an eye out. When she's single again, you can swoop in with a romantic gesture. Buy her some Lindor chocolates. Not the cheap kind, you know, the nice ones in those metallic wrappers that say, 'You're the love of my life'."

Neil tilts his head. "You just said relationships at my age rarely last."

"Oh, don't be sensitive." Mom leans back in her chair, her curly dark hair brushing against her shoulders. "I meant *other* relationships, not yours. Once Lilac sees what a kind and gentle soul you are—so much like your father—she'll never want to let you go."

Refusing to argue, Neil just shakes his head and goes back to his phone.

"Now, speaking of romantic gestures." Mom turns to me right as I'm blowing air over my cup, trying to cool off my tea. I've never understood how she can scald her tongue as if she has no nerve endings there. "How is that handsome boss-roommate of yours?"

I'm hoping she doesn't see the pink crawling into my cheeks, but the flashes of last night—of him taking me in every which way, well into the early morning hours—have my skin heating to the same temperature as the cup in my hands.

My body is bruised and fatigued, but I wouldn't change a single thing.

And then his raspy voice in my ear this morning, telling me that I'd be staying in his room every night from now on. He'd encircled my waist and pulled me into him, burying his nose in my hair before going back to sleep, as if he'd woken up just to ensure I accepted his proposal—*ahem*, demand.

"He's . . . fine. You know, just busy." I take a small sip of my tea, trying to avoid Mom's searching eyes.

"Is he still being gruff and demanding with you?"

Another flash of him telling me to take his cock like a good girl, pumping into me from behind with his hand clasped around my neck and pressing me into the mattress, has me clearing my throat. "Oh, yeah. Extremely gruff and demanding."

My mother is generally open-minded about most things, and while she won't be thrilled that I'm with a man twenty years older than me—who is closer to her age than mine—she won't deem it scandalous or taboo, either. After all, she herself married someone quite a bit older. Still, revealing that I'm in a 'complicated' relationship with my boss will lead to a much longer conversation than I have time for today.

So before she can ask any more questions, I shift the conversation back to Neil. "Hey, twirp, so are you all healed up now? No stomach pains or anything, right?"

Neil nods. "Yeah, all good."

"Good," I respond, turning back to my mom. "Mom, where are the bills from the hospital? I wanted to see how much we owe."

"Oh!" She jumps up off her chair, leaving her cup on the coffee table and heading over to where she keeps all our bills on the counter. Thankfully, the overdue notices have stopped, given I've been paying everything off, so there aren't quite as many on that counter as there normally are. She hands me an opened envelope. "Look at this. It says the bill has been paid."

"What?" My brows furrow as I pull the envelope from her fingers and unfold the papers inside. "What do you mean?"

I scan the various billed items, reading down to the bottom, where an amount well above ten thousand dollars shows that it has been paid. My breath stalls in my chest as I blink up at my mother. "When did you receive this?"

She gives me a guilty look I've seen before. "I've actually had it for a few weeks. I was just too scared to open it—you know how I get around bills, they trigger my eye twitches. But then I finally caved and opened it yesterday. I was so surprised to see your insurance covered it all. What a great company you're working for."

I examine the papers in my hand with renewed shock, as if they just appeared out of thin air, not giving her the truth. That I never enrolled us in the insurance plan, and that this bill was paid by none other than the gruff and demanding man we just spoke about. A man with a soft and generous heart he keeps hidden under a hardened exterior.

"Oh, and I totally forgot to mention," Mom adds, her voice high-pitched. "I was going to surprise you with the news today; your car is fixed and sitting in the garage. The shop called a couple of days ago saying we could pick it up."

"That's great!" I say, relieved. I still plan to buy another used car in Portland, but at least this one will be here for Neil. I had called the shop last week from the office to ask about the status, and they'd said they'd call me to let me know. Apparently, my power steering needed replacing. I wince, wondering how much of a dent that put in our bank account. "How much did they charge for it?"

Mom gives me a confused squint. "What do you mean? Wouldn't you know that since you paid for it?"

"I didn't—" My mouth drops open as more shock registers. Tears prick the corners of my eyes, and I mumble something in response to my mother before excusing myself to my room with my phone, not thinking too much before pressing his number.

"What's wrong?" His husky demand fills my ear.

"Nothing. I just . . ." I laugh as another wave of emotion hits my chest at the concern in his voice. I clear my throat. "Hi."

He pauses for a moment. "You missed me, didn't you?"

I chuckle again, remembering I asked him something similar the night he found me in the throes of a nightmare. "I'd more likely miss a grizzly with a taste for human blood." He doesn't respond, but I have a feeling his lips are twitching. "Are you busy?"

"It doesn't matter if I am."

I curl my bottom lip into my mouth, smiling. "I, uh . . . I know you paid for Neil's hospital bills and my car."

He doesn't deny it. "Okay."

"How did you know which shop I had my car at? I never told you."

He chuckles. "I heard you call them from your office phone, and when you left your desk a couple of minutes later, I just called the last number and gave them my info."

My mouth drops open. The sneak! "You didn't have to do that. You're already paying me a crazy salary and—"

"I wanted to."

"Hudson, that was way too—"

"Kav, I wanted to."

I look down, digging my toes into the carpeted floor. "Why?"

He takes a moment to answer. "I don't want you to have any debt when you start your new life."

And just like that, my heart sinks.

My new life.

A life that starts without him—away from him—in just a few weeks.

I nod, wondering if this is the point I ask him what that means for us, but knowing it's still too soon. We just established something between us last night, and the last thing I want to do is scare him off with questions about our future the day after. "Well, I wanted to say thank you."

"When do you leave for your art therapy class?"

I look at my watch. "I was going to call an Uber, but now I'll just drive there."

"Or I could take you."

I stop pacing inside my room. "What do you mean? How would you take me?"

"In my car," he says, causing my heart to race. "I'm outside your house."

"What?" I'm already running out of my bedroom toward the foyer where my boots and purse are. "When did you . . .? I mean, how long have you been here?"

"Who's here?" Mom hollers behind me, stepping out of the kitchen.

"No one," I yell back, pulling on my shoes and breathing heavily into my phone. I can't believe he's waiting outside my house! "I'll see you next weekend."

"Wait, but you never told me about your friend's wedding. And what about that man she was going to introduce you to?"

"You told your mom about the backup dancer?" Hudson drawls in my ear, unamused, making me giggle.

He's made it clear he's a possessive man, and the feminist inside me should be appalled at the jealousy in his tone, but when it comes to Hudson Case, she's nowhere to be seen. Instead, she revels in being owned and possessed by him.

"I'll tell you about it next week." My voice carries behind me to my mother as I pull my purse strap over my shoulder. "Bye, twirp. Be good!" I holler at my brother as I swing the door open and step out.

I blink rapidly, trying to adjust my eyes to the bright sunlight outside, before finding Hudson's truck across the street. I rush toward him, hanging up the phone.

He exits the driver's side as I run to him, stopping abruptly a few feet in front of him with my breath caught in my lungs. "How long have you been here?"

"It doesn't matter."

"You missed me, didn't you, Mr. Case?" I tease him with a smile between my lips, throwing back what's becoming our familiar banter.

He shakes his head, his forearms peeking out beneath his rolled-up shirtsleeves, hands tucked in his pockets. "I'd sooner miss Chickenpox."

I can't help but laugh as I close the distance between us, wrapping my arms around his neck. He pulls me to him, lifting me effortlessly as I plant kisses from his earlobe down to his neck.

When I reach his mouth, he draws me closer, taking control of our kiss. I tug his hair gently, lost in the sensation of our lips, our connection, feeling breathless and untamed.

This man . . . his scent, his skin, his arms, everything about him. From his rare smiles to his hard-won grins. From his sometimes terse, unapologetic words to the sweetness of his whispers meant only for me. I crave him endlessly.

A familiar throat clearing behind me breaks my spell, and I slide down from Hudson's embrace, turning to find my mother glaring back at me. Her arms are crossed and an expression of both amusement and mild disapproval wrestles over her features.

Her eyes bounce between me and Hudson, and I'm relieved when an upward curl finds her lips. "Pretty sure you've got some explaining to do next time, Kavi."

JOJO'S DAD and stepmom settle into seats in the back of the class. With Jojo's permission, I'd invited them to join us today, letting them know I wanted to speak to them after class.

Last week, Jojo had texted me, telling me that she'd confided in her dad about the situation with her stepsister. From our brief conversation, it seemed he was fully supportive of her. He'd even consoled and hugged her, apologizing for not being there sooner while Jojo suffered on her own.

While I know Jojo and her dad discussed the matter with her stepmom, Jackie, I'm uncertain of their plans to move forward and mend. My hope is to convince them to consider family counseling, but ultimately, it's their decision to make.

"These look great!" I clap my hands together, walking around the classroom.

Each of my students turns to look at the life-sized outline

of themselves on the large white paper stuck to the walls. They helped draw the outline of the person next to them, and I'm proud of the way they all worked together.

And since Hudson has joined today's class, I told him he'd have to participate, too, so we both drew outlines around the other's body on our own pieces of paper.

"Now, here's what I want us to do," I say, picking up my brush and addressing the class. "I want you to pick a color for each important person in your life and paint the inside of your outline with those colors. There's no right or wrong, and you can choose as many or as few colors as you want. Once you're done, I'd love for a couple of you to share your work with the rest of the class, but that's optional. If you'd rather keep things to yourself, that's okay, too. There are no rules when it comes to my class."

Elijah raises his hand and I chuckle, reminding him that, as long as he's being respectful, he can speak freely without having to ask for permission.

"How do we choose the color for each person?"

I shrug. "It's completely up to you. Sometimes the colors will guide you. Remember, there's no right or wrong. Just go with what your heart is telling you."

The kids all get started, and I walk over to where mine and Hudson's papers are hanging next to each other, giving him a smile when I look at the enormous outline of him on the wall.

He picks up his brush, dipping it into yellow paint, while I pick up orange on my brush.

Hudson chuckles. "Orange. Of course."

"It's the happiest color in the rainbow," I quip.

Fifteen focused minutes later, I turn to look at Hudson's painting, assessing the various colors. "Who does the yellow represent over your sternum?"

He studies his work for a moment. "Maddy." He sees my

raised brow in question and continues, "Her hair has always reminded me of sunshine and warmth. Her mom leaving her on my doorstep all those years ago changed my life for the better."

My throat tightens at the emotion in his voice. God, the way this man loves.

If only . . .

I shake my thoughts away, pointing to the blue on the shoulders of his outline. It has gray spots in it. "What about the blue? Who does that represent?"

Hudson's jaw works before he says, "My brother. We were each other's shoulders to lean on for a long time." He pauses for a moment. "There're a few gray spots in that relationship, but . . ."

I brush the tips of my fingers along his forearm, smiling up at him. "But hopefully it's on the mend? Hopefully, you'll be able to find that trust with him again." I look at the orange inside his head and over his heart. "And what's the orange supposed to represent?"

His eyes dip to my lips. "The happiest color in the rainbow. It's taking over my fucking mind, and I'm drowning in it."

I clasp my lip in between my teeth, tracing my eyes down to the other part of his painting where the orange seems to be taking over—his heart. "Are you looking for a life raft?"

Hudson shakes his head. "Not even a little."

He assesses the paper in front of me, his brows furrowing at the light purple and dark green paint covering most of the area inside my outline before it connects with orange on the hands and feet. There's a large red circle over the chest. "I get the orange, but what is the purple and green?"

I lift my brow. "The question is who represents the lavender and pine?"

A small smile tips up his lips, and I know he doesn't need me to answer. He looks at my painting. "And the red?"

"My family and friends."

His brows knot when he sees the red vine crawling up my picture's arm. "What's this?"

My smile withers following his gaze. "My best friend."

Hudson reaches for my forearm, his eyes soft as he puts pieces together in his head. He brushes my scar with his thumb. "Will you ever tell me what happened?"

I'm just about to answer when conversation from the class distracts me, and I walk away to assess each of their paintings, speaking to the volunteers that want to share what they've painted.

Twenty minutes later, with Hudson and the kids helping to clean up the room and put away the supplies, I walk to the back with Jojo, her dad, and her stepmom. Both Jojo and I bring along her artwork from today.

"Jojo, do you want to talk about your painting?" I inquire gently, watching Jojo's gaze shift from her dad to her stepmom shyly.

She begins to explain the various colors on her sheet, revealing fragments of her inner world. She points to the red inside her chest that represents her dad, before explaining a few other colors—her mom, her grandparents, and the dog they lost years ago.

When she gets to the gray colored cloud she's painted in her head, representing Max, Jackie and her father, Alan, exchange similar frowns.

Jackie tenderly clasps Jojo's hands in hers. "I'm so sorry that Max has been so terrible to you, sweetheart. It's no excuse, but she's going through her own adjustments with our new family dynamic. But I promise you that I will do everything possible to protect and support you." She takes a breath. "Your feelings are valid, and I'm here for you, too, okay?"

Jojo nods, glancing at me for guidance.

"I think it's really important for you all to seek family counseling." I offer Jojo an encouraging smile. "I will continue to keep in touch with Jojo, but it's essential that you heal as a family, too. Involve Max. Have her talk out what's bothering her and hopefully, over some time, you all can move forward with mutual respect for one another."

I turn to Alan, reiterating the importance of Jojo's emotional recovery. The defeated way she looked sitting inside that dark shed all alone still haunts me. "Your daughter has felt bullied and threatened. She was brave enough to share her experience with all of us, but it's important that she heals from this. It's important she finds her confidence and inner-strength again."

Alan nods somberly, his lips trembling as he pulls Jojo into a hug. "I'm sorry, sweetheart. I'm sorry I wasn't there for you sooner."

Giving the three of them time to embrace, I take out a list I'd prepared, outlining some family bonding activities and hand it to Alan, along with referrals to family counselors in the area.

Before they leave, I pull Jojo into a hug, reminding her that she can always call me, day or night.

I'm looking out of the passenger window in Hudson's car twenty minutes later, when he reaches over to intertwine our fingers. He brings my hand to his lips, like he's done before, sending a warm current through my body.

I take a breath, my eyes coasting along the oranges and yellows in the sky. "I love the colors of sunsets, don't you?"

"Yes." Hudson squeezes my hand. "But now all I see is orange."

The sound of footsteps on the wooden floor has me glancing over my shoulder at the bare-chested man behind me, clad in dark gray sweatpants. His disheveled hair does nothing to make him look any less sexy. And as usual, his overt display of tattoos, bulging biceps, and stacked abs makes my brain malfunction, and I almost burn my wrist pulling out the tray of peppermint snacks from the oven.

I swear, he does it on purpose—parading around half-naked just to turn me into a fumbling idiot.

I spy the way his lips tip up arrogantly as I place the tray on the counter and close the oven. The bastard knows he looks good enough to cause a highway pileup. He shuffles over, pressing his chest to my back as he lifts his arm to get cups from the cupboard above my head.

Dipping his mouth to the shell of my ear, his salacious whisper sends goosebumps soaring over my skin. "Excuse me."

I roll my eyes. He has two separate cupboards with cups in them, so there is no reason he needs the ones above me. I know he's doing it on purpose to rile me up, and he's succeeding—I just won't admit it out loud.

Placing the two cups on the counter in front of me, he cages me in with his arms and chest. His mouth finds my exposed shoulder and neck, nipping and kissing all the way to my ear, making me gasp.

"I like you in my shirt."

I'd pulled on the button-down shirt he threw on the floor last night and paired it with some tights. I turn my head to run my lips across his jaw. "I like smelling like you. It's my favorite scent."

Hudson grabs my hips and pulls me to him, grinding his hard-on against my ass. His lips find the side of my neck again, his voice raspy with need. "Your pussy is my favorite scent."

I take in a shuddered breath, my body accustomed to being on the verge of an explosion whenever I'm around him.

"You were up early, though," he mumbles against my skin. "Did I not work you out hard enough last night?"

I snort, stretching my neck for him to take as much as he wants. The question should be whether I even slept between the three times he woke me up, only to be buried inside me minutes later. At five AM, I decided to get my day started, trying to be as quiet as I could be in the kitchen.

It's been like this between us for an entire week, minus the two days Hudson had to fly to Portland. We're insatiable for one another—in the office, in his truck, and as soon as we get home. Yesterday, we even put up the privacy window in his chauffeured car and went at it in the back seat.

"Pretty sure I won't be needing to go to the gym with all the workouts I'm getting all day and night."

"You don't need to go to the gym, anyway. You're perfect exactly as you are."

He detaches his mouth from my skin and I see the

sincerity in his eyes. No, I see the way he sees me—wants me—and it leaves me speechless.

He tilts his head at the tray, unaware of the way he makes me swoon. "What have you been up to all morning?"

I wave a finger over the tray. "I made peppermint and rolled oats snacks for Kansas since I'll be meeting her for the first time today. And," I show him the dough under the plastic wrap I kneaded earlier this morning, "I'm making croissants for art therapy class today and to take to the office tomorrow."

Hudson stills behind me, and I look over my shoulder to catch his gaze on my face.

"What?" I whisper, not able to interpret the look on his face.

He shakes his head, his eyes soft. "You made treats for my horse?"

"You said not to call her a horse," I quip, smiling at him. "Anyway, I had most of the ingredients. I just had to go out for the peppermint and—"

"You went shopping this morning?" His brows pinch together, the crows' feet at the corners of his eyes deepening. "Aaron doesn't come into work until nine on Sundays. Why didn't you wake me up?"

I turn around, wrapping my arms around his neck and rubbing out the furrow in the middle of his forehead with my index finger. "It wasn't raining, so I thought I'd take a quick walk to the corner shop. And you've had a busy week; I wanted to let you sleep in."

"Kav—"

I stop the rest of his argument by lifting up on my toes and pressing my lips to his. At first he resists, wanting to argue some more, but after my continued efforts with my fingernails traveling the course of his spine, he gives in.

Our kiss is sensual and deep, our tongues dancing against each other.

Hudson groans into my mouth, bringing my hips flush with his, his erection demanding attention. "You're so fucking stubborn, you know that?"

I smile into our kiss, pressing my chest to his and opening my mouth so his tongue can explore further. He tastes like mint and smells like . . . like me. "You wouldn't have me any other way."

"I'd like to have you every way on this counter," he murmurs, shoving the tray behind me so he can lift me onto the counter.

He scoots in between my legs, dragging his hands over my sides underneath my shirt. His thumbs brush the bottoms of my breasts and I moan into his mouth, feeling that familiar heat building up at my core.

But I have so much to get done today before we head to his farm, including finishing up the croissants, organizing a lesson plan, and getting some supplies together for class later.

I run my fingers through his hair, licking his bottom lip and kissing him until we're both breathless, before pulling away. I peer into his smoldering eyes. "If I don't get stuff done this morning, I'll end up spending the entire day in bed with you."

"I fail to see the problem with that." He nips my jaw, dragging his mouth all the way to my ear, making my center pulse hungrily. I feel like I'm being pulled under by waves, and for the life of me, I can't find the will to resist.

Whimpering at the feel of him against me, I let him pull me into another kiss before he reluctantly leans back, brushing his thumb over my bee-stung lips. "Fine, to be continued later, then." He glances at the dough I have set out for the croissants I was going to bake. "You think we can leave in an hour or so?"

"I'll be ready."

～

EARLIER, I was gawking at the shirtless man with sweatpants in his kitchen. Now, I'm drooling over the same man wearing fitted dark jeans, distressed brown leather boots, and a button-down flannel shirt with rolled-up sleeves that make his forearms look so provocative they should come with a warning.

Tugging the neck of my old shirt that has *Peel With Care* written above a picture of a kiwi, I let the cool breeze caress my heated skin. I trail after him while blatantly checking out his incredible denim-clad ass.

As soon as we got out of his truck, Hudson placed a cream-colored Stetson hat over my head before pressing me against his truck and kissing me like he hadn't just done so minutes before.

He'd gently pinched my chin, his piercing blue irises rimmed with thick dark lashes casting down at me with such intensity, it sent butterflies soaring in my stomach. "You're fucking unexpected, Kav."

But before I could ask him to clarify, he entangled our fingers and led me toward the stables behind his farmhouse.

Anticipation courses through me as the breeze picks up my hair. My boots leave prints on the damp ground, and once again, I note the serenity of the ranch.

Coming to a stop at the wide gates of the stables, I follow Hudson inside with my bag of treats. It takes a moment for my eyes to adjust to the dim lighting, revealing old, weathered beams and a few stalls lined against the wall. With the scent of leather, soil, and hay surrounding me, I feel like I've been transported into a completely different world full of rustic charm.

Noting the three empty stalls, I trail behind Hudson to one occupied by a majestic, sun-bleached, wheat-colored horse standing regally with her ears held high as she watches him—us—approach.

Walking up to the stall, Hudson kisses the air. "There's my beautiful girl." His voice is gentle and admiring, captivating me as he rubs her neck, letting her smell his hair and skin before kissing her cheek. I'm mesmerized watching the bond between them, and somewhere in my head the song, *Dust in the Wind* by the band named Kansas, echoes softly.

"Yeah, yeah, I missed you, too," he coos, brushing his fingers through her mane.

His words and gentle touch seem to calm her while her deep brown eyes study me with curiosity and apprehension.

She's stunning, with a large patch of white under her neck and ears that are tipped with black. Her nose twitches in anticipation, pulling a soft laugh from my lips. Someone knows there are treats in the bag for her.

Hudson extends his hand to me, intertwining our fingers and silently inviting me closer, and I do so, feeling the tension growing in the air.

"Reach out with the back of your hand so she can smell you," he says to me as he continues to reassure her with more gentle words.

Kansas snuffles softly, her breath warm against my hand, making my smile stretch across my face. I want to stroke her velvety fur, but given what I know about her so far, I decide against it, waiting for her cue to tell me when she's ready. When that will be, I'm not sure, but I gather she's still unsure for now.

"You've had her twenty years?" I ask, remembering what he told me last week.

He nods, his expression affectionate as he strokes her neck. "I got her when she was nearly five. She was, and is, the most beautiful girl both Maddy and I had seen, and she came with this ranch we bought."

I notice he stays away from the word "horse" as he speaks about her.

"She's too old for anyone to be riding her regularly, but she'll let me if she's feeling up to it."

"Do you have more?" I ask, hinting at other horses without explicitly saying the word.

Hudson looks out to the pasture through an opening on the other side. "Two more, Lottie and Whiskey. They're both old, but not as old as this girl. They're both retired racing horses that Maddy brought here when she heard they were looking for a new home. We thought they could keep this old girl company." He chuckles, indicating Kansas. "But she's so moody, she barely acknowledges their presence."

Ah, like father like horse-daughter, I see.

I smile at the way he dotes on her, forgiving her for her grumpy personality, almost as if it's endearing. And for reasons I never expected, that in itself makes me fall for him just a little more.

Kansas reaches out her neck to sniff the treats in my bag.

"Looks like she knows these treats are for her." I laugh, looking to Hudson for guidance. "Do you think she'll let me feed her?"

He takes a peppermint cookie from the box, showing me how to feed her, and I follow his lead cautiously. Kansas eagerly takes the treat into her mouth from my open palm before letting out a loud satisfied snuffle, making Hudson and me grin.

"You might have found a way to win her over," he remarks with a chuckle. "I guarantee you'll be best friends if you keep coming over with treats."

I swallow and give Kansas another cookie, wondering how to interpret Hudson's words. Keep coming over . . .

Did he forget that I'll only be here for another four weeks, or did he mean for the short time I'm here?

A few minutes later, Hudson takes Kansas out of the stall, listening to her cues before placing a saddle over her. He pulls her lead as I follow them both, watching her long brown tail swish as she takes slow strides toward the pasture.

Leaving her in one spot, he opens the gates of the closed-in pasture, placing another saddle on an almost all-chocolate-colored horse named Whiskey.

I fiddle the ring on my thumb anxiously when Hudson comes back toward me with Whiskey striding behind him. "I don't know, Hudson . . . I've never been horse riding before."

His hands cradle my face, making me look up at him from under my hat. "I promise, with Whiskey, you won't have to do much. Just hold his reins and let him do the work. He knows the path and will follow Kansas and me."

I nod and he takes my hat off and replaces it with a helmet he finds in a bin inside the stalls. I love the way he focuses on buckling it, making sure it's secure on my head.

I take out another treat from my pocket, offering it to Whiskey, and giggle as the other horse, Lottie, comes galloping all the way to the fence, hoping for the same thing. Thankfully, I'd taken a couple more from the box I'd left inside the stable.

After giving Lottie and Whiskey another treat, Hudson helps me straddle the large chocolate horse.

My heart hammers inside my chest as my thighs clasp the saddle, and Hudson gives me some basic instructions on how to ensure Whiskey follows my direction and what to do if he decides to trot and I want him to go slower.

Five minutes later, Whiskey and I follow Hudson and Kansas on a path around Hudson's property while he points out landmarks in the distance. The soft breeze, laden with the scent of grass and flowers, lifts pieces of my hair from under my helmet.

It takes me a good fifteen minutes to get comfortable riding Whiskey, but I now understand what Hudson meant. The beautiful horse is so mellow and gentle that I relax as we both get to know each other. He does like to munch on the long stems of grass from time to time, so I have to divert his attention back to following Hudson and Kansas again.

We stop at an overlook above a large field where I see a quilt flanked with pots of wildflowers on the ground and a picnic basket sitting on the edge.

I look over at Hudson with my mouth agape as he dismounts Kansas, tying her reins to a nearby tree before reaching up to pull me off Whiskey. "Hudson . . ."

He doesn't respond, leading Whiskey to another tree and tying him there before jogging back to me.

I look down at the picnic with complete surprise. "When did you do all this?"

He unbuckles my helmet, taking it off my head and placing it on the ground before clasping my hand and leading me to sit with him on the blanket. "I didn't." He grins, his eyes gleaming, and I notice—not for the first time—how incredibly beautiful his rare smiles are. "My property manager, Levi, did it for me."

I chuckle softly. "Well then, I suppose Levi should be the one I should thank with a kiss . . ."

Hudson leans into me, gently laying me down on the quilt under the cloudy blue sky as he hovers over me. "What have I told you about my rules on sharing?"

"Hmm." I twist my mouth. "I can't seem to recall. You do have so many rules, Mr. Case."

He nips my bottom lip. "And you seem to like breaking them."

"Maybe I just like seeing you worked up."

"I've been nothing but worked up since you waltzed over to my table that fateful day."

"Ah, yes." I giggle. "That fateful day when you fired me from my first restaurant gig."

He groans. "You're never going to let me live that down, are you?"

I chuckle, dragging my fingers through his hair. "You did have a rather large goose egg on your forehead from where that cork hit you, so I suppose I should let it go."

He tickles my stomach and I giggle and squirm under him. "I did not have a goose egg, but it hurt like a bitch."

I laugh. "Thank God for your thick headedness."

That earns me another tickle and his mouth over my neck.

Our soft laughter turns into something else entirely as Hudson's mouth drags up to my lips and he kisses me hungrily. He untucks my shirt from the waist of my pants, his hand making its way up my stomach and over my breast.

We continue moaning into each other's mouths as Hudson pulls down the cup of my bra, brushing his thumb over my pebbled nipple. My core tightens as he rolls it between his thumb and index finger, pinching until I gasp against his lips.

"Please," I beg.

His eyes focus on me. "Please what, baby girl? Tell me what you need."

"More," I breathe.

"More of what, Kavi? Be specific."

I grasp his hand, dragging it to the waistline of my jeans before unbuckling them. Wiggling them off, letting the wind flutter over my heated skin, I press his hand into my underwear.

I look up at him, my chest rising and falling in time with

the pulsing need at my wet center. "I want your fingers inside me and your mouth all over me."

His jaw works as his hand slides deeper into my awaiting folds. "Just my fingers?"

I lick my lips, shaking my head. "Your fingers, your tongue, and your cock."

A satisfied grin finds his face before his voice turns gruff. "Lay back so I can get started."

Chapter Twenty-Eight

HUDSON

"I appreciate that PowerForge equipment can handle different types of soil and geological conditions, Jake, but Case Geo works with vendors who are committed to the same sustainable practices as we are."

Responding to PowerForge's pitch for Case Geo to purchase their new line of excavation equipment the following week, I put myself on mute, going back to what I've been busy with for the past few minutes while their team drones on.

They're currently walking me through the slides displayed on the projection screen in my office . . .

With her skirt bunched up to her waist, her ass and thighs exposed to me, and her wrists cuffed in my grip, Kavi lays with her chest to my desk while I'm buried deep inside her. Her bottom lip is tucked in between her teeth, her kiwi earrings sliding against her skin, while she tries but fails to swallow her moans. Her soft whimpers have me feeling completely crazed.

She's madness and sin.

A boundless temptation.

Have I ever been so captivated by a woman? I've certainly never been enough to forfeit my sanity—*my rules*—and fuck her on my desk. Not once or twice, but multiple times at this point.

That I have little regard for my own recklessness should be ringing a blaring bell inside my head at how fucked I am going to be in less than four weeks when she leaves.

But I refuse to think about that and tarnish this moment, sullying it for the times I'll remember it in the future.

I made sure she'd locked my door as soon as she came in after our staff meeting this morning.

She was confused at first, noticing the sounds coming from the speaker on my desk. But then her gaze landed on the mute button before it found my curling index finger, urging her closer.

Those same eyes flared with understanding, turning into pools of liquid gold and desire.

I move with speed and force, plunging into her wet heat with feral grunts, loving the way Kavi's entire body thrusts forward against my desk. Her gasps punctuate the space between us while Jake persists in persuading me to invest in his machinery, comparing his costs with other vendors.

I didn't give a shit about the costs before, and I certainly couldn't care less now. Money is a meager sacrifice for ensuring we exceed environmental regulations—it's always been something Case Geo stands on.

Tightening my hand around her wrists, knowing I'm likely going to be leaving marks, I slow down, pulling out all the way. Taking my cock in my other hand, I slap her ass with it. "How many times are you going to come for me today, baby girl? How many times can you come for me on this desk?"

Kavi mumbles something incomprehensible as I sweep my tip from her entrance to the puckered hole in the middle of her ass, covering her in her own juices and relishing the way her body tenses.

We've been at this for a couple of weeks, finding every moment to be together, sneaking glances at company meetings, and being overall inseparable. But I think it's safe to say that of all the spots I love to fuck her, my desk happens to be her favorite. Add to the fact that I'm fucking her while in a meeting, and she's practically dripping down her thighs for me.

Who knew my girl was such a fiend for the forbidden?

The intonation of Jake's voice clues me into the fact that I've been asked a question, and I lean over my curvy admin to unmute my phone. "Repeat that for me."

I shove myself back inside Kavi as Jake starts to ask again, but he stops when he thinks he hears a disturbance on the phone—Kavi holding back another moan.

"Sorry, did you say something, Hudson?" he asks.

"No, please continue." I thrust against her, sheathing myself inside her and twisting in a way that has her eyes rolling back into her head. Her nostrils flare, her mouth pursed so as to not make a sound, as I continue to pull out and push back in.

"Right," he continues. "What I was wondering is what sort of warranties you were seeing with other vendors? As you know, PowerForge has a lifetime guarantee on all parts and labor for all our compound machines and heavy equipment. I could tell you more about them if you'd like."

I'd seen the slides earlier, so I'm clear on their warranties, but since I need to stall for time, I ask him to tell me more about the fuel efficiency of their machines, along with how that would contribute to our sustainability goals.

Jake starts back up, switching to another slide I'd studied earlier, and after pressing the mute button again, I go back to the woman in front of me.

I wrap her long hair in my other fist and bend down to graze my lips over the shell of her ear. "Now, where were we?" I rasp, fucking her to the hilt, harsh and demanding. "Ah yes, you were going to tell me how many times you wanted to be fucked right here on this desk. Once, twice, more?"

She groans, a sheen of sweat over her brows. "As many times as you can manage, old man."

Even while she's got me balls deep inside her, she's going to put me in my place and sass back. There's no fucking end to the ways she turns me on.

"The question is, baby girl," I say, pistoning inside her, my breaths uneven. "Could this pretty pussy of yours manage it?"

A moan leaves her lips, and I know she's close. "Pretty sure she's managing you and your big cock just fine."

"Well, then we might be here the whole night." My cock is so deep inside her, I feel sparks crackling at the base of my spine. My hands are still wrapped around her hair and her wrists. "Fuck, you're squeezing me like a vise. Are you close, sweetheart?"

"Yes," she hisses, a few strands of her raven locks now matted to her forehead with sweat, a flush staining her face. "So close."

I drill into her as Jake and his team continue with their presentation. Thankfully, one of my associates is also on the phone and prompts them with additional questions. It gives me time to focus on the more important things lying on my desk.

I let go of her wrists and hair. "Turn around. I want to see your face as I make you come."

Kavi heaves as she turns around, her body slumping like she's carrying a mountain.

Putting her ass on the desk, I quickly place my hands on the backs of her thighs and open her up. I nudge my cock against her entrance before thrusting forward, and we both moan at the connection and feeling.

This connection. This feeling.

It's unlike anything I've ever fucking felt, and it scares the mother loving fuck out of me.

Like I'm falling without a harness and zero prospects of landing on soft ground. Like this whole time I was tethered and I'm finally experiencing a dose of freedom. Like my stomach has lurched forward, my heart is in my throat, and I can barely catch a breath.

But breathing wouldn't save me, anyway.

I'm falling, and I can't think of a better way to die.

"You're so tight, so wet," I mumble as more words tumble out of me unbidden. "Like you were made for me, baby girl. Like you're everything I've been waiting for. I can't get enough of you, Kav. I'll never get enough."

You're perfect. This is perfect. We're perfect.

And I have no idea what I'll do when it's all over.

My eyes trail over her writhing form, settling on her polished amber eyes, and for the first time in all the times we've been together, my heart cracks at the sight of her. A rough stone scrapes against the walls of my throat and something unwanted pushes to get out from behind my eyes.

But why? Why the fuck am I feeling any of this now? And how did I go from swimming inside her to feeling like I'm drowning all in the matter of minutes?

We were just supposed to be having fun, weren't we? Reckless, stupid fun.

But when did that recklessness turn against my own heart?

My grip on her tightens, as if trying to thwart the words from slipping out, but they're out before I can stop them. They're out before I've even processed the walls crumbling in order to release them. "Make a wish for us, baby."

Kavi's gasp and widened eyes have me halting.

I'm still inside her as she hauls herself up, securing tender palms around my jaw as she does that thing she seems to be so fucking good at—searching, fucking prying, inside my eyes.

I want to squeeze my lids shut, pull myself away from her hypnotic gaze, but like the times before, I'm powerless to her.

Fucking powerless and weak when it comes to her.

She strips me bare, exposing me for what I am. Who I am. *Who the fuck am I?*

Certainly not the person I thought I was before her.

And I'll never be the same after.

The tips of her fingers drag across the bristles over my jaw —her favorite thing to do—before her choked whisper finds my ears. "Every star in the sky is a wish I made for us, Hudson."

My breath gets caught in my airways as she seals her mouth over mine and I let her pull me into her, feeding me with the air I'm dying without.

Our lips mesh as our tongues tangle and she grinds herself against my cock, silently urging me to move again.

Pulling my face away from hers, I clutch the back of her neck to watch every flinch and flex of her features as I drive her up, only to let her fall.

The sounds of our bodies colliding overpower the voices coming from the speakers. Truth be told, I haven't heard a single word spoken in quite a while.

Increasing my speed, I fuck her with abandon, feeling my balls tighten in warning.

Kavi's walls tremble around me, her eyes rolling back into her skull.

"Look at me, baby girl," I grit out. "I need your eyes on my face and my name on your lips when you come."

Pulling her ass closer so I'm deeper inside her, I keep her

neck steady and our eyes pinned. I hold her as her nails claw the sides of my neck and her body tenses against me.

"Hudson!" She comes with a cry from somewhere deep within, her eyes never straying from mine. "Oh, God, Hudson, I'm . . . I'm c-coming."

It's when I continue to drive forward, chasing my own release, that I find the pools threatening to tumble over her lids—pools she's also kept at bay.

My molars grind, watching her force herself not to blink, but it's when the first tear splashes against her cheek that I find myself in the throes of my own release.

My nose and mouth drop to her neck as our chests heave.

And that tear that had broken free trails down her jaw to burn across my cheek.

~

A COUPLE OF EVENINGS LATER, Kavi wrinkles her nose, stepping away from the counter as if there's a carcass lying on it.

I give her a deadpan look, continuing to place leaves of basil strategically around my half-cooked pizza. "It's an egg, not roadkill."

A grunt escapes her lips. "Might as well be. No one puts eggs on their pizza and adorns it with basil to make it look normal. You're one of those people who loves breakfast for dinner, too, aren't you?"

I wipe my fingers on a kitchen towel. "I love brinner. Bacon and pancakes with a glass of orange juice for dinner."

Disbelief and repulsion skitters across her features, making me chuckle. "I knew you were a psychopath . . ."

I throw my head back with laughter, but when I swing my head to look at her, I see her watching me with rounded eyes, gentler as they take me in. I tip my chin in question. "What's up?"

"Nothing." She shakes her head, a smile dancing on her lips. "It's just . . . sometimes my stomach flips when you laugh."

I place my pizza in the oven before turning back to her. "Is that a good thing, because usually that means a bout of nausea for most people."

She giggles, swiping her tongue over her lips. "A pretty good thing. Now, that egg on your pizza, however? Definitely another story."

A few minutes later, Kavi's slicing up our pizzas when her computer dings with an incoming email. She motions toward it with her head since I'm opening a glass of wine for us on the table. "I bet that's the updates from Jett and his team on the work with RCS. They're doing a great job, by the way. Will you scan it and make sure he doesn't need anything from me?"

She plates the pizzas, heading to the fridge to grab something while I click on her mail, confirming it's from Jett and reading out snippets from his team, saying they are still on track to deliver their agreed-upon items.

He's been coming to the office every week to talk shop, but yesterday we went out to lunch at Carl's Catch. I won't say I'll forget everything that happened between us—the shit that separated us for two years—but I'm on my way to forgiving it. I definitely can't deny I'd missed our easy banter and his blasé demeanor. Even when we were younger, Jett had a way of seeing the lighter side of things, and I always appreciated that about him.

Placing our plates on the table, Kavi excuses herself to run to the restroom while I click off Jett's response. Just as I'm about to shut her laptop screen, however, I notice a folder on the sidebar of her personal email application, labeled Nathan-Personal.

Nathan?

I know her brother's name is Neil . . . so who is Nathan?

What's particularly interesting is that it shows over a thousand emails inside it, as evident by the number in parentheses next to the label.

An unsettling sensation—something foreign yet strangely familiar—crawls down my spine as I fight the intense urge to open the folder.

It's a personal folder, clearly marked in her personal email app. There would be no reason, no fucking excuse, for me to rummage through it, but curiosity gnaws at my insides like flesh-eating bacteria. My hand trembles over the mouse as an internal war rages inside me.

Who the fuck is Nathan, and why does she have a folder with his name on it? Is he family, a friend . . . Fuck, is he someone she's talking to? Someone she's fu—

I rake a hand through my hair. My stomach rolls at the thought I can't even finish. A thought I can't fathom.

Shit!

Is she . . . is she . . .?

No. *She wouldn't.*

But do I know her well enough to know she wouldn't? Do I know her that well at all? We've only been in each other's lives for a few weeks, so how could I know her at all in such a short amount of time?

I knew Kenna for way longer and look at what she ended up doing to me.

I don't have much time to contemplate, knowing she'll be coming out of the bathroom at any moment, and I make the decision to peek inside.

Just a quick glimpse, I tell myself. Maybe it'll be nothing at all, but my gut, *my intuition*, says a thousand emails indicate otherwise.

My heart drums as the screen fills with cascades of emails with varying subject lines: *Left in the Lurch, The Waiting Place, You Have Feet in Your Shoes . . .*

My eyes scan the first few subject lines while my brain rushes to comprehend their meaning—something familiar in the recesses of my mind.

Wait . . . are those words from that Dr. Seuss book, *Oh, the Places You'll Go!?* I used to read it to Madison.

What's more is that each email is addressed to this Nathan guy and sent by Kavi, but there doesn't seem to be a response to any.

I open a message at random—one dated from a couple of months ago—skimming the first few lines.

```
I missed you at graduation.
Remember we'd promised each other we'd go
to the same college?

Clearly, you didn't hold up your end of the
bargain. Still, I looked for you in the
crowd. I looked at the empty seat next to
Mom and Neil, pretending you were just
running late.

Remember how you also promised to marry me
in seventh grade because you said you didn't
know if I'd ever grow into my nose and that
my prospects already seemed glib at best?

You were an asshole, you know that? My nose
is perfectly proportionate to my face,
```

thank you very much. But thanks to you,
I've always been a little insecure about
it, especially since there's not a single
prospective husband in sight. I guess you
will have to marry me, then.

Fuck, Nathan, I miss you. I miss you so
much, there are nights I wake up in a sweat
because the thought of wanting to see you
and hug you literally rattles my bones,
and I—

"Wh-what are you doing, Hudson?"

The blood drains from my face at the broken whisper behind me. I turn, coming face to face with a woman who doesn't just look confused or betrayed . . .

She looks downright shattered.

My mouth opens and closes, my mind jumping from one chaotic thought to another as I struggle to process what I just read. But there's no time for comprehension in the face of Kavi's hurt and anger bearing down on my neck like a crushing weight.

So, I retreat to a familiar reaction, drawing upon my own anger and hurt to shield my fucking heart.

"Who the fuck is Nathan?" My expression hardens and the words escape through my tightened lips. It's a defense mechanism I've honed over the years in the face of betrayal.

First Jett, then Kenna.

And now, Kavi.

Anger and remorse rise inside me as I take in Kavi's pained expression.

I force myself not to stand to my full height because, even though I can't quite read the look on her face—guilt, betrayal, hurt?—I hate the look of fear on her even more.

"Is he . . ." I swallow the bile threatening to rise within me as visions of her wrapped up in someone else's arms literally has my breaths coming out ragged. "H-have you . . ." I take a breath and try again. "Have you been fucking someone else while we've been together?"

Her eyes well, bouncing against mine as she tries to wipe the look of astonishment from her face. I know my words are harsh, but *fuck*, I'm feeling like I'm being ripped apart right now.

Maybe I should have seen this coming. Maybe I should have known not to trust someone I've barely known for weeks.

But my soul didn't seem to realize it had only been weeks.

My mind and heart are at war as intrusive thoughts cloud my brain.

She did accept all my offers rather quickly—the additional money, my credit card, the offer to move in with me.

Was I just a quick meal ticket while she was with someone else? Have I just become this joke where people think they can fuck their way into my life, only to fuck me and my company over and find something better?

Is this all my fault and I'm the idiot who refuses to learn? The idiot who keeps trusting the same kind of people?

But even the thought of her betraying me in such a despicable way has my heart ripping from its confines. It seems so unlike her; so unlike the caring and unapologetically genuine person she is.

And then another thought occurs to me.

She never asked for any of those things—not the money, the credit card, or the apartment. Not even the hospital or car bills I paid.

In fact, I don't recall the last time I even had to pay off the credit card I gave her. She never made a single purchase on it. She argued with me at each step, never asked for a single cent, nor has she expected it. If anything, it was I who manipulated her into every part of it. It was I who concocted a reason to make her stay.

So maybe I'm the despicable one here for allowing such thoughts to even filter in and taint my mind, my goddamn feelings for her.

But I do need to know.

I need the truth so my brain doesn't eat me alive from within.

I run a rough hand down my face, letting it settle over my heart, almost as if I'm shielding it from bolting out. "Kav—" I clear my throat, though it does nothing for the broken way her name plays on my lips. "Please, just . . ."

"He's my dead best friend, Hudson."

I take in a staggered breath at her resigned tone, her immovable jaw. Her words echo inside my ears. "Wh-what?"

"Nathan was my childhood best friend who died in an accident. An accident I still believe to be a murder, but there's no way to prove that since it was always deemed an open-shut case of accidental death."

My heart hammers as I process what she's saying, but I stay quiet, letting her speak.

"He was more like a protective older brother to me than anything else." Her lips wobble with a melancholy smile, and I know she's in the midst of a loving memory. "Sure, we joked about marrying each other if neither of us found anyone, but that had more to do with how much we trusted each other than anything else."

I clear my throat again, keeping my voice soft. "So these emails . . .?"

Kavi chuckles without humor. "My therapist told me to write to him as a way to cope at the time. But I still write to him, pretending that, in some dimension, he receives my mail. That perhaps he's alive and well somewhere."

She turns her head, inspecting the ground. "It probably makes me sound crazy, and maybe I am . . ." She shifts to study my reaction. "But I'm not hurting anyone. I know he'll never come back; I've accepted that. But I suppose I rely on the comfort of his friendship, even in the afterlife, hoping he's looking down on me, protecting me from wherever he is."

Her eyes fill again as she tilts her head toward her open laptop. "What you read was a part of my diary. Letters to my dead best friend."

"Kav—" Not able to hold myself back any longer, I rush to her, cradling her face in my palms.

Fuck, I had no clue.

I'm appalled at my own thoughts, my reaction, and my words. Not only did I think the worst of her, but I allowed some of those doubts to slip from my lips and become the reason for her tears.

My voice trembles, wishing I could erase everything about the past ten minutes. "I'm so fucking sorry, baby. So, so sorry. I based everything on my past experiences and thought—"

"That I was cheating on you," she finishes for me as a tear slips from her lids. I wipe it with my thumb, hating the feel of it on my skin. She shakes her head. "I would never do that to you, Hudson. How could I when I'm utterly and painfully in love with you?"

The buzzing in my head comes to a full stop, along with my breaths as her words sink in.

She . . . loves me?

I don't have a chance to process my thoughts or her statement when she wraps her hands around my wrists and pulls me back into her hypnotic gaze. "I would never do that to you. I'm . . ." She steps into me, straightening to ensure I hear her next words. "I'm not her. I'll never be her."

I nod, pressing my forehead against hers. "I know. I feel like an asshole for doubting you, even for a minute."

She rests her hands on my chest. "We're the products of our pasts, aren't we? I mean, look at me. I still sleep with every nightlight on, still shiver at the thought of being inside a small closet or an airplane."

My gaze flicks to the scar on her arm. Somehow, I feel like she'll finally talk to me. "Will you tell me what happened now?"

She hesitates another moment, but nods.

Before she can start, I pick her up—one hand on her back and the other under her knees—and carry her to the couch. We've both forgotten about the pizza and wine at this point.

She settles her head on my chest while mindlessly running her thumb over my scruff. Her voice is ragged against me. "Nathan and I both came from lower-middle-class families. We became best friends in kindergarten, and ended up at the same pricey private high school based on some donations from the wealthy community we lived in.

"Soon after we got there, we ran into a group of shitty kids—bullies, for the lack of a better word. We knew to stay away from them and, for the most part, we did. But Nathan's family was met with financial issues when his deadbeat, drug addict dad ended up owing money to his dealer. And for reasons I still don't understand to this day, Nathan decided to go to the leader of the bully gang, Vance, for help."

Fuck.

A part of me wants her to stop, to tell her I don't really want to know, while the other part needs this just as much as I think she does.

Feeling her body stiffen as she wades through the memories, I hold her tighter. She tells me about how Nathan couldn't pay Vance back, and based on some bullshit rule Vance made up called the 'darkness clause', Nathan would have to carry out a dare of the bully's choosing.

"I got a note from Vance's friend later in the day, saying she knew of a way to help Nathan and wanted to meet me downstairs in the school's boiler room. I knew I shouldn't have trusted her, but I was so desperate to help Nathan, I followed her directions."

Ice trickles into my veins.

My hair stands up at the back of my neck.

My molars grind as she walks me through what happened, and I'm shocked at the wickedness of some kids at such a young age.

"But when I got there, I was ambushed by three of them. They punched me and knocked me out before carrying and shoving me into a tiny, dark closet inside the boiler room."

"What the fuck?" I growl, my heart racing at the images playing out in front of me. Rage settles into my bones, and all I want is to wrap my fucking hands around these monsters' necks and squeeze.

"I tried to get out, but I was stuck in there for hours until a maintenance person saw blood pooled outside the door."

This time, my body stiffens. All I can hear is the roar of blood inside my ears as my pulse quickens out of rhythm. "Blood?"

A tear trickles down her cheek and she quickly wipes it off, as if offended by its presence. I want to applaud her for the strength she's trying to display, while wrapping her up inside my arms and telling her she never has to in front of me, but I stay quiet, letting her tell her story.

"I tried to feel my way through the small space because I couldn't see anything, and my head was fuzzy and pounding." She rubs her lips together, and I notice the slight loss of color on her face. "I'd thrown up on myself, too, based on what I remember. But, somehow, in the process of hurling myself against what I thought was the door, I threw myself against something sharp and metallic. I guess it was hard enough that it literally broke my forearm, lodging itself into my bone."

A serrated breath cuts through my chest as my stomach turns. I try to swallow back the bile terrorizing my insides.

Squeezing my eyes shut at the image of this beautiful woman enduring so much pain, I lay a kiss on her temple, even as my ire liquifies into molten lava inside me at the thought of someone hurting her.

"I tried to dislodge it," she continues, trapped inside her memories. "But I think I made it worse somehow, because when I pulled my arm off it, it ripped my skin further." She heaves in a shuddering breath. "The pain was so excruciating, I passed out in a pool of my own blood. Sometime later, I was rushed to the ER, where they surgically fixed my broken arm."

I hold her to me, kissing her face—her cheek, her forehead, her lips—hoping she doesn't feel the tremble of my lips. Hoping to comfort in any way I can.

It explains so much. Why she wakes up screaming in the middle of the night, why she's still scared of small dark places, why she had such a visceral reaction to one of her students' situation at home, and even why she went on to become a therapist for kids.

I tenderly cradle her arm in my hand, running my thumb over her scar. "Didn't anyone ask how you got into that closet?"

She shrugs. "I was told, in no uncertain terms, that if I told the truth, something would happen to my brother."

My fingers freeze over her skin. "Jesus, Kav."

Her lips quiver. "I told them I'd decided to explore the basement and got myself stuck inside the closet."

"What did those assholes do to Nathan?"

There's no part of me that wants to know more than I already do, but every part of me wants to carry this with her just a little bit.

"They killed him," she states hoarsely in finality. "They took him to these cliffs and made him jump. I know because what they told the police was they all jumped, but he was the only one who never came back up. But I know for a fact that Nathan wouldn't have done something as reckless as that. He wasn't like that."

Did they push him off or did he voluntarily jump? I guess it doesn't fucking matter—the poor kid died, either way.

"The authorities found Nathan's body in the water yards away from the cliffs, and the autopsy confirmed he hit the water hard."

I swallow. "Did you ever tell the police your side of the story?"

Kavi's hands find her face, covering it up before a strangled cry emits from her throat as sobs wrack through her body. I tangle my arms around her as she mumbles incoherently into her hands.

My heart cracks down the middle.

"Hey," I whisper into her ear, rocking her as I plunge my nose into her hair. "It's okay, baby. I've got you. We don't have to talk about any of this, okay?"

She shakes her head, her words garbled and her voice laden with guilt. "I couldn't tell them what had happened because I knew Vance would hurt Neil. The entire school, even the principal, knew what it meant to go against Vance, his cronies, and their powerful families."

Her lip trembles, tears streaking down her cheek. "I didn't sleep, didn't eat, didn't function for months after. My guilt ate at me for the fact that I hadn't sought out justice for my best friend. What kind of fucking friend was I? While he was buried six feet under, these assholes ran free, getting only minor punishments for trespassing in a restricted area where the cliffs were."

"So, you never confided in anyone? You've carried this all by yourself?"

She swallows, wiping the tears from her face. "I told my parents what really happened a few days after the incident, but the truth is, everyone knew how dangerous and influential Vance's family was. My dad made the decision at the time to take me out of that school and move forward with our lives. We even moved into a different home, and my parents put me in therapy . . . even though it cost them a fortune. The therapy helped, but I couldn't tell my therapist everything, you know?"

"God, I'm so sorry, Kav." The words don't seem like enough, but I'm not sure what else I can provide besides reassurance that I understand.

She runs the back of her hand over her red nose before playing with the ring on her thumb. "But my mom was always there for me." She chuckles, finding some of the lightness back in her expression. "She's quirky and can't keep an appliance working to save her life, but she was my rock. She knew the weight I was bearing by not telling the police, but she also knew that doing so would put our family in danger."

My frown deepens as my heart sinks. "So the assholes got away with it?"

She shakes her head, her lips settling into a hard line. "Call it karma, but I heard the four of them were in a major car accident a year later, where three, including Vance, were killed on the spot, and one of the girls was left paralyzed from the waist down." She pauses, turning her ring a couple of more times. "It didn't give me any satisfaction to hear it because I still felt guilty for not coming forward and doing something about it myself, but it gave me peace knowing they couldn't hurt anyone else."

I clasp her face once more, connecting our eyes, our souls. "I'm not going to tell you how to feel, Kav, but I hope you've forgiven yourself by now, knowing you likely saved your brother."

With her eyes rimmed red, Kavi takes in a breath but doesn't speak. She looks completely drained, as if getting it all off her chest took everything out of her, but hopefully, she feels lighter, too.

A few minutes later, I carry her to my room where I undress her, kissing every inch of her exposed skin— including her scar—and making love to her the way I never have.

Slowly, gently.

Heartbreakingly.

Like she's mine.

"Do you think we'll ever be able to look at another cherry again?" I grimace at the now-empty bowl on Hudson's nightstand. "I'm pretty sure they're repulsive to me now."

Hudson's chest rumbles with a soft laugh under my bare arm. He wraps his arm around my back and pulls me tighter to him. "I'm pretty sure you single-handedly increased that farm's cherry sales today."

I groan, my stomach queasy from the excessive cherry consumption earlier. I swear, I never want to even *think* about a cherry again, but I nuzzle into his deliciously bare tattooed chest, feeling content from head to toe.

Hudson returned from his meeting with our RCS clients in Portland last night and wasted no time declaring that we'd be going cherry picking in the morning. Apparently, he'd remembered how much I liked it based on a story I'd told him about my collection of earrings and how they were mostly acquired during fruit picking outings.

The man's ability to file away details and turn them into the sweetest gestures never ceases to amaze me.

So, after waking me up at the crack of dawn this morning, he dragged me to a farm an hour away, where we spent the morning plucking the last of their cherries, giggling and talking as we strolled down each row.

I especially giggled when one of the farm workers stepped out from a canopy of trees unexpectedly, making Hudson yelp in surprise. After apologizing to the worker—who seemed just as startled by Hudson's scream—we continued on, trying to regain our composure. But at some point my suppressed laughter got the best of me, and I doubled over, holding my stomach in a fit of giggles, mimicking Hudson's yelp. His unamused look didn't help the tears that were streaming down my face.

God, I'm going to miss him.

My chest squeezes at the thought, and I shove it away every time it surfaces.

In just two weeks, I'll be moving to Portland.

We've skirted around the topic of our future, tiptoeing past the elephant in the room as if it weren't there. He's walked by my desk in the office when I've clearly been on the phone with my new leasing office or employer. He's also caught glimpses of the two boxes in my room marked for Portland.

But he hasn't said a word about it.

Nor has he said a word about the fact that I am going to be leaving both his company and his home in the matter of days. I'll be hundreds of miles from him, and I can't tell if that fazes him at all.

A part of me wants to broach the subject head-on, but this crushing fear holds me back—fear of his response, fear of his rejection. Fear of finding out that we've been on different pages this entire time.

Sure, he told me at Madison's wedding that he *couldn't*

shake me, that he wanted more with me, and that he couldn't stand the idea of someone else with me.

Sure, he's gone out of his way to make me feel special and seen—introducing me to his beloved horse, taking me cherry picking, and even holding me while I turned into a mess of tears opening up to him about Nathan.

But nowhere in any of those moments, or the moments he's spent over and inside me, has he brought up our future together.

If he has plans for us, I'd love to be clued in on what they are. I know enough to know that he's never been in a long-distance relationship. And though neither have I, I am a *thousand percent* committed to trying.

The question is . . . is he?

When he said he wanted more, did he just mean for the summer? Did he always have an end date in mind?

Hudson's hand brushes over the back of my arm, and I bury my nagging doubts, clinging to the hope that, in due time, we'd confront the inevitable together. After all, it's not like we'd just say, "It's been good, thanks for the mind-blowing sex," on T-o days with a two-finger salute and be on our merry way.

Could we?

"I have something for you."

His husky voice makes my toes curl, even though I'd just been thoroughly fucked not even ten minutes ago. I swear my body is a twenty-four-hour diner when it comes to him. Apparently, it believes he's allowed to *come* inside anytime. Pun intended.

I tilt my head to gaze up at him curiously. "What?"

He shifts to open the drawer of his nightstand, finding a little box and handing it to me.

Sitting up in bed, I inspect the box in my hand with a

surprised look, noting the way his eyes blaze as they drag down my bare body.

My mouth drops open when I peek inside. "Hudson . . ." I swipe my tongue over my lips as if I'm parched. "Wh-when did you—"

"This morning." He watches my expression intently. "You like them?"

"I . . ." I'm still scrambling for words as the prick of tears meet the corners of my eyes. I inspect the delicate cherries with golden stems hanging off shiny studs with the tip of my finger. "They didn't have a gift shop. Where did you find them?"

He steeples his fingers over his broad chest. "I had them made."

My eyes freeze on him. *He did what?*

"You had them made? Are these . . . are these real?" I indicate what looks like diamond studs.

He chuckles. "Yes, baby girl, they're real. Now tell me, do you like them?"

My brows twist together. "Hudson, I love them. How did you—"

"I knew I was taking you cherry picking before the season was over, and you'd said you always purchased earrings at the gift shops when you were younger so you'd remember the day." He shrugs as if he's not causing my heart to expand tenfold inside my chest. "So I ordered them a while ago. Wanted you to remember today when you looked at them."

Somewhere inside my chest, my heart sings, telling me what I want to hear—perhaps speaking on his behalf. That a gesture like this isn't something you'd do for a woman you had no long-term plans with.

And somewhere in my head I decide I like what my heart's singing about, and maybe I accept that as the truth, too.

"Somehow, they got delivered this morning," he continues. "*That* was all coincidence, though; I couldn't have planned that better if—"

I don't let him finish before I lunge at him.

Placing the earrings on the nightstand, I press my mouth to his before I straddle his waist.

His thoughtfulness, his ability to make the most special moments even more memorable, and the colossal heart he keeps hidden under that gruff exterior has tears ripping from my eyes as our lips fuse.

Destined without a destination.

Chaos and harmony.

Tender and raw.

No matter where I go, no matter the distance or time between us, this man who I love with every ounce of me will forever be etched on my soul.

My fingers bury inside his hair as I taste the cherries on his lips. I might have said I never wanted to think of another cherry again, but that was before I'd tasted them on him.

Shimmying my body sensually over his broad and heavy one, I feel him harden under me again.

My tongue demands entrance into his mouth and Hudson obliges, his hands cupping my bare ass as he glides my core over his erection, groaning.

His scruff tickles and scrapes the skin around my lips as I angle my face to let him explore deeper, dragging my tongue against his and moaning into his mouth. I kiss him until I'm breathless before I rip my mouth away and trail it down his jaw. I pepper it with kisses before licking and sucking his neck.

"Do you know how sexy you are?" I breathe, running my mouth over his chest. "Sexy and sweet and perfect."

I can hear the way his heart gallops as his skin heats under my touch. "I've been told a time or two that I'm pretty damn sexy," he muses, and I know it's to make me laugh. "Pretty sure the word *perfect* has been used a few times, too."

I giggle as expected, biting his shoulder. "Yeah, you like women drooling over you, don't you? Wanting a piece of Hudson Case."

The words taste like acid on my tongue, the thought of him with someone else making my chest heavy. I'll be gone in two weeks, and he'll be free to be with whoever he pleases—and there's no denying he could get whoever he pleased.

Hudson pinches my chin, hearing the edge in my voice. Bringing my eyes to meet his thunderous blue ones, he holds me in place even as I try to avert his gaze. "The only woman I give two shits about drooling over me is you, Kav. *Just you. Only you.* And as for having a piece of me? You should know, you've written your name on all my pieces."

My heart sings again, reiterating that my doubts about the future are just those, baseless doubts. That, even though we haven't explicitly spoken about us after this summer, of course Hudson has plans for us. This is *Hudson Case* we're talking about, isn't it? When has the man done anything without a plan?

I kiss him because I can't turn into a sobbing mess again, and Hudson seems to understand my need to take the lead today.

Keeping his hands loose around my hips, he watches me grind down on him. His nostrils flare at the way my slick center slides over his velvety skin, and I press my hands on his chest, rising over him.

Hovering, I wrap my hand around his massive cock, stroking it the way I've seen him do. Satisfaction courses through me when his jaw locks and his eyes hood at the sensation.

To say I love seeing this powerful man surrender control to me—becoming putty under my touch—is an understatement. I feel like a sorceress, commanding oceanic waves and summoning a storm with a mere flick of my wrist.

I'm spellbound in his adoring gaze and bewitched by his touch. This man, who I thought was nothing but a calloused grump, turned out to be so much more.

Running his tip through my center, I drag it to my entrance before pressing myself down on it. My pussy expands almost painfully as I slip down his shaft, creating a hot seal around him, until he's fully seated inside me. We both moan at the overwhelming sensation of connection as our bodies take over.

"Touch me," I demand breathily, wiggling my ass over him. I'm wet and ready, begging for him to create the type of friction inside me that has the potential of making me pass out. "Please, Hudson, touch me."

His large palm kneads my breast before another slides down to my center. His thumb rolls my hardened nub as he regards my face with utmost attention, watching my mouth drop open and my eyes threaten to roll back. With every give and take, he leaves another trace of himself inside me—something I'll never be able to extract.

"You're so fucking beautiful," he gasps, continuing to rub my clit. "So perfect."

I throw back my head, using my knees to guide me up before slamming back down on him. I grasp his shoulders and slide my pussy up his shaft again before taking him back into my body. Over and over. My juices drip down his cock while the slapping of our bodies and the echoes of our grunts fill the space around us.

Hudson meets me thrust for thrust, sheathing himself inside me. His hair is tousled deliciously, every muscle flexing on his chest as he keeps his eyes pinned to mine, pistoning into my body relentlessly from below.

My thighs start to quake as my walls flutter around his shaft. A flush rises over my skin and settles in my cheeks.

"Fuck, just like that, baby girl."

My chest heaves and my movements become sloppy, my body tiring, but Hudson continues to urge me on, clasping my hip as he drives into me. "That's it. Keep going. Don't you fucking slow down on me."

"Slow down?" I ask breathlessly, leaning down to nip his lip. The tips of my damp hair brush his bare chest. "I'm not the old geezer in this relationship. You sure you can handle this?"

Forfeiting a response—or maybe it's how he intends to answer—Hudson takes the opportunity to grab a fistful of my ass. Gripping the back of my neck, he slams into me from below, over and over, until my stomach contracts and I can barely breathe.

His cock hits me exactly in the right places and elation and frenzy duel inside me. My fingers tug at his hair and I scream as he holds me steady, pummeling into me. His hips pound against mine, dragging his cock through my walls relentlessly, and before long, I'm hurtling toward the finish line.

My body shudders and shockwaves of euphoria pull me under while lighting me up. "Hudson! I'm-I'm going to . . . Oh, God, yes! Hudson, yes!"

I come with a start, squeezing his cock, before I feel the heat of his release fill me, like the crescendo to the most melodious symphony. I collapse over him and he murmurs praises into my ear, telling me what a "good fucking girl" I am and how much he wants me.

And, Jesus, how much I like hearing him say those things.

I might not have the reciprocation of the words I said to him when I told him I was in love with him, but I'm not ready to lose hope yet, either. Not when every touch from him says so much more than his words ever could.

Because if every look and every touch doesn't give me a glimpse of his soul, then perhaps I've had my eyes shut this entire time.

We're a mess of arms and legs tangled around each other as little tremors wrack through our bodies and we gather our breaths.

"I love the sounds you make when you're riding my cock," he says hoarsely against the shell of my ear. "So fucking sexy."

"Thank you for letting me ride," I say with my lips pressed to his skin. I'm so spent, I can barely move.

"You're welcome back on anytime."

I chuckle against him.

Grasping him tighter with my palms sweaty over his slick skin, I lift my head to meld our lips once more. They tangle languidly, without any of the frenzy and madness we seem to gravitate to in our lovemaking, before I rest my head on his chest once again, listening to the drum of his heartbeat.

Feeling the type of peace that people look for all their lives but never find.

Hudson lays a kiss on my sweaty temple before slipping out from under me. He leaves me on his bed while I'm still seeing stars on the outskirts of my vision, beyond sated.

A minute later, he's back with a wet rag. Without a word, he opens up my thighs and drags the warm towel over my center carefully, as if he's doing the world's most important work.

Once he's discarded the towel in his hamper, he strolls toward me, letting me shamelessly admire the way his powerful thighs coil and flex with each step he takes. Before he can get into bed, I grab the box I put on the nightstand and hand it to him.

"Put them on me," I whisper.

His Adam's apple bobs as he gently releases one earring from the box. Leaning over me, he gently threads it through my earlobe before doing the same with the other. I take the moment to pepper a kiss or two over that scruffy jaw I love so much.

I lift a curious brow when he's finished, brushing the tip of my finger against the dangly earring. "Well? How do I look?"

His eyes roam over me. "Like the sweetest thing I'll ever have on my lips."

But like the season of cherries, I should have known nothing lasts forever.

Sometimes it even ends abruptly with an unforeseen wintry frost.

"You do that a lot."

Following Hudson's gaze to notice what he's talking about, I look at my thumb. "Fiddling with my ring, you mean?" A chuckle erupts from my lips, and I slide both my hands down to rest on my laptop. "Yeah, I guess I do. Just a habit at this point."

We're both in our pajamas—me in one of his button-downs and him in sweatpants and a distracting T-shirt displaying his pecs—working at his dining room table with our laptops out the following Wednesday evening. The RCS project is nowhere close to being done since excavations of that size take months, but I'm trying to write up the project updates so I can hand them back over to Belinda when she returns from maternity leave.

We've been staying in touch weekly, and not necessarily about work stuff. Not surprisingly, she asks how things are going between Hudson and me at least three times in our five- to ten-minute conversations. As in, frequently.

After Madison's wedding, I'd let Hudson know that I'd

come clean with Belinda. And though I expected him to be angry, he just sighed, saying he'd prepare himself for the barrage of her questions, but that he had no doubts about her loyalty. She wouldn't speak of us to anyone.

Truthfully, having someone I can talk to about him, especially someone who knows him too, has been pleasantly reassuring, unlike the response from my mom.

Where Belinda is more accepting of our situation, Mom's been concerned and somewhat dubious. It's not that she's against us being together; she's just worried about me getting hurt.

Considering Hudson and I have yet to discuss our next steps, my mom isn't completely wrong, either.

Hudson gently pulls my hand toward him, laying a soft kiss on my knuckles and for whatever reason, I decide to share a bit more. "It was Nathan's." I peer down at the silver band on my thumb. "We'd both gotten ones and had them engraved in high school, but I lost mine." I clear my throat, blinking back the mist collecting inside my eyes. "His mom gave his to me after . . ."

Hudson brushes his thumb over my ring as I trail off. "You turn it whenever you're nervous."

Do I? I mull over his words for a moment. I suppose I do. Subconsciously, it helps me relax. Nathan always had a way of calming me down. I suppose, even in death, he's left me something in lieu of his words to do the same.

"Are you?"

My eyes snap back to Hudson's. "Am I what?"

"Nervous," he probes gently, still dragging his thumb over mine.

Yes, I want to admit.

I am. I have been.

After weeks of waiting, I resolved this afternoon to

broach the subject of our future myself. I just can't wait any longer for a conversation we desperately need to have.

I suck in a breath and glance down at our hands. "Yeah, I suppose I am a little."

Hudson's mouth pulls downward, his eyes searching my face for more clues. "About what?"

I swallow, feeling like I'm about to step on thin ice, wondering if it'll support me or crack under my feet. "I wanted to know what you wanted—"

Knock, knock!

Both Hudson and I turn toward the door, and I swiftly rise from my chair. "That must be our food. I'll get it."

I don't know if I'm disappointed or relieved by the interruption, but the short walk to the door gives me a chance to steady my nerves.

My bare feet tap the wooden floors lightly as I mentally prepare for the upcoming conversation with Hudson. Except, when I open the door, there's no delivery person standing on the other side.

It's Madison.

My heart skitters to a stop as I gape at her, my breath catching in a soft whisper. "Madison?"

The smile fades from Madison's face when her gaze travels down my scant clothing and bare legs, her eyes enlarging as she processes what or who she's looking at.

"Kavi?" Both astonishment and betrayal battle over her features as she tries to compose herself. "Wh-what are you doing at my dad's house?"

At this point, I'm positive my face is drained of any color aside from the telltale hue of guilt and embarrassment. I'm . . . speechless.

Madison and Brie weren't supposed to be back from their honeymoon until the end of next week, around the time I was planning to leave Hudson's apartment.

"You weren't supposed to be back until next week," I say hesitantly, though judging by her expression, I'm pretty sure it sounded more accusatory than I'd intended.

"Kav, what's going—" Hudson's voice behind me has my hackles rising. Without even looking at him, I know he's stopped dead in his tracks at the sight of his daughter on the other side of this door, grappling with how to address this strange meeting. "Maddy? What are you doing back so early?"

Madison's eyes bounce between us. In some alternate reality, Hudson and I could have passed this off as a work meeting, but given my attire—or lack thereof—there's no way she would buy it. "Brie's mom was admitted to the hospital for a minor heart issue—"

Both Hudson and I ask similar questions at once about whether she's okay.

Madison waves her hand. "She's fine. She felt pain in her back and arm and thought it was a heart attack. They kept her overnight, but she's okay. After hearing about it, Brie just couldn't enjoy the rest of our vacation. She wanted to see her mom, so we left. I thought I'd surprise you." She cuts a glance at her dad before she chuckles, though the usual lightness in her eyes is missing. "But, clearly, it's the other way around. Care to tell me what's going on between you two?"

I swing the door open further, inviting her in. My gaze shifts nervously from her to Hudson as I tuck my hair behind my ear. "We were going to tell you when you got ba—"

"It's not what it looks like."

To my astonishment, Hudson cuts through my sentence and my head snaps in his direction while my brain rushes to process his words.

It's not what it looks like? What does he mean, it's not what it looks like?

It's fucking *exactly* what it looks like! That we've been sleeping together!

Madison's blue eyes assess her dad before coming back to me, a hint of pain skittering across her features. "I'm pretty sure this looks exactly as it is. But can you just tell me one thing?" Her gaze stays fixed on me, her jaw tense. "How long has it been going on? Since before or after my wedding?"

I take in a ragged breath, standing in front of her in the foyer on wobbly legs. "Since before."

"Wow." She shakes her head in disappointment, huffing out a half-hearted laugh. I know how much she wanted her father to find someone, but for that person to be her friend? I'm not sure she was ever prepared for that. "I-I don't know what to say."

"Maddy, why don't you come in?" Hudson still looks shell-shocked, running a hand through his hair. "Let's talk about this inside."

I clear my throat as heat finds my cheeks. "I'm, uh . . ." I struggle for words. "I'm just going to put on some clothes."

With that, I hastily leave them, almost sprinting to my room as if being chased, before shutting the door behind me.

I lean against the door, trying to catch my breath, when I hear Madison's incredulous question. "Wait. *She lives here? How long?*"

Fuck! This is a disaster.

I had every intention of telling Madison the truth—especially after her wedding when Hudson and I established there was more between us—but with her finding out like this, I look like the world's biggest asshole. Like a friend who not only betrayed her trust, but who exploited her generosity.

She got me this job when I was in a desperate place, struggling to make ends meet, and how do I repay her? By sleeping with her dad.

Of course she'd look disappointed and betrayed. Of course she'd chuckle without an ounce of humor. I've fucking deceived her, and she's literally the only close friend I have.

Not waiting to listen to Hudson's response to his daughter, I quickly wiggle into a pair of ripped jeans and a T-shirt, securing Nathan's old red and blue flannel around my waist.

I step out with my purse in hand, because as much as I want to confess and have this conversation with her, I'm not sure she's looking for an explanation from me first. And if Hudson and I were on the same page with regards to our relationship, I would have tackled this alongside him together.

But given the way it stands now, I decide to go for a walk and give them some privacy to speak alone.

My hope is, once he's spoken to her, Madison and I can have a heart-to-heart about everything.

She's reasonable and compassionate, and I'm confident that once she understands how her dad feels about me, we can have a more meaningful conversation. And given that Hudson's been clear that he does care about me, I can only hope that the tension between all of us—especially the one I felt between Madison and I—will be resolved quickly.

Stepping into the hallway, I pause, gathering my thoughts and my nerves, before striding toward Hudson and Madison on the couch. Our dinner delivery sits untouched on the kitchen counter, the scent of the Thai takeout we'd ordered now making my stomach turn.

I give them both a tentative smile, noting the way Hudson averts his gaze when I look at him. "I'm going to step out for a little bit and give you guys some time to chat."

Madison rises off the couch, stepping toward me with a softer expression than ten minutes ago. "Kavi, I didn't mean to come off so . . . harsh—"

"No." I shake my head as a bolt of sadness hits my chest. I have no idea how to process it, but it feels like everything— her graciousness, Hudson's strange response, and my own guilt—is winding like a coil inside me. It's all I can do to not sob. "Your reaction was completely valid, Madison. I just need to get some air."

With her blonde hair resting over her shoulders, she steps closer, gently taking hold of my biceps. "I get it, but can we talk later?"

God, I wish she'd tell me to fuck off. I wish she'd rage at me about being the deceitful, ungrateful friend I've been.

I can barely keep my tears at bay as I nod vigorously before rushing toward the exit.

But it's not any of that that has me sobbing as soon as I'm outside the door, leaning against the adjacent wall. It's the fact that not once did Hudson object to me leaving. Not once did he utter a word of his usual concern.

And then it's the next words out of his mouth—ones I wasn't supposed to hear, but ones I'm hearing, nonetheless, as I stand outside his front door—that seal our fate, cracking my heart right down the middle.

"Everything just got out of hand. You know me. I can barely manage a relationship in the same city; it was crazy of me to think I could manage something long-distance." He takes a long pause before clearing his throat. "The terms were clear. It was never meant to be more than a fling."

I suck in a frayed breath, my fingers trembling over my lips, trying to hold in my sob, along with my urge to vomit. It's as if I'm being hurled into a past I've tried to lock into that small closet I was stuck inside for hours, bleeding and begging to be let out.

The terms were clear . . .

"The terms were clear for your little friend Nate here: pay up on time or pay the price. The rich don't get richer by making exceptions."

A void opens up inside me, cavernous and unending, as his words swirl around me. The terms were clear? To fucking whom? Definitely not to me.

I wanted to believe he was different—unlike any of the callused rich pricks I'd had the misfortune of running into during my childhood. But clearly, Vance was right about one more thing—the rich didn't get richer by making exceptions. And I wasn't an exception to Hudson, either.

It was never meant to be more than a fling . . .

The two murmur a few more words, but I can't grasp any of it through the blood pounding inside my ears until I hear Hudson deliver his final blow. A blow that seals our fate. "I'm going to have to be honest with her when she comes back. She deserves that."

Walking away on wobbly legs, I nod as streams of tears cascade down my cheeks, dripping onto the collar of my old shirt. This was never meant to be more than a fling, was it?

He'd known. He'd seen it exactly for what it was.

Temporary.

Disposable.

Short-lived.

I now understand why Hudson never returned my proclamation of love. Or why he never broached the subject of my move. Or even why he acted so aloof in front of Madison right now.

I understand it now.

Just a little too late.

I was the one who refused to believe it before, who kept thinking we had a chance. That we could beat the odds. It was I who buried the red flags, telling me we were coming to an end. And it was I who thought I could see it all so clearly —*us* and our happily ever after.

But it's me who's been wearing a blindfold this whole time.

～

AN HOUR AND A HALF LATER, I shut the door to my childhood bedroom, having excused myself from a conversation with my mom that I couldn't handle at the moment.

She could tell something was wrong, given I was home on a Wednesday night when I had work the next day, but I gave her a vague explanation about missing home and wanting to spend time here before leaving for Portland.

I'm pretty sure she didn't fully buy it, but she was so busy trying to fix her broken toaster, she let it slide.

With shards of glass caught inside my throat, I blink slowly, taking in my small familiar room—my bed with its strawberry-printed comforter, the delicate-looking lamp on my nightstand, and the keepsake box sitting on my flimsy dresser.

My feet drag over the carpet as I cover the distance to my dresser, bringing the box toward me.

I haven't opened it in years . . . a decade, maybe.

Lifting the lid, I peer inside as my heart races through a hazy field of memories. There's a part of me that wants to slam the box shut and bury this need, these feelings, but I can't resist the pull today, either.

What is this urge to open it?

I have plenty of reminders of him—his ring, his shirt, his oversized blazer. Every email I've written to an account I created for him, pretending he'd be reading on the other side.

But this . . . this was a reminder I'd promised myself I'd never revisit.

And yet, somehow, like it's a call, a beckoning from deep within me—*him?*---I decide to confront all my ghosts today.

To unravel completely so I can stitch myself back again.

With shaky hands, I pluck the folded-up piece of paper and bring it to my nose.

It no longer smells like him, though I swear it did the first time I'd held it. And that realization, that I've forgotten his scent, bubbles out of me in a choked sob.

"I miss you," I whisper through trembling lips, tracing his familiar handwriting—*Special K*—alongside the words, *Your mountain is waiting! So . . . get on with your day!* scribbled underneath it.

They'd handed it to me a few days after his death. Who's they? I honestly can't recall; a teacher, perhaps. They'd found it inside Nathan's locker, and after talking to some other students, they'd surmised it was for me.

Sniffling, I open the note, but something—God knows what—has my head lifting toward my small walk-in closet.

And for reasons I don't quite understand—perhaps to both unbury my ghosts and face all my fears alone—I find myself hobbling toward it, clutching my phone tightly in my other hand.

Taking a shuddering breath and working through the panic rising inside me, I step inside the dark, enclosed space, shutting the door behind me.

I can do this.

I will do this.

Falling to the floor and finding a wall behind me as an anchor, I heave in a few gulps of air, feeling like there's already a shortage of oxygen. A frenzy awakens at the outskirts of my mind, urging me to run, to free myself, but a voice inside comforts me, telling me I'm safe, that the fear is all in my head.

I reach for my phone, illuminating the small space using its flashlight. It's not much, but it's enough to quell some of the tension and give me a sense of control.

A shiver runs through me as I open his note, shining the light over it, and reading it for the second time in my life.

My Special K,

One flare, one spark can light up an abyss.

You've always been mine.

And I will forever be yours.

~N

Chapter Thirty-Two

KAVI

I t's some time after nine P.M, and I've counted the same glow-in-the-dark stars covering the ceiling in my room at least twelve times. I'm pretty sure I've gotten a different count for them each time, too.

I still remember when Dad helped me stick them on, along with the now half-working string lights around my big window. He'd come home late from work and, despite his exhaustion, he'd seen a glimmer of excitement in my face since Nathan's passing and couldn't refuse my request. He knew how much I wanted my own space after sharing a room with Neil for so long. And if the inexpensive decor was the only way to put a smile on his daughter's face, then he was determined to do it.

My phone vibrates with a text on my bed and the crack in my heart widens. I don't have to pick it up to know who it is, and for a while I stay unmoving, searching my faux night sky for a path forward.

I already know what the text will say; I can feel that in my gut. Something to the effect of, "Where are you?" or "Can we talk?"

What's really left to talk about?

Sure, he doesn't know I was eavesdropping on his conversation with Madison, but do I really need him to rip my heart out of my chest by telling me what I already know in person?

That it was *never meant to be anything more than a fling*. That *the terms were clear*, and he wasn't going to make an *exception*.

That it was fun while it lasted, but he doesn't know how to commit to anything more, nor does he want to. That while I'm sweet and was a wonderful distraction for the summer, I'm not his type long-term.

That I can keep the cherry earrings, but can he please get his keys back? That it's not me, *it's him*.

Oh God. If he says that last line, I'll head back to his condo right then and cut all his stupid neck ties in half!

Still, like the doomed moth to an incinerating flame, my hand reaches for the phone.

CAPTAIN CRANKYDICK

Where did you go? You've been out a while.

My throat feels dry since I never replenished the liquid I lost through my tears this evening, and I have no more to cry.

Is this what acceptance feels like?

Did I miss that phase of denial, or did some part of me already know it was all too good to be true?

My mind wants me to rage, to jab my index finger into his chest and make him admit he duped me—that he'd planned to be rid of me from the beginning, but never had the balls to tell me until I was leaving—while my heart feels too drained and too battered to even hear his rebuttal.

I loved him.

I *love* him.

Madly.

With a certainty that still clings to my bones.

And somewhere along the way, like a foolish schoolgirl, I was convinced he loved me, too.

Fresh tears sting the corners of my eyes as I pull the phone in front of my face and type out a planned response.

> **ME**
>
> Hey! I got a call from my mom while I was out walking. She sounded really sick, so I decided to catch a cab back home.

And though I'd felt no remorse at the time I'd thought of what I was going to tell Hudson when he checked up on me, guilt now unfurls underneath my ribs with the blatant lie.

> **CAPTAIN CRANKYDICK**
>
> Is she alright? Do you need anything?

I stifle a chuckle at the last question.

Do I need anything?

Yeah, Hudson, I need something you'll never give me. Care to ask what, or will you shove that under your overpriced rug, too, pretending you'll never have to face it, much like you did with every other aspect of our relationship?

> **ME**
>
> Just the flu, but I think I'll need to take a couple of days off to help her.

His response comes back immediately. So immediately, in fact, that I have to wonder if he's relieved I've asked for the time off so he doesn't have to see me.

> **CAPTAIN CRANKYDICK**
>
> Yeah, absolutely. Take all the time you need.

> **ME**
>
> Thank you.

CAPTAIN CRANKYDICK

> I'm heading to Portland tomorrow, but perhaps we can talk when I'm back on Sunday evening? I know that was all unexpected with Maddy today, but I need to chat with you about something.

My bottom lip trembles as a bitter chuckle leaves it. *Oh-fucking-sure.* I should have played the lottery today based on the fact that I knew he'd say he'd want to talk in that vague tone that leaves no room for interpretation as to exactly what that so-called "talk" is.

Brushing an angry tear off my cheek with the back of my hand, I pound out my second lie.

ME

> Yep, absolutely.

∼

THOUGH THE LATE morning sky is bathed in sunlight three days later, the weight on my chest remains, unaffected by its brightness. And while that rain has passed after weeks of thunderstorms, my eyes constantly threaten tears.

With my chin resting in my palm and my fingers tapping my cheek mindlessly, I look out the large picture window at the passersby while I wait for Madison at the coffee shop we agreed on.

Since that cringe-worthy evening she caught me in her father's home—wearing his shirt, no less—I've been trying to gather up the courage to face her again. I promised her a chat and she certainly deserves that, given our friendship and the grace she's shown me time and time again. I'd expect the same if the roles were reversed.

The past three days have stripped me of more than just

my hunger, sleep, and smiles, they've emptied me of the pain as well. Now there's just a hollowed me. An anesthetized me.

I laid awake each night wondering if Hudson was as broken up as I was at the thought of a future without one another. Wondering whether he was distraught at the idea of breaking things off with me tonight, or had he prepared himself long ago because *"the terms were clear"*.

Did the past two months mean anything to him? His spoken words certainly made me believe they did, but I suppose it was always the unspoken ones I should have been listening to.

He's messaged me a couple of times to ask if we can chat on the phone, but I've purposely left his messages unread, sending him a pithy response like, `Sorry, was busy with Mom`, hours later.

And if he's wondering whether something is up, he's biting his tongue until we speak tonight.

"Kavi, hi!"

I'm shaken from my stupor at the sound of Madison's voice, and for a second, I wonder how long she's been standing here. I rise to greet her, somewhat on autopilot, when she wrinkles her brows, examining her watch. "Am I late? I thought we agreed to meet at ten."

I shake my head, letting her pull me into a surprisingly warm hug. "No, you're right on time, as always. I just got here a little early."

Putting her designer handbag on the table, Madison settles into a chair, noticing the medium mocha latte in front of her and arching a blonde brow. "For me?"

My face warms, my lips curving up with a hesitant smile. "A peace offering. It should still be hot."

I'd remembered the coffee she'd ordered the last time we'd met here, but unlike last time, when I had all of fifty-nine cents left to my name, I ordered myself my favorite crème brûlée macchiato as well.

She takes a long sip, keeping her blue-gray eyes on me, as if taking the moment to study my sincerity. "I won't lie, that, uh . . . that night caught me off-guard. Though, I really shouldn't have reacted the way I did. I'm sorry about that."

"You have nothing to apologize for, Madison." I steeple my fingers together, laying my hands on the table and circling my thumbs around the other. "I don't blame you for being as surprised as you were. I would have reacted the same way in your shoes."

Madison tucks a loose strand of blonde hair behind her ear, shaking her head and making her ponytail sway. "Truthfully, I had a feeling my dad was seeing someone. Just something about the way he carried himself at my wedding. I can't pinpoint exactly what it was, but there was an air of excitement and happiness around him. I was actually going to ask him after the cake cutting, but got distracted. I even mentioned it to Brie when we were on the flight that night. I figured he'd tell me when I got back from my honeymoon but, yeah . . ." She looks out the window near us briefly, as if gathering her thoughts. "I just didn't expect it to be one of my good friends."

I wrap my hand around her wrist, my stomach going topsy-turvy. "I'm sorry for betraying your trust. Honestly, what happened between Hudson and I wasn't planned." I take a breath, warding off memories of the searing kiss in Hudson's office and all the times we made love. His hands, his lips, those stormy-sea eyes that held me hostage as he ravished my body. "It sort of just . . . happened."

"That's what Dad said to me as well. He also said—"

"Actually," I interrupt, refocusing the conversation for the reason I'm really here, our friendship. I also don't want to hear anything more about what he said to her—I heard enough before I left his place that night. "I'd really prefer not to talk about your dad right now. What's more important to me is whether you and I are still good. Your friendship means the world to me, and I never meant to hurt you. I hope you don't think I took advantage or that this was some premeditated plan in any way."

Madison turns her palm, capturing mine inside it. "We're still good. I know this was something that caught you both by surprise, but I refuse for our friendship to be in question because of it. You're important to me, too, Kavi, so despite what happens between you and my dad, we will always stay friends."

Despite what happens between you and my dad . . .

My nose tingles and I quickly blink back the pricks of tears at the backs of my eyes, knowing she knows more than she's letting on and respecting her for not betraying Hudson's trust.

"I'm so glad to hear that." I give her a relieved smile before taking a sip of my coffee, hoping it tamps down my tumultuous emotions. "Now, tell me more about your honeymoon."

Jojo's smile widens, her eyes wandering down my raincoat. "You kept it? Did you even try taking off the paint?"

I follow her gaze, taking in the patches of purple and navy paint from the night she hugged me inside that dank, dark shed. "Why would I? I think it looks more beautiful now."

She giggles and there's not a word to describe how happy I am to hear it. It's chirpy and young, exactly how a teenager should sound when they're genuinely content.

I'd asked her to meet me a few minutes before our class so I could catch up with her, given this is our last class.

I've gotten close to all the kids, so this class will definitely be bittersweet, but I feel good about having given them a new outlet for channeling their emotions in a constructive way. And though I won't be here physically for them after this class, hopefully they'll be able to rely on what they've learned to persevere and paint their future with vivid colors.

To this day, I'm saddled by my guilt for not having helped Nathan somehow—perhaps if I'd known he was in trouble earlier or if I could have convinced him not to follow those awful kids after school—but with every class I teach and every student I help, some of that melancholy and remorse lessens.

So, in a way, each student has helped me as much as I've helped them.

I give Jojo a hug before gently grasping her biceps. "How are you? Was that a little snort I caught at the end of your laugh?"

She laughs again, bobbing her head up and down. "I'm good. Things are good at home and with Max."

My curiosity piques. "Yeah? Have you guys been going to counseling?"

She nods again. "I think we all needed it. There was a lot of repressed anger and resentment that needed to be addressed. We haven't resolved all of it yet, but we're laughing more as a family and talking things out before they become bigger, you know what I mean?"

A smile spreads across my face. "That's great to hear. And you and Max are getting along?"

She shrugs. "She leaves a spot open for me to sit with her at her lunch table every day, and her and her friends don't wreck my room anymore, so I'd say that's progress. Though she could work on not rolling her eyes with every sentence, but maybe that's too much to ask for at this point."

I laugh. "Yeah, maybe one step at a time."

A few students filter in, and I remember the gift I brought for Jojo. Taking out a raincoat similar to mine from my bag, I hand it to her. I'd asked all the students to bring a shirt or a sweatshirt since we were going to be painting those today.

Jojo's eyes widen to saucers. "You got me the same jacket as yours?"

"You like it?" I ask, my heart squeezing at the emotion on her face. "I thought we could have matching ones. Maybe you can paint this one to look like mine." I pause, clearing my throat. "You might not know this, but that moment inside the shed with you was monumental for me, too."

Because I fought my urge to run, to resist, and to cower. I pushed past the roll of my stomach and the pounding of my heart at the idea of going inside that small, dark space.

Though I may not have conquered all my fears that night, I certainly didn't return defeated.

And while that night was a pivotal moment for both of us —especially Jojo—there's another reason it will always remain etched in my memory.

Him.

The man standing beneath his umbrella, rain pelting down around him in cascades under the inky sky, waiting patiently without a trace of knowledge as to when I'd reemerge from that shed. A man ready to wait indefinitely without me even asking him to.

A man who never questioned me when I came back out looking like I'd fought a war within myself, somehow knowing that was the last thing I needed. He simply walked me back to his truck and took me home.

A man who's no longer mine.

"I'd love that!" Jojo chimes, pulling me out of my memories and into a hug. "Except, I have a feeling you'll want to trade when you see mine."

I'm only minutes from my high-rise, a silhouette against the evening sky, when my phone jolts to life with a text.

BELINDA

> Have you checked your email?

I frown, reading her words, a strange feeling prickling at the end of my spine. Though she's been copied on work emails during her time off, I hate her working when she still has another week at home with the baby. And though I know she will do whatever she wants, because it's just who she is, she hasn't messaged me about work-related items all summer. So the fact that she's messaging me now means it must be something that needs my immediate attention.

Without responding to her, I flip my email app open to search for what she might be referring to when my eyes land on a subject line that has the blood draining from my face. It takes me a second to process before I note who it's from.

My Resignation.

It's an email from Kavi sent less than five minutes ago,

carbon copied to HR and stripped of the snark and humor from the first resignation she left on my desk months ago.

The one that had me chasing her into an elevator and begging her to stay. The one that had me concocting a plan to keep her around, even though all my instincts fought against it.

I was drawn to her like iron to a magnet even then. Even after the unusual way we'd met, the universe decided to drop her back into my life as if it had a predestined plan.

The words, "effective immediately," flash at me like a flickering exit sign, each syllable pricking my skin with a thousand needles. I have to read them multiple times to interpret their meaning as if I'm reading an ancient language.

Effective immediately?

Questions flood my mind like a teeming river. She still had another week at Case Geo . . . Did something happen? Did her mom become sicker, and now Kavi needs additional time to take care of her? Did her new employer change her start date? Did she just need an extra week to sort things out?

But if any of this was the case, why wouldn't she tell me? Why wouldn't she give me a heads up before sending her formal resignation?

Sure, we haven't spoken much since the night Maddy showed up unexpectedly at my apartment, but I thought that was because Kavi was just busy with her mom. She said as much in response to the texts I had sent her.

Did I miss something?

It sure feels like it. It's as if I'm looking at a puzzle from a distance, but not able to point out the missing piece.

Did I overlook a subtle clue or hesitation from her in my eagerness to believe we were okay? Or was I too preoccupied with everything going on in Portland to realize we weren't?

"Fuck." I curse under my breath, loud enough for Aaron to meet my eyes through the rearview mirror.

My leg bounces restlessly as I wait for him to turn into my entryway, each passing second feeling like an eternity. As soon as he comes to a stop, my feet hit the pavement and I rush through the double doors of my building, anxiety and foreboding thrumming through my veins, echoing the drumming of my heart.

Every step forward feels like one toward the unknown, yet I'm inexorably pulled to it with an urgent need to know. To uncover the truth for myself.

Instinct, suspicion, or just plain nerves twist my stomach into knots, but I push through, intent on getting to her. Finding her.

She said we'd talk tonight. Didn't she? I scroll through fragments of my memories from the past few days, recalling our agreement to talk tonight. Or did she?

I repeatedly jab my finger into the button for my floor, as if my impatience will make the elevator move any faster, all the while noting my agitated stance. My shoulders are bunched, a furrow between my brows reflects back at me from the polished stainless-steel doors. I shift uncomfortably on my feet.

She quit?

Sure, she only had a week left, but to just quit without so much as a warning? It doesn't seem right. She's never spared my feelings in the past, having been brutally honest when I've fucked up. So why not offer me that same honesty before quitting?

Something isn't adding up.

Hurried feet take me to my door and I wrangle my key into the lock, swinging it open and noting how even the air feels different inside.

Still.

Vacant.

Lacking the warmth that was here just last week.

Silence reverberates like a cacophony over every space my eyes wander, and I immediately gather the changes.

Like the lack of her baking sheets and cake pans strewn across my kitchen counters. Like the missing lemon-printed hand towels hanging off my oven handle, giving my kitchen a splash of color. *A splash of her.*

Like the removed nightlights, no longer illuminating my hallways.

It's like I'd instinctually known, even before I made my way up here. Like my brain had accounted for the missing limb before my body had processed it.

That she was gone.

But where? And why?

My heart sinks to my toes, my weighted steps dragging me toward her bedroom door, insistent on knowing for sure, clinging to the hope that I'm wrong. That she'll walk out of her bathroom like she was here all along.

But reality proves otherwise.

Her bed is made, the window shades drawn, but aside from the fact that I can still smell her vanilla and lemon scent in every molecule that hangs in the air, I know that's all I'll find of her in here.

~

I JUMP out of my truck, the slam of my door booming against an otherwise quiet, dimly lit street as I stride purposefully toward Kavi's house. It's the only place I can assume she'd be.

After calling her several times only to listen to her voice-mail, I decided enough was enough. She'd promised me a conversation tonight, and I sure as fuck deserve one. I would have preferred a private venue, and I'll try to convince her to step out onto the porch or into my truck to talk, but if it has to be at her mom's house, then so be it.

My fist rises to meet the door, and though anxiety and irritation dilute my veins like a volatile concoction, I force myself back from pounding on it. I draw in a steadying breath, bracing myself as the door swings open, hoping to meet the amber-colored eyes of the woman I'm here to see, only to be met with another pair entirely.

Kavi's mother's gaze flickers with both surprise and expectation before she gives me a tight smile. "Mr. Case. How can I help you?"

Angling forward, I strain to catch a glimpse of Kavi over her shoulder, my desperation written all over my face. "I'm here to see Kavi. Is she here?"

The lines around her mother's eyes deepen before she offers me a weary smile, empathy and resignation etched in her expression. "I'm sorry, but Kavi already left."

Her words pierce the air with a sharp jab, her gentle tone in opposition to the havoc rising inside me.

Left?

The revelation lands like a blow, and I clear my throat, gathering my composure. "Where did she go?"

The tightness in her stance loosens, her shoulders sagging, perhaps as she notes the concern in my face, my voice. Can she see the fissure forming inside my chest, too? "Portland. She left a couple of hours ago. Her flight should be landing in the next hour or so."

The ground feels unsteady under my feet as the finality of her words register inside my brain. Anguish claws at my ribs as I release a breath, but keep everything I want to say—to ask—locked behind my lips.

She's not the person I want any answers from; hell, she probably wouldn't be able to answer my questions, anyway. And the only person who can didn't feel the need to before she left.

"I see," I reply, my voice hollow as I take a step back. In

truth, I don't see at all, actually, but it's about all I can muster up as a response.

I'm half-way to my truck when Kavi's mother's accented words have me freezing in my spot. "Fear is a bottomless pit, Mr. Case. No matter what you pour into it, it'll demand more."

My brows fold and I retrace my steps back to her, my curiosity piqued by her cryptic words. "I'm not sure what you mean."

She swallows as if contemplating her next words. "Some people fear losing," she shrugs, "it's understandable, but did you know some even fear winning? Some fear the dark, but surprisingly, some fear the light, too. We all fear betrayal, don't we? But I bet some of us fear the responsibility that comes with having someone's trust, too. It's a never ending list, to be honest, but do you know the only thing really worth being fearful of, Mr. Case?"

I stand silent and still under the depth of her gaze and the weight of her words.

"Finding love," she continues. "Or a connection so deep that it reshapes your priorities. Finding a person who accepts your flaws, yet pushes you to grow. Someone who understands you in a way that no one else has, who breaches your defenses and grabs a hold of your heart, despite your efforts to shield it. Finding that someone who becomes the sunshine on your gloomiest days, the center of your world amidst the chaos." She nods, as if she's seeing something well past her words. "Because when you find that kind of love, you also find the greatest fear of all . . . the fear of losing it."

Her words hit me like a relentless downpour, creating an ache so fucking excruciating, it threatens to suffocate me.

"My words weren't just meant for you, Mr. Case. I said the exact same thing to Kavi before she left. You've been quite the beacon of light in her sometimes dim world. And though

I don't know exactly what led to her leaving so soon, I do know this . . . she no longer fears losing your love." Her eyes dim, a cloud of melancholy settling over them. "Because she believes she never had it to begin with."

Iᴛ's fascinating how little moments with someone become the only thing you crave when they're gone.

The way her eyes trailed over me when I walked into a meeting.

The gentle glide of her thumbs over my scruff.

Her soft intake of breath when my lips grazed over her neck.

Each memory is like an agonizing echo, a reminder of what's now out of reach.

It's all I can do not to release the roar I feel rising inside me. A roar that would give way to the frustration and sorrow surrounding my insides.

If she only knew . . .

I'm still sitting in my parked truck an hour later, my head leaning against the warm leather headrest, while staring out into the darkened sky when my phone buzzes with an unusually long string of texts.

My heart leaps inside my chest before it plummets like a stone as my eyes wander over the words, each one like a dagger piercing through the fragile barrier that guards my heart.

KAVI

Hey, Hudson. Based on the several missed calls from you, I assume you've read my resignation and have realized I've left. I am sure you have questions about my abrupt departure and want to chat, but please respect my wishes for this to be our final communication.

Per your words, the terms were clear. This thing between us was never meant to be more than a fling, and I apologize for letting myself get carried away. Though I won't apologize for falling for you, for loving you.

Somewhere in the middle of it all, I started believing in forever when, silly me, I should have known better than anyone that there is no such thing. There is only now, this moment, the present. Nothing else is guaranteed. It's the actions we take in the present that matter, and so, I decided to take my present into my own hands and do what was best for me.

I want you to know that I don't blame you. I should have known better and listened to the words you were saying rather than read between the lines for the ones you never did.

I have no regrets about our time together and I'll cherish every moment we shared, but I couldn't stay longer knowing it was going to end, anyway. Knowing my love wasn't enough.

Goodbye, Hudson. I wish you nothing but the best. -Love, Kavi

I read her text again in complete shock, my heart shattering inside my chest, my world collapsing like a sandcastle swept away by a sudden wave.

Pulling up her contact, I dial her number again, clinging

to the sliver of hope that perhaps this time she'll answer. It rings once before sending me to voicemail, leaving me with nothing but the echo of her voice on the other side. I resist the urge to leave her another message, knowing that my countless others have likely been left unheard.

My fingers fly over the keys with a will of their own, the words pouring out before I even have a chance to fully comprehend what I'm even typing.

ME

> Kav, please call me. We need to talk. There are things you don't know . . . things you should know. Don't do this without hearing me out.

I send her another message, the words spilling out in a torrent of emotion—words that should have been said face to face, where she could have looked into my eyes and seen the depth of my feelings for her.

ME

> I do fucking love you, baby. Please, just give me a chance to tell you in person.

Except both texts turn a different color, like she hasn't received them.

Did she block me?

My frustration boils over, my fist slamming against my steering wheel, eliciting a short honk from my car. Clenching my hair inside my palm, I curse under my breath.

Fucking hell, she blocked me!

Not only did she choose to break things off with a text, but she shut down all communication.

But why? Where did that come from? Is it because we still hadn't discussed our future with only a week left?

Yes, it was fucking risky of me to have kept everything

from her, to not have confided in her about my plan, but fuck, I wanted to surprise her!

And as far as telling her I loved her? Hadn't I shown it with every fucking action?

Hadn't I torn my goddamn chest open and shown her my bleeding heart? Hadn't I bared my soul with every gentle caress and every all-consuming kiss, showing exactly how much she meant to me? Had she not heard any of my whispered confessions, felt any of my raw desire?

What were those, if not admissions of love?

I've never said those words to anyone but Madison—not even to my parents or Jett—and even then, they're rarely said. I grew up in a family that never exchanged them freely, so they've always felt foreign and forced on my lips . . . like they were a formality for something that should have been shown instead.

But, fuck, Kavi didn't know that.

She gave them to me without a second thought, with every ounce of sincerity, and expected to have them returned. She deserved to have them returned.

But clearly, I'm too late.

An unsettling feeling tickles the back of my mind like an itch I can't quite scratch. Something I just read in her text but shouldn't have. Something that has me pulling up her message again, searching for the exact words.

Per your words, the terms were clear. This thing between us was never meant to be more than a fling . . .

Per my words?

What words?

My brain races, trying to recollect the words she claims I said. When did I ever—

And then it hits me like a ton of bricks.

Holy shit!

A roll of nausea dances inside my gut as my mind finds the

missing puzzle piece that explains Kavi's strange behavior ever since the night Maddy came over.

She fucking heard me talking to Maddy that night. She heard me, but clearly, she didn't hear everything.

Pressing my fingers to my forehead, I replay every moment from the night Maddy came over and all my plans seemingly went to shit . . .

Chapter Thirty-Four

HUDSON

Stella pops open the expensive bottle of champagne, and I'm reminded of the last time I was at Carl's Catch when a certain waitress in her too-short, hip-hugging black skirt over thighs I'd dreamed about sinking my face in between for days after, opened the same bottle and landed herself firmly in my path.

In my lap, rather.

And while that was an occasion I was celebrating with my friend Dev for his part in his company's recent acquisition, today I'm celebrating something else—my brother joining Case Geo as our COO.

The formalities have been ironed out, the board's nod secured. Now it's just a matter of announcing his new position to the company—that Jett will now be managing the San Francisco office while I open up and head our new offices in Portland.

Though the plan went into motion right after Maddy's wedding almost a month ago, it's been a long time coming. It was a matter of . . . a lot of things, actually, that held me back from this expansion. My pride being at the top of that list.

My ego, my distrust for anyone but myself, and . . . an actual impetus.

A reason that would make me give up everything I have here—my daughter, home, company, and ranch—and move somewhere else.

And that impetus, that spark, that freaking lightning bolt that lit this whole inferno is her.

I've seen what her job means to her, the way those kids look at her and the warmth and courage she instills into their lives. Selfishly, I tried using my connections to find her an art therapy job nearby. I figured it would be something she wanted, too, given her mom and her brother live here. But none were open for working with children, and I know how much she wanted that.

Hell, I even considered opening an art therapy studio for her so she could run her own company, but given how resistant she's been about taking things from me in the past, and the fact that the experience of working at the children's hospital would go a long way for her, I decided on this compromise.

To follow her.

At this point, I'd chase her across every continent, if that's what it took to be with her.

So, over the past few weeks, I've been making extra trips to Portland to secure a lease on some office space, along with purchasing a new home. It's right near Kavi's work, so she won't have to commute far to get there. In fact, I'm leaving again tomorrow to get a few last-minute things squared away for the house.

It hasn't been easy to do all of this right under her nose, given she literally has access to both my calendar and work mail, but somehow, I've managed to keep things under the radar.

Maddy is now settled in her new life, and I plan to ask her

and Brie to look after the ranch for me as soon as they're back from their honeymoon. Hell, they could move into it if that's what they want.

My company has never been as financially stable, and giving the employees a chance to work with their favorite exec again—the one who lavished them with bonuses and company parties, and who'd do anything for employee morale—would only be the cherry on top.

I've gotten better over the past few weeks—snapping a lot less at meetings and really digging inside myself for the nice guy I'm usually not—but I can't hold a candle to Jett. He has a way with people that I've never had and never will. I don't begrudge him for that; I see the benefits of both our ways of working. But I also know my employees won't be shedding any long tears at my departure.

It's not like we'll be that far away, anyway. With both mine and Kavi's families living here, we'll visit often, and if she ever wants to move back, she'd just need to say the word. I'm sure Jett and I can work out a plan to swap offices.

"What are you smirking at?" Jett asks me as Stella pours the champagne into our flutes.

Stella's demeanor has noticeably brightened since we hired more servers and another supervisor. I've also loosened up on my standards for excellence. There's no doubt I still expect nothing but the best, but I'm giving more leeway when it comes to servers in training. Kavi cemented that decision for me.

In some ways, her being a terrible server—though I'd never tell her that, lest I want to lose my fucking balls—was the best thing that could have happened to me.

"Just wondering if there will be an early company shut down the day I announce my Portland move because, let's face it, our staff will be too devastated to focus," I quip with a wry smile.

Jett guffaws, throwing his head back. "Oh, the company will close early, alright. But it'll be because we'll be celebrating the dictator finding other pastures to rule."

I squint at him while Stella giggles, pushing our flutes toward us, and gives me a look like she agrees with him. I might be a broody asshole boss, but I get the feeling none of my staff is really scared of me. I'm not sure what that says about me; I'll have to contemplate that another time.

I pick up my glass, clinking it with my brother's. "Welcome back, little brother, and before you ask, no, you can't have my office. I've asked maintenance to open your old one back up; mine will remain mine for the times I come back to visit."

Jett reels back animatedly. "Dammit! I knew I should have negotiated getting your office as part of the deal before the board signed off." He chuckles before the teasing in his tone softens, giving way to sincerity. "But seriously, though, I'm glad to be back."

We both take sips of our champagne as Stella leaves to place our lunch orders.

Jett clears his throat. "So, have you told your . . ." he makes a confused face as if contemplating the words, "girl-friend? Admin? The woman responsible for thawing the glacial grump that you are?"

I lift a brow. "She won't be my admin for long. I'm planning to tell her tonight now that all the details are finalized. I'm surprising her with a new set of house keys for our place in Portland."

My brother's brows lift. "*Our?* As in, yours and hers?"

"I plan to make everything mine and hers," I say resolutely. There's no question she's the only one I want for the rest of my life.

My brother gives me a long stare, letting my words sink in. "You really love this woman."

I watch a few bubbles rise to the top inside my champagne flute, reflecting on my feelings for Kavi, my amber-eyed ray of sunshine and sass. "I've taken forty-six years to find her, and I won't waste another second without her. Yeah, I fucking love her."

Though I haven't said those three words to her yet.

I plan to—there's no doubt about it—but they're just words, aren't they? Hopefully my actions, especially the surprise I have planned, will speak for themselves.

I have it all mapped out, too. We'll eat dinner, and when we're lying in bed, I'll casually dangle the new set of keys in front of her. The ones for my current apartment have that metal orange attached to it. I got her a cherry keyring for this one. It's silly and simple, but it's her.

It's us.

Jett's grin widens, his teeth gleaming with happiness that matches my own. "I'm happy for you, big bro. She seems like a great girl." His smile wavers a little. "Does Madison know yet? About any of this?"

I shake my head, running a hand over my face and feeling the weight of the impending conversation with my daughter pressing down on me. "Not yet."

While I've spoken to Maddy over the past few weeks, I've held back dropping such monumental news over the phone. My plan is to first surprise Kavi with it tonight, and then inform Maddy next week when she's back in town.

To be honest, I'm not sure how she'll react. She's always been level-headed, but telling your daughter you're in love with her twenty-five-year-old friend and you're moving to another state to be with her isn't your run-of-the-mill conversation.

As Stella sets down our lunches, Jett reaches for his fork, casting a concerned glance my way, no doubt noting my apprehension. "Maddy's a reasonable person. Maybe she won't be thrilled, but I'm sure she'll come around to it. She's always wanted you to find someone." He digs into his shrimp pasta. "And now that you have, it's all upwards from here. What could go wrong?"

Indeed, what *could* go wrong?

Except, perhaps, the nightmare scenario of the woman I love vanishing overnight because my grand gesture came too late.

～

My dad used to say, "When you find the woman meant for you, you'll notice every little thing about her. And you'll collect those little things like a magpie hoarding shiny trinkets, each one more precious than the last. From her throaty laugh to the animated way she speaks with her hands, to the way she plays with the ends of her hair when she's lost in thought." I knew he was admiring my mother, who was standing somewhere in the distance. "You'll notice her because every detail about her will be as significant as a brushstroke on a masterpiece."

He was right.

There's not a single thing I don't notice when it comes to this woman sitting next to me. From her deep sun-kissed thighs tempting me from under my button-down to the ribbons of her dark hair framing her face as she plays with her ring.

She's compelling.

Captivating.

She's never divulged the importance of that ring, but given that I've seen the inscription inside, I'm assuming it has something to do with her childhood best friend.

Each turn of that ring tugs at something deep inside me, an ache I struggle to put into words. An ache for a friend I'll never meet, who knew her in ways I never will. But an ache for her loss, too.

"You do that a lot," I say, pulling her attention to me.

I know she has something on her mind—aside from the work glaring back at her from her computer screen—and I'm willing to bet it's something to do with us.

I have us on my mind, too. She may not know it, but it's all I've had on my mind for weeks now—how to find a long-term between us.

I've never been good at divulging plans until they've solidified. It's another one of the many lessons Dad taught me—not to count your chickens before they hatch—but now that everything is set, I'm dying to tell her.

I just want to do it a certain way . . . something that'll have her gasping next to me in our bed.

"Fiddling with my ring, you mean?" She laughs like a chorus of tinkling bells, bashful and unsure. "Yeah, I guess I do. Just a habit at this point."

I cherish her habits, her tells, like the shiny trinkets I find more precious than all the riches in the world.

Bringing her hand to me, I brush my lips over her knuckles and savor the scent of her lemony fragrance.

"It was Nathan's," she explains, a tremble meeting her chin as she wades through memories. "We'd both gotten ones and had them engraved in high school, but I lost mine. His mom gave his to me after . . ."

I nod, gliding my thumb over her silver band. This is one ache I'll never be able to diminish for her. "You turn it whenever you're nervous. Are you?"

Her eyes widen as if she hadn't realized it herself. "Am I what?"

"Nervous?" I ask.

She regards our linked fingers and I squeeze tighter,

letting her know I'm right here. "Yeah, I suppose I am a little."

"About what?"

Maybe I should just give her the key now. Maybe this whole plan to wait was blown out of proportion. It's not like a proposal or a surprise birthday party. It's just a key to tell her that I can't stand the idea of being apart from her any more than I know she can without me.

That I can't live without her. That I only want to live with her.

A strange urgency springs up inside me, and I'm about to ruin the surprise I had planned when she answers, her face a mix of concern and resoluteness, like she's battling her decision to speak. "I wanted to know what you wanted—"

Knock, knock!

We're both interrupted at the sound coming from the front door when Kavi rushes toward it, announcing it's likely our food.

I take the time to saunter into my bedroom where I have the key resting in my nightstand. I'll give it to her during dinner.

Key in my pocket, I'm on my way out of my room when I hear a familiar voice at the door, other than Kavi's. My mind whirs as I shuffle into the foyer. "Kav, what's going—" My surprised gaze meets identical eyes over the threshold and my heart thunders inside my chest, like I'm about to take an exam I'm ill-prepared for. "Maddy? What are you doing back so early?"

Maddy assesses me and Kavi as if she's trying to trace the lines of an unfinished story. "Brie's mom was admitted to the hospital for a minor heart issue—"

Both Kavi and I jump at once to ask if Brie's mother is alright, to which Maddy confirms that she is before turning hurt and astonished eyes back toward me. "I thought I'd surprise you. But, clearly, it's the other way around. Care to tell me what's going on between you two?"

I'm not sure what overtakes me—my nerves when I'm working without a plan or my anxiety at having been caught in this way. It also doesn't help that Maddy looks like she's been stabbed in the back, and for whatever reason, I speak at the same time Kavi does.

My words, "It's not what it looks like," collide with hers, "We were going to tell you when you got back," and for a moment, time stands still.

For a moment, I wonder why or how I even said what I said.

Of course we were going to tell her when she got back. Of course it is exactly the way it looks. So why did I fumble the way I did? Why was my brain not aligned with my mouth?

I'm about to retract my words, noting the horror on Kavi's face, when Maddy speaks, her hard eyes betraying her bruised heart. "I'm pretty sure this looks exactly as it is. But can you just tell me one thing? How long has it been going on? Since before or after my wedding?"

"Since before," Kavi answers, while a part of me wants to hit pause or rewind or something, just to give myself a moment to figure out how to navigate this entire situation.

"Wow," Maddy says with a strangled laugh. "I-I don't know what to say."

I want to go to her, to hold her by the shoulders and tell her everything. That I've found the person she's been begging me to find for God knows how long. That I'm madly in love and so goddamn happy. But with the way she looks, both disappointed and shocked at having found her father with her good friend, I first need to tend to her wounds.

I suppose the father in me will always put her first in that regard.

"Maddy, why don't you come in?" I ask tentatively, as if

I'm dealing with a wild animal, unsure how it'll react to my attempts at gentleness. "Let's talk about this inside."

Kavi mumbles something about changing her clothes, and I reach out a hand to grasp hers, but she hastily skirts by me, not noticing my crestfallen face.

Looking back, I know there was a better way to have handled this, but it's as if my brain was in slow-motion while everything else was whizzing by. If I've ever thought I was good at thinking on my feet—and I seem to be when it comes to work-related situations—life is giving me a look at myself from another angle, and it's fucking pathetic.

The door to Kavi's room shuts with an inaudible click, almost as if she's trying to stay as unnoticed as possible, and Maddy turns to me inside my living room. "Wait. *She lives here?*" she blurts, large saucer eyes directed at me. "How long?"

I grimace. "Practically all summer."

Her shoulders slump, like all the fight inside her is fleeing. "Wow," she whispers, almost to herself. "All summer, and you didn't think to tell me? Neither of you?"

Rubbing my temples, I explain, "It was supposed to be temporary while she worked on the RCS account. She lived across the bay and was having to take the subway . . ." I explain, knowing I'm not telling her everything—that there was an inexplicable connection I felt with her friend, one I couldn't get myself to break. A connection I wanted to cultivate, despite not realizing that at the time. "I had extra rooms in my condo, so I asked her to stay here to save her time."

Another knock interrupts our conversation and I amble over to bring in our Thai takeout, hunger forgotten amidst all the tension.

Placing it on the kitchen counter, I return to sit by Maddy.

"I just wish either of you had said something to me,"

Maddy says, turning to me. Her expression softens, typical of her forgiving nature. "But you know what, Dad? This isn't about me. This is about you and Kavi." She lifts a brow, giving me one of her serious looks. "Please tell me it's not just sex."

I reel back. "Maddy, not that I've shared much about my sex life with you—"

"Thank God for small mercies," she interrupts, trying to lighten the moment.

"But I wouldn't have asked someone to move in with me, spent every stolen moment with them, if it was just about sex. I could get that without any strings attached if I needed."

She crosses her arms, her nose scrunched. "Firstly, gross. And secondly, you said it wasn't what it looked like not even five minutes ago."

I exhale heavily, feeling like the biggest piece of shit. "Yeah, I mishandled that—"

"I'm going to step out for a little bit and give you guys some time to chat." Kavi's voice has both Maddy and me turning toward her. With her purse in hand, clad in her trademark strawberry-print T-shirt and ripped jeans, she looks both hesitant and resolute.

Madison rises to meet her. "Kavi, I didn't mean to come off so . . . harsh—"

"No," Kavi interjects. "Your reaction was completely valid. I just really need some air."

Maddy's face gentles toward her friend, her hands brushing her biceps. "I get it, but can we talk later?"

Kavi nods before rushing out.

I want to stop her, to have her sit beside me and Maddy so we can sort this out together, but I sense both women need a moment apart to process. I'm not a mind-reader, nor do I claim to understand women or humans in general, but I do what I think is right at that moment.

I listen to Kavi's plea to get some air.

Though, now that she's gone, was that a sniffle I heard as she shut the door?

Fuck, am I doing anything right today?

"God, Dad." Maddy's voice and her rounded eyes have me coming out of my haze. She shakes her head, a smile blooming over her lips, like she's been watching me longer than I noticed. "You really like her."

I gulp in some air, reciting the words I've rehearsed countless times since realizing I was falling for Kavi and needed to tell my daughter. "She moved in with me, and I thought that would be that. We'd work and live together but stay out of each other's ways, otherwise. But no matter how much I tried, I just couldn't resist her pull. And from there, everything just got out of hand. You know me. I can barely manage a relationship in the same city; it was crazy of me to think I could manage something long-distance."

I pause, sliding my hands down my face and feeling surprisingly choked up. Like all the emotions of the day—finalizing everything with Jett, having the keys to our new life in my hand to give to Kavi—are bubbling over, and I can't contain the relief and excitement about taking this next step toward her. *With her*.

"The terms were clear. It was never meant to be more than a fling . . ."

"But?" Maddy prompts me to continue, knowing I have more to say.

"But . . ." I press my hands together, lips against them for grounding. "She came out of nowhere. She stole every thought, every fucking heartbeat." I look at my daughter, unblinkingly. "No, Maddy, I don't just like her; I'm fucking crazy about her."

Maddy's hands fly to her mouth, a teary smile peeking through. "And all that talk about not handling long-distance?"

"It's all true. I can't do long-distance with her," I state

plainly. "And I'm going to have to be honest with her when she comes back. She deserves that."

Her smile falters. "Wh-what do you mean? How else would you guys make it work if Kavi's moving? It'll have to be long-distance with you working here."

And that's when I lay out the rest of my plan.

Little do I know then that I'll never get to see it through.

Chapter Thirty-Five

KAVI

One Month Later

From: Kavi <specialk_jain@gmail.com>
To: Nathan <nathans@gmail.com>
Date: September 18 1:22 AM
Subject: When you're in a Slump . . .

There are times I wonder where life would have taken us if you were still alive.

Would you have been living out your bachelor days or would you have found someone to share every passing moment?

Would we still talk every day or would we have let the arms of time and distance separate us?

Would I have been calling you on a night where I couldn't sleep because all I needed was my best friend to tell me it would get better?

Because no matter how much I want it to, it isn't getting better. This ache in my bones, this void inside my chest. Is this what everyone talks about when they say everything is fixable but a broken heart?

Because there's a black hole where my heart used to be. And now there's only a vortex of grief, of perpetual night.

I keep living out the summer in my head, replaying it as if it were the only movie on every channel, and somehow hoping for a different ending, knowing full-well there's only one.

The funny part about this whole situation is that I can't even yell and scream at Hudson for lying to me. Because he never lied. He never misrepresented where he stood. That was all me, playing out a fairy tale in my head.

But he did rob me, Nathan.

He stole something I can't quite put into words—an indescribable something I'll never get back. Whether I have a right to mourn the loss of him or not, I do have a right to mourn that.

Another piece of me that's gone forever.

xoxo

Special K

"You okay, Kavi? You've been gazing out those windows all morning."

I blink out of my stupor, dropping my fingers from my cherry earrings I was fiddling with, and look toward the voice of Amanda Hitchens, my supervisor at the children's hospital I now work for. "Just admiring the pristine blue skies. It's as if the heavens are pretending they didn't have an all-out melt-down last night with the torrential downpour we had."

Amanda follows my gaze through the window. "Surprisingly, summer rain is pretty rare in Portland. Maybe it's a sign of something unexpected on the horizon. Nature has a way of signaling shifts in the air, don't you think?"

She shuffles inside, looking over the shoulders of some patients—kids who have the misfortune of being at the hospital for extended times—as they put together their 'feelings collage' using newspaper and magazine clippings, while I contemplate her words.

Shifts in the air . . .

That's putting it mildly when I consider all the shifts over the past month. From living in a tiny studio nearby to learning a new city to finding my footing at a new job, there's been a lot of shifts and changes.

Not to mention learning to live with a broken heart . . .

"Why don't you go grab your favorite coffee from that café across the street, and I'll watch the kids for a few minutes?" Amanda regards me with concerned eyes from behind her glasses, perhaps noting my frown. "You look like you could use the walk outside."

Hesitating momentarily, I give her a grateful smile. Some days are better than others, but that's not the case today.

Today, I feel like I'm cracking from the inside, and it seems even my new boss can see that. "Are you sure?"

"Positive," she reassures me, waving me off. "Now, shoo. I'll be here when you get back."

Letting the kids know I'll be back in a few, I swing my purse strap over my shoulder and step out of the hospital's large entrance, welcoming the sun's warmth on my skin. The hospital art room always tends to be chillier than I prefer.

My trusty orange shoes tap over the wet pavement as I navigate around puddles, making my way to the cafe I frequent. I've become a regular there over the past month, even striking up a friendship with the barista. We even went to the art fair together last weekend when she asked me to join her and a few friends.

Being alone isn't anything new to me, but it was a nice change from the several lonelier weekends I've spent at home, talking to Mom and Neil when the silence feels all too deafening. Though, those lonely weekends have helped me get back into painting again. I'm almost done with the one I started a couple of weeks ago.

One I know I'll have to discard or give away once I'm done because I won't be able to look at it much longer. Not when, every time I do, it salts the wounds I've tried to close for weeks.

But I painted it to deal with my heartbreak head on. To close that short chapter of my life once I finished the piece. To remind myself with every brushstroke that waiting for someone who never really wanted me in the first place is futile.

Pining is a silent poison that seeps into the soul.

His terms were clear, and now so are mine. My terms to put myself and my heart first. God knows, it had already been battered and put through the wringer before Hudson came into my life, and now, in the aftermath of his presence, it's barely functioning.

Doing the bare minimum of pumping blood into my veins without a hint of purpose or pride. With mechanical indifference and apathetic duty, a mere shell of what it once was.

"I couldn't erase you if I tried."

"I can't shake you, Kav."

My bitter laugh catches me off-guard when more of his sweet whispered words trek through my mind as they have so many times before. Words that were a salve for my wounded soul. Words I basked in like a parched desert flower under a gentle rain.

But words that now ring false and hollow, having ripped away the flower from its roots, only to fling it across the desert to lay exposed and defeated.

Taking a deep breath, I approach the coffee shop, stowing away my emotions behind a forced smile, before walking through the entrance.

Lena, my barista friend, waves to me after attending to the customer ahead of me. "Hey, chica! Want me to make you your usual?"

I step up to the counter, giving her a smile with a nod. "I think I'll switch it up a little today and do an iced one this time."

She reels back with mock surprise, her brows in the air. "Living on the edge, are we, Kav? I'll have an iced crème brûlée latte coming to you in a flash."

I try to brush off the pang that jabs my heart at the use of my nickname—a reminder of the only two people I've allowed to call me that, and the two who are now absent from my life.

Not that I couldn't, but I haven't discussed anything in terms of my previous relationships with Lena yet. And though I see her as someone I could confide in, the situation with Hudson is too raw for me to relive just yet.

I've exchanged a few texts with Madison and Belinda, mainly about my new life and job. We've all conveniently avoided Hudson's name. And that's probably for the best, considering the strange position I likely put them in when I left him. Perhaps one day we can all laugh about it, but that day isn't today, nor will it be anytime in the near future.

Lena turns over her shoulder to address me while tamping the espresso. "So that hot daddy I was telling you about the other day swung by again just a few minutes ago."

"Oh yeah?" I waggle my brows at her. It's becoming clear that Lena takes stock of the eye candy entering the café, given the number of 'hot daddies' and 'tight butts' she's mentioned to me in the short time I've known her, but I play along, joining her excitement. "What did he order this time?"

"The same thing," she reports, pouring the freshly brewed espresso into a plastic cup. "A cherry turnover and coffee. But," she pouts, puckering her lips, "turns out he's taken. Well, actually, now that I think about it, I don't know if he's taken. I think he's in mourning."

Her hands freeze while her mouth drops open as if she's just put something together. "Oh my God! I think he's mourning his dead girlfriend!" Her eyes mist. "Poor thing. He must be heartbroken. Perhaps I could move my schedule around to give him company in case he wants a shoulder, *or a boob*, to cry on."

I watch a multitude of emotions cross her face—shock, sadness, acceptance, excitement—while I try to keep up. A part of me wants to laugh at how she's made this entire scenario up in her head and has already started making plans to turn it around in her favor, but what if she's right? I wouldn't want to laugh about someone's dead girlfriend.

"What do you mean, he's mourning his dead girlfriend?" I ask, confused. "You asked him?"

"Well, not exactly," she admits, affixing a lid on my iced coffee. "I just asked him what the deal was with him ordering the same cherry turnover each time he's come in, and he said they remind him of the time he went cherry picking with his girlfriend. It totally had a dead girlfriend ring to it."

My heart stutters and another pang punches me in the gut as memories of Hudson and me picking cherries flood my mind.

Stolen kisses underneath cherry trees . . .

His soft groan as he pulled my hips flush with his, brushing his tongue against mine . . .

The heat of his body mixed with the scent of cherries—

"Kavi? Hello?"

I'm jostled from the past as Lena's words and face come back into focus. "Yeah, uh, sorry," I mumble, dropping my hand from my earring.

She quirks a brow. "Don't you agree? He must have been speaking about his dead girlfriend, right? There was just something about the way he said it."

"Yeah . . ." I agree hesitantly. "Maybe."

She gleams. "Then it's set. I'll commence *Operation Dead Girlfriend* by asking him more about her next time, and we can mourn her together over a fresh cherry turnover. Then I'll strategically offer myself up in case he wants mourning sex."

She assesses my horrified face because, at this point, I can't tell if she's joking or not. I don't know her well enough to.

"Don't knock it til you try it, sister," she chides. "It's almost on par with makeup-sex, though not as deliciously savage as hate-sex."

I can't help but giggle at her refreshing honesty. "You do that. Tell me how it goes."

Picking up my coffee after paying for it, I'm just heading toward the exit when Lena calls me again, "Oh! A bunch of people took stubs off your flyer." She points to the bulletin board near the exit. "Hopefully you'll have a better turnout this weekend."

I stop at the wall with the bulletin board to find that five of the ten stubs have been ripped off my flyer.

Not bad, I think to myself. Hopefully, my second free art therapy class will have more than the two kids who showed up last weekend.

Walking back to work, feeling better than I did when I left, I think about Amanda's words earlier.

Perhaps there is something unexpected looming on the horizon . . .

Perhaps the winds of change are headed to Portland . . .

The question is, will that unexpected something—that shift in the air—be enough to fill the gaping hole inside my chest?

"THANK you to those of you who brought empty shoe boxes today," I say, addressing the ten or so kids who came to the free art therapy class I'm leading tonight. I'm thankful to have secured a room at the hospital that allows me to pursue what I love, even outside of my regular job.

"I'm so glad you all enjoyed making the memory boxes during the class project. We chose to fill our boxes with pleasant memories today," I continue with a smile, looking at the faces of students who seem impressed with their own creations. "And my hope is that whenever you find yourself faced with tough times, reading through these uplifting memories will help you remember those past connections and experiences with a renewed sense of happiness. I hope these memories serve as a source of positivity and strength in times you need them the most."

I conclude the class, letting everyone know the assignment for next week, and gather the bag I'd brought filled with empty shoe boxes in case someone forgot theirs. Fortunately, almost everyone brought one with them, probably because I requested it on the flyer.

Heading to my car in the parking lot—a used Volkswagen I bought a couple of weeks ago after giving my old one to my brother—I catch sight of something laying on my hood. Hurrying over, I toss the bag of shoe boxes into my trunk before closing it and rounding to the front for the object.

It's . . . a memory box.

Glancing around the empty parking lot, I can't help but wonder if someone accidentally left it there. But then again, why would someone leave their memory box—filled with their personal memories—on my car?

Upon closer inspection, each side of the memory box is covered with pictures: cherry earrings, wildflowers, a snapshot of me on Hudson's horse Whiskey, a batch of my cornbread cooling on his counter, my orange Doc Martens resting in his foyer, and even my old keys nestled inside a bowl.

A sudden breeze tousles my hair, matching the frantic rhythm of my heart as my eyes scan each image. My hand trembles, a surge of hysteria blooming inside me, as my brain races to catch up.

How did this get here?

When did he put it here?

When did he take these pictures?

With my heart thundering and a well of emotion gathering between my lids, I lift the top of the beautifully decorated box. My stomach catapults as I pluck the picture of the two of us lying on his bed.

I'd taken it on his phone, my teeth grazing his scruffy jaw, my smile evident, while he stares humorlessly into the camera. It was a picture we'd taken right after making love. A picture I'd giggled looking at because, if nothing else captured the essence of Hudson Case, it was that—a man who couldn't be bothered to smile for a camera, for anyone, really, but would freely smile at me.

Beguiling, bewitching . . .

But mostly . . . betraying.

A drop of something wet falls onto one of the papers underneath, and when the breeze touches my face and my cheek tingles, I realize it's my tear. Brushing the back of my hand over it, I pick up a handwritten note.

The night you walked out of your house in Christmas pajamas and bare feet.

A stone lodges inside my throat, a sob bubbling in my chest as I pick up more pieces of paper.

The time you scraped up your hands and knee, and I wanted to hold you hostage in my bathroom and kiss your lips.

The night you told me you were afraid of the dark.

When I heard you crying in your sleep.

The night you went into that dark shed, and I could hear your heart over the thunder that broke the sky.

When you made peppermint cookies for Kansas.

The time I painted orange over my head and heart on the life-size outline of myself. The time I painted you.

More tears drip down my cheek, staining the papers underneath, but I don't dare move or turn around when footsteps tap the pavement behind me.

Footsteps that reverberate through me, setting every molecule alight, every heartbeat dancing, every butterfly soaring.

Footsteps that echo, even in the recesses of my dreams.

He's here . . .

I read the next note.

The night I told you what I was afraid of.

My tears tumble over my lids as I raise my head, barely able to hold myself steady against the gentlest breeze and whispered words I'll never forget—a piece of himself he gave to me even that night.

"Finding someone worth changing for, only for her to realize I'm not worth the trouble."

Chapter Thirty-Six

KAVI

I spin around, leaning against my car for support, to find him staring back at me. Goosebumps ripple over the expanse of my skin under his smoldering gaze.

One month.

One month of happiness flits by like a summer breeze, but one month of heartbreak lingers like an eternal winter.

There hasn't been a day, a waking moment, where I haven't conjured him up in my thoughts. Not a second that's passed where I wasn't feeling like I was suffocating without him.

I shake my head, my chin trembling, indicating the box in my hand. "This isn't fair. *You* aren't being fair."

His hands are buried inside the pockets of his suit pants, and while I look like I'm shattering all over again, he looks confident . . . like he's never been broken.

How dare he look so self-assured and righteous, standing under a beam of light, when I'm over here drowning in the shadows?

Hudson takes a step closer, and I try to melt into my car. "I loved you more with every memory, Kav."

I swing my head left to right, a heaviness I've never felt on my chest threatening to snuff out my breaths.

"Since the day you left that slice of cake on my desk," he continues, taking another step forward, crossing a chasm I'm not prepared for him to cross. "To the day you threw a resignation in my face and sassed at me in the elevator, to the night we stood under your umbrella in the pouring rain."

I blink rapidly, hoping to trap my tears behind my lids but doing the opposite instead.

"I loved you the day you told me your dreams, to the day you shared your fears, your childhood, and your secrets. I loved you when you cried in my arms, and I loved you when you smiled under my touch. I've loved you in every goddamn moment, Kav, and I'll continue to love you more with every new one, if you'll let—"

"No." I shake my head again, pulling the box to my chest as if he's threatening to snatch it from me, all the while wanting to hurl it to the ground. "I heard you. I heard you tell Madison that we were temporary, that it was just a fling. I heard you say that it got out of hand, that we got out of hand."

He nods. "I'm not denying what you heard. But, baby, you didn't hear the best part. The part when I told her that, despite the fact that we started as something temporary, you'd become a permanent part of my heart. That it did get out of hand, but in the best of ways. That I couldn't fathom not being with you, not then and not ever."

I don't move, don't breathe.

Hudson watches my face, recognizing the doubt and disbelief set over my frown before he tilts his head to the box. "Don't believe me? Look underneath the papers and you'll find what you need. And if you don't," his jaw clenches, like he hasn't considered an alternative until now, "then I'll turn around and leave."

My eyes drop to the box and the larger, folded papers underneath the small ones. I pull one out, unfolding it with one hand, and rest it over the open box to read.

It looks like some sort of leasing contract for an office space.

"Read the date," Hudson demands softly, taking a step forward as slowly as one would when assessing an injured animal, so as to not alarm them.

Fresh tears find the corners of my eyes as I read the date —almost two months ago. "Wh-what is this?"

Hudson steps closer, only a foot or two away from me. "Read the other one."

I pull out the other paper with shaky hands, my eyes scanning the deed to a property in Portland, signed and dated a little over a month ago. Days before I left.

My chest heaves.

My heart skips.

"I'd been working on the move for well over a month before that." He swallows, his throat bobbing under an unbuttoned collar.

"You . . ." I blink at him, my stomach feeling hollow. "You live here now?"

He nods. "I opened the Portland branch of Case Geo a couple of weeks ago."

"But, what about . . ." I trail off, trying to collect my thoughts. "What about the ranch? What about the San Francisco office?"

He shrugs, hands still tucked into his pockets. "I decided they weren't as important as the quitter I wanted to chase." A smile dances on his lips. "They'll always be there. Maddy and Brie are taking care of the ranch, and Jett took over managing the office."

He gave the office to Jett?

He left his home, his ranch? He left Kansas?

My heart is in my throat, my voice a hoarse whisper. "You did that . . . for me?"

Hudson closes the distance between us, pulling the box from my hands and placing it on top of my car. Strong arms collect me as he slides his hands to my face, cupping my cheeks. "I'd do anything for you, Kav. *Anything*."

A heated tear rolls down my cheek. "Why didn't you tell me?"

He brushes my cheek with his thumb. "I had a plan to surprise you the night Maddy came over, but I realized later that I should have told you sooner—the moment I started the entire moving process. I fucked up, Kav. I fucked all of it up, and I'm so sorry. But," eyes like cerulean windows mist with a mixture of anguish and hurt, the first crack in his intrepid facade, "you didn't give me a chance to. You left before I could tell you anything."

"So, you've been here for the past few weeks, but you're just now coming to see me?"

I don't mean to sound accusing since I'm the one who cut off our communication, but he changed his entire life and has been here all this time. Why wouldn't he find me sooner?

The corner of his lip tips up. "It took me time to get everything settled here . . . time I didn't want to share once I had you in my arms. And since you didn't want me to contact you, I thought perhaps that time was something you needed, too. But I couldn't wait any longer."

My mouth drops open in an effort to speak, but nothing comes out. How could it when everything seems to be clicking into place, and I'm realizing that I fucked up, too. That not only did I cause myself an entire month of heartache, but him, too. That, had I stayed and given him a chance to talk to me face-to-face, we could have saved each other from this anguish.

I just assumed I knew, and I thought the worst of him.

"I-I thought I was guarding my heart. I thought you didn't feel the same way I did." My chin trembles with remorse. "I'm so sorry, Hudson."

His forehead lands on mine. "This is not on you. I should have told you how I felt about you sooner. I didn't think those three words were important, as long as my actions said enough, but I fucking failed there, too."

A swell of panic rises inside me, and I grab his wrists, shaking my head. "You didn't fail. What you did . . ." I swallow, sniffling, "moving here for me, showing up here today. I don't deserve that, Hudson."

His hands tighten on my face, his eyes steel against mine. "You deserve the fucking world, sweetheart, and I plan to give it to you."

My eyes bounce against his, disbelief still evident in the way my hands grasp him. "So, you're here now? Please tell me you're here now."

Hudson's eyes drop to my lips before he leans in and gently presses a kiss to mine. "If you're here, I'm here, sweetheart. I'm wherever you are." Rare vulnerability, the kind he only reserves for me, shimmers in his gaze. "Tell me I'm fucking worth the trouble. Tell me you'll still have me, baby girl."

A choked sob escapes my lips as soul-stirring relief blankets my entire body.

"You're worth more than I could possibly give you. I'll have you and only you, Hudson Case. I'm never letting you go," I mumble over his lips, watching his eyes squeeze shut and his chest inflate, as if he was holding his breath the whole time. "The thought of never seeing your rare smiles, never feeling your lips against mine . . . It broke me, Hudson. I'd left half of me with you. Thank you for bringing it back to me."

His lips find mine again as he presses my back to my car,

his need heavy against my abdomen. "I love you, Kav. I'd follow you to the ends of the earth if that's what it took to be with you."

Our lips crash together, tongues lashing against each other as I pull him into me. My legs wrap around his hips and his erection grinds against my core while his hands cup my ass.

A feverish growl escapes his lips when his hand tangles inside my hair and he pulls my head back to deepen our kiss.

I feel him inside my chest, in the depths of my soul.

We're a frenzy of lips and tongues, growls and groans, as we rediscover each other.

We kiss until we're both out of breath and heaving against one another before I pull back, my lips still tingling from the delicious scrape of his scruff against my skin. "Wait a minute," I say, still trying to catch my breath, my mind buzzing with disconnected thoughts. "How did you know we were making memory boxes today?"

"It was on your flyer. I looked up a couple of videos online, and then I made it myself."

I reel back, my hands resting on his broad chest. "You found my flyer?"

One corner of his lips lifts. "And your favorite coffee shop."

I let out a soft gasp. "You've been following me? You're . . . you're the hot daddy Lena talks about!"

His brows furrow with confusion. "I don't know what half of that means, but like I said, I'd follow you anywhere, if that's what it took to be with you."

"Yeah?" My smile turns sheepish, butterflies scattering inside my belly. "How about you follow me home, hot daddy?"

～

WE'RE BARELY inside my tiny apartment before Hudson has our lips smashed together.

Parched and famished.

His tongue thrusts inside my open mouth like he'll die if he doesn't get to taste me. Rising up on my toes, I dig my fingers into his hair, moaning as urgent licks of heat travel up my body.

Needy. Greedy. Begging.

My hands work hastily to untuck and unbutton his shirt. In record time, I'm shoving it off him, my palms landing over his wide tattooed chest.

I break away to lay kisses over his collarbone and neck, feeling his erection flinch between us. Sliding my palm down his chest and taut abs, I grasp his cock over his pants. Hudson releases a hard breath and sways against me, as if he's having a hard time staying steady.

His fingers lock on the hem of my shirt, tugging it over my torso before I help him take it off. His eyes flare when they rake down my exposed skin, lingering on the swell of my breasts.

He palms one sheathed breast before he pulls down the cup, his eyes flaring at the sight of my exposed and pebbled nipple. A growl escapes his lips before he leans down to take it in his mouth, sending ripples of blinding lust through my core. His hands slide up and down my torso as his lips and teeth pull at my nipple, sucking so hard I squeak in blissful agony.

Wet heat trickles into my panties as my pussy contracts. My fingers dig into his scalp. "Hudson . . ."

His fingers adeptly unbutton my jeans before he releases my nipple with a pop and falls to his knees in front of me, right at the entrance of my studio. Trailing kisses over my stomach, he tugs the denim over my wide hips and wiggles them down my thighs.

Hudson licks and sucks the expanse of skin on my thighs, groaning while he nuzzles his nose against my pussy. "Fuck, I missed you."

His desperate movements have my panties inching down my legs and off to the side with my discarded jeans before his eyes flash, taking in my wet center. He hooks my leg over his shoulder, and that's all the warning I get before he buries his face in between my thighs.

A cry rips from my lips when he circles my clit with the tip of his tongue, over and over until I'm panting. His hungry lips work over my soft skin, my tender lips, sucking them into his mouth before he tongues my center. Laying open-mouthed kisses over my entrance, he taps his tongue against it. Voraciously. Urgently. Relentlessly.

"Jesus Christ, your pussy is where I want to die, baby girl," he mumbles over my skin. "You're the only one I want on my tongue, morning, day, and night."

I grind my pussy over his warm mouth, loving the way his teeth gently bite my skin and his stubble scrapes my thighs. My hips thrust needily, a heat wave crawling up my body, as I fist his hair with one hand and hold his shoulder with the other. "Hudson. Oh, God."

I whimper and cry as his deft tongue plunges inside me, creating a havoc so intense, I'm threatening to detonate in seconds.

Continuing to lave my clit, his fingers find my entrance—one and two, before he inserts a third for good measure. I'm soaking wet, dripping down his hand as his fingers pummel in and out of me.

He's eating me out and fucking me with his fingers so thoroughly, I'm trembling as I rock over him, my fingernails biting into his skin to keep me steady. I ride his face as he sucks my clit rapidly, knowing I'm close. His fingers curl inside me, and I know I'm going to come.

"Hudson!" I scream as I sway over him, my teeth grinding as the beginning of my orgasm wraps its hold around me. "God, please, keep doing that. Yes!"

Hudson's lips, tongue, and fingers never stop as he growls, desperately eating me out until I'm tensing and arching over him. My sharp cry pierces the air as waves and shudders wrack my body, and I come hard, clamping his face between my thighs.

"Fuck, yes," he groans, his face still buried inside me. "That's it, baby girl, drown me inside this pussy."

A soft mewl tumbles from my lips as uneven tremors ripple through my body before I collapse against the wall, heaving.

Hudson unhooks my leg from his shoulder before leaving a few parting kisses on my thighs, and I coax him back to his feet. Wrapping my arms around his neck, I pull him to my mouth, tasting myself on his lips. We kiss as he presses his thick covered cock over my center, and I'm hungry all over again.

Our chests mesh together. My fingernails scrape down his chest, my whimpers mixing with his growls. "Hudson . . ."

"I know what you need, baby." He smiles into our kiss, picking me up and carrying me to my bed, his raspy voice sending shivers down my spine. "And there's nothing I want more than to give it to you."

Chapter Thirty-Seven

HUDSON

Her back hits her bed, and she unwraps herself from my body, splaying her arms above her. She's a goddamn vision with her tousled hair haloed around her head, that bewitching jewel gleaming over her bee-stung lips, and those golden-brown eyes filled with love and lust.

For me.

She told me once that her name meant poem, and it's fitting. She's a sonnet, a fucking haiku, with her every arc and curve a carefully crafted verse on a page.

I hover over her, my arms caging her head. "You want to be fucked, sweetheart? You want my cock buried so deep, you won't walk straight for days?"

Her response is to stick her chest out—one breast free from when I sucked her nipple, while the other is still tucked inside her bra. I'll get to it later. For now, I like her looking as disheveled and dazed as she does. She juts out her hips to run her bare pussy over my pants, hissing when she feels my erection.

Rising to my feet, I pull off my belt, shoving down my

pants and boxer-briefs. Stepping out of them, I fist my cock, my eyes smoldering. "Get up and show me how much you want this. Suck my cock."

She rises, flipping onto all fours and raising her ass in the air. My mouth waters at the sight, and I almost tell her to turn around so I can bury my face in her ass.

I tuck her hair behind her ear before brushing my thumb over her lips. I press my thumb into her mouth, and she licks it, sucking the way she will my dick.

Her hungry eyes scroll up my body, and I pull my thumb out of her mouth, rubbing it over her lips, before letting her take my cock from my hand. She pumps it before slapping the tip on her tongue, knowing she's about to drive me insane. A low groan rumbles inside my chest as I watch her lick the beads of pre-cum off the tip.

So fucking hot.

"Fuck." My head falls back as my hand wraps around the back of her head. "You're already killing me, baby girl."

She continues to pump my shaft before her wet mouth rolls over my dick and, needing more, my hips instinctively jut forward.

My abs contract and my hand tightens around her silk strands as she sucks me deeper. My dick hits the back of her throat and my need heightens, a tingle playing at the base of my spine. Jesus Christ, I'll never get enough of her mouth.

Her hand plays with my balls and my entire body feels fevered watching her hollow out her cheeks, sucking hard.

Fuck, she's good at this. And to think she'd never done it before me.

A primal sense of pride surges inside me, and I hold myself back from taking control and not fucking her mouth until she's choking on my dick.

With her movement steady, her head bobs over me, her half-covered breasts swinging lasciviously while she laves the bottom of my shaft with her tongue, running it along my smooth, sensitive skin. I hear her gag, but her eyes stay connected to mine, working through it and opening up her throat.

"You like that?" I ask, my voice husky. "You like choking on this cock?"

She moans, her mouth still full, but continues to suck until I'm swaying on my legs, seeing stars at the outskirts of my vision.

Pulling out of her mouth, I breathe heavily, gesturing behind her. Her mouth felt way too fucking good; a minute more and I'd be blowing my load, ending this prematurely. "Get back on the bed. I need to fuck you."

Popping off my cock, she licks her lips before her spine hits the bed again. Within seconds, I'm hovering over her, in between her open thighs, with the head of my cock at her entrance.

Using my hand to direct it, I press the tip inside her, making her hips swing up and her head roll back. Pressing my mouth to the soft skin of her neck, I slowly thrust inside all the way until I'm completely sheathed inside her. "Jesus, fuck, baby. You feel so fucking good."

It's been a month without her. Without her warmth around me. Without her smiles and laughs in the air.

A month where my heart lived outside of me, and I had to watch it continue on as if it was never a part of me in the first place. A month where I did nothing but wait and bide my time, watching her from afar, shattering with every one of her smiles, knowing they weren't for me.

Wondering if they'd ever be for me again.

There were times I felt like a stalker—trailing behind her to see where she went or going into the coffee shop she just left, only to catch a whiff of her scent like it's my goddamn addiction because it was the only way I could feel close to her.

To say the past month has been excruciating would be the understatement of the century. Like being made to watch the same wreckage on tape, over and over again, until your eyes threatened to bleed.

I missed her in a way that was indescribable.

I freeze over her, taking her in—a flush covering her neck, her eyes bouncing over my face, sweat beading over her brows —before pulling out halfway and thrusting back in.

"I love you," I rasp, thanking my lucky stars she fucking took me back.

Her golden-brown eyes mist when she cradles my face. "I know."

She sees it, everything as plain as day written all over my face. My reservations dissolved, my guard demolished. I'm hers. All fucking hers.

Truth be told, I was a goner the day I came into my office and saw her sitting at Belinda's desk that first time, all feigned confidence and uncertain smile.

I knew I was going to lose to her and it scared the living shit out of me.

But looking back at it now, that moment was the beginning of the rest of my life. A life I want to spend with this woman right here.

"I missed you so fucking much, Kav . . ." I take in a stuttered breath, my throat feeling parched. My heart thunders inside my chest, finally alive. Finally whole. "I . . . I—"

I'm not even sure what I'm trying to say, but her wobbly smile tells me she does. "I know, baby. I know."

I melt into her, my face nuzzled in her neck as I ram her deep and hard, thundering into her like a force unleashed. I drive forward as her nails scrape down my back and the wet sounds of our bodies slapping together fills the room.

"Oh, God," Kavi moans and I lift back up, curling my hand over her throat possessively and watching her intently.

Every flicker of her expression is a promise and a revelation. My weakness and strength.

My thumb reaches up to pull down her bottom lip. "So fucking beautiful when you take my cock. Keep making those sounds for me, sweetheart."

Strands of her wet hair stick to the side of her forehead, her skin slick with a sheen of sweat, as I drive into her with deliberate long strokes.

Our breaths are uneven, moans clashing, but we've never been so in sync.

I lean down, taking her mouth in a savage kiss, and Kavi's arms cross around my neck. She locks her ankles at my lower back, pulling me in deeper. We're a tangle of limbs and lips, a knot of yeses and forevers.

Her tongue hits the roof of my mouth and I groan, sucking it, as my hips move with purpose, drawing out this feeling. It's goddamn ecstasy.

Not disconnecting our kiss, I drag my hand down her body, pulling down the other cup of her bra before rolling her nipple in between my fingers.

She whimpers and mewls, her hips arching against mine.

I do it again, pinching harder, and Kavi's mouth goes slack against mine, a moan escaping. Lowering my head, I take her pert nipple into my mouth, laving it with my tongue before biting down on it until she's squirming under me.

I continue to piston into her while my hand slides down to her clit. Rubbing little circles over it with my middle two fingers, I lift up and watch my cock move in and out of her. "Fuck, Kav, I'm losing my mind. Look at how pretty your pussy looks sucking my cock."

She rises on her elbows to watch with me, her chest rising and falling with each thrust before her eyes drag up to meet mine. An electric charge passes between us as our eyes hold and my hips pump into her.

It's fucking magic and fairytales. It doesn't feel like my life and yet, it is.

Soul-crushing, heart-wrenching emotion rocks between us, like we're caught inside turbulent, all-consuming waves, threatening to pull us under. And yet, we'd drown willingly.

Our tattered breaths collide as we watch each other, glassy-eyed and silent, until the walls of her pussy constrict, and she sucks in a hefty breath.

Her body stiffens beneath me, and I quicken the pace of my fingers over her clit as I angle my pelvis to get deeper, focusing on long, punishing strokes.

"Ohh!" Kavi's resolve breaks as her orgasm crescents. Her fingernails dig into my shoulders with enough force to leave marks as she cries out, throwing her head back, "Oh, God, I'm coming! I'm coming . . ."

I'm right there with her, a few pumps of my dick away, as I bury myself to the hilt. Waves of euphoria wash over my senses as I succumb to the sensation building inside me. My eyes squeeze shut and I groan into her ear, my body jerking as I empty myself inside her. I whisper my love and dedication to her—how she's mine and only mine—while I hug her close.

Her hand climbs to my hair, her fingers tangling, as shudders wrack our bodies—tremors of need finally releasing for the time being, until we're lost in each other again.

I roll off her, my cock sliding out, before I pull her back to my chest. Moving her hair out of the way, I wrap my arm around her and kiss her neck.

Heaving chests and heavy breaths, we nuzzle in the wake of our second chance.

A new chapter. Our happily-ever-after.

A silence blankets over us as I hold her to me, like she might fly away if I don't. My eyes roam around the room, taking in the surroundings that had gone unnoticed when we'd first entered. It's a small apartment—cozy, colorful, and warm—just the sort of place I'd expect her to love, with her precious night lights scattered about.

My attention is drawn to a corner near her window where an unveiled painted canvas catches my eye. I study the painting of a suited man standing at a bar, glass in his hand, surrounded by faceless men engaged in conversation with him. But his piercing blue-gray eyes are trained on someone beyond the frame, someone he can't tear his gaze from. The border of the canvas is adorned with wildflowers, much like the ones at my ranch, and I realize the scene is from Maddy's wedding.

Kavi notices my silent fascination, following my gaze. "I couldn't get you out of my mind, and after that time we spent at Madison's wedding, I knew I'd never be able to get you out of my heart, either."

My heart swells and I pull her chin toward me, kissing her with every spoken and unspoken sentiment. Then, for the second time since we met, I ask her the same question. But this time, it's devoid of the stipulations and timeline.

This time it's forever.

"Move in with me," I whisper like it's a secret meant just for her. "Live with me. I can't stand being in that house without your socks trailing the way to the laundry room and your night lights lighting up the hallways." I pause, brushing my lips over the nape of her neck once more and telling her the entire truth. "I can't stand being anywhere without you."

She's quiet for a moment, but I know she's smiling. I can feel it like the warmth that surrounds me.

"I thought you'd never ask."

EPILOGUE

Kavi - Three Months Later

We didn't have a white Christmas, but we definitely had a cold and rainy one.

Though, cold is hardly how I'm feeling sitting around our living room with some of mine and Hudson's closest friends and family.

"Thank goodness Meera and Rayne are finally asleep," Bella announces with a relieved sigh, indicating her two daughters as she descends the stairs. Her eyes are affixed to her husband, Garrett, who is Hudson's closest friend and a pilot for a big airline. "Meera, of course, argued that it was winter break and, as a 'big kid,' she shouldn't have to sleep at the same time as her one-year-old sister. I bribed her with extra screen time tomorrow if she went to sleep now."

Garrett opens his arms to invite her to snuggle up next to him on the couch before planting a kiss on her temple. "I'll take the morning shift. You can sleep in before we have to leave."

I smile at them from my position in between Hudson's legs on the chaise. We're sharing a blanket, my head resting on his chest with his arms wrapped around my midsection, though, his hands have been wandering, mostly lower, and I've had to keep my face inscrutable in front of everyone.

Hudson and I hosted Christmas this year, given our friends and family had yet to see our new home, and surprisingly, almost everyone was available to fly in, with the exception of Hudson's friends Dean and Mala, who are very pregnant and advised by their doctor not to fly.

Aside from Garrett and his family, Hudson's friend Darian and his wife Rani, and their two children joined, too. Darian is Garrett and Dean's younger brother, and one hell of a husband and dad. With his stoic personality—sometimes mistaken for grumpy—he reminds me of my guy, Mr. Cranky-Dick. Though I'd say Hudson isn't mistaken for grumpy; he's actually grumpy to most people, besides the ones he truly cares about.

Like the ones in this room.

And speaking of people he cares about, I am happy to say I've made solid friendships in this short time with both Rani and Bella. And that's saying something, considering I'm generally pretty guarded. Somehow, though, like Madison and Belinda, these two have been able to pull me out of my shell.

The three of us have had fun gossiping about the men in our lives, but also being candid and goofy with each other. Apparently, they'd been trying for years to find someone for Hudson, but the man is not only cantankerous, he's hard to please. As Bella said it, they're just happy I "can put up with his grouchy ass". Recently, they even added me to a group chat with Dean's wife, Mala, and their other friend Melody, who's a complete hoot.

It's unfortunate I wasn't able to spend as much time with Mala this time, but we made plans to hang out the next time I visit San Francisco. And I will be, given my mom and Neil still live there, at least until Neil is in college. If, at that time Mom wants to move, Hudson and I have a guest cottage dedicated to her across our property. Though I've warned him that he'll be on the hook to replace almost every appliance in that little house if Mom decides to live there. Surprisingly, it's a burden he seems happy to take on.

And, of course, Christmas wouldn't be the same if our families weren't here, so aside from my mom and my brother, we also got to celebrate Madison and Brie's first Christmas as a married couple with them. Over the past few days, Madison and I have had a lot of chances to bond, and thankfully, get past the way I left so abruptly last summer. As expected, Madison understood where I came from. She knew her father's plans of moving here and surprising me, but she respected his wishes to not get involved at that time.

Oh, and did I mention that Jett is also here with his girlfriend, Naomi? They've been together for some time now and I get the feeling things are pretty serious between them.

Things between Hudson and his brother have been going really well. Being CEO, Hudson still makes the major company decisions, but Jett has positioned himself to be of great value, running things the way Hudson expects in the San Francisco office.

My gaze travels over everyone, sitting with their significant others, as the fire crackles in our fireplace and the scent of firewood mingles with the scents of the gingerbread cookies I baked and the cups of spiced cider strewn on the coffee table.

It's quieter now that the kids are asleep, though they've had fun the past few days running around the house together, playing board games with us adults, and opening loads of gifts.

My mom and Neil sit side-by-side across from Hudson and me, with mom drinking a cup of chai instead of the spiced cider and giving me a look I can't decipher.

Actually, I've seen that look before—the one where her

brows dance over her cup and she smiles to herself, thinking no one can see it.

She knows something.

My brows pucker at Neil in question, hoping to silently ask him what Mom's deal is, but he just shrugs, not giving anything away. When I squint at her, she continues to play coy, drinking more of her chai.

Hudson clears his throat, holding me tighter but addressing everyone, "Both Kavi and I wanted to thank you for celebrating Christmas with us this year."

"Thanks for flying us all here on your private jet, big brother," Jett says, winking back. "Can't say it was back-breaking work to get here."

Darian chuckles, agreeing as Garrett adds, "Yeah, it was nice to be a passenger for once, too."

"You're welcome," Hudson says, shifting. "I do have another little gift I forgot to give while we were opening presents yesterday." He reaches into his pocket behind me and my brows furrow, wondering what he's doing. "I don't really know how I missed it. Perhaps because the box is so small."

Garrett suddenly announces that he's calling his brother Dean on FaceTime, and I blink in confusion as to why.

Before I can even process what's happening, Hudson pulls out the box he was referring to and opens it in front of me as casually as one would a box of mints.

My hands rise to cover my gaping mouth as I process what I'm seeing—a band covered with sparkling diamonds. I blink, gathering my thoughts, but can't seem to speak.

We were just casually strolling along a shopping area last month when he'd asked me to come into a jewelry shop with him, claiming he needed to get the battery on his watch changed. While we waited, I just happened to smile as I passed a ring situated on a pedestal in the center of a glass case. I've never been one to wear fancy jewelry, nor would I want an enormous diamond that would give me panic attacks at the thought of losing it, but I recall thinking this eternity band with emerald-cut diamonds was classy and subtle.

Of course I never mentioned it to him.

But lo-and-behold, it's now gleaming back at me from its cushioned enclosure. "Hudson . . ."

Jett's voice resounds in the background—something about Belinda and Hudson's friend Dev waiting on standby to be called on FaceTime. His words get muddled with the blood rushing through my ears and the pounding of my heart as Hudson hauls himself off the couch.

I'm still gaping at him on the chaise, while soft *oohs* and *awws* echo in the background from Maddy and the other ladies, as Hudson bends down on one knee.

"Kav, my beautiful poem, living with you isn't enough. I want so much more—vows taken and rings exchanged, children, dogs, and horses. The whole shebang, baby girl. I want forever and nothing less will do. Will you marry me, sweetheart?"

My eyes bounce from him to the ring and back to him. Is this really happening? Am I in dream land somewhere? "Are you being serious right now?"

One side of his mouth rises before he reaches for my hand, setting it over his heart. "As serious as the heart thundering inside my chest." He regards me tenderly, with love like I've never seen, but only seen in him. "Say yes."

"Yes!" I leap forward, wrapping my arms around him, my eyes filling with unshed tears. "Yes, yes, yes!"

His arms gather me, pulling me to him as our friends and family cheer and whoop. It's becoming clear they were a part of this entire stunt.

"Hell yeah! The old geezer's finally getting married!" Dean

yells from Garrett's screen. "Not gonna lie, old man, I almost lost faith there for a minute."

"You and me both, brother!" Garrett chimes in before he gets an elbow in his side from Bella while Darian and Rani both laugh.

Plucking the ring from its box, Hudson lifts my finger and wiggles it over my knuckle while I stare at it in awe.

Of him. Of us.

"Holy shit, did you say *more* children, Dad?" Madison beams from her spot. She's waiting for an opportunity to jump up and wrap us both in a hug. She's been looking forward to her dad finding love more than anyone else. "I can't wait to have siblings, but have you run this by Kansas yet? She can barely tolerate me being your daughter."

It's been tough for Hudson to not see his precious horse whenever he wants, but he's got his eyes on a small ranch right outside the city. Knowing him, he'll be re-homing her and the others here soon enough.

Hudson chuckles. "I'll be sure to get her approval on the matter." He turns to me, whispering into my ear, "What do you say, sweetheart? Will you have my babies?"

I face him before pressing my lips to his, keeping my voice soft. "All in due time, Mr. Case, though I know how much you love having a plan. But, yes, I want to have your babies."

He pulls me to him, meshing our bodies together, ignoring the "reserve that for the bedroom, Hudson," from Belinda chiding him through Jett's phone.

Since her return to work, she serves both Hudson and Jett as their executive assistant. The woman deserves a hell of a raise in my opinion, because there are few who can handle the two brothers and their list of demands and not want to murder one of them.

"Due time needs to start now. Let's tell these jackasses to leave so we can get started right—"

I press my finger to his lips, raising my brow. The man is ravenous, but seriously, we have guests for one more night.

He grumbles something behind my finger before biting the tip teasingly as Madison and Neil both convey similar expressions of horrification with an, "Eew."

Madison then jumps out of her seat, wrapping her arms around us, before the others come forward to do the same, congratulating us.

I'm just unwrapping from my hug with Rani and Bella when my mom rushes toward us with a bottle of champagne and a smile as wide as the Mississippi stretched across her face. "I thought maybe we could celebrate with some bubbles!"

My smile falters, my eyes widening when I notice the cage from the nose of the bottle removed and my mother's fingers under the cork, so much like mine were that fateful day when I slugged my now fiancé in the head with a flying cork.

We're in slow motion, or perhaps we're racing at the speed of light, when both mine and Hudson's hand lands on top of the cork, and we both scream at the same time, "No!"

BONUS EPILOGUE

Two Years Later

"How's my sweet girl?" I murmur against Kansas's neck, combing my fingers through her mane. "You holding up okay? Not letting the young bucks bother you, are you? Nah, I couldn't imagine you'd let anyone bother you."

Kansas snuffles, smelling my hair the way she likes to, before I put one of her favorite peppermint treats in her mouth.

"Dada!"

The greeting resounds behind me and I turn over my shoulder to see my baby boy bouncing in my wife's arms. He's dressed in a long-sleeve onesie with a graphic of a cherry and words that say, I'm the cherry on top, along with denims and orange boots, courtesy of his mom. He gives me one of his wide, toothy grins, reaching out his little hands, hoping to pet Kansas.

At a little over one years old, he's got more energy than I ever remember Madison having, but damn if he isn't the cutest thing I've ever seen with his dark brown hair, amber-colored eyes and beautiful tan skin. And while he looks just like his mother, he's a total daddy's boy.

Though both Kavi and I knew we wanted children together, Nathan Helix Case came about a little earlier and more unexpectedly than we'd planned. In fact, Kavi found out she was pregnant only a month after the Christmas I proposed to her, so we pre-poned our wedding plans and got married that spring at our new ranch here in Portland with Kavi walking down the aisle to me carrying the wildflower bouquet she always wanted, looking like my very own wild-flower dream.

I saunter over to Kavi and Nathan, taking him out of her arms since he's practically trying to fly out of them anyway, and place a kiss on her lips. I hold him with one arm before I wrap my hand around the back of my wife's neck and pull her in to deepen our kiss.

Her hands cup my jaw, her mouth working against mine, before Nathan's tiny hand takes my Stetson hat off my head, causing me to smile against Kavi's mouth.

"I love you," I say against her lips while our son tries to pull the enormous hat over his head. "I love you more than words could ever express, my sweet poem."

She nods. "I know."

We've settled into our life here in Portland, with Kavi still working for the hospital and me running the Portland branch of Case Geo. It's a big change from San Francisco, but it's been refreshing in so many ways, too.

For one, I'm no longer working the hours I used to—I have little motivation to when I've got the most beautiful woman and my baby boy waiting for me to get home in the evenings. For another, I'm just more . . . relaxed. I'll never be the type to not plan and prepare for the future, but let's just say, my wife and my son have ensured I stay flexible and spon-taneous, too. And it's been a welcomed change.

Placing a kiss on my son's cherub cheek, I amble over to where Kansas stands expectantly for us. Surprisingly, she took to Nathan almost instantly. I don't know if it's because she felt closer to him, given Kavi and I regularly visited her in the new ranch, even while Kavi was pregnant, or because she's become more tolerant of babies in her old age, but she has been nothing but patient with Nathan.

Maddy? Now, she's a different story. For whatever reason, my horse-daughter still has a competitive and jealous streak with my human daughter, and I don't foresee that relationship changing no matter how many peppermint treats Maddy tries to give her.

Though Kavi's mom and brother no longer live in San Francisco, we still visit often to see Maddy, Brie, and Jett, who's now engaged to Naomi. But since all our friends—Garrett, Dean, Darian and Dev and their wives—live nearby, too, we usually end up being there for extended weekends. Yes, I said Dev and his wife. He had one hell of a story that started at my stylist, Piper's, salon, that ended with him getting a lot more than a haircut, but that's for the two of them to tell.

Kavi's brother is now at a university in Michigan, surprisingly studying earth science and geology. Depending on what he wants to do after he graduates, I wouldn't blink an eye at hiring him for Case Geo. Hell, my company would be lucky to have him, given how sharp and hardworking the kid is.

Kavi's mom moved in with us shortly after we found out we were pregnant with Nathan and, while I won't deny the woman breaks at least one appliance a week, she's pretty easygoing and a true support for Kavi.

Putting my hat back on my head, I guide Nathan's hand toward Kansas, letting her smell him before he pets her, getting another bounce and squeal out of my little boy.

"Kansas!" He claps, grinning and proud of himself.

I place another kiss on his forehead, breathing in the scent of his baby shampoo. "I think she really likes you, too, buddy."

As the sun begins to descend, I take a moment to soak it all in—my life and my little family. It's a picture-perfect scene I could have never imagined two years ago, but one that has surpassed all my imaginings and expectations.

Kavi runs her hand up my back and I look down at her, at a loss for words and overwhelmed with my gratitude. For her, for us, and for our little boy.

And as the stars start to twinkle overhead, I breathe in the crisp air, mixed with the scents of the ranch and the wildflowers swaying in the breeze, knowing that everything is as it should be. Knowing that I've finally found my happily-ever-after.

The End

Pre-order **PRETEND FOR ME**

Dev and Piper's fake fiancé, forced proximity romcom!

Read the entire **ELEMENTS OF RAPTURE** Series!
Start with **ADRIFT**, Darian and Rani's taboo, single dad/nanny romance.

Like enemies to lovers romances?
What it they also come with a plot-twist?
Read MY DARLING NEIGHBOR, Penn and Sita's enemies to lovers, accidental pregnancy romance.

Your reviews matter!
Please consider taking a few minutes to write a review for ABYSS on Amazon.

ABOUT THE AUTHOR

Swati M.H. writes stories full of humor, heart, and heartbreak. She lives in the Bay Area with her incredibly patient husband, two beautiful daughters, and her pitbull, Sadie Sapphire. Her days start with caffeine and sometimes end with a glass (or three) of wine.

Swati loves staying in touch with her readers. Find her at www.swatimh.com or through Facebook and Instagram. Be sure to join her Sweeties reader group for daily fun.

ACKNOWLEDGMENTS

The Elements of Rapture series is now complete with Kavi and Hudson's story and I can't tell you how bittersweet that feels for me. I've lived in this series for almost two years and letting these characters go feels like I'm letting a part of my heart go too.

But who knows, maybe we'll all see them again in a second gen series in the future. Never say never, right?

Before I thank all the wonderful people who I'm lucky to have in my bookish life, I'd like to thank the people I have in my regular life where I'm a wife, a mom, a daughter, sister, and friend.

Thank you to my incredible family and friends. Your daily encouragement and support is immeasurable and beyond words.

I've met and worked with so many wonderful people throughout my writing journey; people who are not only my incredible readers and friends but who are incredible just as they are and while I couldn't possibly show the depth of my gratitude for them with a few simple words, I'm going to try anyway.

To my PA, Stephanie - Thanks for the daily chats and keeping me organized. More than anything else, thank you for being a friend to me and someone I can rely on and vent to when needed.

To my editor, Silvia - You're a joy to work with and one of the most genuine people I've met. So glad you can deal with all my grammar mistakes without breaking a sweat :) Here's to many more books together!

To my cover designer, Marisa - It's fair to say your work speaks for itself. I am in awe of your talent and your patience. Thank you so much for putting up with my picky ass and for always going above and beyond what I'd ever conceive for my covers. They are absolutely beautiful!

To Rachael P - When you jump into my manuscript and start commenting, it's one of the most exciting moments for me. Thank you for your continued support, friendship, and your fun voice memos. My book world is better because you're in it.

To Rachel C - You have no idea how valuable your insight is for me. You not only challenge me to be a better writer but you cheer me on as I struggle through it and that is the true testament of your belief in me. I hope I live up to it with each book. Thank you so much for your immense support.

To Michelle - I live for your squealing comments in my manuscript. Thank you for helping to make my sexy scenes even sexier and for always being there as a sounding board. I appreciate you so much and am so glad I got a chance to squeeze you this year!

To Namita - It's hard for me to put into words how happy I am to have met you. You're such a beautiful soul and friend. Thank you for supporting me and my books and for always being on my side. I get so happy when you read my books.

To Amarilys - I'm so lucky to have found you as a reader but also lucky to call you a friend. Thank you for alpha-reading Abyss and claiming Hudson as yours pretty much on chapter 1. :-D I know he didn't beat Penn, but he came close and that's a feat in itself.

To Sierra - I have no idea how you found my books but I'm so glad you did. Thank you for beta-reading Abyss for me. Your insights and comments truly helped make this one of the best stories I've written. So glad to have gotten a chance to see you and hug you this year!

To Sarah Beth - Not only are you one of favorite people, you're hilarious and so supportive. Did I mention I'm in awe of your artistic talents? Thank you for beta-reading Abyss and I love that Hudson "almost" kicked Dean out of his spot on your list of book husbands.

To Marla - Thank you, thank you for being so incredibly sweet and supportive. One of these days, I'm going to get to give you a hug and I can't wait for that. Thank you for beta-reading Abyss and for your comments as you read it. They put such a big smile on my face.

To Shauna and Becca at Author Agency - thank you for being so wonderful to work with and for doing such a great job promoting my books.

To my dear friends, Monica Arya, Rin Sher, Emily Silver, Jennifer Hartmann, Steffanie Blais, and Nikki Lamers. Thank you for your friendship, the unending laughs, and for generally just letting me be in your tribe and bask in your glow. You are not only brilliant writers but incredible humans and I adore and cherish you.

To my street & TikTok teams - I am so lucky to be able to chat with you often. Thank you for promoting my books and for all your words of encouragement. I couldn't do it without you!

To my reader group, Swati's Sweeties - gosh, I love you all. Hanging out with you is my most favorite part of the day.

To all my readers — I hope you enjoyed Hudson and Kavi's story. I am so grateful for you and I promise to keep giving you my best work until . . . well, until forever. :)

Made in the USA
Middletown, DE
21 May 2024

54628831R00243